My usually confident self had taken the day off and been replaced by a self I'd not met before, a nervous Nelly self that was as timid and insecure as a country mouse in the city. A burning itch worked its way up my arms and spread across my thumping chest and face, heating my whole body and leaving me feeling as though every breath was an effort.

When Lucy turned to ask me if I was hungry, she gasped. "Addie! What's wrong? Are you feeling bad? Your face looks like it's afire!"

Falling
from the
Moon

Lise Marinelli

Chi-Towne Fiction
An Imprint of Windy City Publishers

Windy City Publishers
Chicago, IL

www.windycitypublishers.com

Falling from the Moon

Windy City Publishers
1935 S. Plum Grove Rd., #349
Palatine, IL 60067
www.windycitypublishers.com

Published in the United States of America

First Edition: July 2009

10 9 8 7 6 5 4 3 2 1

ISBN: 978-0-9819505-0-1

Library of Congress Control Number: 2008943950

Cover design by IntuitDesign

Author photo by J. C. Hatfield

For Thelma and E. L. Hulce

Who never lost their faith

Contents

Harris Family Tree

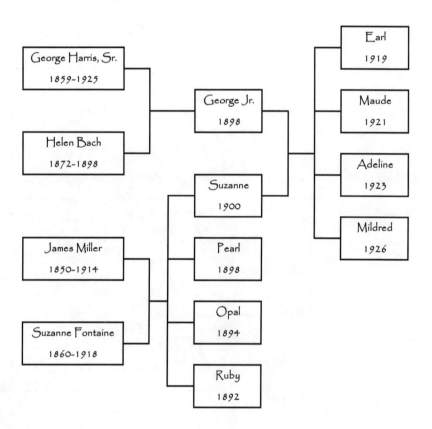

Conklin Family Tree

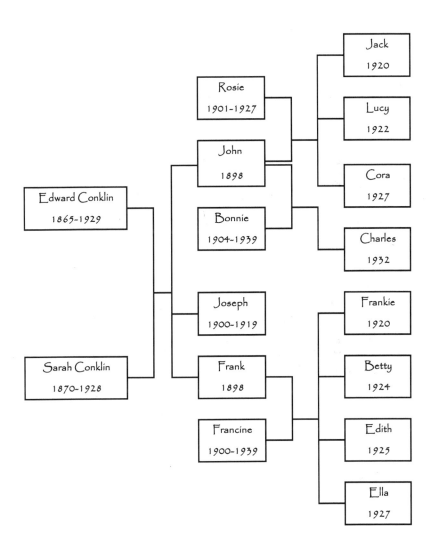

Edward Conklin
1865-1929

Sarah Conklin
1870-1928

John
1898

Rosie
1901-1927

Bonnie
1904-1939

Joseph
1900-1919

Frank
1898

Francine
1900-1939

Jack
1920

Lucy
1922

Cora
1927

Charles
1932

Frankie
1920

Betty
1924

Edith
1925

Ella
1927

Chapter One

Adeline - 1932

I sat on the fence post at the end of the driveway waiting for Lucy. She and Jack never showed up, so I walked to school alone and late. The fresh October air had not yet turned nippy, but the mellow breeze that pushed the falling leaves along the path was a gentle reminder that it soon would.

Playing my latest game of backward hopscotch was no fun; the dusty dirt just turned my shiny black Mary Janes gray. When I stumbled, making a silly face, there was no one there to laugh. I kicked the small stone I had been using as a marker to the side of the road and thought about Lucy and Jack. They didn't have a telephone, so I would have to wait until they returned to school to find out what had happened. I never would go to their home, though. Their father wasn't a pleasant man, and besides, Lucy was always busy doing chores. She and Jack had a far more difficult lot in life than I, and I didn't envy their situation.

As I worried about Lucy and her brother, my attention drifted and my imagination had them kidnapped by the Germans. I became Mata Hari, the exotic spy, called in for a daring rescue. The large fieldstones that marked the boundaries between the farms became my hideouts, and I darted from one to another, out of breath from the run. Huge chasms opened in the earth and I leapt across the gorges, my timing critical lest I misstep and fall down into the bottomless pits. Slipping behind a large maple tree, I spoke into my lunch pail, trying to radio base to send help, but the sneaky "Krauts" had cut off all communications. All of a sudden I felt the sting of a sniper's shot to the kidneys and arched my back in pain, staggering to the side of the road. It had just missed my heart. I was able to remove the bullet with a stick I had converted into a knife, and bravely carried on.

The weeping willows along the banks of the Tittabawassee River were my first clue that I was close to the safe house, a converted school. My fellow spies would be waiting with apple pie and bread pudding—my two favorite desserts. My only hope was that Lucy and Jack had been rescued by the other soldiers, for I had not found them.

As I crouched down beside the steps of the building, looking for the right opportunity to enter, the door flew open and Miss Opal's formidable figure stood in the doorway.

"Would you like to join us today, Adeline?" she asked. "Miss Ruby was just about to take attendance."

"Yes, ma'am," I answered meekly as I stood up. She didn't move, so I squeezed by her considerable frame and walked into the school, the curious faces of my comrades following me as I took my seat.

Our school was situated on the north bank of the Tittabawassee. It was a two-room building with the children younger than twelve in one room and the older kids in the other. The two rooms shared a coal furnace in the middle—it was the job of the older boys to keep the stove full in the winter. Miss Ruby Miller, who just happened to be my mama's oldest sister, taught the younger children. Miss Opal Miller, my mama's other sister, taught the older kids. Miss Ruby and Miss Opal lived in town with my mama's third sister, Miss Pearl, in a large house that their parents had left them. Miss Pearl worked at the small library in town. Between them, the three spinsters knew more information, worthy and useless, than any other ten people in the whole great state of Michigan.

Miss Pearl had a memory like no other and could recall the names of dead ancestors, countries at war in Europe, fancy sea creatures that crawled the ocean floor, and the birthdays of everyone she knew. She was often a fill-in for one of her sisters at our school should they be feeling under the weather, and was by far the most pleasant and prettiest of the three. I heard Mama tell Daddy, though, that Pearl would never marry on account of she was struck by polio when she was younger and was confined to a wheelchair. Miss Pearl seemed proud to be in that chair as her hero, President Franklin D. Roosevelt, shared the same fate.

When Lucy and Jack returned to school the following week, neither would say what had happened, no matter how much I begged.

"Just forget about it, Addie. It's all done with. Pa needed us to do some work." Lucy looked away.

"Fine," I said at last. "It's forgotten."

I sulked for the rest of the day, but I couldn't stay mad at my best friend forever, and I completely forgave her when she agreed that my new game of speaking with an English accent was one of the best I had ever come up with. We played it nearly the whole of fall that year, kicking up more and more leaves as the months passed until there came a time when we hurried so, the gusty winds of northern Michigan reminding us that we would have to wait for spring to continue our game.

I always had a new horse every spring, on account of the fact that my daddy killed so many each year. He was a fox farmer and fed the horse meat to the foxes and their pups, which he raised in a big building out back of the house that we called "the ranch." Daddy even paid the electric company to run a special line out there, so he could grind all the horse meat with a three-phase motor he had specially ordered. It took a stretch of time to skin the animal, gut it, and pull all the muscle away from the bones. He got about 700 pounds of horse meat after the skeleton, blood, and organs were removed. Every now and then the Tri-County Chemical Company would send a big truck out to the farm and they'd haul away all the offal that Pa hadn't ground up.

Daddy told us that when he was growing up they hadn't had the modern luxuries that we did, and he had had to haul all the horse and fox remains down to the grassy area by the river where my grandfather was buried. Except for the one headstone, it didn't look like much of a graveyard to me. The meadow grass was tall and soft, and there wasn't a better place to lie with a good book on a warm summer day.

We kids never cared much for the ranch for a whole lot of reasons, the main one being all the killing and skinning that went on out there. Not to mention that when a fox dug her way out of a pen, it was our job to run after her until she tired and Pa or my older brother, Earl, could catch her with a net. The fox-tending part of the ranch was made up of many small pens where the animal families lived, surrounded by a stronger, higher fence that pretty near made up an acre. In between all the small pens were miles and miles of rows that we did all the chasing in.

"Maude! Addie! Millie!" Pa would call out. "You gals come on down to the ranch. We got ourselves a runner."

Maude would put down her needlepoint and sigh. My older sister didn't care much for the foxes and especially didn't care much for all the running around in the dung and mud, but she would never think of sassing Daddy, as she knew his livelihood depended on it. We didn't have many chores, but fox-chasing was one of them.

We would stand at the gate waiting for Earl to say, "Go," and when it swung open, we'd take off like horses at a race. We'd run around and around those stinky pens, slipping on the dung and the mud, while Pa and Earl crouched in the corners waiting for us to tire that crazed fox so they could pop a net over her and return the rogue to her pen and family.

We didn't mind the first ten minutes or so, but after that we'd start to peter out a bit until Earl would spout some smart talk, urging us on. "Come on, girls," he'd taunt. "You're hardly movin' at all. That old fox is still goin' strong." My brother knew how hard we were working and how much Maude detested what we were doing. He just loved to put it up to her and made sure she saw him wink when she raced by.

Every now and then the good Lord would grant our little track team a reprieve in the form of the most modern of inventions.

"Daddy!" I yelled once. "I think I see an aeroplane over yonder."

He looked up and sure enough, off in the distance, a small single-engine aircraft was working its way across the wide sky. If we were lucky enough, it would pass right above our farm.

"Daddy, it's going too slow," Millie cried. "It's gonna fall right on us."

"No, peanut, it's goin' a lot faster than you think," Pa answered, his eyes squinting in the afternoon sun. "That's the amazin' thing about an aeroplane, isn't it? Jeez, I wonder . . ." and his voice trailed off to a whisper as he tracked the plane across the wild blue yonder.

"Do you think it might be Mr. Lindbergh, Pa?" Earl asked. All four of us turned eagerly to my father, hoping he would think it might be.

He shook his head slowly, one hand covering his eyes, the other tucked in the strap of his coveralls. "I don't think so, son. I reckon he don't fly too much over Michigan. Probably a pilot, come up from Detroit."

We all watched, not saying a whole lot, until the plane disappeared over the horizon, leaving only a small trail of white smoke lingering in the sky.

"Okay, folks, show's over," Pa announced, a little sadly. "Back to work. We got us a fox to catch."

We reluctantly returned to our job, the chasing harder than ever after our short break.

"Daddy, I'm plum tired out, and that mean old fox is lookin' to bite me," Millie wailed after a few more minutes. She ran over to Pa and patted his knee. "I'm only six, you know."

"Goin' on sixteen," Pa grinned. "Come on, peanut, you sit right here." Pa lifted Millie up and set her on the fence post. "Them big girls will run the heat right outta that sly old fox, you just watch."

My daddy was a fair and decent God-fearing man and didn't take any sass from any of his four kids. But he was no tyrant, either. Maude and I didn't mind too much that Millie got to sit out sometimes. We'd been six before and had done the same thing. We knew we wouldn't be running forever, although we sometimes joked in private that Pa would be calling us out when we were so old we'd be hobbling on two canes.

Once Millie was tired out, Maude and I would race around like complete idiots after the fox until about thirty minutes later, when the poor animal would finally tire. Earl would slap a net over her, scoop her up, and put her in a holding pen until Pa could fix the fence from which she had escaped.

We would amble away from the ranch, shoulders hunched, tired as all get out, but never once did my Daddy forget to call out, "You gals did a fine job. Thank you."

We would straighten up a bit as we walked towards the house, our chins a little higher. Suddenly our detested chore didn't seem so bad.

My best friend's mama had died giving birth to her third child, Cora, when Lucy was five. It was then that Lucy's daddy, who'd always had the temper of a hungry bear, just got meaner. Lucy and Jack weren't always at school. Their father often needed them to watch their younger sister or do the daily chores. Not only did Lucy and Jack have no mother, but their younger sister had been born simple. I heard Daddy tell Mama that the Old Doc was so intoxicated when he came to help Rosie Conklin deliver that he left that baby in too long and the oxygen to baby Cora's brain got cut off. If that weren't bad enough, in the midst of trying to get that baby out, Lucy's mama had lost too much blood and bled to death. John Conklin was left alone to run the farm and raise three young children. A few years later, he'd married Rosie's sister, Bonnie, and Lucy's workload had eased some as her aunt resumed her dead mother's duties, including taking care of the baby. Cora was a sweet little thing, but she was thick and needed watching over most of the time.

Lucy was my bosom buddy and we figured we were some kind of cousins twice removed or something, as my Daddy's cousin, Mary, was married to her Uncle Ben. Lucy looked exactly the opposite of me—while I had long auburn hair, freckles, and dark green eyes, she was a dead ringer for Shirley Temple, with strawberry blond ringlets and eyes as blue as the Caribbean Sea that Aunt Pearl had told us about. Despite the fact that her family didn't have much,

Lucy always put herself together nicely and rarely looked dirty or unkempt—something I could not claim. From early on, Lucy had the ability to make any boy forget how to speak, including my brother Earl.

"Mornin', Miss Temple," Earl would squeak when Lucy would come by to pick me up on our way to school. "I mean, Miss Lucy," he would add coyly.

"'Lo, Earl," Lucy would call out, skipping across the wide path to our house. Earl would be grinning like a fool and all puffed up with pride like he'd just discovered water.

"Hey, Earl," I'd yell. "Is that some fox dung on your shoes?" Lucy and I would run off, howling with laughter, and look back to watch Earl checking out the bottom of his boots.

Lucy had a much longer walk to school than I did. It was almost two miles just to our place and another mile or so to the schoolhouse, but the time seemed to disappear as we chatted, and we always got to school sooner than we wanted.

"Did you hear about what happened to Frankie?" Lucy asked one warm spring day as we started out for school.

"Your cousin Frankie?"

"Yes, that Frankie." Lucy pulled absentmindedly on her curls as she continued. "They were getting the fields ready for sowing time and he was on Uncle John's tractor. He was set to go home, so he took a shortcut across the Lewis' field." She looked over to make sure I was listening. "Well, he lost control of the thing, and that tractor went through the field and plowed right into Farmer Lewis' hen house." She smacked her hands together for emphasis. "He run over a mess of hens and a couple roosters and practically tore the whole of the building down." She grabbed my arm excitedly. "He put a big dent in the new tractor, and Uncle John was spittin' mad."

"No!" I exclaimed in horror, picturing poultry being catapulted from the small barn, feathers flying everywhere.

"It's true," she replied, pleased that she could make me cringe at the sheer dreadfulness of the story.

"What happened then?"

"Frankie said he don't know what happened. He banged his head but good... musta knocked the stuffing right outta him. He doesn't remember anything."

"Did he get a whoopin'?" I knew her uncle to be as mean as his brother, and my morbid curiosity was stronger than my good manners.

"I didn't ask," she replied stiffly, and I knew I had offended her. It was common knowledge that her daddy and uncle were drinkers whose anger got the best of them. I immediately took it back, and said that I wished I would think a bit before I opened my pie hole.

"That's okay," she said.

But I wasn't sure that it was. We walked the rest of the way without speaking, and when we got to school I promised her she could have one of my banana muffins at lunch.

When we arrived, Miss Ruby and Miss Opal were greeting the children and helping the younger ones store their lunch pails and sweaters. We took our seats at the same table and pulled out our primers. Even though Lucy was a year older, we were in the same grade because of all the school she had missed. Maude sat a few seats back next to her closest friend, Winnie Mae, who I thought was a silly girl with no sense about her at all. Maude said I was wrong, that Winnie was sweet and they were like two peas in a pod, and when I judged Winnie I judged her. This was actually true. I thought my sister was a bit silly, too.

Miss Ruby stood before our class of sixteen and cleared her throat quietly to get our attention so we could begin the school day. None of the Miller sisters was a loud woman, except when they sang in the choir at church. They commanded our respect through a calm authority that brought even the rowdiest of cowboys to attention. My aunt Ruby was a thin, angular woman with a sharp jaw, a hawkish nose, and small eyes. She was not, oddly enough, unattractive—strange, given her unusual combination of features—but they all worked together to create a pleasant enough face.

"Before we begin, I would like to address an issue that I believe needs to be resolved." She looked around the room and we all wondered what essential rule we had violated. "The honor system for doing the room chores is not working, and that plan has fallen by the wayside. It is apparent that we need to have a schedule that makes everyone more accountable." I breathed a sigh of relief. It was nothing my parents would have to know about.

"I would like an assistant to document these chores and set up a schedule. Volunteers, please?"

Winnie Mae threw her hand up and practically jumped out of her seat.

"Thank you, Winnie Mae." Miss Ruby smiled. "I'll see you at lunch in the courtyard to go over details. Maude may also help." I thought Winnie Mae and Maude would start crying, they looked so happy. I rolled my eyes at Lucy, who gently shook her head.

Only at school was I to refer to my aunts as Miss Ruby and Miss Opal, but it was a hard habit to break. Many a time, during visits or holidays, I slipped up. All of us Harris kids tried our best at school to set an example (Mama's words), as it would be the utmost in embarrassment (Pa's words) to have our aunts telling our parents one of us was misbehaving.

At lunch, Lucy and I sat beneath the large weeping willow on the banks of the river chewing the fat while we ate our boiled eggs and banana muffins. We were chatting about *Little Miss Marker*, a picture show we had seen over the summer at the Bijou. Shirley Temple was the latest craze and Lucy, being that she looked so much like her, felt a special kinship. Most of our discussions about the most popular five-year-old in the world usually ended the same way—we thought Lucy was every bit as talented and good-looking as the matinee idol. When she leaned in and lowered her voice I was all ears, knowing I was in for some good gossip. If anyone was good for gossip, it was Lucy.

"I think Aunt Bonnie is in that way," she whispered.

"What way?" I asked.

Lucy sighed and looked at me with pity. "That way... like I'm gonna have a new brother or sister." She sat back, waiting for the information to sink in, pleased that once again she could deliver news that would shock.

"You mean . . .," I stuttered.

"Yes, I do."

"Dang," I whispered. "Does your daddy know?"

"I hope so, seein' as he was there for the event," she cocked her head. "If ya know what I mean."

I didn't, but somehow I thought I should, so I nodded. "What are you gonna do?"

"What can I do? I guess I'll be watching Cora a little more, doing more of the chores. Ya know…," her voice trailed off.

I reached out and patted Lucy's hand. My friend did not have an easy life and her daddy wasn't anything like mine. He rarely spoke to Lucy except to give orders or dole out a punishment. "Maybe it'll be a boy," I offered hopefully.

But before she could answer, Joey Hicks, a fifth grader from Michigami Lake, ran past us calling out, "There's a fight down by the river!"

We looked at each other and jumped up quickly, following him around the small bend to where the majority of our school chums were circled around two boys. A fight was big news and almost always resulted in one body being hurt and one body being expelled. This was more than exciting. We pushed our way into the tightly knit group, trying to see the fighters, wondering who would be daring enough to cause such a ruckus. Lucy gasped, so I knew she'd identified at least one of them.

"Who is it?" I yelled. I pressed ahead, shoving someone whose elbow had found its way into my ribs.

"It's Jack! Jack is fighting with Bobby!" Lucy cried out. She screamed her brother's name repeatedly until she finally caught his attention and he glanced toward her. Bobby, the class bully, took the offered opportunity to administer a left hook to Jack's nose, and before you could say lickity-split, blood started spurting from his snout, splattering the bystanders who were too close to the action. Jack went wild and pummeled Bobby with a one-two punch that sent him reeling, but didn't knock him down.

Miss Opal showed up just as Lucy jumped on Bobby's back and just as my brother grabbed Lucy and tried to pull her off. With one hand, Bobby was fending off Lucy, who was stuck on him like a June bug. With the other, he kept Jack at bay, and Earl was caught somewhere in the middle. Earl took a punch to the eye from Jack, who, through all the blood, had accidentally taken him for Bobby. Lucy got tossed on her bottom and got right up, ready to throw herself back into the melee, but stopped short when she heard Miss Opal command, "Stop!"

She repeated herself a bit louder, but it wasn't until the third "stop" that the boys put their dukes down. Nobody said a word. The fighters bent over, hands on their knees, trying to catch their breath, while Miss Opal assessed the situation. She looked more curious than she did angry, and for some reason that scared me even more. Boy, there was going to be some whoopins tonight—Bobby's daddy was the town drunk, and I could only imagine what Jack and Lucy's Pa would do.

"Jack, Bobby," Miss Opal sighed, "I'll see you both at my desk immediately." She glanced at the bruised and bloody boys. "On second thought, please clean up before you enter our fine institution of learning. Earl, you may as well come, too." She turned and walked back toward the school, shaking her head slightly as she rounded the bend.

The three boys were barely out of earshot when the squabbling started. Everyone started talking at once, so it was nearly impossible to hear any explanations.

"Jack started it," taunted Fred, Bobby's cousin. "He hit Bobby first. I seen it."

"You're a liar, Fred Cassidy," shouted Lucy. "There ain't no way Jack woulda done that without no reason." She looked around for support. "Somethin' had to happen. What did Bobby say to him?"

No one said anything for a second, until Janet Sims spoke up. "He called your sister a name, Lucy. He deserved a punch. He called Cora a moron…

and simple." Janet turned away quickly, as though it had pained her to inform Lucy of this unpleasant fact.

Lucy looked deflated, like she'd been punched herself. All the spit and fire was gone, and she spoke softly. "Cora ain't but five years old, and she never did anything to that horrible Bobby. Why'd he want to say such a thing?"

Lucy turned and started back towards the school. I ran after her and put my arm around her shoulder.

"Lucy, you know Bobby's got a mean streak a mile long… he ain't nothing but a bully and a coward and an idiot and an ass." I surprised myself with my cursing and Lucy as well. She broke into a smile, unable to help herself.

"Well, I'm glad Jack beat the tar outta him," Lucy said, wiping her arm across her nose. "And I hope Bobby gets a lickin' like he's never seen from his pa."

We walked in silence back to school and sat out on the front steps listening to the murmur of discipline coming from inside. Miss Ruby soon showed up and looked at us peculiar-like before going into the schoolhouse to hear the details of the fight that had interrupted her meeting with Winnie Mae and Maude. Lucy and I knew we would hear the particulars after school. Our brothers were sitting in the hot seat, and would be sure to share on the walk home. It would be a long day waiting to hear what had happened, and the thought of having to sit through spelling and arithmetic was almost unbearable… both Lucy and I were short on the virtue of patience.

The other children started drifting back and the group swelled in size. Soon the whole school was waiting on the stoop for the door to open. When Miss Ruby appeared and finally admitted the eager class, we all hurried inside, curious about what the detainees were doing. To our great disappointment, none of the three boys was anywhere to be seen. No one dared ask what had happened. We could only assume they had left out the back door, presumably sent home to face the surprised looks of their unsuspecting folks. Lucy and I gave each other the "now we'll have to wait till dinner to find out" look and, with great sighs, sat at our bench and began our afternoon of study.

The tick-tock of the old wall clock taunted me unmercifully all afternoon, until I was about ready to scream out to be shot and put out of my misery. Just when I thought my head would explode, Miss Ruby announced that we could put our books away and get ready to leave. Lucy and I shared the "finally!" look and packed up quicker than jack rabbits.

We were on the verge of escape when Miss Ruby called my name, asking me to stay behind. This was almost too much. With my best friend waiting for me outside, I walked to the front of the room, praying to the dear Lord Jesus to make this quick. Our mighty Savior must have been listening that day because all my aunt did was hold up an envelope, waving it slightly back and forth.

"Adeline, I know that you'll respect my wishes when I ask you not to open it." Miss Ruby looked over her spectacles at me as she handed me the letter. "Your sister is staying after school with Winnie Mae to finish the meeting we started at lunch. Tell your mother she'll only be a few minutes."

"Yes, ma'am," I answered, wondering how adults always knew to tell you not to do the things you were thinking about doing. I speculated on whether I would possess this skill when I grew up as I raced to catch up with Lucy, who was dragging her feet through the dust slower than molasses.

"Well?" she said, cocking her head slightly and looking more like Shirley Temple than I could ever remember. I held up the letter.

"For my folks," I explained. "She asked me not to read it."

"How do they always know?" she said, echoing my earlier sentiments.

I shrugged my shoulders. We held the letter every which way, hoping to catch a word or two, but no such luck. The contents of the letter were to remain a secret.

"What's your Pa going to do? Ya' know, about Jack?" I knew it probably wouldn't be good.

"I ain't sure," she answered. "He can't be too mad. Jack was just defending Cora."

"Yeah, but he hit first. My Daddy would have said, 'Just walk away, son. Walk away.'"

"Yeah, well, my daddy ain't your daddy. He don't put much stock in walkin' away from an insulting remark. I bet Jack don't even get a whippin'." She kicked a big stone and muttered "ouch" under her breath.

"I hope not. Jack isn't the type to be startin' a fight."

It was true. For all the bad luck he'd had with his Mama dying and his Daddy being so mean, Jack Conklin was one of the most respectful boys around. He didn't talk a whole lot and he wasn't a teaser like Earl. Many a time I found him and Lucy in deep conversation as they passed our farm on the way to school, but when I joined them he just quieted down and listened to me and Lucy jabber. He was smart as a whip, too. I heard Miss Opal telling my folks that if he could get to school more often, he would make perfect marks. You could tell Lucy and he were kin—they shared the same color hair, though Jack wore his short and had a different nose. He didn't have Lucy's manner, either. He was much more serious, like he had the weight of the world on his shoulders. My daddy often hired Jack to work with him and Earl during tanning time when he needed the extra help. Jack certainly needed the extra money. Sometimes, I wasn't so sure Jack even cared much for me. I'd catch him every now and then giving me an odd look like I'd said something dimwitted, but he was my best friend's brother and my daddy's worker and I knew that if I ever needed anything, I could always rely on Jack Conklin. He was that kind of a person.

Lucy and I were both worried—not so much about Earl, since all he had tried to do was stop the fight; not about Bobby at all; and actually not even so much about Jack, as Lucy felt sure her Daddy would understand—but Lucy and I were happy to be worrying about something on that long walk home.

"I'm worried about two things," Lucy said. "First off, I'm worried that Jack won't be able to go back to school tomorrow, and second, that Bobby broke Jack's nose." She glanced at me. "And he really does have a handsome nose, Addie, don't ya think?"

I agreed on the handsomeness of her brother's nose, but not to be outdone by Lucy, shared my own fears. "I'm worried that Earl won't be able to see as well. Maybe Jack broke something important in his eyeball. Also, I'm worried that Earl might need spectacles and, if he does, I'm worried that he'll get into another fight and break his new glasses. They cost money, ya know."

Lucy looked at me, a twinkle in her eye, and began, "I'm worried that Jack will have to get his nose cut off and Old Doc will try to attach a new one and it'll turn green and fall off and then all Jack 'till have is a big hole in his face." She snorted as she tried not to laugh.

"Well, it's a good thing you're worried," I said.

"Why?"

"Because then Jack would have two pie holes instead of one." We couldn't stop ourselves from doubling over in fits of laughter at the grotesque thought of Jack's face with the gangrene nose.

We were punchy most of the way, but grew somber as we neared our farm. I bid Lucy goodbye, and couldn't help but think that I wouldn't trade places with her for anything.

I walked down our long driveway holding the envelope from my aunt like I was delivering a cup of tea served in the finest china. I turned my nose up, and in a snooty voice softly said, "Excuse me, madam, your eldest is being sent to the loony bin by order of the Queen. If you refuse this command, your whole family will be taken out and shot. And, oh, did I mention this was by order of the Queen?" I loved the way my voice sounded with a British accent and wished I were from England.

My folks and Earl sat at the table talking in a hushed whisper when I walked in. I handed my mother the note and relayed the fact that Maude would be home shortly.

"That's fine, Addie. Please go get Millie from the porch and take her for a short walk to the creek. Your father and I would like to finish our conversation with Earl," my mother said as she opened the letter from her sister.

Sensing my overwhelming disappointment at not being included, my Daddy interjected. "Don't you worry none, Addie. We'll have a nice long talk about this whole thing at dinner. Let's wait 'til Maudy can join us, too. Okay?

Right now, we need to talk to Earl alone." He gave me a weak smile. "Now go get your sister and do what Mama asked you to do." He patted my bottom dismissively and that was my clue to skedaddle.

"'Tis so unfair," I complained loudly in my favorite accent as I headed out to get Millie. "I was the one chosen to deliver the sacred letter. I was the one who braved the dark and dangerous path through the forest. How can they cast me out as such?" I opened the door and saw that Millie had moved to the tire swing. "Mildred," I called out. "Mildred, my dear, please commence with me to a special place of my choosing."

Millie ran over and grabbed my hand. "Why are you talkin' so funny?" she asked.

"'Funny,' dear child? I see nothing funny about my tone of voice."

She stared at me, unsmiling. "If you don't stop it, I'm gonna tell on you."

"Oh, Millie," I said. "Where's your sense of humor?"

"I guess I'm not old enough to have one yet. How old were you when you got one?"

"I dunno. I guess in the third or fourth grade." I thought hard. How old had I been?

"Well, I'm not even in school, so I haven't learnt it yet." Millie ran up ahead. "Addie, will you play hide-n-seek with me?"

Ah, to be six again, I thought as I raced out of sight calling, "You're it!"

A couple of hours later, Maude and I were setting the table for dinner when she glanced around and whispered, "I saw Mr. Van Ostin and Bobby walking into the school as Winnie and I were leaving. He didn't look too happy."

"Really," I said. "Do you think Bobby'll get suspended?"

"If I had to guess, I'd say yes," she answered, reaching over to rearrange the knife and fork I'd just set down. "Addie, you need to be more careful with the silverware. I won't always be here to fix it for you."

Promise? I said to myself. "Sorry, Maude."

"When I get married, Mama said I could have Grandmother Miller's silver, seeing as I'm the firstborn girl and I can't imagine any of the aunts having children at this point. I think they're too old, actually. I wonder how old a woman has to be 'til she can't have any babies?" Maude paused for a moment. "Mama's the youngest, and she's no spring chicken."

"Who's no spring chicken, Maude?" Pa came into the room carrying a plate of sliced beef and set it on the table.

"Mama," Maude answered.

"Why would you say that, Maudy?"

"Well, I just figured that Aunt Ruby and Aunt Opal were too old to have any babies. Also, Aunt Pearl's in a wheelchair and Mama, being the youngest, well…"

Daddy looked amused until Maude asked, "Pa, how long can a lady have babies?"

"Maude, you'll have to speak to your mother about that. I don't rightly know." And with that, he hurried out of room calling out, "Susie!" and glanced back over his shoulder like he was being followed.

The table was set, the food was passed, and we all looked at Mama and Pa, waiting anxiously for the talk about the fight to begin. Earl had a raw horse steak on a plate next to his dinner, and took great pains in applying it to his shiner between bites. Mama cleared her throat and said, "George?" which we all knew was Daddy's clue to begin.

"You know Mama and I don't believe in physical violence in any way, right?" We all nodded, except for Millie, who asked, "What's finsickel violets?"

Mama smiled sweetly at her baby. "'Physical violence,' Millie—hitting and punching."

"You mean like how Earl got hit in the eye?"

"Yes, exactly."

"Sometimes Addie pushes me," Millie tattled.

"Well, that's what we're talking about, Millie," replied Pa, glaring at me. "Now, Millie, I need you to stop talking for a few minutes and listen to your mama and me because we want to tell you why hittin' is wrong, okay?"

"Yes, Papa," Millie replied weakly.

"Hitting is wrong because people have the God-given skills of logic," said Pa, and before Millie could interrupt, added, "This means they can talk about what makes them mad or angry. They don't have to use their fists to settle arguments. You don't see Mama and me hitting, do you?" We all shook our heads. "If something upsets you, all you need to do is explain to the person who is makin' you mad how you feel, and if that don't work, what do we do?" Pa looked at Earl and nodded his head.

"We walk away, Pa," Earl answered.

"That's right," Mama interjected. "It takes a big person to walk away from a bully or a fight. Some people think walking away means being a coward, but it's the opposite. A person who is above fighting can feel like the winner by not engaging with someone willing to bait them into a quarrel." Mama was definitely a Miller sister. We all looked to Pa for a translation.

"It's usually the cowards that start fights because they know they can pick on people and get them all riled up. Especially if they're bigger and they want attention," Pa said.

"Like Bobby Van Ostin?" I asked.

"Yes, like Bobby Van Ostin. Somehow he needs people to look at him and be scared of him. He does this by bein' mean and hopin' someone will take the bait." Pa looked around to see if we understood what he was saying.

Maude raised her hand. "Yes, Maudy?" Daddy smiled at Mama.

"Daddy, Jack Conklin ain't really a coward a'tall. Why do you suppose he went off and socked Bobby?"

"He's *not* a coward, Maude," Mama said correcting her.

"I know he's not, Mama."

"No, Maude. The correct way to say it is 'He is not a coward,' not 'He ain't a coward.'" Mama sighed. Mama wrote a weekly column for the *Michigami Weekly* called "Woman's Work," and she was a stickler for grammar.

"I'm sorry, Mama, I forgot."

"That's okay, dear."

Daddy spoke again. "This is the tricky part, gang. Jack shoulda just walked away from Bobby's taunts, but Jack has a lot of pride. He also has a lot of love for his little sister and he let his anger get the best of him. Jack Conklin is a good boy and Miss Ruby knows it, but he's got to take responsibility for his actions and learn that throwin' a punch ain't the way to solve a problem. He can walk right into the school and tell Miss Ruby or Miss Opal, and they can handle Bobby Van Ostin."

Maude and Earl and I looked at each other like Daddy had told us we were going to the moon. To tell on another kid was like the kiss of death. I could not think of one person who went to our school who would do this, from whiney Winnie Mae down to six-year-old Jane Holcomb. Being suspended would be a million times better than being a tattletale.

"Is Earl in trouble, Daddy?" asked Millie.

"Earl is not in trouble, Millie, but he should be more careful when gettin' involved in someone else's battles. For one thing, he could get seriously hurt."

"I ain't afraid of that," Earl muttered under his breath.

"I'm not afraid, Earl," Mama corrected.

"Sorry, Mama."

Mama patted Earl's hand. "Daddy and I just want to see all of you grow up to be civilized adults who contribute to society and help make your town and surrounding areas better."

"What's 'cibilized,' Mama?" Millie asked, and we all groaned, even Daddy.

We returned to school the next day, but talk of the fight lingered for weeks. Earl proudly wore his shiner, gladly telling anyone who would listen how tough he was, but Jack remained mum about the incident. He left school a week early to help his daddy with the planting and I didn't see him until the summer, when he and his cousin would set tongues wagging again.

Frankie and his family had come to Michigami for the County Fair, and he and Jack joined in as a team for the tug o'war contest. During the game, the two cousins thought they could get a little better leverage with the rope if they wrapped a thick stick around the tugging end and each pulled, using the stick as a handle. Well, that didn't work like they'd expected, because Frankie's pointer got caught up in the rope and was pulled quickly and neatly off his left hand just above the knuckle.

"We done it a hundred times before," I heard Jack nervously tell Frankie's daddy. There was a whole lot of commotion, what with the screaming and yelling, and poor Mrs. Conklin had gone and fainted when she saw all the blood spurting from her boy's hand. Mr. Conklin took off his jacket and wrapped Frankie's fist with it, yelling over his shoulder, "Hey, you kids! You go on and look for Frankie's finger. Hurry, now!"

None of the other girls, except for me and Millie, would look for the finger on account of they were all crying, but I knew maybe the Old Doc could sew it back on. All the boys, excited by the fact that someone was missing a body part, started searching for Frankie Conklin's lost finger among the grassy area of the tug o'war field.

I wasn't quite sure what a finger looked like that didn't have a hand attached to it, but when I spied a fat pink worm that wasn't moving, I was pretty sure I'd found one. It was a strange sensation, picking up that lost finger. It was light as a small stone, and blood dripped from the cut-off end when I squeezed ever so slightly. I ran back to the cluster of adults.

"This it, Mr. Conklin?" I asked breathlessly, holding out my find. He stared in amazement at the neatly severed finger in my plump little hand while I took my first real look at Frankie Conklin. He was a slim, handsome boy of eleven or twelve with streaky hair and dark eyes that were half-closed like he was almost asleep. Lucy's daddy cradled him in his arms, and Frankie groaned softly. He slowly opened his eyes wide and looked at me dreamy-like, as if he wasn't sure I was real. We stared at each other with the kind of open curiosity that only children are allowed, and then he passed out.

"Yeah, I reckon that's it, all right," Mr. Conklin announced. His large hands, rough from years of farm work, picked up his son's finger and set it gently on the bucket of ice that my Aunt Ruby had brought over.

"What's your name, gal?" he asked. His weight shifted as he stood and he placed his hands on his knees to balance himself.

"I'm Adeline Harris. I'm almost nine." I lowered my eyes, suddenly feeling a bit shy.

"Well, you done good, Adeline." Mr. Conklin picked up his son and hurried over to their old Chevy where Frankie's sisters were waiting with his Ma. They took off in search of the Old Doc (best guess was Riley's Pub), and the crowd quickly scattered after the Conklins' automobile disappeared in a cloud of dust.

I stood alone on the tug o'war field, still wrapped in my first cloud of infatuation. The smell of popcorn and hot dogs drifted around me and I heard the neighing of horses in the background, but I was in my own world. I stared at the smeared blood on my palm and recalled how that small finger had felt in my hand and how proud I was to have been the one to have found it. I saw how Frankie's sleepy eyes had looked at me and how it seemed that we somehow had spoken, even though I knew we hadn't. The tickle still was working its way through my stomach when I felt a tap on my shoulder and Earl informed me that the rest of our family was ready to head out.

I sat in the back seat, nestled between Maude and Earl, content to gaze out the window and hum a mindless tune. It was only when I heard Frankie's name that I perked up. My mother and father were speaking in a low voice, and I had to lean forward on the seat, as though I had seen something of interest out the window, in order to hear.

"What about the tractor incident?" I heard my father ask.

"He's only a boy. Didn't you ever do anything you were sorry for?" My mother cocked her head.

"Nothing that cost almost two hundred dollars in damage to another man's property." My father raised his eyebrows as he spoke, "…besides breakin' my daddy's tractor."

"Judge not, lest ye be judged," my mother said as she poked his shoulder lightly. "And your daddy didn't have a tractor; he had a horse."

"You Miller gals," my father replied good-naturedly. "You always got an answer." He tapped the steering wheel a couple of times before he continued. "But I got to tell you, Susie, something about that boy just don't seem right."

Something not right about Frankie? I wanted to defend the fingerless boy, but I was just an unwanted bystander to the conversation, and my input would not be appreciated.

"I'll tell you something else," he added, almost as an afterthought. "I don't see nothin' but trouble comin' his way."

My dander was ruffled even more. How could he make such a forecast? My parents were always speaking of treating people fairly, and I was incensed that they were talking of my Frankie that way. I sat back in my seat and crossed my arms on my chest, unable to listen in on any more of their discussion. The conversation soon died down and we rode the rest of the way home in silence, my parents caught up in their own private thoughts.

Frankie and his missing digit soon faded into a favorite memory, and it would not be until years later that my father's prediction actually would come true. He had been right about Frankie, but for all the wrong reasons.

Chapter Two

George

My name is George David Harris, Jr. I am five-feet-eleven-inches tall and have weighed between one hundred seventy and one hundred eighty pounds since I was twenty years old. I resemble my paternal grandfather, Earl, and have his thick hair, broad shoulders, and flat stomach. Because my papa always told me, "You act the way you dress," I always wear a white shirt and tie, and a dress jacket or suit when going to church, a play, restaurants in the evening, and weddings and funerals. I also take an overcoat, gloves, and a hat if the weather is cold or windy.

I am an honest man, sometimes to a fault, and I have learned tactfulness the hard way as a result. I don't envy the material possessions that others have, and I have accepted my life—not unhappily, just with a little curiosity as to what God has planned. But I am what I am because of His doings, and I try not to question Him. He has a plan, and I recognize this. I love my family, my home, and my town, and I wouldn't trade places with no one, but I sometimes wonder how my life could have been different. Ain't that always the case, though? The grass is always greener...

I speak now as an adult, and as I listen to my solemn self, I wonder where the boy I once was went. Can my crosses be so heavy that I have forgotten the wonderment of life? The curiosity? The excitement? The enthusiasm? Are these feelings only for children? Is that an adult's lot, to be saddled with concerns about taxes, employment, dismal affairs of state? To shoulder the responsibility for the safety of his family? Of his neighbors? Where does it stop?

I am not the man I thought I would be. That I even have these thoughts is proof enough. A respectable man takes his knocks. He goes on with his life, taking the curve balls thrown by some higher power. But somewhere along the way I took a turn that set these thoughts forever in my brain. At one time I felt right enough to share these opinions and beliefs with another, but that was a long time ago. I ain't complaining, just taking notice. I don't like to even give it much thought, but every once in a while it occurs to me that as a young boy I would never have accepted my lot so easily. I would have put up a fight. I would have stood my ground. I would have just said "no." At least, I'd like to think so.

I ain't smart enough to have figured out what happened. All I know is that, bit by bit, my life moved further from my dreams and the fight left me. I figure this must happen to everyone, because we don't have a world overcome with baseball players and statesmen—just everyday Joes, like me.

My mama died soon after I was born, and my papa never remarried, having done had "the great love of his life." He seemed content to live in the large home in which he raised me without the advantages that a wife would bring. Mrs. Singer, who had come north as a young woman, had been with Papa for years and helped with all things female-like. She and her husband Washington, a mulatto from Georgia, lived in the two large back rooms of our home, and betwixt them took care of me and Papa, until Mrs. Singer returned to the South and to her kin after Washington died.

I don't rightly know the whole of the story, but as a young man, Papa had gotten involved in securing homes and work for the flood of newly freed slaves come up from the South after the war ended. Mrs. Singer and Washington lived with my papa and his family, and after Papa married they stayed with him to help his new bride get settled. After Mama died there weren't any question as to what would happen, and Papa thanked the Lord daily for their loyalty. Washington helped Papa with the foxes, and them two were friends, seeing as there weren't much difference in their ages and they were both healthy, sturdy men looking to make a living. My Papa respected Washington and Mrs. Singer, as they did him, and I spent my boyhood with these three adults fussing over me. Mrs. Singer and Washington never did have children, and they worried about me same as my papa, sometimes even more.

"Junior?" Mrs. Singer would call up in her fading southern accent as I was getting ready for school. "Y'all don't forget your hat today. It's fixin' to be a cold one."

I would hear her mumbling about catching a bug that would put me under, and I'd reluctantly put down my baseball mitt and groan. School in April weren't my favorite place to be. I was of the opinion that I should be practicing my game, as my intentions were to play shortstop for the newly formed Detroit Tigers Baseball Club. I figured I didn't need schooling to play ball.

Baseball was the most exciting thing ever to have happened to me. In 1902, when I was only four years old, the Detroit Tigers came back to win their first game ever in the American League, beating Milwaukee, and I thought I would burst like a split watermelon. Even though the news were a couple days old, I relived every minute of the exciting game as Papa read the full account of the match from the *Detroit Free Press*. My biggest goal in life that day was, by hook or by crook, to get to Bennett Park and watch Frank "Pop" Dillon slug one out.

"I promise you, son," Papa told me, "one day I'll take you to Detroit to see a game. I can't rightly say when, but I got business there every few years or so and we'll see what happens. But you'll go."

I lived for that day, and bothered Papa so much that he said if I done said another word about it, he'd change his mind. From that day forward I kept my yearnings to myself, but the idea was never far from my thoughts.

Since I never knew my mama, seeing as she died when I was two days old, I never really missed her. Papa wasn't one for speaking much of her, though I knew her name was Helen and she was twenty-six years when she passed, and that she was beautiful. Mrs. Singer would tell me about her as she sat on the edge of my bed, the flickering kerosene lamp lighting her handsome ebony face.

"Your mama was about the best seamstress I ever done seen. Why, she could make curtains outta a hankie, that woman could," Mrs. Singer would say as she tucked the quilt around me.

"Do you think she would have liked baseball?" I asked.

"Well, now, I 'spect she would. 'Specially if you do," she said.

"I wanna be a baseball player so bad, Mrs. Singer. Every night I pray to the Lord and ask Him to help me be better, and every day I try to practice like crazy so if He sees fit to let me play, I won't disappoint Him."

"Oh, baby, you can't never disappoint the good Lord, don't y'all know that? He loves you no matter what you do."

Mrs. Singer looked so upset I sat up and gave her a quick hug. "I'm glad I don't have no mama."

"Why, Junior, why would you ever say that?" she asked with a look of wonderment.

"Because I like you here. It's like you're my mama. I don't need no one else."

I meant what I said. She was everything I imagined a mother would be, and I had nothing to compare it to. What more could I want?

She got up quickly and kissed my cheek, her eyes wet. "Go on now to sleep, Junior. God loves you."

Her voice suggested that it was not just God who loved me, and I snuggled under my covers, safe and happy. I closed my eyes, imagining the opening season for next year and hoping I would be there. The last thing I heard was her whispering voice telling Washington that I would be the death of her yet.

Mrs. Singer was always Mrs. Singer, even to her husband. Papa felt that a lady, no matter what her color, should be respected, so in our household she was never referred to by any other name. I once saw a piece of paper that listed her name as Leona, but she was no more a Leona to me than Papa was. It was funny because we all called Washington just that, but when Papa first told Washington and Mrs. Singer to call him George, they flatly refused.

"That wouldn't be fittin'," they told him.

"But Washington, I'm askin' you to call me George. This is equality. This is why we done had a war. It's your right," Papa pleaded.

"Don't take no offense, Mr. Harris, and I do appreciate you makin' the offer and all, but this here Negro got a long history of knowing what to say and when to say it. I been durn lucky so far as I ain't seen a noose yet, and I aim to keep it that way. North and all." He and Mrs. Singer nodded together, and Papa could tell there was no changing their minds.

"'Mr. Harris' it is, then," he conceded. "I can't say I've ever walked in your shoes, and if that's what you're feelin', then I respect it as such, though it don't make much sense to me."

"That's because you white, Mr. Harris. You a white man."

Papa and Washington looked at each other for a moment like they was seeing the other for the first time.

Papa reached his hand out, and Washington slowly shook it. "I'm sorry, Washington, I truly am. I know firsthand life ain't always fair. I forget that sometimes."

"The Lord, he work in mysterious ways," Washington said.

I asked Papa later about what Washington meant when he talked about "not seeing the noose." I knew about the Civil War and how Lincoln had freed the slaves, but not much more. Papa told me of the hate that drove some folks to do serious harm to the Negro population, or any population that wasn't exactly like them, and that they had so much hate in their hearts that they would kill.

"Are these people Christians, Papa?"

"They say they are, son, but they sure don't act like it. Violence ain't never the way decent folks solve their differences. Some people don't see that others can also have a side to the argument. They just want to be right no matter what, and they're willing to do anything to prove that, even if it's plum wrong."

"Papa, that ain't fair."

"No son, it's not. But I said it before—and you always remember this—life ain't always fair. We all got our burdens to shoulder and our crosses to bear."

"You got a cross, Papa?"

He didn't say anything for a moment, just stared off into the distance like he was doing some serious thinking. "Yeah, I got a cross, son."

He pushed his hat back on his head and looked over to me, the smile returning to his face. "Hey, Junior, let's go throw a ball for a few minutes. Whaddaya say?"

"Oh, boy, I say 'Whoopee!'" I ran off to get my glove, forgetting about crosses and burdens and anything else that wasn't baseball.

One spring day I come back from school to find Papa and Washington unloading timber and stacking it in piles.

"What's up, Papa?" I asked.

"Washington and me's building a little apartment out by the fox pens. We been using the shed for too long and we got too many foxes for it to be useful anymore. This here building's goin' be plenty big to do all our skinnin' in. Right, Washington?"

"That's right, Mr. Harris."

"Can I help, Pa?"

"Whaddaya think, Boss? He old enough?" My papa looked to Washington.

Washington looked me up and down; I crossed my fingers behind my back, hoping he would agree. "I reckon he is, Mr. Harris. He gettin' big."

"Yippee!" I shouted, jumping up and down.

"Go run in and get a bite from Mrs. Singer, and then you can come back." Papa grinned as he looked down.

I couldn't get back fast enough, and over the next few months that spring, we built a fine apartment and workroom from the 200-year-old pines felled from the banks of the great river that ran through our back lot.

Once a year, in late November or December, depending on the lot size, it would be pelting time. Papa would put the mature foxes, one by one, in a wooden box where they couldn't move and inject them with a needle full of chloroform. He'd throw the carcasses into the freezing room, a small unheated shed outside, where the dead animals would be safe from hungry varmints until it was their time to be skinned. Papa was a skilled tanner and could skin ten to fifteen foxes a day—pretty good, seeing as it took most men almost an hour to do one. When he was finished, he would hand the hide carefully to Washington, who would lay it fur side down on a flat board and pin it there to dry. After a week or so, they would flip the hide over, comb out the fur, and let it continue to dry out for a few more days until they felt it was finished. Drumming was the last step in the process: the furs, some sawdust, and a bit of mineral oil were put in the steel drum and spun, and then the pelts were brushed carefully in order to bring out the shine and softness. The finished pelts were carefully packaged in wooden crates and put in a locked room in the cellar until Papa could ship them off to auction in Detroit.

Papa and Washington spent most of that winter out in the new apartment they called the ranch, working by day and sleeping in the small bunkroom at night, keeping a close eye on those pelts. They always slept with a shotgun close by, and when I asked Papa about the gun, he replied that those furs was worth a lot of money—his whole year's earnings—and he didn't need no funny business. He said there was a difference between defending your property and just plain fighting, and he wasn't gonna let no one take what was his. My granddaddy had been a fox farmer before him, and Papa had inherited his business. It had kept Granddad and my papa in a healthy way; Papa said that even during hard times, the wealthy still needed their fur coats. We lived a good life. No one would call us rich, but we never wanted for much.

Papa and Washington worked them foxes every day, all year long, from dawn to dusk. They were always busy: mending fences, cleaning and fixing cages, helping deliver litters, and killing horses. Papa killed the horses and Mrs. Singer cut their meat into ten-pound packages that either went to feed the foxes and their young or were sold to the neighbors as dog food.

In 1906 we got ourselves a gas-powered single engine, or a "one-lunger," as it was known, to grind the horsemeat, saving Mrs. Singer the time-consuming act of cutting it up. She was rightly pleased to be relieved of that job, seeing that it could take a couple of days for her to dissect a large horse. Papa and Washington would also salt and cure the horse hides, and they would be packed along with the fox furs to be auctioned off, as well. They wouldn't bring in the same price a fox fur would, but they added to Papa's take enough so that the extra work was worth it.

My daddy's hands were always busy, and after the arrival of the one-lunger more so than usual, because that "dang machine," as Papa often referred to it, was always bustin' down. I asked him why he even used it, if it was so much trouble, but he just grumbled a bit and Washington scooted me outta the way, telling me to find something else to do. I'd go sit in the corner, waiting for the familiar *fump fump fump fump* followed by two dying wheezes to let me know that the engine was once again up and running.

"Hey, Papa, I done figured out why they call it a one-lunger," I shouted out over the din one day. "Don't ya think it sounds like a body with only one of its lungs?" I demonstrated with a loud *fump fump fump fump… wheeze wheeze*, taking in large gulps of air.

"Well, now, I never woulda thought of that," Papa said, as he raised his eyebrows at Washington. "I thought it meant a one-cylinder engine. How'd you get so smart, boy?"

I beamed and smacked the dead horse hanging upside down in front of me with one of the sticks I used for a baseball bat. A hand winch had been used to suspend the carcass from a double track that made the trimming out of the bulky animal easier. A large metal bucket caught the dribbling spurts of blood that seeped from the slit jugular.

"Junior, don't be hitting that hide," Papa told me. "You could do some damage, and then it won't be worth as much at auction. Why don't you make yourself useful and load up some of that rubbish and take it down to the graveyard?"

"Sure, Papa," I replied, walking to the tool shed for the hand wagon. I shoveled up some innards and bone and headed out, my old mutt Grady keeping me company.

The graveyard was a small area down near the river, toward the back of the property, where we dumped the unsellable and unused parts of the horses and foxes. Almost immediately, the leftover flesh would be picked from the bone by the predators that now waited for their supper to be delivered, but the bones would take longer to be consumed, if they ever were. Field mice, squirrels, and such would cart away the smaller pieces, but there still remained a sizable pile of leg and thigh bones in addition to some skulls that were too large for the rodents to run off with. Walking down past the graveyard on misty days was just plain eerie, 'specially when the fog settled unevenly over the river and the buzzards circled silently above. Most times I didn't think too awful much about going down there; just every once in a while, usually towards dusk, when Mrs. Singer said the dead were restless to get up. Papa said he didn't believe in ghosts, he ain't never seen one, but Mrs. Singer and Washington swore they'd not only seen them but spoken to them, as well. I weren't so sure either way, but I wasn't fixin' to take any chances. On those gloomy evenings, when the shadows jumped and the weeping willows swayed, their graceful branches leaning out as if to grab you, I couldn't get home fast enough.

Baseball was our favorite topic of conversation, and sometimes arguments. Mrs. Singer said she didn't have no concern for the game, but before long she was joining in the discussion with as much interest as the menfolk. She had a memory like a steel trap, and soon had a substantial knowledge of the players and their hits against just about every team in the league. She and Washington became devoted supporters of Mr. Ty Cobb and felt a strong connection with the Tiger center fielder, because he come from their home state of Georgia.

"Why, Mr. Cobb had a battin' average of .350 last year, and considerin' he's just gettin' more experience, I 'spect it a go up a bit. Don't y'all agree,

Washington?" Mrs. Singer once asked her husband as she brought lunch out to him and Papa at the ranch.

"I 'spect you be right, Mrs. Singer." Washington gazed at his wife proudly. "They don't call him 'Georgia Peach' for nothin'."

"That's about right," she nodded.

"What about 'Wahoo Sam'?" Papa asked. "He got a pretty good average hisself."

"All due respect, Mr. Harris, Sam ain't got the speed that Mr. Cobb do. Ain't that right, Junior?" Mrs. Singer looked to me for confirmation.

"She's right, Papa. Last season he got caught at the bag 24 times."

"I done told y'all I was right," she mumbled as she marched back to the house.

"You think they're goin' all the way again this year, Papa?"

"They got a good chance, boy. That new manager, Jennings, he's a character all right, and I 'spect he got the talent to take them to the end. Whadda you think, Washington?"

"If he don't get hisself kilt, I 'spect y'all be right, Mr. Harris," Washington answered. "But Mr. Cobb, he gonna be the man who save that team, I tell ya. You jes' wait and see. They don't call him 'Georgia Peach' for nothin'."

I played baseball during recess at school, after my chores were done, and sometimes in the dawn of a warm spring morning when I caught Washington before the milking. He fancied himself a pitcher and would wind up like I never seen anyone do. Tapping his chest three times, spitting once, and flailing his arms like he was swattin' a fly was his usual routine before letting one rip. If Papa happened to be passin' by, he would call out, "I think you done killed that bug dead, Washington." But for all his flapping around, Washington could throw a ball pretty hard, and as a young catcher, I got challenged every time that leather ball came across the plate.

In the spring of 1908, when I was ten, Papa surprised me by telling me we were going to the Tiger's season opener against the Cleveland Naps. He had business that year in Detroit, so we would accompany the furs on the train ride to Detroit, drop them off at auction, then make our way to Bennett Park and my first ball game.

My excitement quickly turned to worry. I had waited so long for this event, I was spooked it wasn't going to happen, that something would prevent us from going.

"Papa, what if it snows?"

"They'll still play, son."

"What if it rains?"

"'Less there's lighting and hail, they'll play, son."

"What if we get there and there ain't no tickets left?"

"There'll be tickets."

"Papa, how can you be so sure?"

"Junior, if you keep this up, I'm gonna be too tired to go. I know they'll have tickets, they ain't sold out yet. You'll see them play. I promised you I'd take ya, and I've yet to break my word." Papa looked at me sternly.

"I'm sorry, Papa." He had eased my mind slightly, and over the next few weeks my worries faded and the excitement crept back in, spreading to Washington and Mrs. Singer as well.

"Now, Junior, when you see Mr. Cobb, y'all hafta give 'im our regards. Tell 'im his biggest cranks is from Georgia, too." Mrs. Singer made me give my word. "I'm goin' to make him my best apple pie, and I want you to give it to him. Promise?"

"Mrs. Singer, I don't know rightly if I can do just that," I answered, wondering how I was going to get a pie to Detroit without either dropping it or eating it.

"Don't you get smart, Junior. Y'all do what I say," she scolded me.

"Yes, ma'am," I replied, thinking I would have to ask Papa about how we was to take a whole pie on our journey.

Washington had a mental list of things I was supposed to remember and relate to him, not forgetting any one detail.

"And I wanta know how tall Mr. Cobb be and how much he weigh and what color his hair be, should he take off his hat. And I wanta know what that ball park look like, every tree and fence and rock. And I wanta know who hits first and every player after and how they hit." He scrunched his face like he was forgettin' something. "Oh, yea, I also wanta know, if you get a chance to be speakin' with Mr. Cobb, if he done talk to his poor Mama. Shame about his daddy, God rest his soul."

"How'm I supposed to remember all that, Washington?" I complained. "I'll do my best, but geez, that's a lot."

"Well, you just try, ya hear?"

"I will, I will."

Every night I went over our plan and everything I was supposed to do and remember. As our departure date drew closer, it was all we discussed. Papa, always bein' the cautious one, had Mrs. Singer sew hidden pockets into our coats and trousers to bring back the money he would make at the auction. We would be carrying back a few thousand dollars, "enough to kill someone for," he said, and he didn't want to take any chances about losing either his year's work or our lives. I was thrilled to be an accomplice to this scheme and took my role seriously, practicing my reaction to a holdup, should one occur.

Not only would I be seeing my first ball game, but I would be taking my first train ride, as well. We were to leave Midland the day before the game, sleep on the train, and get to the auction first thing the next morning, then go on to Bennett Park early that afternoon with plenty of time to spare. That night we would stay in a real hotel, eat at a real restaurant in Detroit, and then return the next day on the train. It wouldn't be until midnight that we would get back to Midland, but Washington would be waiting with a team to take us back to our farm and back to our lives as we knew it, with only memories of the previous day's excitement. I missed the park already though I hadn't even left Michigami, and spent many sleepless nights trying to figure out how to make our time in Detroit last longer.

April 16 was cold and crisp, but the sun was shining and I coulda run to Detroit if Papa woulda let me.

"It'll be a spot warmer further south," Papa predicted, "but it'll still be chilly. Take your hand warmers, Junior."

"Aw, Pa, do I have to?"

"Do what your Daddy say, boy." Mrs. Singer frowned at me. "Y'all don't want to catch your death of cold afore you meet Mr. Cobb. Now I got here some meat sandwiches, eggs, biscuits, milk, apple pies… this here big one is for Mr. Cobb, y'all don't forget."

She packed the huge basket into the carriage where Washington and Papa waited and came around to where I stood. "Y'all have a good time." She pushed my hair back. "And Junior, we countin' on you to remember everything to us."

"Yes, Mrs. Singer. I'll sure try." I jumped up into the back seat. "Bye! See you in a couple days," I called out, as Washington said "Giddyup!" to the team and we took off, waving good-bye to Mrs. Singer and Grady.

I'd seen the train a hundred times, but the feeling of a constant speed that was smooth and soothing was a sensation I'd never felt. A horse would jostle a body and follow the grade of the road. You had to be on notice at all times should something spook your ride, and running a horse constantly wouldn't last too long.

I spent the whole of the day gazing out the window at the country racing by, and after our supper that night, the train lulled me to sleep like a cradle would a baby. It weren't until Papa shook me slightly and whispered, "Junior, it's daybreak" that I woke up. The early morning sun was but a glimmer in the sky as I made my way to the toilet car and cleaned myself for the day. Papa believed that a well-dressed man showed that he respected hisself and others, so we dressed in our Sunday best for the auction and the game and stepped off the train appearing smart, like we was looking for a band box.

Papa had employed a large wagon with a team of four and two drivers who were waiting for our train. The two hired men helped Papa load his boxes full of fox and horse furs, and they drove us to the auction house a mile or so away. Detroit was bustling with all kinds of activity in the early hours: milk wagons were out, newspaper boys tossed bundles to the unopened storefronts, and construction workers carried their lunch over their shoulders on the way to sites that kept pushing out the city limits. The hired hands shared their coffee with Papa, and they talked business until we pulled up in front of a large warehouse just north of the Detroit River. I sat in the wagon while Papa went in, and when he came out about 30 minutes later he was with a large redheaded man who glanced at me and nodded. They spoke for a few minutes longer and shook hands, and then Papa came over and said, "It's time to go, son."

"Who was that, Pops?" I asked, as I grabbed my knapsack and jumped out of the cart.

"Pops?" Papa looked at me. "You ain't never called me that."

"Well, I just decided, setting in this wagon, that I'm gettin' to be a man, and a man don't call their papa, 'Papa.' It sounds like a baby or a girl. I want to call you 'Pops'." Truth told, it had just come to me, and I realized as I looked into Papa's wounded face, it had sounded better when it was a thought.

He sighed and put his hand on my shoulder. "I guess you're right, boy. You are almost a man, ain't ya? 'Pops' is good enough for me." He smiled over at me. "Hey, I think I like the sound of it even better."

"Well, okay then," I said, my head spinning with all that was new and unfamiliar. Even my own father was not who he had been a minute ago. "Who was that man you were talking to?"

"He's the middleman—the fellow that will sell my lot to the highest bidder."

"Do you pay him?"

"He gets a percentage of the take. That way he has incentive to get the most for the lot."

"Do you trust him, Pops?" I tried out the new name. "He wouldn't do you wrong, would he?"

"No, I don't think so, son. He's been doing this for a while, and he's got loyal customers that come back every year. I don't think he'd risk it, but you never know." Papa looked like it wasn't the first time that thought had occurred to him.

"When do you get your money?"

"We'll come back after the game. Come on, let's go get some breakfast, then go watch Mr. Ty Cobb in person."

We walked back towards the city, away from the industrial buildings, and pretty soon we came to an area with shops and bakeries and meat markets just opening their doors for business. We stopped at a small restaurant for a quick bite, then continued on our way, the chilly mid-morning air rousing us as we headed out toward Bennett Field.

My heart pounded in my chest as we neared the ball park, and I pulled my coat around me and jumped up and down, trying to shake the willies that had crept in. I was secretly glad to have my hand warmers; the brisk breeze off the lake made my hands shake even more than the nerves did. We passed a lumber mill and there, seemingly out of nowhere, stood the park. I could see the peaked roof of the grandstand and a few seats scattered with early fans, or "cranks," and I excitedly tugged on Papa's arm.

"Is that it, Papa? Is that where we get to sit?"

"I hope so, boy. Let's see if we can afford a ticket," he teased.

We paid our two dollars and made our way to a row of benches five back from home plate.

"Wow, Papa, I can see everything. This is great! Where are the players?"

"Why, I rightly don't know," Papa said as he looked around, pretending he didn't notice I had been slipping up and calling him Papa.

"They'll be out shortly to warm up," a voice from behind us said. We both turned around to see a large, portly gentleman with a handlebar mustache and a black bowler hat sitting on the bench behind us. "This your first game?"

Papa and I nodded yes, and the fellow held his hand out to us. "William Flannigan's the name. My friends call me Big Bill."

Papa and I each shook his hand as he continued. "Been coming here since they joined the American League back in '01. Missed two home games in '04 when my wife passed, but other than that . . ." he raised his eyebrows at me and pulled out a big cigar. "Where you fellows from?"

"Northern Michigan, place near Midland."

"You boys are a long way from home. You come just for the game?"

Papa looked at me, and I understood I was not to say a word. "I got a little business down this way, and me and Junior decided to take in a game. He's quite a fan." Papa ruffled my hair.

"That so, son?" Big Bill looked at me like he didn't believe it. "Who led the team with doubles"—he paused—"*and* triples last year?"

"That'd be Mr. Sam Crawford. He had 34 doubles and 17 triples," I answered confidently.

"By Job, he's right," Big Bill threw back his head and laughed. "Can I buy the boy a Coca-Cola?"

I looked at Papa pleadingly. A Coca-Cola! "That's right kind of you, Mr. Flannigan, but I was plannin' to get us both one in a bit. Thank you for the kind offer, though." Papa wasn't a man to take charity, and I could tell he didn't know what to make of the character who called himself Big Bill.

"Suit yourself," he shrugged. "Hey, here they come." Big Bill stood up and started whistling with two fingers pressed against his teeth. "Let's go, boys!" he yelled.

"Can I yell, too?" I asked Papa.

"Well, I guess so, seeing as it appears okay." Papa looked around at the other cranks cheering and hooting.

"Go, Tigers!" I screamed at no one in particular. Every now and then I let out a hoot or a holler, until the players took their positions and began to throw the ball to one another.

"Where's Ty Cobb?" I asked. The players were all dressed exactly alike, with a fancy "D" on their jersey.

"He's right over there." Big Bill leaned in and nodded to a fellow in the outfield. He proceeded to point out all the players on the field, each man's position, and his own personal opinion of them and their usefulness to the team. Big Bill knew just about everything about the Tigers, and Papa and I listened, our attention focused on his every word and his colorful descriptions of the players.

"That Ty Cobb, well, he's just about the meanest S.O.B. to come around." Big Bill didn't even glance at me while he swore. "He's meaner than a snake and just about as honorable." He leaned in. "You know what happened to his daddy?"

"He passed, we done heard," Papa said.

"He passed, all right, but it was his own wife that put the bullet through his noggin." Big Bill exhaled, the smoke from his cigar curling up around his head. "She thought he was robbing her."

"That true, Mr. Flannigan?" Papa looked stunned.

"True as I'm sittin' right here. They had her in for murder, but let her out after a bit. I figure that's why Cobb's such a mean S.O.B." He sat back calmly, and I figured swearing was just a part of his regular vocabulary.

"Well this day's just gettin' more and more exciting, ain't it, Junior?" Papa looked at me like anything could happen.

"Wait till Washington hears about this. He ain't never goin' to believe it," I said, the last few words lost in the roar of the crowd as Charles Bennett took the field to throw out the first pitch.

"You know about that unlucky fellow, don't you?" Big Bill whispered in our ear. Papa and I shook our heads. "That poor S.O.B. fell under a train fifteen or so years ago and lost both his legs. You know, the park is named for him, and he's been throwing out pitches ever since 1896. You're watching history, boy." Big Bill touched my shoulder, making his point.

As I sat in the park on that bright, frigid day, watching the greatest game in the world, I looked around, trying to burn the memory into my brain. I saw Papa stand, his hands shoved in his pockets, leaning over trying to see "Germany" Schaefer slide into first base. I watched as Big Bill shook his hand at the umpire, calling him a "crazy S.O.B.," his cigar ashes drifting down like snow around my head. I committed to memory the taste of my first box of Cracker Jacks and my first Coca-Cola, which was guaranteed, according to the sign on the outfield fence, to relieve the fatigue from overplay, overwork, and overthirst. I burned into my mind Hughie Jennings and his wild antics:

jumping up and down, screaming "Ee-YAH!" every time he wanted to distract the other team. I felt the disappointment of the Tigers' loss to Cleveland that cold spring day, but it only fueled my desire to make a difference, to be a part of this sport in any way I could. I sat there, my eyes closed for the briefest time, and swore I would do whatever it took to be a Detroit Tigers ballplayer. That was the promise I made to myself that day.

As I had expected, our journey soon faded into the past, and life returned to normal in every way, except for my newfound pledge to be a ball player. At fourteen, I started playing on the city league in Midland, strengthening my skills on the field and sharpening my ability as a team member. I learned about the value of cooperating, not just for the benefit of the individual, but for the group. A couple of evenings a week, Pops put together a home practice; he, too, felt I had a chance to make it to the big leagues. He played the field while Washington pitched and Mrs. Singer played catcher. Though she was a petite, slender woman, years of working had left her lean and strong. She was no hindrance on the field and could throw the ball out to Pops if need be.

"Come on now, Washington," she'd call out. "Y'all can't let him get a hit." Then she'd whisper to me, "He's gonna throw it on the inside, take notice."

Washington went through all his gestures, convinced that he was making the signals that any pitcher would. He tapped, spit, and wiggled his fingers, and threw a burning fastball to the inside. I'd swing, sending the ball out past Pops and sometimes out toward the graveyard, where old Grady would happily retrieve the now spit-covered leather ball. I studied the sports paper every chance I could and, when I earned some extra money, got myself a subscription to the weekly periodical called *Sporting Life*. I just about devoured every article.

When I turned eighteen and graduated high school, Pops said I could try out for the Gunners, a minor league team that was starting up in Bay City, thirty miles away. It was all I could concentrate on, and I stayed up late at night going over possible plays and outcomes, as well as the rules of the game. I kept getting tripped up on the infield fly rule, and it was just this notion I was thinking about on my way home from an errand I had run for Pops. I was so caught up in my thoughts that it wasn't until it started misting that I even took notice of the dark skies and the swirling clouds looming above.

"Go on, now." I smacked Lucky, my horse that year, and pushed him into a fast trot, the rain coming down harder. Summer storms could come up as quickly as they could wane, and my only concern was the wet clothes I would soon be wearing. Past experience told me that it was just a thunderstorm passing through. It wasn't unusual to see a rainbow and sunshine through the clouds while the rain still fell; such was the nature of a Michigan storm.

Nothing can spook a horse more than thunder, except maybe the crack of lightning, and when they happen at the same time you know the storm is right above you. At the instant I heard the thunder and felt the ground tremble, I saw the lightning bolt hit a large evergreen beside the road, splitting it down the middle and sending out a crack so loud I thought they musta heard it in Detroit. Lucky neighed and reared up on his hind legs, and I held on tight and prepared myself, knowing he would bolt when he came down.

What I didn't count on was the destroyed evergreen falling on me, knocking me off my mount and pinning me underneath it. Instantly, Lucky reared up again, and when he came down on my ankle and the bone suddenly appeared, I wondered briefly whose leg it was. The shock of the pain was immediate, leaving no question as to whose bone was sticking out at such an odd angle. My last thought before passing out was that I had never figured out when a player needed to tag up before advancing on a caught infield ball.

I was unconscious for three days, and I don't remember nothing but the strange dream I had. In my vision, I was aware of my accident and was recovering in my room when Mrs. Singer announced I had a visitor. "It's God, come to see you, Junior," she said, as she led a bushy red fox in, and pointed to the chair in the corner of my room.

The fox made himself comfortable and looked at me, his snout sniffing about.

"You're not what I expected," I said, sitting up.

He looked at me slyly. "I know."

"Why are you here? Am I going to die?"

"Not yet." He grinned hideously, showing his long, pointed teeth. "You have to suffer a bit."

"Why would you want me to suffer?" I asked, confused.

"For reasons you don't need to know," he answered, slinking off the chair and coming over to my bed. "Now you have your cross to bear."

"What do you mean?" I asked, alarmed. "What cross?"

He swelled in size until he loomed as large as a horse next to me. Bending over and pushing his great snout up to my ear, he whispered, "You'll find out soon enough." He drew back, then bent down again and bit my injured leg, sinking his long teeth into my calf. Excruciating bolts of pain shot through my body and shook me from head to toe, causing me to cry out.

"Soon enough," he repeated, as he slipped away into the recesses of my mind.

I have no recollection of anything past my fall. What I know is what Pops told me. On that stormy day, when Lucky returned to the farm without his rider, Papa knew something had happened. He and Washington set out to find me, and it wasn't until they come right up to the felled tree that they seen me caught underneath. It took three hours in the pouring rain, using the team and chains, to pull the evergreen off me. Papa said he thanked the Lord I was passed out because he thought no body coulda stood the kind of pain that it would have received while moving that tree. They put me in the cart, and Papa brought me back to the farm while Washington ran on foot into town to fetch the doctor, then ran back to the house while the doctor rode.

The break wasn't a good one. Setting my leg proved more difficult than the doctor had expected, and both Papa and Washington were needed to pull it back in line. Washington later told me that I cried out in my sleep and my body shook like I was fixin' to die. I suffered the fever for three days, and Mrs. Singer said that all three of them prayed at my side, barely eating and only sleeping when they fell from exhaustion. When I awoke, there wasn't a dry eye in my house; even Grady whined and cried when I reached out to pet him.

"You's lucky to be alive," Mrs. Singer clucked as she fed me the broth she had prepared. "I was never so scare't in my whole life. Lawd, I thought you was goin' to your maker, Junior. Your daddy, why, I thought he was goin' join you, he about worried hisself to death. And poor Washington, he done run almost three miles that day and he ain't no young man. Boy, you had us so worried."

She tucked my covers around me and patted my hand. "Y'all get some rest, Junior. And don't forget to thank the good Lord for all he done for you."

"I won't, Mrs. Singer. Thanks." I took her hand and pulled her down, kissing her on the cheek.

She straightened up and patted her hair. "None of that, y'hear. Y'all just get your rest, Junior. Remember, God loves you." She smiled down at me, then turned to leave.

"I will," I said. "I need to get all my strength back to make tryouts next month."

She stopped, but didn't turn around. "Good night, Junior."

The next morning Papa told me that my leg had been broken in two places, one being the ankle, and the doctor didn't know how long it would take to heal properly. He didn't expect that I would be walking, let alone running, in two months. Matter of fact, he wasn't even sure when I would be able to stand without the aid of arm crutches.

"When can I start playing ball again, Pops?"

"We ain't sure, Junior." Pops wiped his brow with his cap and looked out the window.

"I am going to play, right?" I wasn't about to let a stupid broken leg stand in the way of my baseball career.

"I can't rightly say, son. The doctor, well, he don't know how that ankle's going to heal. You had a pretty good spill. You're lucky you ain't dead." Pops leaned in and pulled my covers up. "You need to take this one day at a time."

"It don't even hurt, Pops. Really, I could stand right now. Watch." I struggled to sit up.

"Whoa, boy!" Papa helped me lay back down as my strength gave out.

"It don't hurt, Junior, because you're so doped with morphine, you can't feel nothing. You got a serious injury, boy. The doctor don't even know if you'll ever walk again."

Papa had said what needed to be said. He looked at me, waiting for his words to sink in. "You understand?"

"It's just a broken leg," I shouted. "I'm not only gonna walk, I'll play ball, too. You'll see. I'm going to be a ball player!" By then I was screaming. "I'm going to walk, you just watch me!"

"I hope so, son. I hope so." Papa said softly as he left the room.

I was right on one account. I did walk again. It took six months and I was left with a limp, but I did lose the arm crutches and then eventually the cane, and managed to drag my bad leg less and less. I would never run fast again and my ankle would pain me for the rest of my life, but I shuffled along and got by. I could not keep my promise to play ball, though.

I insisted that Pops let me go to the minor league tryouts. "I know I can do it," I told him, sounding more sure than I felt.

"You're fallin' from the moon, son. It just ain't realistic that you can compete."

Pops spoke gently, but his words hit hard. He did take me to the tryouts, and his prediction came true as we watched the players in action. My career in baseball was over. I could never run the bases or sprint to catch a fly ball. I couldn't even stand up straight or jump. Pops suggested I look at being a part of the team in another way, but my heart wasn't in it. I was no longer the talented young man batting and running his way to the top. I was the gimp, the one that people pointed to and whispered about under their breath. Pops said I was exaggerating, that people hardly noticed the limp. But I knew differently, and after a while I just stopped caring... about anything. My dream in which the fox had told me of my coming burden came true. I now had my own cross to bear, and I joined the rest of the folks who every day went through their joyless routines, dragging the crosses of their unfulfilled dreams.

Pops belonged to a group called the American Pacifists, a small set of locals who discussed current affairs and how they thought issues could be resolved peacefully. He went into town monthly for meetings, and when he returned one night he said he had some good news for me. Mrs. Miller, one of the members, was teaching piano, and Pops thought it might do me some good to get a hobby. Now, I didn't know much about any musical instrument, but I had a fine voice and I knew my mama had played, so I agreed. Once a week I would go into town and meet with Mrs. Miller at her home on First Street. I knew that Mr. Miller had worked at the bank before passing the previous year; I also knew that there were four Miller girls, none of whom had attended our local school.

"Their Mama educated them at home, Junior. She's French," Pops said, sounding impressed. "And they're good people," he continued. "They have the same peace-loving values as we do."

"Sure, Papa," I said. I didn't give a care either way. It was something to do.

Mrs. Miller was a tall, handsome woman as were her four daughters. Their home was as different from our farm as up was from down. It smelled of lilacs and talcum powder, and Miss Opal, one of the Miller daughters, was always baking some treat for the students who came for their musical lessons. There weren't no dirty hides or lye soap or muddy boots anywhere, just soft pillows and low-lit candles and full skirts that swished when a female walked by. Of late I had been edgy and ornery, but when I walked into that house I found myself to be a different person. For the first time in some while, I felt consoled. It weren't baseball, but I took satisfaction in the piano. I had promising talent, Mrs. Miller told me, and I began to enjoy the music I was playing.

Mrs. Miller's daughters also held a newfound interest for me. Mrs. Singer was the only female I had ever really known, and she was tough and lean and smelled of lard and vinegar. I ain't talking down on her—I smelled like that, too, when I wasn't cleaned up—but I had a new appreciation for the more feminine side of the women who fawned over me each week.

"Oh, Mr. Harris, do come in," they would say as they threw open the great front door. "You must be so cold." They'd help me off with my wrappings and call out to their house girl, "Francine! Please make Mr. Harris a cup of hot tea. He's half frozen."

"'Mr. Harris' sounds like my Pops," I told them. "Please call me Jun… George."

"George it is," they replied, and never knew that I had been Junior my whole life.

They would wander in and out of the parlor as I sat with their mother, making suggestions every now and then as to how I might improve. "Have him play it *fortissimo*, Mama," they would say as they carried a vase of flowers past. Or, "That sounds lovely, George, but pick up the tempo a bit."

Mrs. Miller had long, delicate fingers that could leap and jump across the keys or wander, like a fat, lazy cat, picking their way through some haunting melody. She spoke with a French accent and would nod and smile to her daughters as they made suggestions, whispering to me, "Zay should be teaching you. Zay know so much."

Miss Pearl told me that her Mama hadn't been the same since their daddy passed, and that for a while they thought they might lose her to a broken heart. She played with a melancholy spirit that I was familiar with, and it weren't unusual to hear one of her girls sniffing back tears while they dabbed at their eyes.

There weren't a finer baker in all the county than Miss Opal, the second of the sisters, and she was always tempting me with one of her inventions. French tarts with thick sweet cream, molasses cookies that were crunchy on the outside and chewy on the inside, and raisin bread pudding with a rum custard sauce were some of my favorites, and she took special care to make them when my lesson was scheduled. She looked the part of a baker, with a full, doughy figure and plump, rosy cheeks. Her dark hair was piled high, and almost always had a bright ribbon wrapped around the swirled bun. She and Miss Ruby, the eldest, were no-nonsense women. They said what they meant, and their kindness was likewise sincere. They were sisterly to me and fussed over me in a way that made me feel doted on, not nagged.

"George," they'd say, "would you please take this apple pie home to your daddy? I know it's one of his favorites. And you might want to bundle up, George. There's a chill in the air this evening."

None of them women ever mentioned my limp, though I knew Pops had probably told them what had happened. They acted like I was normal, and would even ask me to help them now and then with lifting a heavy pot or moving a piece of furniture. They were always grateful; I never felt more useful than when Miss Ruby touched my arm and said, "Sometimes, George, I don't know what we'd do without you."

Susie was the baby, but you would have never known it by her big personality. She was the only redhead of the group, with freckles and a quick laugh that could change just as quick to a temper. She sassed her sisters, and even her mama once, but she was funny and entertaining, and clung to me like a second shadow. I got used to her hanging on me and it didn't bother me none to have her tagging along, running off her mouth about anything that would cross her fickle mind.

"George, do you think women should have the vote?" she asked one day.

"Well now, Susiekins, I never give it much thought."

"George!" she admonished, "you must. Don't you think women are as smart as men?"

I thought about the women around me, and about Mrs. Singer. "Yes, I do."

"Do you think that we are inferior in any way?"

Again, I thought of the women I knew. "Probably just the opposite."

"Well, then, you must join the suffragette movement with us. We need men to help give our cause credibility." The sixteen-year-old stood with her hands on her hips, daring me to answer differently.

"Suzanne!" Miss Pearl exclaimed. "Don't be a bully. If George wants to join us, you can tell him what we're about and let him make up his own mind." Turning to me, she added, "It is a right cause, George. If you want to know more about it, I'd be happy to speak with you sometime."

Out of all the sisters, Miss Pearl was the nearest to my age. We had a close connection, as she, too, walked with difficulty; she had polio. But as I got better, she got worse. As the months went by, she went from a cane to crutches, and finally took her place in a wheelchair, never to walk again. She didn't seem as bothered by the development as I would have expected, and as I carefully carried her out to the garden one warm spring day, my bum leg slowing me a bit, I asked her how she could feel no bitterness for the cross she done carried.

"This is my destiny, George." She brushed back her long black curls and smiled sweetly at me. "For some reason God has chosen this life for me, and I try not to question why. He has a plan, and I must accept it." She had on a blue flowered dress and her equally blue eyes brimmed with tears as she continued. "I wish it were different, but all I can do is pray and hope for the best. I try to remember to count my blessings."

"I'm sorry, Miss Pearl. I didn't mean to make you all upset." I was ashamed for bringing this sweet girl to tears. "I feel sorry for myself sometimes, and I say things without thinking." I looked into her blue eyes and realized suddenly that the affection I felt for her went far beyond the sisterly devotion I had for her sisters.

"That's all right, George. I know what you meant. Our lives throw us curve balls sometimes, don't they?" She grinned mischievously.

"You know what happened?" I asked.

"Your daddy told us about your accident. I am sorry, George. I'm sure you would have been a fine ball player." She reached out and touched my hand.

"You're very nice to say that, Miss Pearl. You're just so..." My words floated away from me as I lost my thoughts. I felt the heat from her silky hand and struggled to finish my sentence, "...so ...very ...nice."

I looked into her eyes, and my heart gave a flip in my chest. Her cheeks flushed, and I knew she had felt the same. She held my gaze for a moment before shyly looking down, and more than anything in the world, more than playing baseball for the Detroit Tigers, I wanted to kiss her.

In the spring of 1918, U.S. involvement in the Great War began, and the young men of the area started drifting off to the service. My bum leg was reason enough for the Army to turn me down, never mind the fact that Pops and the other American Pacifist members did not support the conflict. When it became against the law to be a dissenter toward the war, the group became a "book club," but still met once a month to continue whispered debates on how they thought the government's war effort was an insult to the American intelligence. Me and the Miller sisters joined the "club" as the next generation of free thinkers. Not only did we discuss the war hysteria, but we also talked about the vote for women and the many measures the President was taking to raise money, such as the increase in the personal income tax. These were spirited discussions; my mind was introduced to the world of adulthood and analytical thought, and I found I had a skill for debate and negotiation.

Because of Miss Pearl's illness, Mrs. Miller asked me to consider helping them out on a permanent basis. My limp weren't too bad, and I could now easily perform duties around their house. I had no problem lifting Miss Pearl in and out of her chair, and spent more and more time sitting in the garden with her and Susie, discussing current affairs. Opal and Ruby had taken on the responsibilities of the local teacher, now gone off to war, and spent their days at the school house. Because the staff had gotten so small at the paper, Susie had taken a job as a junior reporter for the *Michigami Weekly*. She covered the local politics and meetings, and time and again would run her ideas and plans by us.

"I think it would be wonderful if we could do a piece on all the local women who have taken jobs because of the war." She sat on the step below me and looked up at me. "What do you think, George?"

"I think you got a good idea, Susiekins. There's a lot of womenfolk who are doin' men's jobs and doin' 'em well."

"Susie, you must be careful not to sound too disconcerted about the war. Go at it from a suffragette's point of view. That's much more acceptable." Miss Pearl, as perfect as ever, sat straight in her wheelchair.

"Your sister's got herself a point, you don't want no trouble." I looked at Miss Pearl and smiled, sharing our unspoken secret.

"I'm so tired of being afraid to write something." Susie's voice rose, reflecting her frustration. "This is not what our forefathers intended, I can guarantee you that. Whatever happened to freedom of speech? I am a responsible American obliged to overstate my patriotism so I'm not persecuted—is this what we've come to?" Susie stared off into the distance, shaking her head.

"I'm afraid so, dear. These are the modern times we live in." Miss Pearl patted her sister's shoulder.

"More like the Stone Age, I think."

Susie's character was more passionate than the rest of her sisters'. Many a time she was moved to action, and her enthusiasm for charitable causes was contagious. More often than not, it was her who put forth the ideas that the club acted on, and more often than not it was her who done the leading.

September of 1918 came, and brought with it the dreaded Spanish Flu. It overcame the population, not only of the U.S., but of the world—it ravaged the war-torn European countries, taking over two times as many lives as the war itself did. Mrs. Miller was taken, her constitution so weak after her husband's passing that she had no chance. Susie took ill and put up the fight of her life; she won, but lost her gumption, either from the infection or from the passing of her mama.

Washington weren't so lucky. After a long struggle, he passed on a rainy October morning. Grief stricken, Mrs. Singer told Pops she wanted to return home to her kin, and Pops nodded miserably, saddened by the death of his best friend.

Mrs. Singer could barely look at me as she packed and wept silently. I was losing the only woman who had picked me up when I'd fallen, wiped away my tears, and encouraged me to try again. She had mothered me since I was born, and to watch her packing to return to a place as far away and unfamiliar as China was devastating. I sat quietly on the chair in her room as she finished, closing her case and setting it on the floor.

"Well, I 'spect I'm done," she said, dabbing at her eyes with her kerchief.

Papa came in to help her load her belongings in our new Tin Lizzie.

"Mrs. Singer." Pops cleared his throat.

She turned to look at the man she had come to know as a brother.

"Yes, Mr. Harris?"

"Mrs. Singer, I want you to have this." He reached his hand in his pocket and pulled out a wad of bills. "You and Washington been with me for twenty-three years, and every spring, after auction, I tried to give your stubborn old man his pay. He never would accept nothin', and I took the liberty of settin' it aside for just some day. That day done come, and what I got to give you is yours. I won't take it back, so don't even try."

Pops walked over and put twenty-three hundred-dollar bills in Mrs. Washington's hand, closing her fingers around it. "Now don't you go crying none, or I'll think twice about sending you home."

Mrs. Singer hung her head, and her shoulders shook slightly. My Pop was the kind of man I wanted to be, and I knew why. He reached out to lay his hand on Mrs. Singer's arm, and she lifted her head.

"Thank ya kindly, Mr. Harris. You and Junior done been the world to me and Washington. We ain't never had better friends." She came over and lifted my chin with her hand. "Always remember, Junior, God loves you." She kissed my forehead and, with her head held high against her grief, walked out of our home for the last time.

I sat in the dark house after they left and knew my life was going somewhere that weren't familiar to me anymore. Too many things had changed; too many people had been lost. Things could never be what they were, and it was a daunting and peculiar feeling. As I sat there, a vision gradually became clear to me. I was twenty years old. I was of marrying age, and there was a woman I genuinely cared about. Truthfully, I didn't just care about her, I loved her. Why hadn't I seen this before? This was my future. This was what I wanted: I wanted to make a life with Miss Pearl, to bring her out to the farm. Pops and I could make a ramp for her chair, and I could help her with the chores, and we could be in love forever. I would have the farm one day, and we could live happily for the rest of our lives.

The dark skies warned of a coming storm, but I couldn't get Rusty, my horse that year, saddled fast enough. I had to see Miss Pearl, had to tell her of my revelation. She would be so pleased. She would share my excitement. We could announce our engagement over the holidays and get married soon after. Her mama and daddy wouldn't be there, and for that I was sorry, but her sisters would, and…

I would have sisters! They would be my new family, and I would be theirs. Pops and Miss Pearl and I would have the sisters to our house and they would have us over in turn. We would share holidays and birthdays and good times, and in bad times be there for each other. Out of bad sometimes comes good, and this was proof of it.

I raced into town as the wind pitched the cold rain at my face and neck, stinging my skin like the buck shot from a pellet gun. I ran up the front steps, out of breath, banging on the door. Francine opened it, and when I gushed, "Where's Miss Pearl?" she could only point towards the parlor as she stared at my frantic demeanor.

Miss Pearl was sitting by a kerosene lamp, reading. She looked up, pleased. "Why, George, how nice to see you." Then, noticing my appearance, she asked anxiously, "Is something wrong? You look in disarray."

"Where is everyone?" I asked, finally catching my breath.

"They're at the school play this evening," she said. "What's wrong, George? You're scaring me."

I knelt in front of her, brushing my wet hair back, and picked up her tiny hand. "Miss Pearl, do you have feelings for me?"

Her eyes widened and she shook her head. "Of course I... we do. You're like family to us."

"No, you, Miss Pearl."

An uninvited breeze escaped from the storm and slipped through a cracked window, sending a chill through the room. "Why are you asking me this?" she said, flustered, pulling her shawl closer.

"I need to know, Miss Pearl, because I want you to be my wife. I want to marry you. I love you!" I looked at her, waiting for the surprise to wear off and the happiness to sink in.

She sat there, not moving an inch. Instead of the joy I expected to see, I saw a cheerlessness that caught me by surprise. The thunder rumbled in the distance as I realized something was wrong, terribly wrong.

"What is it? Tell me—what's the matter?" I felt there must be a mistake, a misunderstanding. She didn't realize what I was saying. "Don't you love me?" I asked hesitantly.

"Love you?" she asked incredulously. She stopped suddenly, appeared to have a silent conversation with herself, but took a deep breath and continued.

"How can I not love you? You have opened my heart to joy that I never thought possible—I, a woman resigned to a chair, with no hope for any kind of a normal life. You, George, have brought me to a point that I only imagined was possible." She smiled through her tears. "You have gone the distance with me. You have taken me as far as I can go, and it is here, with a heart as heavy as stone, that I must leave you. This is the end of my journey."

"I don't understand. What do you mean, the end of your journey? You... we have our lives in front of us, not behind! What could you possibly mean?" I begged. The rain had turned to hail, and it beat relentlessly against the tin overhangs, creating a deafening noise that added to my befuddlement.

She straightened her shoulders as her cheeks flushed, and spoke softly. "A person in my position must have realistic expectations as to her station in life. I have exceeded mine. I will always know that I had your heart, as briefly as it may be, but I will cherish this feeling forever." She closed her eyes for a long moment and then took a deep breath. "Thank you, George. I shall always be grateful to you for giving me something that I thought I could only dream about."

"Oh, Miss Pearl, I'm giving you my heart. I don't want it back; it's yours for the keeping." I was at a loss, and I felt a divide beginning to grow between us. "You can't give up. You can't quit me. I won't let you," I said.

"You must, George. I love you with all my heart, but I cannot marry you." She looked me square in the eyes. "I won't marry you."

"Why, Miss Pearl? Why do you say this? You talk of stations in life. You talk of your journey, but what does that mean? What does that mean to me? I'm handing you my heart, my soul, my love, and you're just saying no. You tell me you love me, but you're breaking me. I would give you everything I have. I would make you happy. I know it."

"I know you would, but look at me." She spread her arms out in exasperation. "It wouldn't take long before you would grow tired of this. George, you would start to resent me, and I just couldn't let you live like that. I love you too much."

"That's it? That's why you won't marry me?" She didn't know I had this all figured out. "Miss Pearl, I already thought of all that. Pops and me are going to build a ramp to the house and I'm going to help you. I can help you do everything, you'll see. Me and Pops can take good care of you." I took her face in my hands. "We can do this."

She pulled back and said in a surprisingly flat tone, "*You* don't see, George. You are blinded to the reality of what I am. You find me dressed every day, reading and doing the normal things a person does, but you don't understand how much more there is to taking care of me. How do you think this happens?" She opened her arms.

"It is a painstaking process that only my sisters can participate in. I don't want you to see what goes on. I don't want you to see me when I need to go to the outhouse. Who will take me then? Who will help me when it's my womanly time?" She lifted her chin proudly, and her unspoken words carried her message loud and clear. "There is a good chance that one day I'll be a complete invalid, and then what? Will your love be there then? Will you be as blissful then? I think not." Her faced showed an irritation I was unfamiliar with, and I cringed as her harsh words struck my battered senses, making me feel as though I were outside, taking a beating from the raging squall—a beating that was crushing me over and over.

"Has it ever occurred to you that I can't have children? George, I can't have children. One day you will want them, and I can't have them." She dropped her head and silently sobbed, saying the words I knew must have been her cross to bear.

"No, Miss Pearl, that's not true." But even as I said it, I realized that I hadn't even considered that. Pops and I sometimes kidded about the grandkids he would one day have, and I wondered if he would be disappointed if that never happened. Would *I* be disappointed?

"You would end up cynical and disappointed." She looked at me, reading my thoughts. "George, I can't give you the life you will one day want. You don't think so now, but some day you would realize you settled for less than you could have had, and I would bear the responsibility for that decision. You would see parents playing with their children and wish it were you. You will want to experience the joy of fatherhood, of a boy who will look just like you or a little girl with curly red hair who calls you 'Papa.' You will, George, and right now, I know that more than you do. If you love me, you must trust me. Do you trust me, George? Do you?" She looked at me, begging me to believe her.

The eye of the storm had passed, taking the heavy winds and hail, but a steady drizzle continued to fall. I heard Francine in the front room, putting another log on the fire, and I listened to her rearranging the timber with the poker.

"Yes, Miss Pearl, I trust you," I finally said, exhausted. "You're smarter than me, I know that much. All I wanted was for you to be my wife. I just wanted that. I thought we could be happy, but you tell me that ain't possible. How do I know what's right? I'm a broken man, Miss Pearl. You done busted this man's heart, and I don't know what to do. I'm a lost soul."

I know a man ain't supposed to cry, but for the second time my life wasn't working out for me, and I buried my head in her skirt. My crosses were becoming many, and shouldering them was wearing me thin.

"There, there, it's all right," she said softly as we cried, sharing our heartache. She smoothed my head and we rocked gently back and forth, not wanting to let go of a moment that would never again happen. The unbroken drone of the diminishing rains enveloped us, closing me out of everything that wasn't her.

"It's all going to work out, you'll see." She leaned down and whispered in my ear. "Marry Susie, George, and you will always be close."

Chapter Three
Adeline - 1936

I come sick for the first time when I was twelve. Maude started when she was eleven, and for a whole year I thought something was wrong with me, even though Mama assured me it was different for everyone. It wasn't long after that my body began changing so fast that some days I didn't know who I was anymore. My dresses had become so tight that Mama had Aunt Pearl let them out at the bust and hips, and even I could recognize my moods swinging back and forth, changing as fast as Michigan weather. Lucy guaranteed me that it would all even out after a bit, but I heard Mama tell Pa, "We're in for the long haul with this one." I couldn't help but wonder if there was something different about me.

I grew self-conscious about the attention that I now drew from the boys I had grown up with. They seemed more awkward with me, their squeaky voices offering to carry my books rather than shouting the insults that had been routine. For the first time, I felt the control a girl could have over the opposite sex. As much as it thrilled me, it frightened me, too; it was unclear where the boundaries stood.

Lucy had been aware of this influence long before she'd even come of age. She always seemed to be in the know about things and how they worked before I even knew there were things worth knowing. When I asked how this was, she just shrugged and replied that she had an older brother. Well, I did, too, but sometimes I thought Earl knew less than me, should he even be willing to share, and so was no help whatsoever at being in the know.

Mama had a long talk with me about the birds and the bees and pollination and being a respectable young lady, but I didn't want to disappoint her by telling her that I already knew everything she seemed ill at ease explaining. What I did not know, and no one really seemed interested in telling me, were the specifics. My mother, for all her talk of modernization and equal opportunity, turned bright red when questioned about the particulars of a certain act. "I'll need to speak with your father, Addie. I'm glad you feel comfortable asking me."

She quickly left, calling "George?" and not looking glad at all. I heard the murmuring in the next room, and when I put my ear to the door as I so often did, I heard her frustrated voice announcing that she was simply not good at this part of mothering. My father agreed that this was a tough spot they were in; Earl and Maudy had had the common courtesy to just listen. These must be some very interesting explanations, I thought, to throw my parents into such a spin. They usually knew everything. I was more curious than ever and quickly returned to my seat before the door opened and both my parents stepped into the room.

"Addie," my father said, his voice full of authority. "Your mother and I think that it's best we put this here discussion off for a spell until you're a little more mature. Right, Susie?" He looked at my mother, nodding with the air of a person who had just had his say.

"Absolutely," she piped up. "Addie, maybe in a few months we can continue this conversation, but right now just isn't the right time, okay?"

They both looked at me so pitiful-like that I didn't have the heart to disagree, and when I said, "Sure," I thought they'd die of relief.

"Great," Pa replied. "Let's go have us some supper."

Though the talk of babies and the making of them died down (and was never really addressed again) I didn't forget that I still had no answers. Oddly enough, it would be Lucy's brother, Jack, who would be the most helpful in clarifying this mysterious situation. And, oddly enough, it would be Earl who instigated it.

In the winter of 1936, spurred on by the local Parent Teacher Association, my three aunts decided to put on a show to help raise money for some new playground equipment. The PTA was a small group of civic-minded women whose concern for better education could move mountains when necessary. Most folks weren't familiar with the PTA, but when they found out that the show was to be a musical and that the talented Miller sisters were involved, it was the biggest news to hit the county since the tornado of '32. It was decided that all the school children would take part in one way or another, as we would all benefit from the experience as well as from the swings.

"Children, we need your attention, please," Miss Ruby asked quietly as she and Miss Opal stood together in front of the combined classes. "We have some rather exciting news and it affects everyone, so your attention, please." Miss Opal clapped her hands; the clamor died down, and we looked to our teachers expectantly. Miss Ruby spoke first.

"With the endorsement of the PTA, we would like to announce that our school will be involved in the production of a musical. It will be the story of Julius Caesar, the great Roman emperor, and the music and the dialogue will be written by Miss Opal, Miss Pearl, and me, and based on Mr. Shakespeare's famous play. All of you will either have a part or be involved in the production in some form or another."

Millie's hand shot up. "Yes, Millie?"

"What's the PTA?"

A few of the older children snickered until they saw Miss Opal frown. "That's a good question. Thank you, Millie. PTA stands for 'Parent Teacher Association' and is a group of parents and teachers that advocate for the education and well-being of school children across the country."

Millie beamed and turned her nose up, vindicated, as she thanked her aunt.

"To continue," Miss Ruby said, "we have assembled a sign-up sheet for anyone who would like to be involved behind the scenes rather than appear on stage. This includes a student director, wardrobe personnel, set designer, and various other jobs specific to the production of the show. But before we pass that out, we would like to ask who would like to audition for parts in the play. You will be expected to memorize lines and in most cases sing, either as a character or as a part of the chorus. May I see a show of hands of those interested in a role, please?" She looked expectantly around the room.

Not a single hand went up. Miss Ruby did not look happy.

"This is one of William Shakespeare's finest plays and Miss Opal, Miss Pearl, and I have worked very hard to adapt it to our vision. A show of hands, please?"

Again, not a hand went up.

"The bard would be very disappointed in this group, as I am currently," she said with exasperation.

Millie's hand rose and Miss Ruby smiled as she nodded and asked, "Are you interested, Millie?"

"Yes, ma'am. I'm interested in knowing who the disappointed bard is."

I thought my aunts would break down right there. They looked at each other and shook their heads slowly. This wasn't the way they had envisioned the announcement going, and all the hard work they had already done seemed a waste of time. They had a school full of northern Michigan farm children who could make enough noise to raise a barn at recess, but were too shy to say "boo" to a goose on stage.

"Miss Ruby," I spoke up, "I would like to volunteer to be student director. I'm very organized and I think it would be a good job for me."

"Adeline, we're not filling those positions yet." Miss Opal looked at me, annoyed that I didn't understand. "You heard what Miss Ruby said."

"I know, Miss Opal, but you know I'm the only one of Mama's children that can't sing. I'd be of no good to you on stage." It was true. I couldn't carry a tune in a bucket. "But Earl, now, there's a different story. Why, I bet he'd make a fine Julius Caesar." I turned to smile at my brother and caught a look that said I would be sorry, very sorry, probably for the rest of my life.

My aunt's eyes brightened as they turned toward Earl. "What do you say, Earl?" She asked hopefully. "You do have a beautiful singing voice."

Earl chose his words carefully as he speared my soul with the daggers shot from his vengeful eyes. "I'm not sure Papa can spare me from helpin' out with the farm. Otherwise, I'd love to."

"Oh, my goodness," my aunts exclaimed, their voices alive again. "Students, because this is a school function, we will be spending school time studying William Shakespeare and practicing the play. No one should have to miss any chores or work time, except for the dress rehearsal and the day of the production. This play will not interfere with your schedule at home, and we've put together a whole lesson covering the Roman Republic. It should be very exciting," they added.

I looked around the room at the resigned faces and knew we'd lost. All I could hope for was that I would be given the job of student director. After all, I'd called for it first.

A renewed energy had crept into my aunts as they scoured the room, searching for victims.

"How about it, Earl? Would you do us the honor of playing the leading role? He's only on stage three times, but the whole play is named after him."

Earl knew he wasn't going to get any better a deal than this. "Sure, I'd be delighted to be Julius Caesar." His sarcasm was lost on our aunts. "That is, unless anyone else wants to?"

I saw most of the boys lean over to tie their shoe or pick up a dropped pencil.

"I guess not," Miss Ruby said, noticing no takers on the offer. "Don't worry, fellows, there are plenty of juicy parts for everyone."

It was downhill after that. All the roles got handed out quickly, with Jack taking the lead role of Mark Antony and Winnie Mae grabbing the role of Calpurnia, Julius Caesar's wife. Miss Ruby happily gave me the role of student director, knowing full well that she could count on me to be her right-hand woman.

After school, Lucy (who was playing Brutus' wife Portia) and I ran ahead, looking to scoot far enough in front of Earl so as to not bear his wrath. But I couldn't outrun my brother; he caught up with me halfway home and gave me a knuckle sandwich to my arm that set my teeth a-chattering. I hung my head and rubbed the sore spot as he yelled, "That's for bein' too smart for your own good, crybaby!"

"I ain't no crybaby and you know it, Earl Harris," I said defiantly, as I lifted my head and looked him straight in the eyes, proving my point.

"Hey, Earl, lay off." Jack walked up behind my brother and then stepped between us.

"Mind your own business, Jack," Earl threatened. "This ain't any of your affair."

"Hey, buddy, she paid her price. Leave her be." In the next breath Jack added, "Ain't that swell that we get to kill you? I mean, in the play."

Earl cocked his head and decided that he was through with me. "Yeah, let's practice me dyin'. Go ahead and put a sword through my gullet." That was all it took, and Earl and Jack, preoccupied with killing each other, kept their sights off me.

"I'm sure glad I'm not a boy," I told Lucy, holding up my injured limb. "They act so dumb all the time."

"Most of the time, they sure do," she agreed. "About as dumb as a doorknob. Or a poked pig. Or a rock, for that matter." And with that, we both broke into giggles.

March 15, 1936 was a warm winter day. The spring thaw had come early that year, and it seemed to be a good sign, as *Julius Caesar: The Musical* would be performed on the large stage of the Bijou that evening. The twenty-five-cent tickets had sold out, and our small town was abuzz with talk of the exciting production that would feature the children of Michigami Consolidated School. The play had taken months of preparation, and the fifteenth fell on a Saturday that year, making it the perfect time to celebrate the death of one of Shakespeare's most popular character: Julius Caesar had met his maker that very same day almost two thousand years earlier.

"Beware of the Ides of March," sang Millie, the Soothsayer, as she danced around the house early that morning.

"Millie," I explained for the umpteenth time, "it's not 'Beware *of* the Ides of March.' It's 'Beware! The Ides of March!'" As the student director, it was my responsibility to make sure the lines were read or sung correctly, and Millie refused to sing her line the right way.

"Well, I think it sounds better my way. Don't you, Daddy?" Millie asked Pa as he walked into the kitchen.

"I sure do, Peanut," he said, winking at me.

"But Daddy, that's not the way Mr. Shakespeare wrote it. It ain't right," I argued.

"It *isn't* right, Adeline," my mother, with her exceptional hearing, called from upstairs. Daddy and I smiled at one another.

"I don't think anyone's really gonna notice, sister. Let her be," he said quietly. "Where's Earl?"

Mama answered as she came down the stairs. "He's complaining of a stomachache. He must have jitters about the show tonight."

Earl had better *not* have the jitters, I thought. If he didn't shape up right quick, we'd be in a mess of trouble. Earl did rodeo and should be used to coming under pressure.

I stomped upstairs to set a fire under him and get my show on the road. "What's wrong?" I inquired sternly as I threw open Earl's door.

"Jeez, did you ever think of knockin'?" He glared at me as he pulled his shirt down over his head.

"Sorry. Mama said you were feeling ill, and I was just checking on you."

"Well, I'm fine."

"Do you have the jitters?"

"No."

"Then what's wrong?"

"I'm fine, Addie. I just got some kinda stomach bug, but I'm feeling better."

"You sure? We can't do the show without you, ya know?" Earl wasn't on stage much, but he was full of spirit, and the show, well, it just couldn't go on without him. As much as Earl could be a tease and a pain in the behind, he was a fine actor and had taken the role seriously. When he sang the "Death of Cowards" song to his wife, Winnie Mae, his engaging tenor pulled the goose pimples from your skin.

"No, I'm really okay. Maybe I do have jitters." He smiled weakly. "You're just worried I won't do well."

"That's not true. Really. You'll do great. You play Julius just fine." I turned to leave and added, "Finish up and come down for some breakfast. Maude has a nice hearty meal done up for us."

"I'm on my way, I promise."

Earl was melancholy all day during dress rehearsal, and after, when we went to the Bijou to prepare for the opening, he looked downright spooked. His face was ghostly white, and he walked hunched over like he had a bellyache. Aunt Pearl sensed something was wrong, but Earl insisted he was fine; he was just tired from a late night of thinking about the show.

"Earl, you look so peaked, are you sure?" Miss Pearl wheeled over to him and set her hand on his forehead. "You're burning up!"

"Aunt Pearl, really, I'm fine. Please, just let me be."

"Can I get you some water? Something to eat?" She turned and called out to me. "Adeline, get your brother some water, please."

"I'm not thirsty, Miss Pearl, thank you. I just want to rest a bit before the show. Really, I'm all right." He gave her a reassuring smile before he leaned back and closed his eyes.

Aunt Pearl was called on to help organize the orchestra she was directing and reluctantly wheeled away, looking back solemnly.

There was so much to do and such a short time in which to finish before the curtain went up! Winnie Mae had a ripped hem and Maude, as head of wardrobe, bustled over to fix it. Mama and Daddy were occupied with last-minute scenery adjustments, and Miss Ruby and Miss Opal were busy organizing the chorus and the other players who roamed the theatre floor and stage. I thought we would never be able to pull it off, but as evening fell and the seats began to fill up, everything began to fall into place. Even Earl looked better; the nap had done him good.

"Good evening, ladies and gentlemen, and welcome to Michigami School's performance of *Julius Caesar: The Musical*." Aunt Ruby welcomed the packed theatre. "We hope you enjoy our unusual performance of William Shakespeare's tragic tale of honor, patriotism, and friendship. The songs you will hear were written by Miss Pearl Miller, and the updated dialogue by Miss Opal Miller and me." She stopped briefly for the applause that rocked the theatre. "Without further ado, I present to you *Julius Caesar: The Musical*." She bowed slightly and walked offstage.

"Quick, Flavius!" I pushed Fred Cassidy out onto the stage where a small group of townfolk had gathered, and breathed a sigh of relief as he spoke the first words of the play. "Why aren't you people at work? This is not a holiday!"

The play moved swiftly along, and I looked for Earl, as his scene with Winnie Mae and his solo were coming up soon. I saw him on the other side of the stage, bent over, hands on his knees, breathing deep. I couldn't tell what he was doing until he straightened up and, glancing over at me, waved gently. Earl took the stage, walking tentatively, but when he and Calpurnia began their discussion and he broke into song, I felt full of pride to be his sister. His voice rang clear through the hall, and the audience was mesmerized by the sad melody that filled the theatre.

Afraid of death? Why should I be?
The mystery is for the dunce;
Again and again the coward dies—
The hero, only once.

I looked over to Aunt Pearl, who was leading the small orchestra. She mouthed the words to her own song as her nephew performed and, when he finished, closed her eyes as the thundering applause drowned out the last notes of the musicians. There was no doubt about it, my brother had talent. Mama and Daddy were clapping wildly, and looked at each other like Earl had just grown wings. The curtains closed, and Earl walked unsteadily off stage and slumped down next to the curtain to wait for his last scene. I walked backstage as the actors took their places, and as the curtain went up I squatted next to Earl.

"You did great, Earl. You really did."

"Thanks, Addie." He looked up at me. "Sorry about the knuckle sandwich I gave you. This really ain't so bad," he added as he nodded towards the stage.

"That's okay." I looked out to the stage, watching as Bobby Van Ostin took his cue correctly.

When I looked back, Earl had closed his eyes and was breathing in short, shallow breaths. Alarmed, I shook his shoulder and whispered quietly, "Earl! What's wrong? Should I go get Miss Ruby?"

He opened his eyes and sat up quickly. "Don't, Addie. I only got just one more scene to get through; I'll be okay. But I think when I'm done you should go get Daddy. I think something's wrong in my gullet." He doubled over, clutching his stomach.

"Earl, you gotta go now. You're gonna pass out. You can't stay here." I was scared stiff. Earl looked as though he would die backstage, right before he was to die onstage.

"No, Addie. I can finish. I'm done after this, so . . ." He sat up. "See? I'm all right. You just do what I told you. You go fetch Daddy as soon as I'm done." He looked out to the stage and stood up unsteadily. "It's just about my time."

His cue came up, and I watched my brother walk out to face his last battle against the Roman senators waiting to cut him down. I looked out to the audience and saw Mama and Daddy watching him, both with a peculiar look on their faces. Aunt Pearl wore the same odd expression. They knew something was not right. Even Jack, as Mark Antony, could tell that Earl was not delivering his lines with the same enthusiasm he had displayed so many times before. I was frozen in place, watching the scene unfold in front of me. I watched Earl as he painfully delivered his last lines, and I watched him as he took a well-practiced sword to the gullet. I watched him as he fell to the floor, and I heard him as he haltingly cried out to Johnny McCade, "And you,

Brutus?"

It wasn't until the curtains closed and Earl began to vomit onto the stage that I sprang into action, running through the closed curtains and calling out to my father through the intermission crowd.

"What is it, Addie?" Aunt Pearl grabbed my arm as she wheeled her way through the exiting musicians.

"Earl's real sick. He told me to get Daddy."

Aunt Pearl's face turned ashen and she looked frantically about, searching for my parents, shaking her head as if to say, "I knew it."

Mama and Daddy must have known something was amiss, too, because they were backstage in two shakes of a lamb's tail. Daddy carried Earl out the back door; Mama told me to tell my aunts that they were taking him to the hospital in Midland. After Lucy's mama had died in the Old Doc's care, I appreciated the fact they didn't want the same fate for Earl. As they were leaving, Mama looked at me like she had so many things to say, but the words seemed to stick in her craw.

"Don't worry, Mama," I told her, "we'll be okay."

She nodded, and without saying another word, turned and walked out to the car waiting by the door.

Daddy phoned us later that evening at our aunts' house, where a small group of concerned thespians were discussing the night's success and waiting anxiously for some news. Earl's appendix had burst on the way to the hospital. Poisonous pus and the contents from his intestines had filled his abdominal cavity, temporarily relieving the intense pain but setting him on the far more dangerous course of peritonitis. Earl would have to go in for surgery, and they were lucky that the young doctor at the new hospital had recognized the signs of appendicitis. It was not uncommon for folks to die from the curious ailment that had only recently been discovered to be treatable. Daddy asked that Jack, who was already familiar with our farm and the foxes, help out until he could get back, God only knew when. Maude could take care of Millie and the house, and I could help Jack. They would call later when they had more news, but they had to go; the doctor was waiting to speak to them.

We sat silently as Aunt Ruby replaced the phone on the hook and repeated what Daddy had told her. The very fact that Earl was to have an operation was terrifying. An operation almost certainly meant death. It was considered a last resort, something doctors turned to when options ran out and hope ran low. All of a sudden it occurred to me that I might not ever see my only brother again, and I felt a heaviness in my chest so painful that it made me gasp for a breath of air. Frantically, I looked to my aunts, needing the calm authority of an adult to ease the sorrowful situation and assure me that all would be fine, that Earl would be all right.

Every face in the room turned expectantly to the three Miller sisters. They were the leaders, the teachers, the repositories of all answers. They would tell us what we were supposed to do, how we would manage. As a teenager, I could not understand the intricacies of this unfamiliar situation, and all I could do was pass the burden to them and follow their instructions. It was not within me to do anything else.

The sisters stood together, a united front of strength, recognizing the need for leadership and, as usual, stepping up to the challenge. Miss Ruby took a deep breath, then looked to her sisters as if to say, "Here I go."

"We will get through this. We must pull together and make the best of this difficult situation. Earl is in the best care in the county, and I'm sure the doctors know what they are doing. We must put our trust in them, and in God, to take care of Earl. Jack?" She looked over to where Jack and Lucy were standing. "Would you please take our automobile and drive the girls back to their farm?"

Jack nodded in agreement as they continued.

"Finish up any chores that Mr. Harris may have for the evening. Adeline will help you. Drive to your place, and then in the morning you can go back. Seeing as it's the weekend, maybe your father can get his brother and your cousins to help him while you work the foxes. Would you like us to speak with him?"

"No, ma'am," Jack answered. "My daddy would want me to go. There's no problem."

There was a rumor floating about that Jack and Lucy's daddy had found the good Lord and was thinking of getting baptized. I had not worked up the courage to talk with Lucy about this. She was a bit sensitive about speaking of her daddy, but Jack's confidence in his father's approval fueled my curiosity about his daddy's salvation.

Miss Ruby handed out more instructions, and our anxiety began to wane as we slipped into the comfort of well-being that my aunts tucked around us. Jack went out to start up the Chevy, but before we could leave, Miss Pearl announced that she would like to say a prayer for my brother. Aunt Opal agreed, tears streaming down her pudgy face.

"Please, dear Lord, keep Earl from death's door, as he is just a young boy and deserves his time on your marvelous earth. Please keep your heavenly eyes on my sister and her husband as they, too, must be suffering. You are our savior, and we look to you for guidance and salvation, and pray that you will take care of our family in this time of need. Amen."

A murmured "Amen" rose from the small group, and Aunt Pearl wiped a heavy tear from her lashes as she wheeled over to where I stood with Millie and Maude. "I am so sorry, girls, that we can't be of more help to you. It is really my fault. I can't manage without both Ruby and Opal. It's too difficult for just one of them." She wiped away another tear as we crowded around her chair.

"Oh, Aunt Pearl," Maude said, "please don't say such things. Why, we can look after ourselves, it's no problem at all." Millie and I nodded in agreement. "You know I can cook even better than Mama, and with Jack's help, why, we'll be just fine. Right, girls?"

Millie and I assured her that this was true, but it was heartbreaking nonetheless to see our favorite aunt so full of despair. She had a real soft spot for Earl—he was the only boy—and her anguish was disconcerting. We always saw her as a pillar of strength, and here she was, saying it was her fault that she couldn't do more.

"It ain't your fault you're in a wheelchair, Aunt Pearl." Millie kissed her cheek.

"It *isn't* my fault, Millie." Old habits die hard, and she and Mama were cut from the same cloth.

"That's right. It *isn't* your fault. See? You're feeling better already." Millie patted her shoulder, the correction going unnoticed.

Aunt Pearl choked back a laugh, and wiping back her last tear, said, "I *am* feeling better. Thank you, Millie. Thank you, girls." She smiled weakly at us and Aunt Opal shooed us away, urging us to get back to the farm, since it was getting near midnight.

The ride home was quiet. Jack concentrated on the unfamiliar nuances of the new Chevy as he anxiously navigated his way over the dark roads. His daddy had a beat-up old Ford truck that he drove occasionally, but here he was, in a new automobile that wasn't his, with the responsibility of getting all these girls home safely; he took his job seriously and shushed us when we asked him how he was doing. He and Lucy stayed briefly at the farm while we closed her up for the night, and Jack promised he would be back at daybreak to open up. He told me that I should be ready to go; he would be needing my help. They left, and Millie, Maude, and I entered our dark home and spent our first night ever away from our parents, our brother, and the presumed security that we took for granted every night when we lay our heads on our pillows.

Jack kept his promise, and at daybreak I heard the horn blowing as he pulled into our drive. I watched from my window as he stepped out of the car and walked confidently toward our side door. Jack had grown into a young man, tall and broad-shouldered, and while he wasn't as handsome as his cousin, Frankie, he was attractive enough to draw the attention of many of the girls at school. As Maude was letting Jack in, I saw Mama and Daddy pull in the drive and I hurriedly shook Millie to wake her, urging her to be quick, that there was sure to be news.

We raced down the stairs, almost running into Maude as she took Mama's coat and hung it on the peg in the pantry.

"How is Earl?" I blurted out, before I could even notice how worn and tired my parents appeared. They looked at me with bloodshot eyes; their weariness filled the kitchen. Jack stood awkwardly by the door, ready to start the chores, but uncomfortable taking the lead since my father was now here.

Daddy's hands shook as he reached for the cup of coffee Maude offered.

"Thanks, Maudy." He took a sip of the hot liquid, letting it replenish everything that had been drained from him. "Earl has what the doctors call 'peritonitis.' That means that he has an infection in his gut where the poison was... is." He took a bigger drink and continued, "The operation that Earl had supposedly cleaned out all the infection, but now Earl has a fever. He has this fever because that's his body's way of fightin' the infection. When he doesn't have a fever anymore, his body will have beaten the sickness, and he should recover in a couple weeks."

"What happens if the fever doesn't beat the infection? What will happen then?" I asked.

"We're not going to think about that, dear," Mama interjected. "Right now, we're concentrating on how to get Earl better."

"Is Earl gonna die, Daddy?" Millie asked the question that we were all leaving unasked.

"We hope not, Sweet Pea." My father looked at my mother. "But Earl's body can't keep up the high fever for too long; it would hurt his insides. For the next day or so, Earl's body is going to be doin' some serious fightin'."

"I thought we didn't believe in fighting." Millie started sobbing, and my mother comforted her, pulling her onto her lap and stroking her hair.

"It's not that kind of fighting, honey. Earl will be just fine. You'll see. He'll be back in no time, teasing you girls worse than before."

My Pa looked up, noticing Jack standing at the door, staring uneasily out the window. "Jack, I can't tell you how much I appreciate your being here. I don't know what I'd do without you. You going to be all right with just Addie helping?"

"We'll be fine, Mr. Harris. I'm happy to lend a hand."

"Your daddy okay with you being gone?"

"He don't mind at all. He wanted me to pass on to you that you and Mrs. Harris are in his prayers and you keep me as long as you need. My uncle John is coming over to help him out until I get back."

"Well, you tell your daddy that's right Christian of him, and I do thank him for his well-wishes. We need all the prayers we can get." My father looked at my mother once again and nodded. "Susie, you best finish up what you need to do while I go out to the ranch with Jack and Addie. We need to get back soon as possible."

Within the hour, Mama and Daddy had left, and the emptiness of an adult's absence once again returned. Knowing that we were in charge and my parents were depending on us cleared away any thoughts of shenanigans; we were as solemn as Sunday while we finished our breakfast and cleared the dishes. I put on my work clothes and followed Jack back to the ranch as Maude and Millie started the weekend chores in the house.

Jack was so intent on following Daddy's instructions that it was well over an hour before he even spoke. "How you doin', Addie? You know, with Earl and all."

"I'm okay."

"Earl's gonna be just fine. He's a fighter." He looked at me and smiled, I assume because he was remembering the knuckle sandwich.

"Yeah." I was unaccustomed to Jack's full attention, and my customary boldness was overcome by a sudden shyness that colored my cheeks red.

"Cat got your tongue today, Addie?" he teased. "Usually I can hear you chatterin' when I come ten feet from your front drive. You ain't said but two words all mornin'." He had stopped shoveling the fox dung and leaned on the long wooden handle, waiting for a response.

The trouble with your mind being somewhere it isn't used to is that you're just not sure what you might say or do. Maybe I was overcome with the fact that Earl could be dying, or maybe it was Jack standing so close, but I was having trouble finding where I stood. I wanted to tell him how much I liked having him around and how strong he looked and how capable he was, but my thoughts lost their way from my brain to my mouth and came out differently than I had planned.

"Here's two words for you, Jack Conklin. Shut up. Why don't you mind your own damn business?" I snapped, sorry I had said it as soon as the words crossed my lips.

Jack just stared at me like I had three heads, then picked his shovel up and continued working as if I hadn't just sworn and been obnoxiously rude to him. After all, Jack was the fellow that was helping my Pa out while my sick brother lay on his deathbed.

Jack continued the silent treatment all through the morning and only spoke to me when he called out orders and when it was time for lunch. I knew I had kicked the dog for no reason and that I owed Jack an apology, but my insufferable stubbornness stopped me in my tracks every time I began to speak. Instead, I followed Jack's orders meekly and spoke the words silently in my head that I should have said out loud. My head ached from my uncalled-for outburst, and my stomach ached from the thought that Earl was fighting for his life. I was exhausted from all the turmoil, and when I remembered busting into Earl's room to hound him about having the jitters, I couldn't believe that only a day had passed. It seemed like a distant memory.

Things took a turn for the worse when Mama called in the afternoon and said Earl's fever was raging and they would be at the hospital for the night, sitting vigil and praying. Jack drove Maude and Millie over to sit with Aunt Pearl while Aunt Opal and Aunt Ruby took the car to Midland to stay with Mama and Daddy for a few hours—and to be there in case of the worst. They dropped Jack back off at the farm on the way to the hospital, assuring us that they would call with any news, good or bad. My aunts drove off, waving sadly and leaving Jack and me alone as the late afternoon sun began trading places with the chill of the evening shade.

Maude called later and said that she and Millie were staying in town for the night with Miss Pearl. They didn't know when the other aunts would be home, and I was to make supper for me and Jack. I wasn't the cook in the family, so Jack and I sat down to a cold meal of sliced pork and potatoes, the usual noisiness of the family replaced with an icy stillness.

The grandfather clock ticked loudly in the hall, the sound echoing through the empty house and amplifying the screaming silence that had settled in between Jack and me. After dinner, Jack told me he would be sleeping out at the ranch and that I should be up and ready at sunrise to help him open up. The door banged shut as he walked out into the dark, and I wondered how events had come to pass in such a way that had left me in this miserable predicament.

I sat paralyzed at the prospect of spending the night alone in the large, empty house. I didn't move a muscle as the clock ticked on and the night pushed forward, taking me unwillingly along. I had never been afraid before, had never even thought of being afraid in the home I had spent my entire life in. But in the murky darkness, my heart rate began to steadily increase, picking up speed as my imagination noticed sinister phantoms lurking behind every sofa and chair. I couldn't move, my limbs frozen in the panic that gripped me from head to toe. I wanted desperately to scream out to Jack to save me, but I had lost my voice to the terror that filled my lungs and throat. The fear expanded in my mind and body like a balloon filling with air. When the clock in the hall struck the top of the hour, my fear burst, sending me running outside and racing out to the ranch, my body surging with a strength and speed that seemed superhuman.

"Jack," I managed to shriek as I burst into the small apartment where he was making up his bed.

"What is it, Addie? Are you okay? What happened?" He got up swiftly and came over to me. "Here, sit down and tell me what's goin' on. Did you hear from your mama?" He led me over to the cot and took a seat beside me, the light from the lantern flickering and sending shadows across the room.

"N... n... no..." I stuttered, out of breath. My relief at reaching safety was so overwhelming that I closed my eyes and settled up against him, trying to catch my breath and thanking the good Lord for sending him to us.

"What's wrong then, Addie?" he asked, confused.

I could hear the barking of the pregnant vixens in their pens as they smelled me, a potential predator. They knew Daddy, Earl, and even Jack, but I didn't visit the ranch much anymore unless Pa had an emergency, so I could understand the mild uproar taking place in the animal territory outside the walls of the ranch.

"Jack, I am so sorry I was cross with you this morning. It was uncalled for, and I hope you accept my deepest heartfelt apology." I kept my head down, ashamed for my actions, but the pain eased on my conscience as I unloaded the words that should have come much earlier.

Jack sighed. "That's all right, Addie. You've got a lot on your mind right now. Just forget it."

"I'm just so worried about Earl. What if the worst happens and he dies? What will we do? How will we ever get past it?"

"People got resilience, Addie. They can live through the worst of things and learn to move on. Bad things happen and you adjust. You pick up and go on." Jack stared off into nowhere, and it occurred to me that he was speaking from experience. He and Lucy had lost their mama a few years back and were left only with a sister that had the brain of a baby. Losing Earl would be horrible... but if Mama was gone? I shuddered just thinking about the devastation that would shatter our family.

"Do you miss your mama?"

"Every day, Addie. Every day."

"How's your daddy doing, Jack?" This seemed like an opportune time to bring up the subject that I had been so curious about. I snuggled in closer, feeling the warmth of his body through my sweater and the strength of his arm around my shoulder. I could smell Jack through his jacket, but the hard work from earlier that day made an intoxicating perfume that wasn't at all repellent. Just the opposite—it drew me in, and unfamiliar thoughts filled my head.

"He's doin' good. He stopped with the whiskey and got religion somehow when Charlie was born, and now he talks a lot like a preacher, but it's better than back when my mama was alive."

"Little Charlie's like a charm, huh?" Jack's baby brother was four, and his whole family doted on him. Lucy's spirits were way up since his birth, even though it had meant more work for her, but that little boy had done wonders for his kin. And on top of it, his Daddy had found the good Lord.

"He sure is, Addie. Why, just the other day he told me he was gonna drive Pa's tractor all the way to town. And when I asked him why he don't take the truck, he says it's because he don't know how to drive a truck, only a tractor." Jack laughed, clearly captivated with his younger brother. "Imagine that! A child saying he was fixin' to drive a tractor. Why, my daddy was so tickled he put him in the seat of the truck with him and let Charlie steer that old bucket of rust around and around the yard. 'Course, Aunt Bonnie about threw a fit when she seen them toolin' about with her baby at the wheel. But it sure was funny." He smiled at the memory. "That boy's got a personality big as life, I tell ya."

I yawned, done in by the events of the past two days, and I struggled to keep my eyes open in the warm comfort of Jack's presence. "Keep talking, Jack. I just want to listen," I murmured. The uneasy foxes had settled some, and only occasionally would one cry out, as if to warn the others I was still there.

"You need some sleep, Addie. You're plum tuckered out. Come on, I'll take you back inside."

"No!" I came alive quickly. "I don't want to be all alone in there, Jack. Can't I just stay out here with you?"

"Well, now, Addie, that just don't seem like it's the right thing to do. Your daddy's been good to me and it wouldn't be fittin', us two out here all by our lonesome."

He didn't look like he was all that sure of his words, so I pressed on.

"Oh, please, Jack. I can't go back in there, I just can't. I won't tell a soul,

I promise. I'll be still as a mouse." I looked into his face; his eyes betrayed his confusion at the dilemma facing him.

"Jeez, Addie. You're about impossible." He looked away, and I felt him giving in. "You just get some rest." I lay down, and he covered me with his blanket.

"Where are you going, Jack?" I asked, alarmed, when I saw him getting up.

"Nowhere, Addie. Just blowin' out the lantern. I don't want to burn your daddy's ranch down while he's gone. Now go to sleep." He blew out the flame and then sat at the end of the bed. "Go to sleep," he repeated.

As I started to drift off, relaxed and safe at last, I heard Jack begin to speak softly, his words like a lullaby. "You know, my daddy ain't the most understanding fellow in the world, or the nicest. He's way different than your pa, Addie, but he's had a different life. He and my Uncle Frank, well, they been on their own since they was young boys."

He stopped talking and I wondered sleepily if that was all he was going to say, but he began again. "When those boys were just eleven years old—they were twins, you know—they run away from home. See, their own daddy used to beat them so bad he once broke Uncle Frank's arm. Their mama was just as mean; she didn't have no sense of love for those boys, including their baby brother, Joe. They was just two bad seeds that God seen fit to give children to. I met them once or twice before they passed, and they didn't have much to say then, but they was old and had lost all recollection of the years that had passed.

"But my daddy tells me that one day, not long after their eleventh birthday, he knocked over a bucket full of fresh milk. They didn't have much money and that was their milk for the week, but Daddy swears it was an accident; he wouldn'ta done nothin' to enrage his pa, for fear of a whippin'."

Jack stopped and listened to a particularly noisy female, waited until she settled, and then continued.

"Well, my granddaddy went into the house, and when he come out, he was carrying his shot gun. My daddy says that he saw that big ole gun and just started runnin'. Runnin' across their vegetable garden, runnin' across their corn field—he just took off runnin'. Uncle Frank joined up with Daddy when the shotgun got turned on him, and they both just took off and never looked back. They jumped the fence and hid out in the neighbor's barn 'til 'twas dark, and then they went back to their farm and took their little brother, who was but nine at the time. Those three boys lived in haystacks and barns and stole corn and raw vegetables and anything else they could get their hands on, till they found work in the picking fields. They lived in the woods until they saved enough money to take a room in Roscommon with a kindly old spinster. Their mama and daddy never went looking for them, though. They probably figure it was just as well; they didn't seem to care for them much, anyway."

"What happened to your Uncle Joe?" I asked, captivated by the story.

"He died of the Spanish Flu in the Great War."

"I'm so sorry, Jack. I didn't know about your daddy."

"That's all right, Addie. I just try to remember that it's hard to judge a man until you done walked in his shoes. I ain't makin' excuses for my daddy or my uncle. I know what they are. I just remember where they come from. And where they come from ain't so nice."

"Thank you, Jack." I whispered, overcome with sadness for this man I had only thought of as hateful. "I sure appreciate your sharing that story." I wanted to see his face, but there was just a faint glow coming from a far window that was no help.

"Good night, Addie. Sweet dreams," he said from the dark.

I tumbled into a deep sleep, where my dreams were anything but sweet. They were harsh and real, and kept putting me into one impossible situation after another. I tossed and turned, unable to shake my sleepy uneasiness, and only when I felt the cot shift and Jack lie next to me did I begin to rest. All through the night I would wake, reaching out to assure myself that he hadn't left, then drift back off as I felt his body close by.

I awoke before the sun, poorly rested but happy to put the night behind me. Rolling over in the tight quarters, I came face-to-face with Jack, his sleepy eyes half-open as if he were waiting for me. Though no words passed his lips, I knew what he wanted, and I closed my eyes and gave in to the overwhelming desire for my first kiss. His hold on me was unyielding but his manner was gentle, and when he pulled me in and put his lips to mine, I was both willing and reassured that the thrill I felt was shared.

My inexperience was no match for my intuition, and nothing seemed more natural than having Jack's lips and body pressed against mine. It didn't last but a few seconds, though, before the rooster's crow interrupted us, announcing the beginning of the day; our fervent kiss was over. Jack pulled away reluctantly, his eyes glued to mine until he got up from the bed and disappeared through the door and into the back of the ranch, where I could hear the loud complaints of the foxes awaiting their breakfast.

Dazed for more than one reason, I hummed the *Death of Cowards* song absentmindedly as I brewed the morning coffee. Only when I heard a car coming down the drive was I jolted back to reality and the dire situation our family faced. I slammed back into the present, my daydreams evaporating as I realized that my parents could soon be telling me that my brother—their only son—had not survived the night. I saw Jack walking up from the ranch; he had heard the car, as well.

We met the slowing automobile. Jack opened Mama's door, and she directly burst into tears. I saw straight away, though, that they were tears of joy. She confirmed my hope, sobbing, "His fever has come down."

My first instinct was to hug Jack, not my mama, but I quickly realized this was one can of worms I couldn't open and so I let my mother wrap her arms around me.

Jack shook Daddy's hand excitedly as we all made our way back into the kitchen for the details of Earl's miracle recovery.

"I'll tell you what," my father began. "That new hospital's somethin'. They got the latest machines that tell you just about anything. And the doctors... some of the best in the state, I hear. Dr. Anson, why, he couldn't a been but thirty years, but he's smart as a whip. He's the one that knew just what was wrong with Earl. If it hadn'ta been for him, well..." He didn't finish his thought, thankful that he didn't have to.

"And the nurses," my mother continued. "They stayed by us day and night, getting us coffee and rolls when we were so tired we couldn't see straight." She shook her head, and I could see that she hadn't slept much in the past two days. They talked on about the hospital, Jack and I listening politely until they both stopped as if they'd hit a wall.

"I'd best go check on the foxes," my father said, his words sluggish with exhaustion.

"Mr. Harris, why don't you get some rest? Addie and me, we got it all taken care of. Looks like you could use a little shut-eye." Jack deliberately did not look at me.

"You really should get some sleep, Daddy. We've been working them for the past couple of days, we're okay for a few more hours, really," I added.

"You two..." Pa choked up a bit, but gave in without difficulty. "I just can't see straight, I'm so beat. What about it, Susiekins?" He looked to my mother, who had dropped her head to the table.

"That's fine," she answered simply, not even picking her head up.

Daddy stood up slowly and placed his hand on Jack's shoulder. "I don't know how to thank you, son. You been a lifesaver."

"I'm glad I can be of help, Mr. Harris. That's what neighbors are for."

"You're right, Jack. You're so right."

Mama and Daddy went upstairs, reminding us that Millie and Maude would be home later that afternoon. Jack and I ate our breakfast in silence, not trusting that our words would fall on sleeping ears. What we didn't say with words, though, we made up for with hushed giggles and animated faces. At one point he reached over to tickle me and I backed up playfully to escape, almost taking the chair over top of me. He pointed out to the ranch, and we hastily finished our coffee and headed out, a whole day's worth of work ahead of us.

Our energy kept up through lunch, but after a meal our lack of rest began to catch up and our work slowed to a snail's pace. By mid-afternoon we were downright exhausted, and just lifting a shovel or cleaning a pen was proving to be difficult. Jack carried the brunt of the responsibility and the work, and offered to help more than once.

"Here, let me get that for you, Addie," he said, grabbing a pail of water from me that had spilled when I lost my footing.

"Thanks, Jack," I answered, grateful for his assistance.

"Addie, what do you think you'll be when you grow up? I mean when you're an adult, 'cause you're kinda grown already." He stumbled over his words, not wanting to offend, but I understood what he meant.

"I don't know, maybe a schoolteacher like my aunts, or a writer like Mama." I stepped off of a bale of hay. "It seems like it'll be forever 'fore I'm old enough to even learn how to drive. Daddy says I have to wait until I'm fourteen. That's well over a year from now." I groaned loudly at the thought. "What about you, Jack? What you thinking for your future?"

"I dunno. I thought it might be swell to be a police officer, or maybe a fireman, but I'll probably get stuck right here doing farmin', just like my Pa." He sat down on an overturned milk bucket.

"That's not so bad, is it?" I sat down on the straw next to him.

"Naw, it ain't so bad. I just thought it would be excitin' to be savin' people's lives. Ya know, to help folks in need." He sighed, and I could see his dismal attitude breaking thru his fatigue.

"Maybe you will, Jack. You'd be a great police officer. If that's what you want, you should set your sights on it." I patted his shoulder encouragingly.

He looked at me longingly. "I got my eyes set on somethin'." Then he looked away, embarrassed.

I was caught off guard and wasn't sure how to respond, so I didn't. At least not out loud. My heart started up real fast and my body was flooded with the yearning to be right back where we'd been that morning.

"Addie, will you give me another kiss?" Jack looked at me like a tiger spying his last meal. "It just felt too quick this morning—like it was over before it even started."

At that moment, I understood fully the command a simple kiss could conjure.

"I will," I said hesitantly, feeling like this was a perfect time to strike a bargain. "But you have to do something for me."

"What?"

"You have to tell me how babies are made."

Jack burst out laughing and I felt the flush of embarrassment rise in my cheeks.

"Well, that's a fine how-do-you-do. I sure appreciate you making fun of me. Thank you so much, Jack Conklin." I turned away, furious that I had become the butt of the joke. I picked up a piece of straw and jammed it angrily between my teeth.

"I'm sorry, Addie. That wasn't very nice. You're right." But he was still smiling, so I turned my back on him again.

"No, really. Don't be mad." He leaned over and spoke softly in my ear. "I'll tell you, if you really want to know."

"Well, I do," I answered defiantly.

"And you're gonna give me a kiss. You promise?"

"Yeah, Jack. I don't go back on my word."

"Addie, why don't you give me that kiss first? Then I won't be thinkin' of it while I'm givin' my explanation." He smiled shyly.

"You're the impossible one," I sighed, agreeing.

He cupped my face in his hands and gently kissed first my forehead, then my nose. When he settled his mouth on mine and pulled me in close, I found instinct once again leading the way. We swayed together in a perfect, silent dance. My hands found his neck; I caressed his shoulders, then ran my hands upward through his thick hair, its silkiness inviting me to linger.

It was only when I heard his breathing step up and he shifted me even closer that I felt a fleeting panic. My common sense gave me sudden voice.

"That's enough, Jack. You got your kiss." I pushed him away and stood up straight, trying to shake the fervor of our encounter. "Now it's my turn."

"You really want to know?" he asked, smoothing his hair back and rearranging his shirt.

"Jack, don't stall. I wouldn't have kissed you if I didn't."

"Yes, you would. You like it as well as me, I can tell." He grinned slyly.

I scrunched my nose and started to give him a piece of my mind, but he stopped me and continued.

"Addie, I'll tell you. Don't work yourself into a fit." He looked around, as if expecting someone to pop out of hiding. All that peered back was our old cow, Betsy.

He leaned over and whispered into my ear the explanation that I had waited so long to hear. There were a couple parts that he wasn't exactly sure of, but I got the general idea. No wonder my parents were in such a stitch. Neither Jack nor I looked at each other when he had finished, and when he coughed nervously and stood up, I followed suit.

"You sure, Jack? You positive that's the way it's done?" I inquired, figuring I wouldn't put it past him to pull my leg.

"Yeah, I'm positive." He grabbed a pitchfork and started throwing hay into Betsy's stall. "Let's finish up here, Addie. Your sisters will be coming home any time now, and I imagine your daddy'll be up soon."

"Yeah, sure." I couldn't stop thinking about what Jack had told me. I kept glancing at him, expecting that any minute he would look over at me and break out into gales of laughter, telling me how gullible I was, but Jack kept his nose to the grindstone and didn't even glance up.

I had lain next to Jack, pressed against him all night, and spent the morning with my lips on his, but I couldn't imagine that anything else might have happened. To ever envision that I would participate in such a bizarre act was beyond belief, and to think my parents had—four times! And not just my parents, but any adult who had children... Thank goodness my aunts were safe.

My world was now a different one. I had been let in on one of the biggest secrets of the adult population and I supposed that made me one, too, but all I felt was that I was in way over my head. I wasn't ready to make that leap, and I even regretted kissing Jack, kind of.

What would I be one day? Would I ever do that thing that Jack had told me about? The uncertainty of so many things was a tremendous weight, and all I wanted was to curl up next to my mama with a good book while the rest of my family sat nearby, in our warm, safe home with food on our table. I clung to that vision, even as I felt it slipping through my fingers. There was no going back.

Chapter Four

Susie

During the first year of my marriage, my husband visited my bed once, on our wedding night. I had just turned nineteen, and already I couldn't imagine a more abysmal state than that of being married. Either my parents had done a magnificent job of misleading us as to the joys of matrimony, or I had made the largest mistake of my life. Nothing was what I expected. I had neither the joy nor the love that Mother and Father had modeled, nor did I have the companionship and respect that I would have assumed came with the vows and promises so recently exchanged.

At the risk of sounding presumptuous, the problem did not lie with me. I married George with my heart full and my mind open to our future together. I loved him intensely. He, I came to believe, did not share the same feelings.

Nothing overt betrayed him. He never raised his voice to me, belittled me, or threatened my person in any way. It was much more subtle. My husband avoided me—he went out of his way to make sure I had left the kitchen before he entered or was asleep in bed before he joined me. George spent many a night sleeping in the small apartment out at the ranch—"watching the foxes," of course—while I huddled, deserted, in our marriage bed and Pops slept in the room down the hall.

I took the blame originally, and enlisted my sisters to help me make the house a home—the meals more enticing, the curtains more eye-catching. But it was all to no avail. My husband never noticed the changes, though my father-in-law didn't miss a beat and was always complimentary about my attempts at cooking and the updates to the old house.

Pops became my friend. We continued our discussions from the "book club," debating such topics as Woodrow Wilson's health and the practical functionality of the Versailles Treaty. Reading the paper was a daily ritual, and we laughed at the advertisements suggesting that a bald head could be cured by rubbing Ed's Magic Elixir on it clockwise, or that drinking Theo's Tonic could help a woman lose ten pounds overnight. He, at least, enjoyed having me around, and without him—well, I don't know how I would have handled a bad marriage, in addition to the fact I had become pregnant during the single time George had been intimate with me. My husband had no clue that I was expecting, but Pops noticed it even before I did, when I was just a few weeks along.

"How you doin', Suze?" he asked suspiciously one morning, when I can only assume my face looked as green as I felt. "You're looking a bit under the weather."

"I am, Pops. I don't know what's wrong. I only pray it's not… something serious." I had barely recovered, and only just recently, from the Spanish Flu, and had lost my dear mother to its insidious grasp. I was terrified I would get sick again.

"Your back hurt?"

"It does."

"You feel like you got a bug in your stomach?"

"I do."

"You got no energy?"

"None. Oh, Pops, do you think I have the flu again?" I asked, my heart pounding in my chest.

"Nah. You'll get over what you got, say, in about nine months or so." His Cheshire cat grin gave away his obvious joy, and he hugged me as he whispered in my ear, "You'll be a wonderful mama, I just know you will."

"A baby?" I asked wonderingly. "How can that be? Why, we only…" I stopped before I embarrassed myself even more. "I mean…," I faltered.

"It only takes but once, Suze." Pops looked away—it was his turn to be uncomfortable.

This new turn in an already bad situation did not make me happy. My mother was gone, my sisters were busy with their careers and the care of Pearl, my husband was nonexistent, and I, an ignored mess of a wife, was now to become an ignored mess of a mother. I was not the maternal type. Pearl was. I was not the housewife and cook. Opal was. I was not the organized housekeeper. Ruby was. I was not anything. I loved the excitement of working, of creating words that inspired people and piqued their curiosities, but I had lost my job at the paper when the war ended and I got sick. Then I got married. And now I was with child.

I was but a young woman and already I had nothing to look forward to. All I needed was another person to care for who would not speak to me. I had stepped into someone else's bad dream, and everything around me, from the beat-up old dishpan to the threadbare rugs, was foreign. How had I missed the road to happiness? Who had led me astray? I could only look to my handsome husband as the reason things had slipped past my control and turned me into something ordinary and dull. Something I'd never been.

"You told him yet?" Pops asked me in my second month as he passed a dish to me to dry. George had gone into town for some supplies and it was just me and Pops. Again.

"No. I'm waiting for the right time."

"No time as the present," he said.

"I know. I will, soon. I promise." The truth was, George hadn't even slept in the house since I had found out about the baby, and I never could find a time when he didn't seem exceptionally busy. I wasn't nervous or excited about telling him; I was apathetic.

"Whatcha think? Boy or girl?" Pops picked up another dish.

"Oh, I don't care," I said absentmindedly.

"Don't care or don't know?"

"Did I say 'don't care'?" I asked, surprised. "I mean, of course I care. I guess I don't have a feeling one way or the other." I spoke the truth. This baby was just another faceless stranger to me that was using me, using my body.

Pops looked at me like he was reading my thoughts, as though they were written out on a sign I was holding. "Suze, you'll grow into it. It's a big adjustment and a big responsibility. Tough thing to wrap your arms around."

"I suppose."

"Why don't you and Junior take a walk tonight? It ain't too cold out, and it'll do you some good to get in some fresh air."

I smiled at hearing him call George, "Junior." It was such a young, lighthearted name, and I pictured George as anything but.

"What was he like, Pops? You know, when he was a boy."

"Well, now," he began as he sat with his coffee, "he was always a real fine-looking boy. Girls always took notice of him, but he ain't got no notion they was sweet on him… he was always talkin' baseball. He lived for that game, I tell ya. Couldn't get enough of it. Until the accident." He stopped and stared out the window. "He changed some after that."

I wiped down the wooden cutting board that held the stains of countless dead animals and nodded in understanding. My illness had changed me. Being so close to death and then watching my beloved mother pass had marked my mind and soul in a way that was never to be reversed. Laughter came with a guilty price tag, and enthusiasm for the outwardly significant seemed an unreasonable use of time. The unborn child that I carried had so far refused to ignite the spark that had once driven my ambition and enlivened my visage, and I feared that my only relief from despondency were the memories that I carried of a more contented era.

"I think you're right, Pops. A walk would do me good." I reveled in the parental concern that my father-in-law felt for me. Being the youngest in a large family, my sisters and my parents, until recently, had continually fussed over me, and it had come to a screeching halt after my marriage. To have Pops pick up the dropped reins was my saving grace.

"I'll go get my wrap," I said, feeling enthusiastic about the change from my usual routine. "When George gets back, I'll be ready to go."

"Ready to go where?" George stood in the door, back from his errands.

"A... a walk," I stammered, startled at his sudden appearance.

"I thought you and your beautiful wife could take a little stroll down by the river," Pops said.

"That sounds like a right idea, Pops, but I have to finish fixin' a busted pen. Maybe another time." George smiled weakly in my general direction.

"Well, now, Junior, I suppose that busted fence will just have to wait a spell." A look passed between father and son, and I sensed there would be no negotiation on this point. Pops wielded his silent authority with a conviction and strength that was unmistakable.

"It's just too nice of a night to let it go unnoticed, and your bride here needs a break from all this housekeepin' and such. I'd join ya, but my old back is achin' tonight." He reached around and pressed on his spine. "But you two, you go on, now. Take your time; I'll hold down the fort." He pushed his chair back and rose slowly to his feet. "Nice night to get out," he muttered as he moved to the front room and the comfort of his easy chair.

George and I stood uncomfortably in the kitchen. He kept his gaze to the floor, and I glanced around the room. I broke the silence. "I guess I'll just get my wrap, then."

"I'll be on the porch." He turned and headed out, the wooden screen door banging loudly as it swung shut.

We walked down toward the river, our shoes sinking in the spongy green grass of spring. The fading sun gave more light than warmth, casting long shadows between the budding leaves on the great oak trees that dotted the grassy fields near the river. The river was at its highest and rushed noisily past us, telling us how busy it was, that it didn't have time to sit and chat. Water splashed on the rocks by the shore; when I put my hand in, the cold bit back and I quickly pulled away.

"When I was a boy, we called this here spot the graveyard."

I looked up, surprised that George had spoken. He stood in profile, and I couldn't help but admire his lean physique and attractive features.

"Why?" I asked. "Was anyone you know buried here?"

"I don't think so. We just used to bring all the waste from the fox and horse carcasses down here for the critters to eat. Seemed so much more... I don't know... spooky, I guess, back then."

"It's so beautiful down here," I said, admiring the weeping willows, their long heavy branches hanging over the Titabawassee, occasionally dipping their slender limbs in the river like a child trailing her fingers through the water.

We sat in the stillness of the evening for a bit until I ventured a thin, "George?"

"Yeah?"

"George, I'm... I'm with child," I blurted out.

He turned to look at me straight on, and I saw right away the confusion in his every movement. He nodded gradually, as though he had figured out when and where this unlikely event had occurred, and then sat down hard on a flat stone while he looked off over the river.

Nothing could have made me feel any worse, and I promptly burst into the tears that had been building for so long. "I'm not—any—happier than you," I sobbed. The tears racked my body, and I cried for all my misfortunes of the past few years.

"No... no... I didn't...," he said, rising and coming to my side. "Don't cry, Susie, this is a blessin', really. I'm sorry I give you the wrong impression. Really, I'm just surprised, that's all." He looked at me earnestly. "I don't want you to get into a fit, please."

I sniffled and accepted his offered hand as he pulled me to my feet. My bottom was damp, and he smiled as he helped brush the loose grass and twigs off my skirt. We started back towards the farm, his gait a little slower than usual. His bum leg was normally unnoticeable, but tonight I could tell he was dragging it. He spoke just as I was about to ask him if he was all right.

"I can't believe I'm goin' to be a daddy. It don't seem possible." He looked almost happy, and my heart found a place where it hadn't been in a while.

Just thinking that it was me who had brought him this pleasure picked up my spirits immeasurably, and when he held my elbow and guided me through the darkening wood, I thought I would burst with joy.

"Does Pops know?" he asked as we picked our way through the tall grass.

"He knew before I did."

He shook his head, grinning. "That don't surprise me at all."

"He's something, isn't he?" I practically skipped through the violets that grew out behind the ranch. "I think of him like I did my own daddy. He's always so concerned for me. It's so sweet the way he watches out for my welfare—he's more excited than I am about the baby." I realized what I had just said and added, "I mean, just as excited. He just can't wait." I looked over at George, who had gone quiet during my discourse. "Can't you just see Pops with a grandson? He'll be beside himself," I added.

"Yeah, I suppose so," George replied as we picked our way through the muddy area next to the fence where the horses had cleared out any sign of grass. My heart pounded in my chest as I contemplated my next question, but despite how difficult it had suddenly become to breathe, I forced it out.

"Are you happy about the baby?"

"Sure. What man don't want to have a son? Or a daughter," he added.

"Doesn't," I said, instinctively correcting him.

"What?" George starred at me.

"Oh… I was just saying—nothing. Really. Nothing." I realized my mistake and tried to backpedal. "I was just making a comment."

"Did you just tell me I weren't speaking correctly?" George looked at me like he had just knocked a block off my shoulder and the fight could begin.

"It's no big deal," I said, trying to brush off the remark. "I was just saying that the word is *doesn't*, not *don't*. That's all."

He stopped in his tracks and turned to look at me. "Let me tell you something right now, Susie." He spoke slowly and in a tone that told me he meant business. "You're more than welcome to correct our child—in fact, I want you to. But never, and I mean never, again do I want to hear you correctin' me. Is that clear?"

I stood there, meeting his intent gaze. "Perfectly," I said. "It won't ever happen again."

In that moment a little spark from the Susie of the past ignited and, fiercely, I determined not to yield to any bullying from this man who persisted in sending me mixed signals.

We stared at each other, speaking volumes in the charged silence, until there was nothing more to be declared.

I stalked into the house, the door banging shut as I hung up my wrap, and walked into the front room. Pops looked up, surprised to see me so soon.

"Well?" He pulled his spectacles down on his nose and set the paper on his lap.

"I told him."

"And?"

"Well, you should just ask 'Junior' what he thinks about it." I used his old nickname sarcastically. I couldn't help feeling like a child that had come to tell a parent about a misbehaving sibling.

He pulled himself to his feet. "I think I'll do just that," he said, heading for the kitchen.

"And I'll be in my room if you need me," I called after him. I started up the steps, but stopped halfway when I heard the murmurings of George and his father talking on the porch. I hadn't eavesdropped since I was a child, but I wanted too much to hear my husband's explanation for his peculiar—and insulting—behavior. Catching only the phrases "grow up" and "responsible," both of which were emphasized loudly enough to overhear, did not offer enough to piece together a sentence, let alone provide an explanation for George's lack of sentiment towards me. I gave up and went to my room.

George's footsteps warned me of his approach. I composed myself enough that I was sitting in wait when he knocked on my door and softly said, "Susie?"

"You may come in," I replied.

He poked his head through my—our—bedroom door. He looked around the room as if seeing it for the first time and appeared ready to comment on it before changing his mind.

"Susie, I'm really sorry about our argument. I *am* excited about the baby." Then, almost as an afterthought, he added, "How you feelin'?"

"I'm feeling fine, thank you." I wanted him to come in, to sit down and talk to me, but he stood at the door like an unknown neighbor who didn't want to bother me. "I'm sorry, too," I added, disappointed in myself that I could give in so easily. I willed him to come in, wanting so badly to return to the brief contentment we had shared down by the river, but he avoided my gaze and traced a knot in the doorjamb with his finger, studying it intently. This was not to be the night that he declared his undying love for me. So before my voice could convey the desperate tone that was sure to come through, I let my irritation take over and concluded our meeting with a curt "Is there anything else?"

"Uh, no, I guess not." I thought I detected a note of relief in his voice. "I think I'll just run out and see about that busted pen." He turned, softly pulling the door shut behind him, and left me alone in a darkened room without an ear to bend or a shoulder to cry on.

Not much changed over the next few weeks. Maybe George was a little more attentive, or maybe I was just imagining that his passing comments held secrets he couldn't yet share with me: secrets of hidden passions, of adoring admiration, of anything other than the perfunctorily performed task of communicating with another individual in the house.

One afternoon, as I stood staring at George's mother's silver, thinking that I would rather toss it down the old well than polish it, Pops surprised me.

"Suze?" he called from the back room.

"In here." Delighted that I could postpone such an unbelievably boring job, I closed the drawer and met Pops in the kitchen as he was pulling off his overcoat.

"Suze, I just run into Mr. Bonmiller at the lunch counter in town."

"My old boss?" Mr. Bonmiller was the editor of the *Michigami Weekly* and had hired me during the Great War, when I was just seventeen. He was the fatherly type, with bushy white hair and fingers stained forever with dark printing ink.

"The very same."

"I haven't seen him in ages." I thought about it. "Right before I got sick, I guess." I wiped my hands on my apron and sat down. "How is he?"

"He's doing just fine. We had an interesting conversation and your name come up." Pop's eyes twinkled.

"Really? Why?" I asked curiously.

"Well, they're lookin' for someone to write a weekly column, and he thought about you."

I looked at Pops, letting his words sink in. Did he mean that Mr. Bonmiller thought I could write the column? My thoughts raced with the possibilities. Women would soon be getting the right to vote, Prohibition was the latest talk, and... and I couldn't wrap my arms around the multitude of possibilities that could be mine. I waited for him to continue, my voice lost in anticipation of his next words.

"He thought maybe you was the right person for the job." Pops smiled broadly.

"He did?" My head spun with the news and I jumped out of my seat. "Oh, Pops, you're the best," I sang out as I wrapped my arms around his neck and kissed his cheek.

"Well, now, you don't rightly have the job yet, Suze. He wants you to come on in and talk to him."

"Oh, my gosh, of course."

But I sensed that I did have the job. This was where I could fit in, where I could belong. I plopped my growing body back down in the chair.

"Pops?" I had realized something. "Does he know I'm... expecting a baby?"

"He does, Suze. But he said it don't matter. You can write from home—after all, what better place to write a column about women's work than from home?"

"What do you mean, 'women's work'?" I was bewildered. I wrote about current issues, not housekeeping.

"The column's being called *Women's Work* and he's wanting a young woman's perspective about keeping house and caring for her family. Now that you're in a family way, it's right up your alley. You can offer recipes and tips for the homemaker, stuff like that."

I was taken aback by the explanation Pops offered. I knew next to nothing about keeping a house, not to mention that I wasn't even interested in such things. Pops sensed my confusion and quickly offered, "I know it ain't what you been used to, honey, but it's a start."

The term of endearment struck a chord. I felt embarrassed and guilty for even thinking that I should be entitled to such a prominent position as that of current events writer on a paper that I hadn't even worked at in over a year.

"You're right, as usual, Pops." If I had to pay my dues, then so be it. I patted his shoulder. "I'm going to be the best writer on women's work north of Lansing." I paused and added, "I just have to learn how to be a homemaker in the next couple of weeks." I smiled ruefully at him.

"You'll do just fine, Suze. Somethin' tells me that we don't have to worry none about you."

Mr. Bonmiller did offer me the job. My husband accepted the news with "Congratulations! Sounds like a good idea," and showed up the following week with a shiny new Smith Corona typewriter. I suspected Pops was behind the gift, but I was happy to attribute the thoughtfulness to George, and he seemed happy to accept it.

My new job offered a release from the tedium of my days and allowed me to exercise my writing ability, though in a much different way than I ever could have expected. I became an expert in the uses of vinegar (removing the smell of dead rodents and cleaning toilet bowls) and baking soda (gargling to eliminate bad breath and polishing silver) and began to keep a recipe index with the most popular requests of the day. I could tell you how to get a coffee stain out of a china teacup or recommend a potato salad recipe, but had a hard time making my bed in the morning or baking a batch of cookies to save my life. It was the ultimate irony, but I was writing and that was all that mattered.

My belly expanded as the summer months passed, and every now and then I caught Pops looking at me as if he were gravely concerned. I knew he had lost his own wife in childbirth, and I suspected he was worried that something might happen to me or the baby. My thoughts were confirmed when he suggested that instead of having the Old Doc deliver the baby, I should use the midwife from Hillside, a small farming community about five miles away.

Sarah McGillis was an older woman who walked with a slight limp and carried a small kerchief that she continually used to pat her lips. When the handkerchief wasn't in use, it was stored in the alcove of her bosom and pulled out as needed. Her strong hands and confident manner assured me of her capability, and when she examined me it was with an expertise that could not easily be imitated. She pressed her head against my protruding midsection, her long silver braid falling on my arm, and listened intently, moving her head around my belly, listening for what I presumed to be the primitive sounds made by an unborn child. When she finished, she stood up, pulled out her kerchief and dabbed at her mouth, looked me in the eyes, and said bluntly, "There's a problem."

I sat, unable to move, stunned by the news. She let Pops and George into the room and repeated to them what she had told me.

"See here," she said, as she laid her hand on the top part of my belly. "This here spot is too hard and high." She pressed down firmly. "I feel a head here, and when I listen for the heart, I hear it right here." She pointed to the middle of my belly.

"Why's that a problem?" George asked, echoing my sentiments exactly.

Before Sarah could respond, Pops answered flatly, "Because the baby's upside down, son."

Sarah McGillis nodded her head in agreement and explained further, "That baby's gotta come out headfirst, and if it don't turn in the next month or so, we got us a predicament."

We all sat in shock at the astounding news. George and I stared at one another, not quite sure how to react. Pops shook his head as if the situation were somehow his fault.

"How can I turn it?" I finally asked. I recognized a unique panic, one I had never felt before, one in which I wasn't the central figure. I realized that I was worried for my unborn child.

"You can't," Sarah answered simply. "Either that baby's gonna do it alone or I gotta do it for him. Ain't no use getting in a pitch quite yet; we got a bit of time for it to come to that. Let's leave it a rest for now. I'll come back in a couple weeks and check up on you. See if we's made any progress." She reached for her hat and Pops led her to the door.

I was devastated at the thought that my baby might be in danger. My maternal instincts kicked it at that moment, and they kicked in hard. I knew that I would do whatever I had to in order to have a healthy baby and be there to raise it. Nothing so far in my life, including the loss of my parents, had touched me as deeply as the news I had just recently heard. I felt that my motherhood was being tested by God, and I was determined not to fail.

George was lost in thought, as well, but when he reached for my hand for the first time as my husband, I was never so grateful in my life. "Don't you worry none, Susie. I ain't gonna let nothing happen to that baby. Or you." He patted my hand.

I noticed Pops and Sarah still talking, and when she reached out to clutch his elbow, it occurred to me that Pops had somehow known about the baby's position. Clues flew at me. It didn't take much to piece together a possible reason for George's mother's death—George had been a breech baby, too. Pops had seen that I was too big on top and had recognized that I would need someone skillful with this type of delivery, should it come to that. I glanced at George, who was getting ready to go out to the ranch, and asked, "How did your mother die?"

"I don't rightly know," he answered after thinking a bit. "Pops just said she died a couple days after I was born. Why?"

"Just wondering," I replied, certain I was right.

"Susie, you ain't thinkin' you're gonna die, are you? I told you that nothing's gonna happen to you or that baby. I promise you."

He looked so sincere that I had to smile. "I believe you," I said, and I did. The fact that he was so adamant about my safety and the baby's safety gave me hope that our marriage could survive.

Pops came back in, looking so serious and solemn that I had to say, "It'll be okay, Pops. We're going to be just fine. I'm doing well, considering."

"Well, you ain't gonna be doing much, I'll tell you. Me and Junior's takin' care of all the house chores. I want you to rest. I don't want to see you doing nothin', you understand?"

"Pops, Sarah didn't say I was an invalid."

"Just so, you need to be takin' it easy. You should probably tell Mr. Bonmiller you're takin' some time off."

The thought of not having my work, no matter how trivial it might be, was overwhelmingly depressing. All I could say was, "Oh, no, Pops."

George spoke up. "I don't think that's such a great idea. Susie needs to fill her time doin' something productive instead of dwellin' on this... problem. She needs her work; it'll be good for her."

I was flabbergasted. My husband had stepped in and taken up my cause. What had just happened?

"Pops, George is right," I added, resolute in supporting the theory that had been so generously put forth. "I would go stir-crazy just waiting. I need to keep my thoughts occupied." I gave George a look that I hoped conveyed my deepest gratitude.

Pops thought for a moment. "I suspect you two are right, and I don't need you gangin' up on me." He feigned irritation at his authority being overturned. "If that's what you need to do, Suze, then so be it. But I ain't kidding when I say I don't want you doin' nothing except sittin' at that typewriter. Got it?"

"Got it," I said

"Junior?"

"Deal."

"Then that's that." Pops left to make a pot of coffee, and George and I were alone again.

"I really appreciate your coming to my defense, George. I don't know what I would do without my job. It keeps me sane."

George appeared embarrassed at my show of appreciation.

"That's what a husband should do," he said as he stood to leave. "I'm headin' out to the ranch. And you heard Pops—no house chores," he added emphatically.

"Yes, sir," I replied, saluting him, excited at the length of our exchange. Not being able to participate in chores wasn't the least bit concerning to me. Frankly, I didn't have many anyway, and those that I did have I knew I performed with the distracted air of one who dearly wished to be doing something different.

Sarah returned two weeks later to inspect the situation, and I knew when she clucked and shook her head that nothing had changed.

"We're going to try to turn that baby afore he gets too big." She rolled up her dress sleeves and asked for Pops and Junior to come into the room to help her.

"Here's what we gonna do," she stated. "I'm goin' move that baby, pushin' and pullin' to try to force his head down." We all nodded in agreement as if this happened every day. "It's goin' to be downright uncomfortable," she looked at me, "but we gotta try. Now, I need you two fellas to hold her arms and give her some leverage against my force. We all ready?" Again, we all nodded silently.

She delicately pulled my dress up, covering my legs with a blanket. I was determined to conceal my embarrassment and squared my shoulders, preparing for the procedure. Her strong hands took their place on my belly and she began to feel for head and limb placement, gently pressing down on various parts of my midsection.

This isn't so bad, I thought, and I began to relax, brushing off my worries of pain.

But very rapidly her hand movements became harsh and quick, and I had to bite my lip to keep from crying out. She pushed against my lungs, and I had a difficult time catching my breath. When she pressed against my stomach, I felt my lunch threaten to reappear, and when she flattened that baby against my intestines, I was sure I was about to embarrass myself in a way I had never done before. My body automatically recoiled against the force she was exerting; Pops and George had to use their full strength to hold my shoulders down as my torso rose to defend itself. I couldn't believe that she could cause so much agony, and I couldn't help but think about my baby and pray that she was not breaking every little bone in its body. Small moans escaped me while she twisted and manipulated my belly as though she were kneading a stiff bread dough. I closed my eyes for fear that they would give away my anguish and Pops would force her to stop. I knew that baby had to come out headfirst. There was no other way.

When she stopped, I couldn't believe that only a few minutes had passed. It had seemed an eternity, and I was utterly exhausted. I knew Pops and George had felt the same—they were both dripping with sweat.

"You got a stubborn one," Sarah declared as she pressed her head against my stomach to listen for a heartbeat. "But he's doing just fine." She looked up at me. "How about you?"

"I'm all right," I answered weakly.

"We only got a couple more weeks afore we can't do this from the outside." She raised her eyebrows at me.

"And if it don't happen?" Pops asked.

"When she's ready to birth this baby, well, I gotta do it then." Sarah put her head back down, avoiding everyone's gaze.

"Sarah, how many breech babies have you delivered?" I was powerless to stop myself from asking the questions that I knew would only add to my distress.

"Too many to count," she answered

"Have you lost any?"

Pops and George looked at me, torn between wanting her to stop and wanting to hear the answer themselves. They, too, needed to know where we stood and what our chances were, and so they remained silent.

Sarah patted her lips with her kerchief and took her time tucking it back into her cleavage. She sighed, and I imagined her thinking that she was getting too old for this line of work. She looked at me with a kind but honest mien, and said in a low voice, "I lost a couple, dear. Sometimes God don't let me make the choices." She pulled her kerchief out again but did not wipe her lips. "All I can tell you is that I saved more than I didn't, and there ain't no one more experienced than me. Not even any of those fancy doctors in that newfangled hospital. I done delivered over a thousand babies, and any that God took... well, it was all for the better. They wouldn'ta had much of a life on this here earth."

She put her kerchief back in its place. "You're in good hands, and I don't aim to have anything happen to you or that child of yours. You're a healthy, strong girl and you got the love and support you need to get through this. You gonna be all right."

Pops got up, walked over to the sideboard, took out two glasses, and filled each with a jigger of port. He handed one to Sarah, and they both threw it back, shuddering at the shock of the bite.

"I ain't losing no one," he said resolutely.

"That's right," George added. "We're gonna have a healthy baby—and mama, too." He set his hand on my shoulder and didn't move it until he was forced to, when I had to stand to arrange my dress.

"That's the spirit, boys!" Sarah exclaimed. "I'll be back in two weeks and we'll try this again.

I dreaded her next visit and spent my time writing columns, hoping to keep my mind occupied. I found new uses for baking soda (cleaning stubborn grime from pans) and wrote a whole column comparing recipes for sugar cookies (add sour cream for a smooth break). I couldn't stop writing and racked up a whole year's worth of columns in the next few weeks, writing about everything from gardening (sprinkle red pepper on the plants to keep the deer away) to, oddly enough, child care (a high temperature can be controlled with aspirin and a cool bath).

I begged Pops and George to keep the distressing news from my sisters. They would be terribly upset, and I felt that it would be too much of a burden for all involved if they knew. It was difficult keeping up the pretense when they visited, but it was necessary if I was to triumph in my battle.

"Susie, you are positively glowing," Opal stated during one of their visits.

I smiled demurely as I adjusted my wrap. "Thank you, sister."

"Now, you must let us know as soon as you start your labor," they gushed. "Of course, we want to be the first to know."

George sat securely by my side, not saying a word but solidly planted. In these trying times, he had risen to a staggering challenge and shown me support I never would have imagined him capable of offering. He was still not in my bed—for fear of hurting me or the baby, he said—but had moved into the spare room on a small cot he had set up. If I so much as got up to get a drink of water, he would rush out into the hall to check on my well being.

My days were filled with writing, but at night I lay, awake and alone, wondering about my upside-down (or, rather, right-side-up) baby. Was it a boy or a girl? What name would we choose? I felt acutely the absence of my mother, who would have adored being a grandmother, and the sting of my father's death returned in full measure. My gratitude to Pops, and now to George, brought tears to my eyes. I cried more than once in the solitude of my bedroom, thanking God that I had these two strong and capable men looking out for me.

Sarah returned two weeks later and was again unsuccessful. Twice more she came back, each time failing despite her efforts. We all grew increasingly anxious, the tension and anticipation building, until one day I sat at the Smith Corona and decided I would not write again until after the baby. The summer had slipped into fall, and I had begun to experience sharp pains that sometimes stopped me in my tracks. I mentioned these to Sarah in private, not wanting to add fuel to the fire, but she assured me that they were normal.

I soon rivaled the size of a barn. One late fall day, Sarah announced that she would be giving me an internal exam. She shooed the men out of the room and proceeded to insert what felt like her fist into the place where, up until now, only my husband had been. I arched my back, holding my breath, until she was through, and only relaxed when she told me to get dressed and meet her in the front room with Pops and George.

"She's gettin' ready," Sarah announced as we gathered together, the early evening light fading. Her clothes were clean but unmatched, and I wondered if she was married or had any children. Now didn't seem to be the time to ask. "You need to come get me soon as her water breaks or she's having pains seven minutes apart."

"Junior can be at your place in fifteen minutes, right?" Pops looked to George.

"Tops. Probably quicker." George seemed eager to do his part.

"Good. Now here's what we gonna do." She pulled out her kerchief and wiped her perspiring upper lip. "I'm gonna need some help. If you boys ain't up for it, we gotta get someone who is."

Pops looked offended. "There ain't no way anyone's gonna be here but us. Ain't that right, Junior?"

"That's darn right, Pops. I'm gonna help my baby… and my wife. No one else."

"That's what I like to hear." Sarah grinned at their enthusiasm.

I was paralyzed by their talk of planning, and could only listen as they discussed their strategy as though I wasn't there. Sarah sensed my discomfiture and turned to me. "You're gonna have your hands full; don't you feel left out. You'll see."

I nodded, knowing she was right. They decided they would convert the dining area to a delivery room—the bedroom was upstairs and away from a ready water supply. Pops would make a pad for the table and it would be covered in sheets and blankets. Sarah had George write down a list of items she would need, and when she alarmed me by including a sharp knife, she rapidly assured me that it would only be used to cut the cord.

I wanted desperately to ask Sarah how she was going to turn the baby, but she carefully avoided any talk of the actual delivery. Pops and George didn't seem concerned with it either. When I caught them later in a whispered discussion, I realized they had already spoken of it.

"Suze, save your strength, honey. You're gonna need all your reserves. You don't need to be spendin' time worryin' about somethin' that we got under control." Pops gave my enormous frame a much-needed hug. "You know we got your best interests at heart, don't you?"

I did, and tried to relax and get some rest. I was so uncomfortable in almost any position, I never felt like I had a full night's sleep under my belt and was constantly tired.

I woke one chilly morning from an unfit night's sleep and found George sitting on the rocker in the corner of the room.

"Is everything okay?" I questioned as I sat up awkwardly in bed.

"It's fine. I'm just thinkin'. Go on back to sleep, you need your rest."

He was slouched in the chair, dressed in his work clothes, but he had never looked so handsome and appealing to me. His casual position and attitude were beguiling, and his scent reached out to me, stroking me encouragingly. I forgot my condition and imagined him sliding beneath the sheets and reaching out to me, whispering his love into my ear and holding me as a man does a wife. I closed my eyes to better watch the intimate scene unfolding in my mind, and when I was content with the conclusion, opened my eyes to find that George had left. It was such an ethereal situation that I later wondered if I had, in fact, dreamt the whole scene.

The first snow was falling one afternoon and I was watching an owl in the large birch outside the window, when my water broke. Pops and George walked in at the same time, and when Pops noticed the pool of liquid beneath my feet, he wondered aloud if I had spilled my drink. I could only shake my head, so stunned that the time had finally come that I stood there like a frightened child waiting to be told her punishment.

It was George who finally said, "That ain't her drink." Then all hell broke loose.

Pops missed the counter trying to set his coffee cup on it and shattered china flew everywhere. George began racing around, looking for his motoring glasses and asking no one in particular where his brown coat was. Amniotic fluid and coffee mixed together at my feet, and Biscuit, one of our labs, started slurping it up.

"Out, Biscuit!" Pops yelled, as he tripped over the stool that George had inadvertently placed in the center of the kitchen. In all the chaos, I managed to slip out unnoticed and went to my room to change and clean myself. The pains had not started and I thought it best to finish the few brief personal chores that were probably the last thing I would do that day—except have a baby.

I heard the Tin Lizzie roar off, and the sounds of Pops cleaning up the kitchen drifted up the stairs as I washed myself. He knocked on my door, and I assured him that all was well and I would be down as soon as I was finished. I straightened my bed, and as I washed my face I studied my reflection in the mirror. My long auburn hair fell in soft waves that lay about my shoulders. George had helped me wash it the night before, so it smelled of lilacs and spring. My green eyes were vivid and unblinking as I stared at the face of one who was soon to become a mother. I prayed for the safety of my child and asked of the Lord that if one of us had to die, to please let it be me. I whispered "Good luck" to the terrified girl I saw standing in front of me and tried to smile at the reflection, but it was a wan one, so I gave up and instead touched my fingers to the glass.

Pops and I waited nervously in the front room, the ticking of the grandfather clock loudly reminding us that time was a-wasting. When I asked him how he was, he answered with a confused "What?" like he'd forgotten I was even there, so I gave up on conversation and we sat silently while the light snow floated about outside and the minutes ticked by.

By then I had felt some obvious pains but had concealed them from Pops. I knew he would get overwrought. They weren't too bad and I wished that that would be the extent of all of them, but I knew that that would be highly unrealistic.

George and Sarah arrived within the hour and a sense of relief imbued our home as we gave up control to the woman who would work the miracle that we needed. She examined me inside and out as Pops made coffee, and then we sat down and discussed our situation.

"Here's what we gonna do," she said as she sipped her coffee and nodded her approval to Pops. "That baby's still coming out the wrong way. There's but a brief time I can get up in there and flip him around, so I got to be ready." She looked me up and down before she spoke again.

"You scared?"

"Yes, ma'am," I answered.

"That's okay. You got a right to be. I can do this, but you gotta help, you understand?" She watched me closely. "You gotta do exactly what I say and when. I can't say how important that is."

I nodded.

"You get the smellin' salts?" she asked George.

"Yes, ma'am."

She looked back to me. "Now, you're gonna feel pain like you never done felt before. I ain't trying to scare you, but I don't want you to believe otherwise. You pass out and you ain't no good to me. You got it?"

I nodded again, certain that today was the day I was going to die.

"That ain't the most important part." She put both hands on my shoulders and pressed her nose close to mine, her breath smelling of coffee and mint. "No matter how bad you want to push, until I tell you to, you can't. You understand?"

I was ready to follow her off a bridge if she told me to and so I nodded, completely terrified.

"I'm going to need you to repeat back to me what I just done told you."

"I am not to push until you give me direction to do so," I repeated like a machine.

"What else?" she asked.

"I am not to pass out. I am to stay awake and help you."

"Good girl." She patted my leg. "She's a smart one, all right." She gestured towards Pops. "You boys are gonna need to hold her down. She's likely to have the strength of ten and you're gonna have to control her. Can I count on you?"

"Yes, ma'am," they replied in unison.

"All right," she said happily. "We got a plan and I got complete confidence in my team. We're gonna have a healthy baby and a healthy mama." She sat down in Pop's easy chair and leaned back, closing her eyes.

"What should we do now?" I asked, bewildered.

"I'm gonna take a nap," she said without opening her eyes.

"What should I do?"

"The same," she answered, and within minutes she was snoring softly.

I looked at over at George, who shrugged his shoulders.

I wasn't in the least tired. The blood was surging through my veins and I couldn't imagine resting, let alone taking a nap. Pops suggested we take a turn around the yard to pass the time. He would finish the soup he had started yesterday.

I grabbed my wrap and waited outside for George. Biscuit and Barney barked happily and gamboled around me until George came out and ordered them down. He held my elbow as I stepped carefully off the porch, and we started off down the drive and towards the road that led into town. The snow that had fallen earlier had disappeared into the dirt, and the muddy ground held on to our shoes, making our walk sluggish and slick. George guided me to the side of the drive and we continued in the grass, stopping occasionally so he could clean the mud off our shoes with a stick.

The pains increased, moving in that short time from spotty and uncomfortable to severe and regular, and settled into a new territory of misery, one that I had never encountered. My steps became staggering and I grew nervous, as though I were a balloon that could float away from Sarah and her safety. I yearned to get home before I popped.

"You doin' okay, Susie?"

"I think I'm ready to get back," I replied, thankful as we turned and headed for the house.

George helped me up the steps, and when Pops saw me, he hurried over to take my wrap and help me to a chair. He fixed me a cup of hot tea, but after only a few sips I put it down. I wasn't thirsty or hungry. I was restless. As soon as I sat, I wanted to get up. As soon as I got up, I became exhausted and couldn't wait to sit. Then the pains would come, gripping my belly like an invisible vice, and neither option was comfortable. When the contractions began to come, seemingly without pause, Pops woke Sarah up and she examined me again.

"She's only at five fingers."

"What does that mean?" George asked for all of us.

"She's gotta get to ten afore we can even start. We got a ways to go yet."

I shook my head, trying to dislodge the disbelief I felt toward the news. Another pain hit me, racking my body, and I couldn't believe I was only halfway there. The intense pressure came in waves and washed through my body. My ongoing persecution turned my thoughts dark and ugly. More than anything, I wished I had never married George, had never even met him. It was entirely his fault that we were in this predicament, and I felt a hate for him that I would never have thought possible.

My legs soon began to shake uncontrollably and felt as though they were ready to give out. Pops and George helped me change into my nightdress and hoist myself up onto the table and the soft mattress Pops had made for me. I lay back while the pains subsided. I went from hot to cold and back again in a matter of minutes, and volleyed between wanting to be left alone and wanting bodies around me—belligerent in either situation.

Sarah checked me again and announced that I was at eight fingers.

"It's gonna go quick now, so be on guard." Then, to me, she said, Don't you push, no matter what. You got that?"

I felt like a trapped animal. I snarled back, "I haven't forgotten."

The pain became unbearable. Each time a contraction came, I retreated into a fetal position, and communication with the others became impossible. I heard Pops asking George if he was hungry and heard his negative response, but I was an observer that had no voice. I saw Sarah and Pops talking quietly in the corner of the kitchen and somehow knew he was telling her once again about his wife. I sympathized with them and felt part of all that was happening, but as a ghost, a passive observer, sent to witness my own circumstance. I heard myself moaning and saw my body turning, but was so disconnected that I watched in interest as Sarah ran over, yelling for Pops and George to hold me down.

I was jolted back into reality and the torture that came with it when the smelling salts were held under my nose. The sounds were turned up to a deafening roar. I turned my head and vomited on the floor from the pungent ammonia that filled my lungs and forced me to breathe.

"She's at 10!" I heard Sarah yell, and then to me she shouted, "I'm going in! Do—not—push."

As soon as she said the word "push," my body responded and all I wanted to do was just that.

"I have to," I managed to utter as my brain screamed "push" in pictures and languages I didn't even know existed.

Sarah's face loomed above mine and grew ugly. "Don't you dare," she growled.

I plotted swiftly that, if I did live, I would hunt her down. Until then, I gritted my teeth and prepared for what was to become a pain so excruciating that I would recall it to my dying day. George and Pops held my shoulders and legs as Sarah's hands disappeared inside me and awoke a monster the size of a small pig, twisting and pushing against my every organ. I felt the beast's hooves pushing through my stomach and then my muscle and skin, cutting open every vein it met along the way. The brute clawed and kicked and bit me, sinking its razor-sharp teeth into everything in the way and leaving a bloody trail in its wake.

"Get it out!" I screamed as I struggled against the cataleptic state that beckoned me enticingly. I was ready to die. No human body could endure the kind of torment that mine was going through, and I couldn't hold out. I felt bad that I would be leaving Pops and George, but I hoped the baby would live and they would at least have that. I readied myself to meet my maker, but before I could go, everything stopped.

I opened my eyes to find myself lying alone on a table in our dining room. I heard a smack and then the scream of a human so small I knew it could only be a baby—my baby. George, Pops, and Sarah stood up from the end of the table and held out a wrapped bundle to me.

"You did it, Suze. You birthed a baby." Pops' eyes were misty as he handed me the child. "It's a boy."

I burst into tears as I took my son, setting off a chain reaction. George sobbed uncontrollably at my side as he clutched my arm, and Pops turned his head, but his shaking shoulders gave away his emotions. Even old Sarah was dabbing at her eyes and couldn't stop telling me what a fine job I had done. I hugged her close and thanked her with all my heart for saving me and my child, ashamed that I had just recently wanted to do her bodily harm.

After finishing the birth and cleaning me up, Pops and Sarah took the child to give him his first bath. George carried me up to my room as carefully as one would transport delicate china and set me down gently in my own bed, pulling the blankets up around me.

"I can't believe you done it," he offered. "You were so brave, Susie. I don't know if I could have done what you did. You're amazin'."

I reached out and stroked his cheek, taking a liberty I never would have before.

"I don't believe that. You would have done the same thing."

He gazed at me, slowly shaking his head. "Things are gonna be different now, you'll see. They ain't—they aren't—gonna be the same. I promise you that." He smiled through the tears streaming down his face. "We got us a son now. Can you believe it? A son! I never thought I could feel this way, I can't believe the love I have. Thank you, Susiekins. Thank you." He looked away, overcome.

My heart exploded at his use of the nickname I hadn't heard since before we were married. He didn't say it in as many words, but this was the day I heard my husband declare his undying love for me—the day our son was born was the day I became George's wife. I fell into a long sleep, awake only for brief intervals to feed a squalling baby and lulled back to sleep by the happiness that would now become routine. I wasn't allowed to do much for the next couple of weeks and had to fight both my father-in-law and my husband just to have my turn at holding the baby. All of us loved him intensely, including his aunts, and I was over the moon as I settled into motherhood.

George and I had three more children, and each one brought us closer. We built our love and our marriage around these four miracles. There were, thank the good Lord, no more breech births. George always held his secrets, but he tucked them deep within, and soon they were so remote that I forgot even to wonder about them. I was content with the love he offered, and he appeared to feel the same.

Every day was a new and exciting challenge. Earl was the kind of child I imagined George had been before his accident. Maude was the spitting image of Opal as a child and had her same propensity for the kitchen and the needle. Adeline took after me, though she was even more willing than I to speak her mind. Millie was the frosting on the cake—the sweet, precocious child that everyone admired.

Pops lived to see all but the last of the girls. He adored the children and reveled in the large family that was now his. He meant the world to me, and when he took ill with cancer, I wasn't sure how life could ever return to what it had been. As he shrank down to the size of a boy, the skin stretched itself

so thin that you could see the outlines of the numerous tumors filling his
stomach. He stopped eating and eventually turned away even water. Pops died
in his own bed one spring morning, George holding one hand and I holding
the other, watching as he took his last breath. We buried him down by the
river in the area they used to call the graveyard, and it finally became what its
name had always suggested.

Sometimes at night I think about old Sarah McGillis, dabbing her lips
and tucking her kerchief into her bosom, and what we went through together.
What a strange thing, to be beholden to someone you barely knew, but I was.
She had given me everything.

Chapter Five
Adeline - 1938

Cross-eyed Mary was rumored to have received her affliction from her mother's witnessing a murder while pregnant. My father said the only murder he knew of in the history of Michigami took place two years after Mary's birth, when Old Mrs. Kearney caught her husband sneaking around with her house-girl and shot him dead.

There was scuttlebutt, though, that another murder had occurred—one that had gone unreported because of its ties to the devil. One that Cross-eyed Mary's mother was involved in—but no one even seemed to know who the victim was. Still and all, the tale endured, and poor Mary carried with her the stigma that the story bestowed. Even after her mother married a minister and died a few years later in the church rectory from a heart ailment, the rumor persisted, and Mary was politely avoided. It was as though her damaged eyes had become the windows to her soul and those who looked inside were doomed.

Frankly, I never gave Mary much thought. She was almost two years older than I and had gone to live with her Uncle Jethro, a barber, and his wife on the far side of town after her stepfather decided he could not raise a young girl on his own. The only time I was even in her vicinity was when she boarded the bus at the stop after ours, on the way to the new high school over in Midland. It was a forty-five-minute trip one way after we got picked up, and Mary always sat behind the driver, by herself, unless crowded conditions forced another student to ask her to move over. I don't recall her ever speaking to anyone, and though I never joined in, there were plenty who did take part in the ridicule and mockery that would sometimes start up when boredom set in on the lengthy drive.

Lucy and I started ninth grade in 1938 and were the first class of freshmen to attend the new high school. The population had grown so in Michigami and the surrounding areas that a large new senior high had been built and the neighboring communities bused their teenagers in to attend. We were now thrown into a mix of students that came from as far away as Lake St. Clare— even the Indian offspring from the reservation in Mt. Alma were allowed to attend. We no longer received our education in a two-room schoolhouse, which was now only for the elementary children, and our social circle expanded beyond the small crowd we had grown up with.

Fancying ourselves trendsetters, we grew out the bobs that the movie stars no longer favored into long curls that we would wear close to our heads during the day and up in a chic chignon when attending church or school functions in the evening. When the models in the fashion magazines started wearing bright and colorful clothes, we followed suit. We discussed in earnest during the first few bus rides that year what clubs and organizations we and our small set of followers should join. The end of the Depression had inspired a whole new language, and our conversations were speckled with the latest slang that we picked up from radio programs, the comics, and magazines.

"There's no question," I asserted one morning a few weeks into the school year, "that the Glee Club is our fave and number-one priority. My only problem is that I can't sing. I'll have to do a lot of humming."

"I agree," seconded Lucy. "Everyone knows that the most popular girls always join the Glee Club. And popular boys like popular girls," she added.

"What about the Art and Needlework Club?" asked Hazel Wade, a new friend from the adjacent community of Freeland. "I hear they do lots of fun projects."

"That's too iffy. Let's leave that for Maude and Winnie Mae," I answered, glancing back to where my sister and her best friend were huddled together.

"We can't be in everything. We just don't have the time."

The small group agreed and the discussion moved on to a more important topic, that of the upcoming fall celebration, the Harvest Moon Dance. We were all planning on joining the dance committee, which met during lunch period, to help organize the decorations, food, and music. Freshman weren't typically asked to the dance, but we had plans to attend, one way or another, even if it meant we would just serve punch.

"I have a question for you," Lucy said, lowering her voice as she leaned in. She was dressed immaculately, her blue checkered dress clean and pressed, her blond curls pulled to the side with a barrette. "If you could go to the dance with anyone, who would it be?"

"Real or made up?" asked Marion Winters, a petite redhead from Lake City.

"Real," I answered for Lucy. "It has to be someone that could actually ask you. Not like Cary Grant or Mickey Mouse." We all chuckled as the bus bumped along the country road and past the landscape slowly turning to its fall colors.

I looked around the small group. "You go first." I motioned to Rebecca Hughes, a big-boned blonde known for her sweet disposition.

"Oh, I couldn't. Someone else go," she giggled shyly.

"Okay, I will." I thought hard. "I guess I would choose Floyd Stader."

"Floyd Stader, the junior on the football squad?" Lucy asked, clearly in awe of my bold choice.

"The one and only," I declared.

"Do you even know him?" asked Hazel.

"I do not, but he could ask me. I mean, it *is* possible. Anyway, that's my choice." I looked around. "Who'll go next?"

"I'll go," Marion volunteered. Marion was a pleasant enough girl, but she had a habit of sighing constantly, as if she were forcing herself to speak. "I would choose Dwayne Haskett. I think he's awful dreamy. And besides, he goes to my church and," she looked at me, "I actually know him. So it's not only possible, it's probable," she finished, using recently learned algebra terms to emphasize her point.

I groaned inwardly. Dwayne Haskett was no dreamboat; I could attest to that. He was, in fact, something of a drip, although I would never say that to Marion. Lucy and I avoided eye contact, knowing it would be too difficult not to laugh, or at the least, smile.

"What about you, Hazel?" Rebecca inquired.

Hazel chewed her lip for a moment and then answered, "Kenneth Miles. Definitely Kenneth Miles." Kenneth met with everyone's approval, as he was a cute sophomore, sang in the boys' Glee Club, and was president of the local 4-H chapter.

"Okay, Rebecca, your turn," Marion said.

"Oh, well," she looked down and gnawed at her fingernails. "I think your brother, Jack, is awfully cute." She looked at Lucy. "And he's awful nice and, well… swell." Rebecca looked as if she would burst into tears. "Oh, but please, please don't ever tell him I said anything. I would just die if he knew."

"Don't worry, I won't," Lucy reassured Rebecca as she patted her arm.

Rebecca had a crush on Jack! I turned around to look for my childhood sweetheart, but only caught sight of my own brother, who was now a senior. He winked at me and waved his fingers effeminately. I rolled my eyes at him and turned back around just as Rebecca clutched my arm and said excitedly, "Don't look at him!"

"It's okay, Rebecca. He ain't in school today. Don't worry," Lucy told her. "He had to stay home and help my dad put up a new pole barn."

"Why's your daddy putting up a new pole barn?" I asked Lucy curiously.

"Well, um, he's settin' up to be a preacher and he's building a church to do his sermons in." Lucy looked away, embarrassed. "Frankie and Jack and my uncle are all helping out."

"He finally did it, huh?" Lucy's dad was still mean and ornery, though not like he used to be—he'd stopped with the drink. But now he was to be spreading the word of the Lord? This was downright interesting news.

"He did," Lucy said, somewhat shortly, and I didn't pursue it.

Rebecca was sweet for Jack. Lucy's dad was to be a preacher. So far this day was full of surprises, and we hadn't yet gotten to school.

It was halfway through sixth period before I even realized that Lucy had not answered the question of who she would choose to go to the dance with. We had gotten sidetracked and left the subject without her answer. I caught up with her in the hall and pressed her on the issue.

"I didn't?" she asked, in a voice that told me she knew perfectly well she hadn't told us. "Let me think some on it and I'll tell you on the way home."

What was up with Lucy? I knew her well enough to know she was keeping something from me. But I wouldn't have to wait long, because she shared it on the bus that afternoon.

"All right, Lucy." I got right to the point as we all settled in for our long ride home. "Who would you go to the Harvest Moon Dance with?"

"Well," she started coyly, "I'm *goin'* to the dance."

We all gasped. Rebecca put her hand to her mouth.

"With who?" everyone asked in unison.

"With Earl."

Silence reigned as we digested the news.

"My brother Earl? *That* Earl?" I couldn't have been more surprised if she had told me she had grown wings and was going to fairy school.

"Yes, that Earl. He asked me today in study hall." Lucy smiled sweetly. "Of course I said yes. I mean, after all, he is a senior."

"I am *so* jealous," groaned Marion. "You're only a freshman, and you have a date with a senior." She sighed a sigh to beat all.

"I think it's great, Lucy," Hazel volunteered. "Congratulations."

We all offered her our less-than-enthusiastic well wishes, our envy lost on Lucy in her overwhelming excitement.

I couldn't believe it! The worst part was that I didn't have anyone to discuss this turn of events with. I would normally have shared my horror with my best friend, but she was part of this incredible conspiracy. I would be forced to confide in Maude. We didn't always see eye-to-eye, but I hoped she would appreciate my concern.

"Adeline, it sounds like you're jealous." She surprised me with this unlikely statement after I related the news. She folded her sweater and tucked it in the bureau. "Why would you give a care who Lucy goes with?"

"I… I don't. I really don't," I repeated, "but Earl?"

"Why would you care who Earl went with?"

"Jeez o'petes, Maude!" I practically screamed as I stomped out of the room. "You just don't understand."

"More than you think," I heard her mutter under her breath.

The old parlor had been turned into my mother's office when she restarted her career at the paper, and it was here that I found her, typing furiously away on the old Smith Corona that my father had given her in the first year of their marriage. She didn't look up from her work when I threw myself into the overstuffed easy chair next to her desk, but asked, "What are you up to today, Adeline?"

"Nothing. Absolutely nothing. It's an absolutely nothing kind of day," I said.

She stopped typing and turned to look at me with a puzzled expression. "When your Aunt Opal makes the sauce for her bread pudding, is it rum or whiskey that she puts in it?"

"I think you can use either one, depending on which you prefer," I answered.

She grinned at me. "Good girl. I think you're right. I can never remember."

She finished her sentence and peered at the sheet of paper. "Well, it's not front-page news, but it's the most requested recipe in the whole county." She pulled the paper out of the typewriter, tucked it in a folder, and sat back. "Why is it an absolutely nothing kind of day?"

"Dunno, just is."

"How is the dance committee going?"

"Fine, I guess. You'd think it was a coronation, everyone's in such a tizzy."

"A tizzy?" My mother raised her eyebrows at me.

"A flap... a panic... a state." I enjoyed that my mother had to ask me the definition of one of the latest expressions.

"Ah, a tizzy. I'll have to remember that." She smiled and sat there patiently as if she hadn't a care in the world.

I waited a moment before pressing the issue. "Did you hear that Earl asked Lucy to the dance?"

"I did."

"And you don't find that interesting?"

"In what way?"

"I don't know. It's like... well, like they're brother and sister or something. It just doesn't feel right. Don't you think?" I looked at her hopefully.

"Well, I can certainly see your point. They *have* known each other for pretty much their whole life"—she tapped her mouth with her finger thoughtfully—"but that could make them just good friends. I don't know if Earl is getting ready to propose marriage to her just yet, and I like Lucy, so that doesn't bother me." She paused for a brief moment. "How would you feel if Jack asked you? It's a similar situation. Would you go?"

I opened my mouth to speak but found I had nothing to say. Would I go with Jack? The thought had never occurred to me, and I had to stop and think about it. Jack and I were friends. I had even kissed him back when Earl was sick and he was helping out at the ranch, but that was over two years ago. I was fond of him and enjoyed his company, and there was something about him that was... familiar, I suppose. He was a nice-looking boy. Even Rebecca wanted to go with him. If I had to answer my mother's question, I admitted silently that I would.

I couldn't look at her and she took this as a sign of my answer. "Things aren't always what they seem, Adeline. Be careful about placing a judgment on people and situations. You have to walk in someone's shoes before you know how they feel." She stood up and kissed my cheek.

"If Lucy is your friend, and I know she is, be happy for her. She's had a difficult life and if a little happiness comes her way, don't begrudge her—even if it is with your brother." She ruffled my hair and left me sitting in the big easy chair that had been my Grandpa George's.

She was right, of course, and I felt a little childish as I sat there thinking about Lucy and Earl. I admitted to myself that I probably was a little green, but on the other hand, it was still just our freshman year and not having a beau didn't mean I couldn't go to the dance. I knew Floyd Stader would not be my date—Marion was right, I didn't even know him—but the other girls and I could all go together, even if we just hung coats or ladled punch.

I made up my mind to be happy for Lucy, but when Marion boarded the bus the following Monday and announced in a voice the whole bus could hear that she was going to the dance with Dwayne Haskett, I was sure I could not feel the same for her.

"Addie, I heard she asked him," Lucy whispered to me during gym class as we did our calisthenics.

"Really?"

"Yes, really. Rebecca said during church yesterday that she saw Marion whispering in Dwayne's ear and then his face got red and then he nodded yes, so I don't think that counts as a real invitation." Lucy bent over to touch her toes.

"Thanks, Lucy, you're a real pal," I snuck in before Mr. Goulet, our instructor, came over to warn us to be quiet.

Now it was down to just me and Rebecca and Hazel stuck being punch servers. That is, until Hazel announced that she would not be going because she and her family would be attending her cousin's wedding ceremony that weekend in Frankfort.

"Actually, it takes the pressure off," Hazel confided, and I began to hope that some long-lost relative would show up with an emergency wedding that we simply could not miss.

Maude was asked by George Cassidy, and she and Winnie Mae, who was invited by a fellow I didn't know, were set to double date. Things went from bad to worse when Lucy got on the bus one week before the event and said excitedly, "You'll never guess who got asked to the dance!"

"Who?" I asked unenthusiastically.

"Cross-eyed Mary!"

"What?" I came awake at the news.

"Here's the even bigger news. Guess who asked her!"

I thought a second before I replied, "I couldn't even begin to guess. Tell me."

"Frankie Conklin."

"Your cousin Frankie?" I couldn't believe it! Her cousin was practically the best-looking boy, and certainly the most popular, in his county. "How does he even know her? Lucy, you must tell me everything." I was in shock; there must be some kind of mistake. Lucy must have heard it wrong.

"Oh, it's the truth," she replied, keeping her voice low. "You know my daddy set up his little church and started his ministry?" I nodded. "Well, Mary and her uncle started coming on Sundays. And of course, Uncle Frank and his family've been coming as well, so they seen each other there."

"I thought Mary's stepdaddy had his own ministry," I said, confused.

"Apparently, her Uncle Jethro and him got in some kind of row, and Uncle Jethro quit going. So he come to my daddy's place with his wife and Mary, and that's how she met Frankie."

"But he doesn't even go to our school. Can he come to the dance?" I wondered.

"There's nothing that says he can't."

"Lucy, why would Frankie ask her? That just doesn't make any sense. Her glasses are as thick as the bottom of a Coca-Cola bottle. If he wanted to go, he could ask any girl in the county and she would say yes." I knew I certainly would. Frankie came around every so often with Jack to help Earl and my dad, and I became tongue-tied every time he even said hello. He had an easygoing sense about him and a smile that would melt any girl's heart. He was a real dreamboat.

"I don't know why. Frankie's got his own way about him. He don't care much for anyone's opinion of what he does." Lucy shook her head, and her blonde curls bounced around her shoulders. "I can't rightly say why he would ask her and I'd rather fight with a mad bear than question him about Cross-eyed Mary. He don't need to say nothing, just the way he can look at you will make you wonder why you ever opened your mouth." She touched my arm. "And Addie, I don't think Frankie would take too kindly to hearing us call her 'cross-eyed' anymore. She's just Mary."

I understood and nodded. We had called her "cross-eyed" out of habit, but that was the talk of children and that time had passed.

We watched with interest as Mary boarded the bus that morning. It did look as if there was something different about her. She seemed to hold her head a little higher, and I thought I detected a bit of a smile on her face as she stared straight ahead, intently watching the road through her bulky glasses. I observed her closely for the hidden charms I must have missed, but I couldn't find anything, and I speculated that she might be that-kind-of-a-girl. What else could it possibly be?

This was a conundrum. I simply could not understand how Cross-eyed Mary would have been asked to the dance by Frankie Conklin. As I lay in my bed that night, I thought about Mary. I confessed to myself that she had a decent figure—actually, a very nice figure—and her thick curly hair framed her face agreeably. But could that have enticed someone like Frankie to ask her? As I finally fell asleep, I decided I knew nothing about the opposite sex.

I was resigned to serving punch and wondering how Cross-eyed Mary and I could possibly trade places when Jack plopped himself down next to me on the bus the following morning.

"Howdy, Adeline."

"Hey, Jack, where's Lucy?"

He motioned with his thumb over his shoulder toward the back of the bus. Lucy had somehow made it past me and was sitting with Earl, captivated by some story he was telling her.

"So, who are you goin' to the dance with?" he teased.

"You know perfectly well that I haven't been asked, Jack," I snapped. "If you're here to rub it in, I'm less than interested."

"Hey, Addie, I'm sorry. I didn't mean it to come out so disagreeable." His face gave away his disconcertment. "I'm not very good at... oh, just forget it." He turned away. The bus rambled past the orchards now turning fantastic shades of orange, and we sat in silence for a few miles before Jack turned to me and without hesitation asked, "Would you like to go to the dance with me?"

Well, there you have it, I thought. My mother not only had eyes in the back of her head, she was also apparently clairvoyant. But almost instantaneously, just being asked had straightened out all of my tilted feelings, and the scale in my brain closed in on balanced and normal within seconds. Whether I would even go or not didn't have a darn thing to do with the fact that I now had moved from pathetic to desirable, and I wallowed in my own high regard.

"Gosh, Jack, it's awful late in the week to ask a gal. I don't know if..." I trailed off, leading him on shamelessly.

"Well. That's okay, Addie. I got someone else in mind," he offered as he lifted himself out of the seat, calling my bluff.

"Oh, no... no..." I grabbed his arm and pulled him back. "I didn't mean I wouldn't go, Jack"—I couldn't get the words out of my mouth fast enough—"I would be delighted to attend the soiree with you."

"The what?"

"The dance." I amended my words. "I really would like to go with you."

He looked at me strangely, like he wasn't sure he had done the right thing and every time I opened my mouth he was less inclined to go. I thought it best that I sit there quietly and just enjoy the fact that I would be a guest rather than a punch server, so I did exactly that until Rebecca boarded and saw Jack next to me. Her hand flew to her mouth, as it so often did, and she quickly moved past us and took a seat on the other side of the bus a few rows back. Jack didn't notice a thing. When we arrived at school, all he said was "See you later," and he took off for shop class.

Rebecca avoided me for most of the day, but I finally caught up with her at lunch and begged her to stop and listen to what I had to say.

"I promise I did not campaign for the invitation in any way. Really, Rebecca, I didn't."

She stared at me unflinchingly.

"Rebecca, Jack and I have been friends since we were small—he probably just asked me because of that. We're just friends, that's all. There's nothing more," I added, as I brushed away thoughts of our shared kisses. *That was years ago*, I reminded myself.

Rebecca looked as though she were warming up to my explanation.

"I don't really even want to go with him. I just feel bad for him, that's all. Jack means nothing to me," I added. Even as I was saying these words I knew they were inappropriate. Jack didn't deserve to be treated as a pauper of love. But it was too late—they had had their desired effect.

Rebecca melted and hugged me briefly. "That's okay, Adeline. I know you really wanted to go with Floyd Stader and I would have done the same thing as you, I suppose." She looked hesitantly at me. "I guess I'll be the lone punch server."

"Oh, it'll be fun, you'll see," I predicted, but my words rang hollow long after I spoke them.

Lucy and I wanted to double date, but Jack had promised his cousin Frankie that he would go with him, so in order to accommodate everyone, we all went together. Earl and I drove to Jack and Lucy's in my father's large Chevy. It was a crisp October evening and the crescent moon followed us, playing peek-a-boo behind the sweeping willows and oaks that stood stoically along the back road to the Conklins'.

Earl looked as if he were nervous, but I was too, so we shared the tense ride in an unspoken agreement of silence. We pulled in the drive and sat, each taking a deep breath and sighing at the same time, an unplanned action that got a quick laugh from each of us.

"Let's go, Toots," he said as he adjusted his fedora and hopped out of the car.

I hadn't been to Lucy's in ages, certainly not since her daddy had taken to preaching, and I was curious to see the dynamics of the new situation. I did notice the new pole barn, and I tugged on Earl's jacket and nodded in that direction. He raised his eyebrows at me as he knocked on the side door.

The door flew open and little Charlie, who must have been about six, stood there flashing the grin of a toothless old man.

"Hey, buddy," Earl said, ruffling Charlie's hair, "where'd all your teeth go?"

"I lotht 'em."

"I sure hope you find them," I offered as we stepped inside the kitchen.

"Luthy! Jack! Everyone! Addie and Earl ith here," Charlie shouted in a voice sure to wake the dead.

Lucy walked in and motioned for us to follow her. "We're in the front room," she said. I could tell Earl was overwhelmed and rendered speechless by Lucy's appearance, because frankly, I was too. She looked stunning in a light green frock, her long blond hair loose around her shoulders. She walked with the grace of an assured woman, her long tapered fingers following the lines of a chair, looking back at Earl as if he were the sun that had just risen.

Jack greeted me as I stepped into the room. "You look very nice, Adeline," he said as he handed me a small pink corsage to pin on my coat.

"Why, thank you, Jack. How sweet of you." I glanced around the room and noticed Lucy's daddy and aunt sitting on the sofa.

"Good evening, Mr. and Mrs. Conklin."

"Hello, Adeline. Earl." Mr. Conklin spoke in the confident manner of a preacher who knows his place at the head of the table. Lucy's Aunt Bonnie just nodded.

Earl mumbled a greeting while fending off little Charlie, who was begging for Earl and Jack to play catch with him.

"Not tonight, little buddy," Jack said as he pulled Charlie off Earl's back. "We got business to attend to."

"Can I go, too?" Charlie begged.

"Not tonight."

"That'th not fair," he argued.

"Come 'ere, son," Mr. Conklin called out to Charlie. "Let them big kids alone."

"Papa, I wanna go," Charlie continued.

"Not tonight, boy." Mr. Conklin's voice was stern but not cruel, and I saw the difference being off the bottle could make.

We said our goodbyes, Mrs. Conklin saying faintly, "Have fun," and we went outside to wait for Frankie, who would be arriving soon on his motorbike. We hopped around on the porch to keep warm in the chilly evening while discussing the particulars of the upcoming event.

"I hope Rebecca has gotten over her little tizzy," Lucy said. I watched in amazement as Earl took a package of tobacco out of his pocket and rolled a cigarette.

"Earl! What do you think you're doing?" I knew my parents would not approve, and I was astonished to see him defy their authority.

"Addie, mind your own business. I'm a big boy. I don't need you to be telling me what I can do. Or tattling on me, either," he added.

I stuck my tongue out at him while Lucy whispered in my ear, "I think he looks handsome when he smokes."

"I think he looks like an idiot," I said under my breath, just as Frankie roared up.

No one that I knew had a motorbike besides Frankie, and he looked every bit the part of a rogue cowboy with his windblown hair and oversized goggles. We all watched in admiration as he coasted up next to the porch and turned off his bike, then sat back as he pulled off the glasses and smoothed his hair with his hand.

"What's shakin', bacon?" he sang out as he swung his leg over the seat and hopped off.

"He certainly knows how to make an entrance," I said quietly to Lucy. Frankie sauntered up to the porch, slapped Earl and Jack on the back, and gave Lucy and me a slow once-over.

"I don't think I ever done seen two prettier girls than you two," he said, with such sincerity that it was difficult not to believe him. "Hello, Adeline," he added as he bent down and whispered in my ear. "Your hair looks really nice put up like that."

"Thanks," I managed as we headed for the car. I sat between Jack and Frankie in the back seat and we settled in for the ride to pick up Mary on the other side of town. Lucy cozied up next to Earl in the front seat and he casually set his arm around her shoulder, pulling her close and whispering in her ear. We all joked and kidded one another, and when talk turned to the latest popular songs, we boisterously sang at the top of our lungs Ella Fitzgerald's hit, "A Tisket, a Tasket."

"Was it red?" crooned Jack and Frankie as they leaned in towards me.

"No, no, no, no," Lucy and I sang back, as Earl tooted the horn in time. When the song was finished, we all clapped wildly and collapsed on one another in a fit of giggles.

The mood changed quickly after we picked Mary up. She squeezed in between me and Frankie, giving me a slight nod and a quiet "Hi, Adeline. You look pretty." I nodded my acknowledgment and whispered "Thanks—you too," but after that there was no more singing or even loud talking, and we spoke in hushed tones only to our dates if we spoke at all. Frankie and Mary were deep in discussion, prompting my great interest as to what they could possibly have been talking about, but I was content to sit, nestled under Jack's protective arm, and listen to the hum of conversation that swirled around us. Sitting so close to Jack brought back memories of the last time we had been together, and the effortless comfort of the past appeared and settled in like a long-lost friend come back to visit and take tea.

"Isn't the crescent moon lovely?" I said, making small talk.

Jack didn't answer, but pulled me in tighter and squeezed my shoulder gently.

"It's actually a waxing gibbous moon," a soft voice next to me offered.

I glanced over and found myself staring into Mary's thick glasses.

"Excuse me?" I said, taken aback by her contribution.

She cleared her throat nervously before continuing. "The phase the moon is in tonight is actually called a gibbous moon, the stage between a crescent and a full moon. This one is considered waxing because it's moving toward a full moon rather than a new moon."

Mary's willingness to participate and educate the group stopped us all in our tracks, and the hum of conversation stopped. Even in the darkness, I could feel the heat from her face as it turned red, and she shrank back in her seat as though she was instantly sorry she'd spoken out.

"Is that so?" Frankie offered up at last. "Now, how in the world do you know that?"

"I'm in the astronomy club," she said weakly.

"I thought that was only for boys," Lucy said, turning around to partake in the discussion.

"It's mostly fellows," said Mary, "but there aren't any rules that say girls can't join."

"Why would you want to?" I asked.

"Because I'm interested in the stars and the planets," she said defensively.

"Well, I think it's a fine hobby," Frankie chimed in again. "And I'd like to hear more about the gibbious monkey moon that waxes."

His comment sent a round of giggles through the car, and the mood lifted. With his encouragement, Mary talked for a bit on the cycles of the moon, and I admit I found her and the subject interesting. I wasn't the only one. We all asked questions, and her easygoing manner and willingness to share her knowledge on the subject endeared her to us in a strange and intimate way. In the dark, where you couldn't see her eyes, she wasn't the Mary we all thought we knew.

It was a long ride to the school. When we arrived, the dance had already begun. Students were spilling out the front doors and parked on benches and rails, casually smoking as they entertained their dates with stories of epic feats accomplished in their younger days. We all walked up to the school together but soon were separated, and out of the corner of my eye, I saw Frankie and Mary slip away and walk out toward the football field. I turned to tell Lucy, but when I looked back, she and Earl had disappeared onto the dance floor, and I didn't figure Jack would think it any of my business to be discussing his cousin's whereabouts.

"Let's go say hi to Rebecca." I pulled Jack along to the refreshment table. "She's at the punchbowl," I shouted over the music.

"Sure," he shouted back as we wove in between the dancers towards the back of the gym, waving to friends and acquaintances who popped up along the way. I spied Marion draped over Dwayne, dancing; she waved and blew me a kiss, never taking her arms from around his neck.

We found Rebecca dipping out cups of punch and setting them down in neat, perfectly aligned rows. She scowled as a thirsty dancer grabbed a cup from the middle of her handiwork and swiftly replaced it, but brightened when she noticed Jack and me.

"Hi, Addie." Rebecca smiled sweetly at me and turned to Jack. "Hello, Jack," she purred. "How nice to see you here tonight. Are you enjoying the dance?"

"We just got here, but it seems like a good time." Jack looked off in the distance. "Hey, Addie, I want to say hi to Larry Guy. I'll be right back, okay?"

"Sure," I answered. "I'll wait right here."

"Thanks," he said over his shoulder as he took off in search of his friend.

"He sure looks spiffy tonight, don't you think, Addie?"

"Yeah, I guess so," I replied as I helped myself to a cup of punch from the row closest to me, careful not to upset the overall design. Rebecca quickly replaced it with another.

"I saw Floyd Stader. He's here with Rosemary Russell. Do you know who she is?"

I shook my head and looked around the dance floor for my car mates. I found Earl and Lucy chatting with Maude and George, but failed to locate Frankie and Mary.

"She was princess of the 4-H parade last year. She's very popular."

"Bully for her," I replied good-naturedly. I had lost interest in the boy that I had never even been introduced to, and he and his date held little concern for me. When I caught Jack's eye as he stood with his buddies, he flashed me a bright smile. I had to agree with Rebecca on one point: He sure did look spiffy.

Marion and Dwayne sauntered over, her hand clutching his so tightly that her knuckles were white. He was a nervous boy who seemed to cough a lot, and he cleaned and adjusted his eyeglasses often, as though that were the most important thing he had to do that day.

"Hi, girls," Marion called out gaily as they approached. "Everyone, this is Dwayne. Dwayne, this is everyone." Jack had returned, and we all murmured polite greetings.

"Isn't this a killer-diller dance?" she exclaimed, sighing one of her cheerful sighs. "We are having so much fun, aren't we, Dwayne?" Dwayne didn't get a chance to answer before she added, "I am absolutely parched from all that dancing. How about a glass of punch, Rebecca?"

"Coming right up." Rebecca handed Marion a cup. "How about you, Jack? Are you thirsty?"

"Sure," Jack responded, as he took the cup Rebecca held out seductively to him. He threw his drink back, then took my hand. "Let's go cut a rug, Addie. Whaddaya say?"

I followed him out onto the dance floor, eager to leave the uncomfortable setting at the punch table. I was surprised at Rebecca's boldness and irritated with Marion's annoying behavior, so it was a relief to leave them, Rebecca rearranging the cups and Marion adjusting Dwayne's necktie.

Jack and I found a spot next to Earl and Lucy and for the next couple hours had the time of our lives. Swing was the latest rage and the band played many of the latest hits. We sang and danced to "Boo Hoo," "Thanks for the Memories," and "Cry, Baby, Cry," pretending we were infants bawling as we fell into each other laughing so hard it brought real tears to our eyes. Maude's crowd danced next to us and we switched partners and dosie-doed back and forth between the groups, linking arms as we skipped by. Frankie and Mary showed up at some point. They held each other close and swayed to the music, eyes closed, even during the fast tunes.

It was over much too quickly for everyone, but we all agreed that this was the best dance party we'd ever been to. We were exhausted on the trip home, and I settled into Jack's arms without a care in the world. When he bent down to kiss me, I eagerly returned his affections.

It was a quiet ride back to Michigami. We dropped Mary off, waiting patiently while Frankie walked her to the door and kissed her goodbye. *What an odd couple*, I thought, but I had newfound respect for her—and I liked her. She was different than I had imagined her to be. My mother's words echoed in my mind about placing a judgment on someone, and I realized yet again how true her advice was.

When we arrived at the Conklins', Frankie scooted inside and Jack and I bid farewell on one side of the car, Lucy and Earl on the other.

Jack nuzzled my neck. "I had a wonderful time," he whispered into my ear. "And by the way, you smell really good."

Thanking him for the good time, I kissed his cheek and waited in the car for Earl. We left, like overstuffed guests at a banquet, happy and contented.

Our parents were waiting up for us. My mother never took her eyes off her book, but asked, "Well?"

"It was wonderful," I gushed, gliding up the stairs.

"Did you have fun with Jack?"

"Oh, yes. It was great. Wasn't it, Earl?"

"Yeah, it was okay," he said, rolling his eyes at Daddy. "You know, lots of girl-type stuff."

"And you managed with that?" my father asked as he hid his mouth behind the newspaper.

"Yeah, I guess." Earl shrugged. "Lucy's pretty fun." He started up the stairs after me, calling, "Goodnight."

I glanced back at my parents, who were smiling at each other like they had just shared some big secret, and I wondered if they wished they could be young again and go to dances and have fun like we did. Did they long for their lost youth?

Lucy and I chatted nonstop on the ride to school the following Monday morning, discussing every single event, dress, and conversation we could recall. Marion joined in when she boarded, but Rebecca just smiled and walked by, pushing her way past Hazel to sit next to Jack.

"That's funny," I mentioned to Lucy, but soon entered into a conversation with Hazel, reviewing every song the band had played.

Jack gave me a funny look as we got off the bus, but it wasn't until after school that he grabbed my arm and stopped me outside the gym.

"Ouch," I said, shaking my arm. "Why did you do that?"

He got right to the point. "Did you tell Rebecca that you really didn't want to go to the dance with me? That you just felt sorry for me?" I'd never seen Jack so furious; his dark eyes raged with anger.

"Why? Did she tell you that?" I was stunned. Could she have shared my words with Jack?

"And more," he scoffed. "Did you tell her that? Yes or no?"

"I don't remember exactly what my words were, Jack, but whatever I said, I didn't mean it the way it came out."

"What did you mean, then?" he asked. "How could you even talk about me with her, Addie?" His hurt showed through in his voice and expression, and my heart pounded in my chest, reminding me what a despicable person I was. "I thought things were different between us. I can't trust you." He looked at me like I was less than dirt and walked away slowly, shaking his head and dragging his feet.

The still air around me slammed into my head and I had to sit down before I fell. Rebecca had not only betrayed me, she had done it spitefully, turning Jack against me. She wasn't the sweet, quiet girl I had thought. She was an insidious, deceitful monster, slithering out from under a rock to spew her venom on those around her. Before I could crucify her entirely, though, I heard my parents' voices calling from my subconscious, "It's not her fault, Adeline. If you'd never said such things, she couldn't have repeated them. You're as much to blame as she is—even more so, because Jack has been nothing but a friend to you and you have betrayed him."

I wanted all the voices in my head to stop, but there was no end to the badgering that came my way. Rebecca whispered repeatedly, "You got what you deserved," and Jack shouted "I can't trust you," while my conscience beat me unmercifully and my parents just clucked and shook their heads. The bus ride home was torturous, Lucy sitting stoically next to me. She didn't want to desert me, but she was loyal to her brother and felt his pain as well.

Over the next few months, I tried in vain to offer up my apologies and Jack finally accepted, but only reluctantly. Our conversations were cordial, but we had lost the intimate friendship that had been ours for so long. Rebecca asked him to the Sadie Hawkins dance that February, and I resigned myself to the fact that he was no longer available to me. I had no desire to go to the event and stayed home with my parents, remembering the exuberance that the last dance had brought, while Earl and Lucy went alone. Lucy had forgiven me completely, but I longed to have Jack feel the same and missed his calm and gentle companionship.

The dreary winter pressed on, the monotony of the snow and the cold wearing thin on everyone. The Tittabawassee River froze every year, but the rushing water underneath was quick to melt the ice, which could be thin in places. Every adult and child growing up near the water knew the stories of other less fortunate individuals who had literally skated on thin ice, only to drop through into the freezing waters below. The lucky ones got pulled out, but the legends and stories were legion about those who hadn't been. We had been warned, threatened, and scared stiff about not going near the ice until my daddy had tested it by drilling down with a steel rod to check its depth. But there were others who didn't feel the need for that assurance and took their chances, even as the warm spring sun began its ascent to summer highs.

Michigami County Cemetery was located on the south side of the river, down a mile or so from our place, and it was here that Lucy's Uncle Sam would have his funeral one warm spring day in March of 1939. It was Lucy's daddy's first funeral at which he would officiate as an ordained minister, and she told me later that he had been up till the wee hours practicing his sermon before his wife. Tensions ran high, and they were late getting to the cemetery because of a flat tire on the old truck. No one was in a very pleasant mood. Uncle Sam had died of gangrene after it had set in from a nail in his shoe gone infected, but he had lost his foot and then his leg first before the Old Doc figured they hadn't ever really got it. I didn't go to the funeral, but my parents did—Uncle Sam bought the horse meat my father sold for his many dogs. I do know it was a beautiful sunny day—the kind that reminds you that summer hasn't disappeared forever—and that the ground was still damp and muddy from the melting winter snow.

Lucy told me later that there was so much commotion from them being late and Uncle Sam's wife being in such a state that no one had reminded little Charlie it was too late in the season to go near the river. It was only after the funeral had started that she observed that Charlie wasn't even there. She said that she and Jack both realized it at the same time, and that as they stepped back from the crowd to find him and assure themselves that he was safe, they noticed him out on the ice, jumping and running around.

"I swear," she recounted days later, her eyes still red and puffy, "one minute I seen him standing there and before I could even shout out to him, poof! he was gone. Like he fell through a trap door in some magic trick."

The funeral party quickly turned to a rescue attempt. All the men ran downstream, trying in vain to pull up any piece of thin ice in hopes that they might grab an arm or leg. The women tried to comfort Lucy's Aunt Bonnie, but she had gone hysterical and finally fainted, her body unable to handle the shock of the catastrophe. The rescue effort was unsuccessful. The spring waters were high and moved quickly, and it wasn't until three days later that his small, battered body was found, a mile or so downstream.

The horror of the tragedy settled over Michigami like a mist that is barely visible but constantly felt. Our whole family attended the funeral, and I watched in sorrow as the despondency of a child's unnecessary death affected all those I loved. Aunt Bonnie sat, dazed, in a chair by the casket. She couldn't even stand without assistance. Jack and Lucy cried outright, and even Cora understood that her baby brother had died and bawled uncontrollably. Lucy's daddy kept repeating that the good Lord must have needed his baby, but by the end of the funeral words had deserted him, and he fell silent.

After the last handful of dirt was thrown down on the small casket, my Aunt Pearl, looking fragile and older than ever before, silently held up her hand. Lucy's daddy nodded and she began to sing, a capella, in her sweet, high voice, of the angels that would be watching over little Charlie in heaven. I couldn't bear the sadness of the song or the occasion and stepped back, wiping my misty eyes and collecting my thoughts.

I bumped into Jack, who had apparently done the same. Our eyes met, and I instinctively reached out to him. He held me tightly, his grip fierce, and we stayed that way until I felt his embrace loosen and noticed Rebecca standing behind him.

"It's time to go, Jack," she said firmly. She nodded at me. "Hello, Adeline."

I nodded in response and watched as she led Jack away and back to the disbanding funeral party.

I walked back to my family. My father came up to me, put his arm around me, and hugged me. "Just for no reason," he said softly, and I could only imagine how a parent might feel at the loss of a child.

We dropped off a casserole that Maude had made, but didn't stay long at the Conklins' place. It was crowded with their own grieving kin, and the mourning and unhappiness was overwhelming.

I didn't see Jack and Lucy for the next few weeks, but they were constantly on my mind. Everything seemed out of whack, like we were going through the motions of life ten minutes out of time. It got even stranger when, in June, right after school let out for the summer, Lucy's Aunt Bonnie walked into the river at the deepest part and did not come out. Her body was never found. I heard my father say that there were too many hungry critters out and about at that time of the year.

Lucy and Jack had lost two mothers and a brother, and their daddy two wives and a son, and it was agreed by both my parents that their cup of grief runneth over. The Conklin family's misfortunes allowed my family a new appreciation for our good fortune, and we thanked the Lord daily for watching out for us and permitting us to have the blessings that we did.

Days became weeks and the mist of misery lifted, but it left a stench that blew through every now and then, reminding us that misfortune is always hovering and no one is immune. My heart ached for so many reasons that when I looked back to that ride we'd taken the previous fall to the Harvest Moon Dance, the joy I had experienced was nowhere to be found. I wanted desperately to relive that night, to go back in time and pick up from there, to start over fresh and take back everything that had happened from that moment on, but the magic needed for that miracle was nowhere to be found.

My parents counseled us that time would heal our wounds and this was part of growing up. Bad things did happen to good and innocent people, they said, and we should take from these trying times the lessons that would help us cope as adults. At the time, their words were just words, offering a brief but unsatisfactory explanation of the unexplainable, and I was somehow disappointed that they couldn't fix the hurts administered by the hand of God.

As I grew older, the exhilaration and elation I had felt from that ride to Cross-eyed Mary's house and to the dance did return, separating itself out from the tragic events that followed. I was able to appreciate the pure and simple joy that had been ours on that late fall evening. It became the embodiment of unblemished happiness, a time when adult thoughts and worries were on the horizon but carefree love and unbridled enthusiasm were still acceptable. It would be the last time my life was relatively uncomplicated, and I wished that I had known this—as though it somehow would have made a difference.

Chapter Six

Francine

I always knew I wouldn't live to be an old woman. I can't say why; I just knew. I remember when I was a small gal my granny tellin' me that when I got to be her age I'd be movin' slower, sittin' down a little more, and probably needin' spectacles to boot. I didn't know much at such a young age, but I known she was wrong.

When I closed my eyes at night I seen my whole life in front of me. I seen pictures tellin' my story, pictures that turned into people, changin' color and jumpin' around my mind like a fish on a hook. Pictures like I was readin' a book, but it was *my* book. But about halfway through the book there weren't no more pictures. It was just blank. Everything went dark.

That's how I knew. That's how I knew Granny was wrong. I think I even suspected how it would happen. Or maybe I done made it happen the way I suspected it should. Either way, it don't likely matter so much. End result's the same.

I couldn't do that much, and Lord only knows I weren't much to look at, but one thing I could do was see my life lay out in front of me. I knew I would marry a man just like my daddy. I saw my babies, plain as me, scared of their own shadow for fear of God only knows what. I felt a darkness so heavy that I didn't see no way out. Only thing I never seen was Frankie—he come from someplace I ain't never been and he come with things I never give him. He made me think for a while that I musta been wrong about the things I saw, about my darkness. But that weren't the case.

My daddy did everything religiously. He got up with the sun every morning, he ate his supper every night at five o'clock, and he went to church on Sundays, rain or shine. He also give us beatin's religiously, every Saturday morning, whether we needed it or not. He told Mama that he was beatin' the devil outta us, and if he didn't, the devil would steal our souls forever. Poor Mama couldn't do nothin' but sit back and watch as he picked up one of her babies and gave 'em the strap. If she was to say anything he woulda taken the strap to her, and she needed to be there for comfortin' when he was through. He started the beatin's when we was three, and every year on the day we was born, he added one more lickin'. To this day I don't care much for birthdays. The regular beatin's stopped when we was thirteen, but that didn't keep my daddy from handing out his punishment for just about anything that made him angry—from not having his supper on the table to missin' a spot while sweepin' the floor.

My mama willed herself to live till her last baby left the house. She died one week after my brother Ebner joined the Army—he told the United States Government he was 18 when, fact was, he was but 15 years old. I was the only one of Mama's five babies to come to her funeral, but I know she woulda understood and not held it 'gainst any one of 'em for not coming to pay their last respects.

The funeral was on one of them days that couldn't be prettier. I remember thinkin' it was a perfect day to be buried, and as the soft wind blew across the land and I turned my face to the warm sun, I imagined it was me bein' lowered into the earth. My tears started from the joy I felt, knowin' that I would one day know the relief Mama musta felt as she left her earthly home.

Even though I weren't married, I left my daddy's house when I was seventeen. I hired out to a widower about fifteen miles down the road. I helped with the babies and the animals and the farm. I never seen the widower beat his children, and they were very spirited, but I just couldn't help but wonder how he was goin' to save their souls. He seemed a decent man, though, so I weren't surprised when two days before we laid Mama to rest he told me he was takin' a new wife and wouldn't be needin' my services no more. I was taken aback, though, when he give me a week's wages and a letter of reference to a family he knew in Michigami County lookin' for a house-girl.

I didn't have no clue as to what I was goin' to do, my only hope being the Michigami position, and it was just these thoughts I was ponderin' as they lowered my poor mama's pine casket into the ground. I hadn't as yet spoke with my daddy, but he had heard I was outta work and after the funeral he said he wanted to have a word with me. He told me that, seein' as my mama was dead and all, he thought it would be for the best if I came back home to help him with the household chores and such. The breath left my body for a short passin' before I heard myself thankin' him for his generous offer but, meanin' no disrespect, said I'd already taken a job with a family in the next county over. He glared at me as I kicked a small stone with my toe and I shook with jitters as I finished my lie, tellin' him I would be gettin' room and board in addition to a small wage, so again, meanin' no disrespect, I would have to decline his kindly offer. Matter of fact, I told him, I needed to head out right quick, as the next coach to Michigami was leaving soon.

I turned and started off, but not before my daddy grabbed my arm and, giving it such a squeeze as to leave a blue mark, whispered in my ear that he knew for a fact that the devil had gotten my soul and one day I would meet my mama in hell, and that if we wasn't in a public place he woulda tanned my hide. His words terrified me. I told him I was sorry I had disappointed him and that I would do my best to repent. I hurried off, holdin' my arm, shaken by my daddy's harsh words, to face my uncertain future.

I didn't know no one in Michigami County, and when I got off the coach I was the scaredest I'd ever been in my life. Even though I'd left my daddy's house a good year ago, they was still just down the road. With Mama gone, I felt like I had no one even interested if I was alive. I didn't know if the family I was goin' to see had already taken on a girl, or if they would even like me. My daddy had told me often enough that I sure weren't that much to look at, so maybe they wouldn't like my appearance. I was sick to my stomach on the way over to the Millers' house—sick with all the worries I had.

I never had so much relief as after meeting the Millers. Them folks were the kindliest people I ever met. Mrs. Miller done lost her husband a while back, and she lived with her four girls in a big ole' house on the edge of town. The third daughter, Miss Pearl, had taken ill with a fever that turned into the polio pox, and the poor girl was havin' trouble walkin'. It wouldn't take long till she was in a wheelchair, but for now she was gettin' along on hand crutches.

They put me up in a back room behind the kitchen that was surely the sweetest room I ever did sleep in. The room had a little window that looked over the garden in the back, and in the spring I could smell the sweet perfume of the apple blossoms. I smiled more than I ever did in my eighteen years with my daddy, and one time I heard myself outright laugh. Them girls and their mama was smart, too—most every night was spent talking about stuff I ain't never even thought about. They told me of the women in England that'd gotten the right to vote, and they thought that soon we would too. Imagine that! They called themselves "suffragettes" or somethin' like, and they said they could speak their mind about anythin' they wanted, just like they was men. Them girls laughed at what they thought was funny and would raise their voices when discussing politics or somethin' serious. I wondered what my daddy would do if he knew I was in hire of the Millers, and I had such dark thoughts that I swore I would never think those things again, as if somehow doin' so would send him runnin' to Michigami County to fetch me up and take me away.

I never seen girls that didn't have no stones draggin' 'em down, and not once did I seen the Miller girls cry, 'cept when they was speakin' 'bout their dear sweet papa. They didn't talk of beatin's, and somehow I knew there weren't never been any. It was like watching folks from France or someplace from the other side of the world. It almost didn't seem like they was real. But I know they was, 'cause I helped Miss Opal in the kitchen and I dusted the tiny glass figures sittin' out that their daddy bought 'em. Best of all, I could hear them sweet voices when they decided they was in the mood to warble. Them Miller girls could all sing sweet as bluejays, and I knew it was the closest I'd ever get to heaven when they sung whilst their mama played the piano. Sometimes I found myself cryin' as I listened to the melodies that danced around the room in an' outta my head. It weren't from sadness, but because it was all I could do that was as perfect as them singin'. I knew I weren't any way near as good and decent as them, but when I dropped my tears it made me feel like somehow I belonged in a strange world of people that let me watch as they lived their lives.

When the Great War started, menfolk were gettin' more and more scarce as they ran off or got called up to join the effort. My three brothers were sent overseas, and men all over the country got struck with the fever to fight the Germans. Bein' as there was fewer and fewer men around, it weren't a strange sight to see Mrs. Meade deliverin' the mail or Mrs. Hoekstra slicin' meat at the grocer. Why, even Miss Ruby took over schoolin' the older children when young Mr. Higgins got called up. Miss Ruby was pleased as punch with her new assignment, and was certain to share amusin' stories of her day with her mama and sisters, keepin' them in stitches even at the dinner table. Her eyes was always smiling, even when she was relatin' times when she said she was spittin' mad. When I ventured to ask her one day if she used a switch, she looked at me like she didn't understand the question. It was a piece before I come to realize that beatin's weren't no part of any of their lives—or mine either, anymore.

For bein' such a tall lady, Miss Ruby had tiny feet and hands, and they fluttered like a hummin'bird when she was excited. She had a delicate look about her appearance, and her speakin' voice was the same. I would have almost thought she was singin' when she talked, but I knew better. When that woman opened her mouth to sing, I could swear my mama could hear her from her grave the next county over. She had the biggest voice I ever heard for a woman, one that started deep in her gut and exploded from the top of her head. She shook a person down to their bones and sent a shiver through your spine, 'specially when she stood at the front of the choir on Sundays.

I weren't the only body in that house that greatly admired Miss Ruby. Her mama counted on her to help with the runnin' of the household, and also to assist with Miss Pearl, who was now sittin' in a wheelchair full-time. Without no menfolk around, it was up to Miss Ruby to find a handyman to help with the few things around the place us women couldn't do, no matter how strong we was.

Mr. Harris was a piano student of Mrs. Miller's and had been comin' around for a while. He weren't much of a talker, but he was plenty able to shoe a horse or fix a leak high on the rooftop. He weren't really a handyman—his daddy owned a farm down the road a piece—but he was an able body in this time of war, and he appeared more'n happy to help the sisters and their mama. I heard some scuttlebutt that he weren't in the war because he was a gimper, but his daddy didn't have no other babies to help at his farm, so Mr. Harris woulda been excused from the service anyhow. He always had a kind word for me and the animals, and I could see in his eyes he was a gentle soul.

It weren't long before I could tell he was sweet for Miss Pearl. I could see it in the way he handed her bonnet to her so delicate-like, and the way he set her down so softly, like she was an egg that he was afraid to break. Now this was a strange occurrence, as she weren't no good to anyone. She was pretty and sweet enough, but she couldn't even dress herself without help from me or her sisters. How could she give him any babies or put up cannin' or do any of the chores a body would have to do as a wife? It just wouldn't make any sense in my head, no matter how much thought I give it, but Mr. Harris, he didn't appear to care 'bout those things. He just sat for hours listenin' to her soft voice and askin' her questions just to keep her talkin'. He would carry her like she was a baby, his bad leg draggin' ever so slightly, out to the garden to look at the prize-winnin' roses Miss Opal grew, or down to the cellar to pick out some canned peaches for that night's meal.

He had another admirer soon enough. Susie, the baby of them girls, started sittin' with him and her sister out on the big front porch, listenin' to the summer crickets. Susie was the only girl in the family with red-brown hair, and surely the most talkative—she always had somethin' to say about anything, from the weather to how much eggs cost that week, and it weren't beyond her to argue with her older sisters, and sometimes even her mama. That poor Mr. Harris listened to that girl again and again, and when Miss Pearl tell her baby sister silence is golden, he just smiled so patient-like and said, That's okay Miss Pearl, I don't mind none.

Mr. Smith had taken leave of his position at the grade school for the war, and Miss Opal had replaced him in teachin' them younger children at the school. She and Miss Ruby left every mornin' and walked the short distance to the schoolhouse like two peas in a pod, so happy they was to be addin' their piece to the family pot. Miss Susie was helpin' her mama at home, but when her mama took ill with the influenza, Mr. Harris was around that much more, takin' charge, and them girls were happy to let him.

The summer of 1918 weren't a good one for many folk around this area—and even all over the world, as I come to understand it. I didn't get sick, nor Mr. Harris, but Miss Susie and her mama done caught the bug, and poor Mrs. Miller ended up passin' away after a month of bein' on her deathbed. Miss Susie got better real slow, but she didn't have the gab like she done before—the sickness pulled it out—and that whole house fell silent for what seemed like ages. If the war didn't kill you, all a body had to do was wait, and the influenza bug would. Mr. Harris lost his daddy's worker, and my only sister passed as well. Many of the menfolk gone to war never come back, includin' every last one of my brothers. There weren't no one nowhere that didn't have some loss, either from the Germans or the 'flu, and everyone that year seemed to have some cross to bear, as Mr. Harris was fond of sayin'.

That Christmastime was a sad one, and them girls was desperately missin' their mama, but Mr. Harris and his daddy come over to have supper and cheer 'em up. After the meal, the young Mr. Harris stood up and spoke to them of hopes and dreams for the future. He said the war was endin' and our fellows was coming home, it seemed the worst of the influenza bug had passed, and we all had so much to be thankful for, especially havin' each other. This made all the womenfolk cry, includin' me, and as we were sniffin' away he says he got another announcement to make.

He says it's high time he got married. He looked at his daddy, who nodded his head like he was givin' him permission to go on. He says he got a farm and a good life to offer one of the sisters, and they gonna make a life together in these tough times. It's right important to have family. Now he's gonna have a bigger one, and he's so thankful it's with the Millers.

I turned to see Miss Pearl and saw the smile on her face, but when I looked real quick to her heart and seen the pain, I knew it weren't her. Miss Susie was smilin' to beat the band, and the news brightened the mood real quick. Miss Susie would be movin' to Mr. Harris's farm, but it weren't too far, and she would see her family often and Mr. Harris could still be helpin' the sisters whenever they needed him. Miss Pearl smiled and laughed with the others and showed no bad feelin's whatsoever, but she done closed the window to her heart forever, and I never saw inside again.

I met Rosie when I first come to the Millers' and she became my first real friend. She worked for a family up the road a piece, and she come to visit every now and then, bringin' gossip from across the county. She told me that Mr. Van Hopkins, the old man from the bank, was sweet on Miss Ruby, and that Miss Opal had lost her true love in the war. She was happy to tell me of how a girl gets a beau and how to rub rouge on your cheeks to make 'em red, but sometimes I weren't so sure as to her honesty, as her stories seemed a bit farfetched. She had a younger sister, Bonnie, who followed her around just beggin' for us to include her, but we would lock arms and skip away, tellin' her to go find her own best friend.

The Great War had ended, and to celebrate the Doughboys comin' home there was to be a cotillion. Rosie and I would be there. All the sisters were goin' and were fixed to sing with the marching band at the ceremony. It was to be the most thrillin' day in my life, I just knew. The evenin' was fine and the juices were flowin', as Prohibition was still around the corner. I weren't much of a drinker, but Rosie convinced me I was bein' a wet noodle, so behind the backs of the Miller sisters I had a pull or two off a bottle someone pushed in my hand. I got dragged to the dance floor by a serviceman in uniform, and when we whirled by Rosie she whispered she was with his brother. I couldn't say what that boy I was dancin' with looked like—I was concentratin' on keeping my head straight and my innards intact. But the fact was, he was holdin' on so tight and spinnin' me so fast that I had trouble catching my breath.

I finally broke away and ran to get some water and stand outside the hall, where the cool of the night soothed my achin' head and body. It weren't but a moment later that I felt someone grab my hand and pull me off to a path that headed down to the river. I recognized the rough outline of my dancin' partner, and when I tried to stop he jerked real hard on my hand, and as he stumbled he said isn't this what you wanted anyway? I didn't know what he was talkin' about, as all I wanted then was to go home, but that man scared me and I didn't know what I should do. He pulled me off the path for a spell and pushed me down real rough-like in a grassy stretch next to the river. I was shakin' so hard and my heart was pumpin' so fast I couldn't find the breath to push my voice out, so I just sat there like a caught rabbit. He looked at me a stretch, like I was a German tryin' to shoot him or somethin', and it was the first time I really seen his face. Maybe it was the drink, but that man, he got the same eyes as my daddy, and I knew his intentions weren't no good. We stared at each other until I finally had the breath to say I wanna go. That was all it took for that man to put me back where I come from in a way my daddy never done. I been beat pretty good before, but this man done things to me that, before I would say them aloud, I would die first.

I lay in the soft spongy river grass, smellin' the springtime blooms and hearing the song of the crickets, while the man who just molested my person lie sweatin' on top of me. It weren't long afore I felt my mind walk away from my body and head over yonder a bit to pick up somethin' that I recognized as belongin' to me. My mind slipped it over my shoulders and I felt the warm, comfortable blanket of darkness I thought I done lost. Ain't it funny when you think you come a ways from where you started, but then it only takes but a brief minute to set you back?

Later that week, as I was sittin' by my lonesome on the Millers' front porch, comfortable, wrapped in the mist of a light rain, I saw a figure comin' down the street. I didn't rightly know who it was until he turned up the steps leadin' to the porch and I seen the eyes of my attacker. They wasn't mad now, just empty, and he spoke like he was real nervous, coughin' a lot and searchin' for words he couldn't find. When he catched his breath, he told me he was liquored up bad that night and he done lost his senses. Weren't no excuse, he said, but he hoped I would accept his apology 'cause he was a soldier that served his country and a good man. As he was tellin' his story, I looked into him and saw he was a good man. A good man, just like my daddy was. A good man who went to church and provided for his family and would walk five miles to pay back a nickel he done borrowed. That kinda good man. But he got the temper like my daddy, and the drink pull it out right quick.

Problem is, when you're bein' dragged down it don't take much to give you a false hope. Even when you know this to be the case, you're forever thinkin' this time is different. You forget that each time you get disappointed, even if it just happened. You always have hope. The hope is what keeps them stones from pulling you down where there ain't no comin' back. And this was my mindset when I said I would go to the picture show with him that weekend.

When I told the sisters I was going out with a man, they was all excited and wanted to know all about what they call my "soldier friend." Problem was I didn't even get his name when he come to the house that afternoon to give me his apology, and what I known about him weren't the thing to share with proper folk. But when he showed to pick me up, he was all pleasant and such, and I began to think maybe I had remembered the incident wrongly. Did it really take place like I recollected? Now my thoughts were fuzzy, and I had trouble puttin' myself back in that grassy spot by the river. I knew somethin' had taken place, but was it as bad as I thought?

Rosie and me went to the show with Frank and his brother John. *Tarzan* was playing, and I swear it was the best movie show I ever seen, what with that

man livin' with the monkeys like that. We all drank orange sodas after the
show, and them two brothers tell us stories from the war and how they killed
so many Germans it would make your head spin. They come quiet, though,
after they tell us they lost their baby brother to the 'flu overseas, not Germans.
How 'bout that for funny business?

I didn't have much to say and they all done most of the talking, but Rosie
told me later that she wanted to marry John and I should marry Frank. These
thoughts was floating in my mind as we was walking, but they sank when I got
back to the house and the sisters told me my daddy had passed. I hadn't seen
nor spoke to him since I left for Michigami County over a year ago, and hearin'
the news bring all kinds of memories back—and they ain't the kind that make
you smile. The sisters, meanin' well, ask me what was he like, Francine? Tell us
about him. But I say I like my mournin' in private, my hurt runs deep. They
don't say no more, but truth is, I got no tears for the man I call my daddy. I
don't feel no sorrow, but I don't feel no joy neither. I just don't feel.

Couple weeks later, a man from the county come around and tell me I'm
the only kin of Mr. William Baker and I inherit two things, my daddy's house
and all the back taxes he don't pay over the past two years. He tell me I got
six months to start payin' or all kinds of bad things'll start happenin' to me. I
tell Frank I don't want the house, I don't want nothin', but he say that's crazy,
Francine, you gotta do somethin'. He says he'll fix my problem, and the next
day he come up with the idea of us gettin' hitched and working my daddy's
farm. I told him Miss Pearl needed me and I couldn't leave, I had my job with
the sisters. Why, those rich bitties, they don't need nothin', and they can get
along just fine without you, he says. But when I see the ugliness in his words,
he changes his tune and says he means they'll just hire a new girl. He tells me
this is our chance, Francine, to have a farm and maybe a family and start our
lives on our own with no help from nobody.

Frank and I married the followin' month, on the same day as Rosie and
John, in the county courthouse. Weren't no big deal, but the sisters, they have
everyone over for cake and coffee, and as a gift they give me a handsome glass

bird and sing the most beautiful song about everlastin' love. I hear Frank mutter real low that that ain't going to pay the piper, but I think it's the best present they could give.

I got a kiss on the cheek from Frank when the ceremony come to an end, and if I woulda known it was the only kiss I'd ever get from the man I now called my husband, surely that mighta given me cause for concern. Guess I don't know what I woulda done different.

But I don't have no dark thoughts that day until Frank go out to celebrate with his brother. I wait up for him to come home, but as the time goes on that darkness comes creeping back. When he gets home I seen he was drunk, and after he raped me a second time I understand what my life will be. This time there ain't no apology, just a grunt in the mornin' and a demand to have his lunch ready by noon, as he's now workin' my daddy's farm for me. But I don't care; I sense a light inside me I never known. It gives me reason to make a home for a man that don't seem to care much for me.

Rosie and John settle in her daddy's backhouse in Michigami, and she was in a family way quick as me. I don't get to see her much but when we can, we laugh and share stories 'bout our expanding bellies. As I get bigger Frank don't come near me, which only makes me hope I'll be pregnant forever. I get nine months of peace and every day I thank the small baby growing inside me for allowing me this time. It don't last forever, though, and on a windy day in September, I give birth to a boy we call Frankie. Big Frank about burst with pride and tell everyone he knows, and some he don't, how good-lookin' his boy is. He is beautiful, which surprises just about anyone who sees him. I ain't pretty and Frank, well, he's no looker, either. Frankie has light curly hair and dark eyes, and he's got a peaceful presence. When he cries, it's but a whimper. He takes to my breast like a duck do to water and he grows like a weed, fillin' out all over. Rosie too had herself a boy they call Jack, the day before me, and when we get together, them cousins play like they was brothers.

It don't take too long for Big Frank to start swattin' at me or givin' me a kick when I don't move fast enough. I stay outta his way much as possible, try to serve meals when he wants, but that man has it out for me. He's always complainin' he's takin' care of my farm, payin' my taxes, and I don't seem to be thankful. He sometimes looks at me like he don't know me, like he's confused why he's here with me. But his boy? The sun rises and sets on that baby. Big Frank always wants to know when he eats, why's he cryin', what am I doin' to him. And that baby, turns out he's my guardian angel. He's protectin' me, and Big Frank's always respectful when the baby's around. It took but one time Frank lifted his hand to me when Frankie was 'bout three. That boy done the oddest thing. He don't cry out or run to his mama. He goes over to his daddy, who's spittin' mad, and he says in his sweet baby voice, don't, daddy, don't. He takes his daddy by the hand and pulls him outside to look at the new litter of kittens in the barn.

After that, Big Frank, he don't ever lift a hand to me again. He just stopped talkin' to me. He'd just say, Frankie, tell your mama I'll be home at noon, or I'm headin' to town, let your mama know. Except for the times he forces hisself on me, we don't speak none. I know he hates me for the same reasons my daddy did. I just can't say what they are.

He still gives me three more baby girls, but they're all just like me and even their daddy sees this and don't pay them much attention. Frankie, though, he's different. He's got a light around him that make him look like he always shinin'. Even the sisters, they see this and they tell me, Francine, he's so smart, and handsome, too. He's gonna be somethin', maybe President or a movie star, he's got a special quality about him. Big Frank gets all puffed with pride because he sees it, too. Everybody who meets Frankie sees it. Now, I don't see nothin' but harm in tellin' a boy such things. He feels he's gotta live up to folk's expectations all the time, and for a child that's too big a cross to bear.

Frankie and them girls, they're all I care about. I know I ain't the best mama in the world, but I do the best I can. I tell them kids about their kin and how my mama woulda loved 'em. I tell them 'bout their daddy's brother who never come back from the war, and I tell them they livin' in their granddaddy's house that I grew up in. I tell stories of all my dead brothers and my sister and how we swam in the river when we was kids and how one day when they was small my older brother David shot my baby brother in the bottom with some buckshot and how my daddy tanned his hide. They loved hearin' the stories of when we was in trouble and would say to me, tell us more, Mama, tell us more. It was all I could give them kids—stories that weren't always nice as I made them to be, but them kids didn't need to know any more than what I done told them. They didn't need to know about the darkness that we lived in.

My little girls liked to hear 'bout the time Frankie got his finger pulled off, and I tell a long tale, full of oohin' and aahin'. I tell them how I gone and fainted and how the Old Doc tried to sew Frankie's finger back on. We remember when the finger didn't take and turned all green and gooey. It smelled like rottin' flesh, and finally Big Frank just had the doctor cut the bad part off. They like hearin' the blood and guts and I tell it like it's never been told before. I see Frankie smile at me like we got a secret, and I wink at him as he rolls on the floor pretendin' his finger still has blood spurtin' from it.

I known for a long time, since I started rememberin', where my life was headed. Sometimes I wish it to be different, but it can't be changed. I feel a force pushin' me in a way that I got no control over. I can't fight it and I give up tryin' long ago. I just go where it takes me and hope I'll be standin' for the end. I ain't too sad 'bout it. I seen it happen to my mama, and it ain't no surprise I be doing it too.

Big Frank always loved the drink, even when it weren't legal. I tell him that moonshine'll rot his gut, but he just looks away. He stays at Green's Tavern many a night, which I don't care nothin' about. After my last baby, he never come back to my bed, which don't make a woman feel too good even if she don't care much for her man. It's better to take a beatin' then have him actin' like you was dead. Like a ghost, I live with him. He walks right through me. He talks like I can't hear. I go through the motions of bein' his wife and a mama, but I ain't alive. My voice was never one to be heard, and even now, it echoes silently from the grave.

No one can save me, not even Frankie. I had hope for a time, but that didn't work out. He ain't got the strength, he's just a young man. He sees a darkness that sticks to my skin like glue, but he don't know how to help. Why you so sad, Mama, he say, why? I can't answer, I don't know. I shake my head and shoo him away, he's too young to see that he got a ghost for a mama. I don't know if Frankie's got any darkness. If he does, he's hidin' it real good. He wears such a beautiful coat it's too hard for me to see past it and find the ugliness beneath. All I tell my babies is that I'm their mama and I have love for them. They should remember that.

I last almost twenty years with Frank. My mama done better, but she's a stronger woman than her daughter. My days crawl by, my chores always comin' one after another, but I don't regret nothin'. Some days, usually when Frank's been gone, I even forget that I got the darkness, but it's just teasing me, waitin' for me to get comfortable before it rears its ugly head to remind me I ain't goin' nowhere.

I'm havin' one of them days, them good days, when the air smells like clean sheets and the sun warms your neck when you bend over to pick a spring flower. I've got energy like two, and I clean my house spic n' span, make a large pot of soup and finish all my laundry. Me and the girls play kick-the-can until Frankie comes back from Michigami on the beat-up old motorbike his daddy got him. He's been workin' with his cousin during the week, and we all miss him terribly and jump all over him with hugs and kisses when he gets off the scooter. It's Friday, so I know Big Frank won't be showin' his face till well after we've gone to bed, and he'll be sleepin' in the barn tonight.

After the girls get to bed, I have Frankie all to my lonesome. We sit together, not sayin' a whole lot, just lookin' out on the forest trees slow-dancin' in the breeze like they got nowhere to go. We make small talk of this and that, and all I wanna do is hear his voice. He tells me all about his cousins and the work they been doin' over in Michigami—he likes it real well over there. Then, all nervous-like, Frankie asks me, do you love my daddy? I open my mouth to say course I do, but the words don't come. I truly don't know how to answer my boy, and my brain begins to slow down like a machine comin' to an unhurried death, the motor just barely runnin'. For a short spell, I become nothin'. Then, without no warnin', my mind gets a new life like the devil himself come to save the day. My mind starts putterin', then gathers speed as that devil picks up the rocks of past hurts and throws them. They smash into my head one after another like a boxer gettin' a bad beatin' that he can't stop. I relive times I thought were gone forever, but that ole' devil wants to get one more lick in. He does, and when it's finally done I'm buried in stone, and all I can do is reach for a breath. I can't seem to get air, and I cry out to myself till I feel a hand on my shoulder and realize my boy is watchin' me. I hang my head, plum worn out from the silent outburst.

Frankie, he ain't heard nothin' but me moanin', and he says to me I'm sorry, Mama, I don't mean to pry. I bring my head up and look him in the eye. Tonight I can't speak nothin' but what's in my heart, and I finally say I don't rightly know if I love your daddy. I tell him that I got four beautiful children from him and for that alone, I'm thankful. I tell him I know the love a mama has for her babies, but I ain't sure what love is between a man and a woman. I seen the love on the movie screen and heard it on the radio, but I ain't never felt it for my very own. I tell him I wish I was stronger, but somethin' in me broke long ago and it weren't never able to be fixed. He's lookin' at me like he understands, but he's just a boy and I can't be puttin' this on him, and I'm sorry I said anythin'.

I change the subject and ask him about his sweetheart, the one he took to the dance. He says he's just friends with her, that she's different than people expect, but he ain't in love. Why, I tell him, one day, you'll find the perfect girl just for you. He says he likes a lot of girls, but don't plan on gettin' married or havin' any kids, not for a long time. I know he sees the hardship I got in my marriage, and he don't know it can be different. He don't know how a man and a woman can be good together, but I can't tell him, I don't know myself.

I look at him and wonder if he got the same darkness that I been carryin', but I can't see nothin'. I touch his arm and tell him he's the best thing that I ever did and I don't know how I woulda made it without him. We sit for a long spell, and it's only till I see his eyes half-closed that I can bear to let him go up to bed.

There's a beautiful wolf moon risin', and it makes me think of my granny. There's something special about a moon that's almost full, she done said. If you look real close, you see a big wolf a-howlin' to get out. I used to see it as a girl, but I don't see it none tonight. I sit there the whole of the night, drinkin' my coffee and countin' the stars in the sky. I get to over two hundred before I lose my place and think I been countin' the same ones over and over.

I see Big Frank's old Buick pull in the drive real late, but it's dark and he don't see me sittin' out on the porch. I watch him stumblin' and mutterin' to hisself as he makes his way to the barn. He stops before he goes in, and by the light of the wolf moon I watch him relieve himself and I have to cover my mouth lest the laughter escapes. I giggle to myself and pull my wrap tighter. Knowin' I seen him do this makes me feel like I got a secret on him.

I make fresh coffee when the sun comes up and don't feel the least bit tired. When Frankie gets up I ask him to check on his daddy, and when he comes back he says Big Frank's snorin' up a storm in the barn, it's a wonder he hasn't woken up all the neighbors.

After breakfast I ask him to run into town with the girls for some salt I need for cannin'. Sure, Mama, he says. You want me to take all them kids? If you don't mind, I tell him, and I give him some money I got saved and tell him to treat everyone to a nickel's worth of candy. The girls jump all over me and run out to Big Frank's car. Drive safe, I call out. You got all my babies. I will, he says, his handsome face smilin' back at me. I see him today, for the first time, as a man, and I wonder how I missed the change. See you soon, my boy calls out, and he leaves with my girls.

I sit at the table and even though the morning sun has filled the room, I light the kerosene lamp. I think 'bout what I missed in my life, and what I have. I ain't sad or nothin', it's just what my mind wants to remember. I seen my two sisters-in-law pass and one of their babies. I seen Frank's brother turn to preachin', and I seen Frankie with his first sweetheart. I think on how I ain't never been outside of two counties. I think on how I never been to school after I done turned twelve years. And I think on how I ain't never been kissed by a man.

But I am grateful for my time with the sisters and my babies, 'specially my Frankie. I ain't had so bad of a life.

I sit here, still as a mouse, thinkin' I stopped time, and only when I move will it start again. It's so quiet that it startles me when I think I hear Frankie callin' Mama, and I jump up, so surprised that I knock the lamp over. I watch as the flames follow the oil down the table and back up the hem of my skirt. I see the fire spread, catching the clean laundry on the table and exploding as the lamp bursts into flames. I wait as the heat fills the room and the smoke swirls around my head, pluggin' my nose and mouth. I hear screamin', and I stumble to the window and see my children runnin' back to their house. Frankie come back because he knows. But it's too late. I fall back into the burnin' room where the flames devour the world around me, and I know the same relief my mama did.

My daddy was right. I'd be burnin' forever in eternity, but I was at ease knowing I'd be in good company with my mama, and I hold tight to the pain as I pass through the gates of hell.

Chapter Seven

Adeline - 1939

Earl started his freshman year at Michigan State College in September of 1939, the same month that Germany invaded Poland and started what would become World War II. Our parents vowed that all their children would receive the higher education they had never had, and Earl was first in line, set to study agricultural engineering.

The whole family was anxious about having one of our own so far away. The threat of an impending conflict overseas cast an even more somber mood over his departure, as though the war machine could magically make him disappear and we would never see him again. My father made the long drive to East Lansing and helped him move into Wells Hall, where he lived with 250 other young men who attended MSC, and Earl began his college career in our state's capital.

Back on the home front, talk centered constantly on the war in Europe. Except for Earl, it was all my parents seemed eager to discuss. Mr. Bonmiller, Mama's boss at the paper, had retired after thirty-five years. His replacement, a much younger man named Mr. Elwin Leigh, had been so impressed by some current events pieces Mama had submitted that he'd promoted her to junior reporter, covering the local politics. After twenty years, she retired from her weekly *Women's Work* column and jumped into her new duties with a vengeance. Mama's enthusiasm and passion for anything other than her children was unusual, and we were in awe of her spirit and fortitude. She became a different person, immersing herself in any news that didn't concern baking soda or bread pudding. Daddy said that she reminded him of a girl he once knew in his youth, and it was only when my mother smiled that we understood he was speaking about her.

It seemed as though every month Germany invaded another European country, and war and the talk of it was the gloomy cloud overhead that never dissipated. The relentless gossip and rumor drained me. I grew restless and tired of it, and yearned for talk of anything but. I discovered a kindred spirit in my newfound heroine, Scarlett O'Hara. Her charm and confidence inspired me, and more often than not I found myself saying "fiddle-dee-dee!" when I was bored with a subject and ready to move on. I drew a parallel between her war and ours—the Germans and the Confederates blended together as the villains in the epic movie battle I imagined in my head.

Lucy and I had a longstanding argument as to who was more handsome, Clark Gable or Cary Grant. She preferred Grant's comical and wholesome appeal, while I favored the dark mystery of Gable's most famous character, Rhett Butler. This was an important issue, one that needed to be settled before I went to Hollywood to become a film star. I had to decide which gentleman I would like as my leading man.

"What about Tyrone Power?" she inquired, as we held our daily meetings after school in my room.

"I suppose he would do in a pinch, but Clark is really who I'm leaning toward," I answered, not wanting to be unfaithful to my crush. "He has the versatility to do comedy as well as drama."

"So does Cary," she insisted as she set her books on my nightstand and threw herself on my bed.

"Maybe so, Lucy, but I'm still partial to Clark. It's just my personal preference."

I had taken a job in January of 1940, the winter of my sophomore year, at the Bijou, the movie theater in town. It hadn't been difficult to convince my parents that Saturday afternoons were not spent doing schoolwork anyway, and that I could earn and save money by taking tickets at the local movie house. I had ulterior motives, of course, and would spend hours before and after my shift watching the pictures that came and went weekly. *The Wizard of Oz* was my favorite. When the picture went from black and white to Technicolor it was miraculous. The colors burst from the screen and brought the picture to life, changing my movie-going experience forever. Judy Garland was wonderful. She was my inspiration—until, of course, *Gone with the Wind* was released.

"You can't sing, anyway, Addie," Lucy reminded me. "How could you have played Dorothy?"

I contemplated this problem and conceded that my best friend was right. But Scarlett, that was another story. I knew her inside and out. I felt her very presence in everything I did, in every word I said.

"Do you think I resemble Vivien Leigh?" I asked Lucy of the actress who had made Scarlett famous. Lucy had gotten off at my bus stop one blustery winter day. Jack was to give her a ride home when his shift was done.

"You have the same hair color, I guess," she answered diplomatically. "But I think you're a bit taller. And maybe a bit more buxom," she added. "Besides, I think she cried in the scene where Rhett left." Lucy looked at me sternly. "You know you ain't prone to tears." She picked up my teddy bear from the bed and straightened his bowtie.

"I think those were crocodile tears," I muttered under my breath.

But she was right again. I had been misty a couple times in my life, but I wasn't a crier and never had been. That simply would have to change, and I vowed to start bawling at anything that was remotely sad, even if I had to pinch myself to get it started.

"How's Earl doing? Have you heard from him?" Lucy changed the subject and inquired after my brother, who had since returned to school after the winter break. He'd done well his first semester and had come home even more cocky and self-assured than when he left, if that was possible. His physique had filled out and his appearance was that of an adult—so much so that when he walked through the door after catching a ride home with a friend, my first thought was, "Who is that man?" College seemed to agree with him, and I knew Maude was set to go to nursing school the following year, but I wasn't sure how my parents would receive my big plans for going to Hollywood to star in films. I figured I would have a fight on my hands, but like Scarlett, I also figured tomorrow was another day. I would think about it then.

"He's fine," I answered. "He'll be home in a couple months for spring recess."

Lucy looked at the floor as she spoke. "He's really liking school, huh?"

I had a sneaking suspicion that they had something going on, something that I wasn't privy to, but she didn't share with me and I knew better than to ask. For being my closest friend, Lucy was very private and always had been. Her secrets ran deep—and, I suspected, dark—but I loved her like a sister, sometimes even more than Maude and Millie. She never spoke of anyone but Earl, and though she had been asked out by others, she always refused. But ever since he'd left for MSC, she'd been anxious and unsure about my brother, her confidence somehow shaken by his absence.

"I guess so," I replied, wishing I could reassure her of my brother's affections, but frankly, I didn't know where they were directed.

"It sounds like he's met lots of new people." She looked at me squarely, and I could almost hear her fear—"smart, rich girls"—in the words that she didn't say.

"Maybe," I answered. "But you know Earl. He's loyal to his friends and family here. This is his home, Lucy. Earl's not likely to forget that."

Lucy smiled at me. "You're right, Addie. I guess I'm a little green. It must be wonderful to be able to get away from… everything," she trailed off.

My heart went out to her. The Conklins' streak of bad luck had continued after Charlie's death with the fire that consumed Frankie's house and took his beloved mama. His kin had been forced to move to Michigami and in with Lucy's. The small house was nearly busting at the seams with the two families crammed in together.

"Well, I've got to be getting home. There's twice as much work now." She smiled weakly. "Did I tell you we're set to get the juice soon?" She put the bear down as gently as one would a baby and smoothed her skirt.

"That's wonderful. When?" We had had electricity for as long as I could remember, though many of our neighbors did not. Getting dressed and washing by candlelight or lantern had been the norm for Lucy her whole life.

"I'm not rightly sure. Soon, I hope." Lucy stood up and replaced the books that had fallen out of her bag. "I'll see you tomorrow, Addie. Jack's probably waiting for me." She kissed my cheek and walked downstairs, her yellow curls swaying under the red knitted cap she had made.

I watched through the window as she headed for the ranch to look for her brother. Jack and another fellow, José, a Mexican who had immigrated to the U.S., had begun working for my father full-time when Earl left for college. The fox operation had become fairly large, and Daddy was unable to handle all the work. He was getting older, and every now and then his back would act up, a lingering consequence of an accident he had had as a boy.

But he was lucky in other ways. He had come through the Depression financially unscathed. As he said, the rich still needed their fur coats and the poor still needed their horsemeat. I overheard him telling Mama that he figured the horsemeat he sold in five- and ten-pound packages wasn't always going to the dogs—that during the toughest times, our friends and neighbors might have made a meal from it.

Between my father, José, Jack, Earl, and sometimes Frankie, the work load was absorbed, and I didn't go out to the ranch much anymore. Jack had devised a gate system for any fox that burrowed from her pen, so us girls' job of chasing her was eliminated.

I lay back on my bed and thought about Lucy and her family. Jack was roughly Earl's age, and he had no chance for college. He was lucky he would get to finish high school in a couple months; his cousin Frankie had not been as fortunate. Frankie had left school after the fire and taken up doing odd jobs, some for my daddy, some for the local farmers. Lucy's lot was even worse. Her only chance of getting out of that house was to get married, and

I had the feeling she was counting on Earl to propose. Although I would be thrilled to have Lucy as my sister, I had no idea what Earl's thoughts were. He would never share them with me. I felt that it could all be settled so easily if Earl would just see that it was a perfect match, and that he should tell Lucy he would marry her when he finished school. It was so frustrating that people couldn't see, as I did, what was clearly the right thing to do. I thought about Scarlett and her determination to make things happen, to get what she wanted. I knew I could not be so bold—I had neither the experience nor the years to allow for that—but maybe I could work my will in a more subtle way.

"I've got an idea!" I gushed at the dinner table that evening. While my parents had been discussing the expulsion of Russia from the League of Nations for attacking Finland, I had been hatching my plan. "Daddy, why don't you let me drive to Michigan State to pick up Earl when the winter term ends?" I smiled brightly. "I'm a swell driver, and maybe someone could go with me." I scrunched my brow, pretending to think about it. "Maybe Lucy could go and keep me company. What do you think?"

"I think that ain't likely going to happen," my father said without skipping a beat.

"Addie, the drive there and back takes almost a day, and you aren't sure of the roads. Besides, you're only sixteen. You're too inexperienced." My mother passed the peas to Maude and smiled.

"There is such a thing as a map," I countered hotly. "And I'm sixteen and a half."

"Adeline, be careful of your tone," my father cautioned.

Millie scoffed under her breath. "Besides, Addie, what would you do if the tire blew out? How could you fix it?"

"Millie, you best stay out of this," I warned her. "This is none of your business."

"Well, she does have a point, Addie," Maude added, throwing her two cents in.

I glared at her. "Thank you for your support, Maude."

"Well, the fact of the matter is that Mother is right. You're too inexperienced." She nodded in Mama's direction.

"Thank you, Maude, Millie, for helping your mama and me out with the parenting." Daddy looked sternly over his glasses at them. "We are well-equipped to handle your sister." He looked at me. "Give me and Mother some time to talk about it, and maybe you and Lucy can go with me. Is that an answer more to your liking?" he teased.

"Oh, yes! Thank you, Daddy." I made a face at my sisters, wishing all the while that Lucy had a phone so I could call her and tell her the good news.

"Don't count your chickens before they hatch," Mama counseled as she apparently read my mind. "Nothing has been decided yet."

I didn't even mind that Maude and Millie were snickering behind their napkins. I knew there was a better-than-good chance that my father would take us with him, and the prospect of a trip with Lucy was exhilarating, even if Daddy would be sharing the ride with us. Once again, Scarlett had come through in a pinch.

Two days later, my parents agreed that Lucy and I could go with my father, so Mama wrote Earl to let him know we were coming. Lucy and I could talk of nothing else for the next eight weeks, and when Earl wrote back and said there was an end-of-term celebration dance, suggesting that maybe we could all go and he would get a date for me, the two of us were in heaven. That ship sailed, though, when my father said he had to be back as soon as possible and could not spare the extra time away. We were disappointed, but the dance had been the icing on the cake, and we were happy just to be going—Lucy especially so.

"What are you going to wear, Addie?" Lucy was more nervous than I had ever seen her, and was in a constant quandary about the upcoming excursion.

"I think I'll wear my yellow dress with the pink flowers. You don't think it's too summery, do you?"

"Oh, no, it's perfect. It shows off your figure very nicely." She pulled her hair back. "Up or down?"

"It looks nice either way, Lucy, but I think Earl prefers it down."

She looked up at me, surprised. "Did he tell you that?"

"No," I answered tentatively, not wanting to make something from nothing. "He just mentioned how nice it looked at the Harvest Moon Dance, that's all." That quickly settled the discussion, and we moved on to Earl's favorite foods and the large basket of goodies we would pack for the long trip.

Spring took its sweet time rolling in that year. The snow had barely melted when our departure date finally rolled around. The late April morning was chilly, and we were glad we had spent the previous afternoon packing the car with blankets, food baskets, and bottles of milk and water. Lucy had been allowed to sleep over. We had spent most of the night giggling in nervous anticipation until my mother finally came in to warn us that if we didn't get some rest, we might not be awake to leave. We quickly fell asleep, but were up before the rooster crowed and were ready and waiting at the kitchen table when my father came down.

"I just need to get the fellas set up before we go," he explained as he pulled his coat on. "Frankie's comin' over to help Jack, and I want to tell them boys a couple things. I'll be quick, so you girls be ready."

He looked at us, sitting in our coats and boots, handbags on our lap, and laughed. "I guess that ain't a problem. I'll be right back." He walked out, chuckling as the door banged shut. My mother appeared to set us up with coffee and some warm rolls before we left.

We were quietly discussing our plans for the day when Frankie came racing up to the door and opened it wide enough to announce, breathlessly, that we had best come out to the ranch quickly. My father had hurt his back.

Lucy, Mama, and I hurried along behind him and found Daddy lying in a pile of straw, moaning.

"Jack, Frankie, grab his arms and help him to his feet." My mother called out directions calmly, but her voice was tight with worry. "José, get the animals back from the door. Addie and Lucy, make sure the path is clear to the house and up to our room."

We all scrambled to follow my mother's orders. This was not the first time that my father's back had gone out, and we all knew the routine. He would spend the next week or so recovering in bed, slowly make his way downstairs, and then a few days later make his way back to the ranch. It would be a good month before he felt right again. It was a slow process, and he would be groggy the first couple days with the pills the doctor had already given him for the overwhelming pain that would rack his body.

I realized that my father would not be making the trip to MSC; he was in no position to drive so far. I speculated as to how Earl would get home. I wanted desperately to ask, but knew that I'd receive only a curt answer from Mama, so I bit my tongue.

After my mother found Daddy's pills and got him settled, she asked Frankie and Jack to come upstairs and talked with them for a bit. Lucy and I shrugged our shoulders, wondering what they were planning, and sat down at the kitchen table to wait, fidgeting all the while.

When they came downstairs, we sat up straight and waited for the news. By this time it was past eight o'clock and we should have been well on our journey.

"Your father is in a bad way," my mother announced to Lucy and me. "Obviously he cannot make the trip, so he has asked Frankie to make the drive with you."

Lucy and I looked at each other, eyes wide. I was distressed about Daddy, but if this was the result of the accident, well...

"Frankie has agreed. Jack and José will take care of the ranch." She sighed and wiped her hands on her apron. "We would like you to stay overnight at the college. We don't want anyone driving in the dark, and you're already leaving too late to make it back at a decent hour." She looked at me when she spoke next. "Please ask Earl to have one of his female friends put you up for the night. And please don't take advantage of this situation in any way. Do I make myself clear?"

We both answered, "Yes, ma'am," as we stood up hurriedly. Lucy and I tried to control ourselves, but it was difficult not to jump for joy at the prospect of having the whole weekend to ourselves with Frankie as our chaperone. I couldn't have imagined a better way to get to Lansing than having Lucy's handsome cousin chauffeur us. Frankie had often come into the movie theater on Saturday evenings, almost always with a different pretty girl on his arm, but he was nothing but polite and went out of his way to ask me how I was. I was anxious and excited at the same time about the opportunity to spend so many hours in the car with him. This was a perfect way to get to know him better.

As we hastened to leave, Lucy took hold of my arm and whispered in my ear to go grab a couple of extra dresses. It was only when she murmured "The dance!" that I understood that the end-of-semester celebration was now a possibility.

This latest realization tipped the limit on my scale of opportunity and turned my mother lode of excitement into a mother lode of anxiety. Would Frankie think he had to be my date for the dance party? What if he didn't want to? Lucy would be with Earl all weekend, and I would be... with Frankie? Frankie had unsuspectingly invaded the plans, taken them over, and I was unprepared for the implications that had unfolded. Why did my father have to pick this day to throw his back out? The very wish that had been mine for so long came true too suddenly. I was ill-equipped to both juggle my emotions and organize them in a way that would offer Frankie a glimpse into the kind of girl he might find appealing—whatever that might be.

Lucy sat in the middle during the car ride, and she and Frankie chatted on endlessly while I tormented myself as I pretended to gaze out the window. I knew I was overreacting, but I couldn't get past the fact that there was a possibility that Frankie and I would be going to a dance together—oddly enough, a situation I had daydreamed about only a couple months ago. The phrase "Be careful what you wish for" played over and over in my head, accompanied by the annoying refrain, "I told you so." I cursed the individuals who had had enough time to come up with these infuriating sayings.

My usually confident self had taken the day off and been replaced by a self I'd not met before, a nervous Nelly self that was as timid and insecure as a country mouse in the city. A burning itch worked its way up my arms and spread across my thumping chest and face, heating my whole body and leaving me feeling as though every breath was an effort.

When Lucy turned to ask me if I was hungry, she gasped. "Addie! What's wrong? Are you feeling bad? Your face looks like it's afire!"

Her concern was genuine and so was Frankie's. He pulled off the road and told us to get out and get a breath of fresh air. We stepped out of the car, and I excused myself as I scurried out into the pasture spreading in front of me. The cool morning air lingered, but the sun was burning through the early clouds. The fresh breeze that blew through filled my lungs, salving the irritation on my skin and soothing my frazzled nerves.

I heard footsteps, and when I turned, Frankie stood there with a bottle of water.

"Addie, have a drink. It'll calm your person."

He handed me the water and I drank, the cold liquid flowing through my veins and replacing the hot blood that had only just scalded me. He was right. The rash started to dissipate, and I began to regain my composure as I walked carefully around the cow patties and back towards the automobile. Frankie held open my door and I climbed in. Even when Lucy said she was going to lay out in the back and rest, I held my own.

That kind of nervousness was uncharacteristic of me, and I reminded myself that Frankie was just like any other person who put their pants on one leg at a time. Sure, I'd had a crush on him ever since I'd handed his father his finger on that day so many years ago, but it wasn't like I didn't know him. I had even been in the car with him on the way to pick up Cross-eyed Mary last year. We had sung together. He was like… kin.

"How's your finger?" I asked bravely as we started on our way.

"It ain't grown back yet." He smiled as he took his hand off the wheel and wiggled the stump at me.

Could I have asked a dumber question? I felt my face begin to heat up again and decided my best bet was not to say anything. If I couldn't ask an intelligent question, I'd be better off sitting in an uncomfortable silence than looking like an idiot. I resigned myself to the status of a deaf mute.

We rode without speaking for a few miles, but as the car bumped along, passing by farms with only an occasional cow taking notice, a voice in my head went from a hint of a murmur to a stage whisper that I couldn't ignore.

"Why, I do declayuh, Miss Adeline, that I nevah expected to see you so scahred of a silly boy."

There could be no mistaking the honey-tinged southern accent, and I felt the presence of my mentor, Scarlett, come to help the handicapped and offer advice.

"Oh, Scarlett," I answered silently, *"I can't believe it either. All my common sense has flown the coop, and I'm stuck like a pig in the mud. What do I do?"*

"Well, first of all, you need to sit up right straight and square your shoulders, Miss Addie. Y'all look like you been shot," she told me.

I realized I had slid down in the seat and was hunched over like an elderly lady sitting by the window watching birds for the afternoon. I sat up straight and took a deep breath, glancing over at Frankie and wondering if he could sense the internal discussion taking place, but he was maneuvering the car through some fallen branches in the road and was oblivious to my imaginary conversation.

"That's bettah already." I imagined Scarlett smiling, her charming dimples setting off her sparkling green eyes. *"Now, the way I see this here predicament is that y'all got your heart set on this young man and you're just looking for him to give you some notice. Well, Miss Addie, a man's like a fish in a pond. You have to dangle some bait in front of him so he knows you're even a-fishin'. Now, put a smile on and show me your best fishin' bait."* She became serious and nodded at me to begin.

I wasn't used to having to work for my love interest. Jack had come without any pomp and circumstance, but Frankie was a different story. I batted my eyelashes like crazy and gave the cow outside the window my coyest look.

"I suppose that's a start." I felt her scrunch her nose and could sense her

disappointment. *"Y'all need to remember you're not clearin' grit out of your eye—you're a beautiful doe who slowly bats her beautiful doe eyes, then looks bashfully away."* She demonstrated for me, fan in hand, smiling demurely as she gently batted her eyes before shyly looking away. It did remind me of the first scene in the movie, in which Scarlett captivated the Tarleton twins with her charms.

"Why don't y'all try it that way?" she suggested.

I could see another pasture up ahead and a herd of cows. As we passed, I made eye contact with a large brown heifer, smiled sweetly, batted my lashes softly, then looked away unhurriedly.

"That was perfect," she praised, clasping her hands together under her chin. *"Now y'all need to practice that with your beau. Good luck, honey. I've got to go. Mammy's a-callin'."*

Scarlett was gone, and once again it was me and Frankie, alone in the front seat.

"Hey, Addie, how'd you like *Of Mice and Men*?" Frankie asked unexpectedly. He had come to the Bijou a few weeks before with a shapely blonde on his arm.

"I loved it," I replied, grateful that he had not only broken the silence but also asked me a direct question.

"Did you think George did right by shooting Lenny? I just don't know if I could do such a thing to my best friend." Frankie shook his head as if trying to erase the scene from his memory.

This is it, I told myself as I readied my person for what would become my first planned flirt.

"It seems like he really had no other choice," I answered as I looked over at Frankie with smoldering eyes, made contact, then looked away slowly. I let my eyes wander back to his gaze as I postured for my next statement. "It was either that, or watch his best friend be lynched by the mob."

Frankie looked bewildered, like he wasn't sure if what he'd seen was really what he'd seen, but it was enough. When he glanced over at me it was with a new-found interest, and I knew I had hit my mark.

"I suppose so," Frankie answered in a voice that told me my wiles had worked. I could tell that his attention had wandered from the movie to the seductive pose I had adopted. A feeling of control inched its way back into my awareness, my confidence soared, and I said goodbye to the pitiful girl who had originally occupied my seat.

"I can tell you this, Frankie," I said, saying his name with commanding conviction, "that was one difficult scene to watch, when George had to shoot Lenny. I had to cover my eyes each time I saw it—and I saw the picture four times." I had slipped into pleasant conversation so easily that my nerves didn't even tingle. The car had warmed to a pleasant temperature, the morning sun high in the sky, and the sunlight came streaming through the windows.

"I just can't get that picture outta my head. It's like I feel so dang helpless, like I want so bad to see Lenny be treated rightly, but after what he did to Curley's wife… it's like there ain't no fair and right justice. Know what I mean?" He glanced over.

"Yeah. It's like a big ball of yarn that keeps getting knotted and tangled as you roll it up, and there's no way to even find the beginning, to start over. It's very frustrating." Boldly, I reached over and touched his arm.

"Yeah. You put into words the pictures I was seein' in my head." He turned and looked at me with a gleam in his eye. "You're smart, Adeline. I like smart girls."

"Are all those girls you bring to the shows smart?" I ventured to tease, finding a new security in my ability to hold his attention.

"Well…" He smiled brightly and then laughed—"I also like pretty ones."

I laughed along with him, blushing modestly and hoping that he thought me both. Frankie had such a pleasant disposition, in light of all the bad luck his family had been through recently. I was curious about his mama and the fire, but Lucy had said it'd hit him hard, and my common sense told me it was none of my business to bring it up. I was also enjoying the light, easy conversation we were having and didn't want to spoil the pleasurable mood.

Frankie was quiet for a moment, and then in a hushed tone he asked, "Do you think that if Lenny woulda killed a Negro woman, there woulda been such a hoopla?"

The thought had never occurred to me. I had to think for a bit before I answered.

"I can't rightly say, Frankie. I have to wonder how far a mob of black men, hunting down a white man, could have gotten without some kind of setback arising. I don't know if I've ever heard of such a thing happening. What made you think of that?" The question was interesting, and I enjoyed the thought process it challenged me with. It also reminded me of the Jim Crow laws that were still in place some seventy years after the Civil War, though not so much in Michigami.

"I don't know. I was just thinking about how unjust our world is sometimes. Look at them Jews in Germany. That crazy Hitler has really got it out for them. Them and the Negroes, they got it real bad over there. Seems like the world's done moved in the wrong direction." He shook his head and slowed down as a flock of geese crossed the road up ahead.

"Do you think we'll get drawn into the war?"

"I can't say. I hope not."

"Would you join the service?" I asked.

"I guess if I had to. I ain't crazy about the idea."

"My parents don't support the war at all. They don't believe in it," I admitted. Even though we were raised to be peace-loving folks, I wasn't so sure that fighting the Nazi regime was wrong, but this was a thought I kept strictly to myself.

"Sometimes it takes a fight to right a cause. Look at the Civil War. If that didn't happen, we might still have slaves, and that ain't even remotely a just cause. I can't say I like war or the idea of it much, but I do think there's times when there ain't no other way. Appears some folks have forgotten we're all just people."

"It's strange," I added, "that we don't take notice of an animal's color. It doesn't matter if your cow is black or brown, but somehow a person's color, or for that matter their gender, makes them less of a person." I was thinking that it had been fewer than twenty years since women had received the right to vote, and then only after a long, hard fight. It had never been offered to us—it had needed to be taken.

"Would you ever marry a Negro?" Frankie looked at me seriously.

Frankie's questions were complicated, and the answers in my heart didn't seem to be the answers I wanted to give. "Probably not," I replied truthfully.

"Now, after everything you done told me, how can you say that?"

"I… just don't know, Frankie. You're asking me something I've never even thought about. I can't answer. I just can't." It was uncomfortable, having Frankie quiz me and feeling like I failed.

"That's all right, Addie. It ain't no big deal. I was just curious." He glanced over at me, and his smile set things right.

"Would you?" I asked, turning the tables.

"What?"

"Would you marry a Negro girl?"

"That would depend."

"On what?"

"On whether she was smart." He looked at me and winked before adding, "Or pretty."

We both chuckled, and I acknowledged privately that he was as charming as he was handsome. I couldn't have been happier in any other place than right there with him.

"Hey, Frankie, whatever happened to Mary? You know, the girl you took to the dance last fall." She had disappeared soon after the dance, never to ride the bus again, and no one seemed to know what had happened.

"Her uncle inherited some property in Wisconsin, so they up and moved." He stared straight ahead, and I couldn't detect whether it bothered him or he was just passing on information.

"That was one fun dance," I reminisced, remembering back to when I had had no worries, back to when Jack was still my friend, back to before tragedy had struck the Conklin family.

"It sure was," he said softly, and we sat silently, our memories drifting back to a time we could now only wish for.

We were jolted back to the present when we heard a loud *pop* and my side of the car seemed to sink a couple of inches. Frankie held tight to the wheel as the car veered sharply to the right, making a deep, pounding thump that slowed and finally stopped as we coasted to the side of the road and came to a halt.

"What happened?" Lucy had awoken and was sitting up in the back, rubbing her eyes.

"I think it's a flat tire. Damn," Frankie swore as he got out of the car and came around to my side. "Sure is," he called out. "You gals are gonna have to get out while I fix the darn thing."

Lucy and I huddled together as we stood at the side of the road. In the car the sunlight had been bright and warm, but outside under the shade of the large oaks that lined the country road, the air had a bite. We blew on our hands and rubbed them together as Frankie brought out the tools needed for his project. The cool wind blew around our dresses, creeping up our legs, and we jumped from one foot to the other to shake off the cold.

We were all grateful when a passing farmer stopped and asked if we needed assistance. Changing a tire wasn't easy. It took all of Frankie's and the farmer's strength to jack up the car and replace the tire with the spare my father had recently checked and deemed satisfactory. Lucy and I quietly discussed what a horrible mess we would have been in, had Frankie not been with us. For the first time that morning, I thought about my father and wondered how he was doing.

It was well past noon before the tire was replaced and the farmer was on his way. We huddled in the car and ate our cold sandwiches. We still had a ways to go, probably 65 miles or so, to the campus, and I knew that Lucy was desperate to get there and make the dance. We finished our lunch quickly and continued on our way, full and warm once again, and this time I sat in the middle, nestled between the two cousins.

We soon turned off the bumpy road and onto the smooth Highway 27 that would take us downstate. Absorbed in our own thoughts, we all sat quietly, and the warm sun and monotonous sounds of the road soon lulled me into a light sleep. We had spent most of the previous night chatting, and with all I had put myself through earlier, it didn't take much before I faded. I felt my head drop against Frankie's shoulder. When he didn't move, I didn't either, and I drifted off, wondering whether Scarlett would have approved of my performance. The next thing I remember was Lucy gently shaking me to let me know we were there.

MSC's campus was bustling with young men carrying piles of books or bags slung carelessly across their shoulders, whistling and calling out farewells to their friends and colleagues. Our traveling party was in awe of the scene set out before us. The coeds exuded an air of confidence and self-assurance that was obvious and intimidating to our country bumpkin selves. We needed to get our footing—and we did, when we stopped a couple of fellows to ask directions and they gave Lucy and me the once-over, asking us if we were attending the dance that evening. We giggled softly and answered coyly that we might, before Frankie interjected that we needed to find my brother and get the directions, please.

We dug our heels in when we reached my brother's dormitory and a group of young men, led by Earl, gathered around the car, wrangling over who would open the door. Earl announced that it was his girl and the others backed away, but Lucy took her time getting out, her slender leg held out daintily as she waited for Earl to help her. It was obvious that my brother was proud to be her beau, and I could sense her lost self-assurance returning as the young men of Wells Hall expressed their approval of his choice.

Young women were a minority on the campus. MSC was a farming school and the majority of the students were boys like Earl, first-generation coeds, their parents beaten down by war and depression, wanting their children to have a better life. Females usually attended a smaller college that graduated nurses and teachers, so it was fairly uncommon for a girl to attend a four-year university, especially one that specialized in agriculture or business. But there were some young pioneers of the feminist movement that had forged a path through the male-dominated world of college education, and MSC's female enrollment had increased, especially since the school had recently added an unrivaled Home Economics program. Morrill Hall, or the "hen coop," as it was known, was on the other side of campus, and it was there that Lucy and I would lay our heads that night, with Earl's roommate Harold's girlfriend.

Lucy and Earl made a handsome couple—he was tall and broad-shouldered, she slim, blonde, and blue-eyed. They held court as we traversed the campus, and Frankie and I followed behind, content with our comfortably shielded subordinate position. I can say in all honesty, though, that I garnered my fair share of attention. More than once I heard catcalls and low whistles. The rest of the afternoon was spent touring the campus and meeting Harold's girlfriend Anne, the gregarious redhead from Grosse Pointe who would be offering us a bed for the night.

After a quick supper at the commissary in the dorm, Lucy, Anne, and I cleaned up and met the fellows in the lobby of Wells Hall for the Last Chance Dance. The night sky was frosty and clear, but we brushed off the cold, our excitement racing through our blood and warming our insides as we hooked arms with our dates and headed to the Pavilion, where the dance would be held. As we walked to the auditorium, Anne explained this was actually not the big dance of the year. The J-Dance, sponsored by the juniors, was in February.

"It's very expensive," she explained. "And it's held at the Hotel Lansing, downtown. But it's absolutely magnificent. I adored going."

Anne was very sophisticated. Her father was a surgeon and her background of money and pedigree was apparent in every word she spoke. She was friendly and unassuming, but Lucy and I were intimidated by her class and upbringing and offered only commentary to her chatter, preferring to let her stand in the spotlight.

"How nice," we murmured. "It sounds lovely."

"Oh, it is." She smiled as her name was called out by a beautiful platinum blonde in a stunning red dress. "Laureen! You look marvelous." Anne turned to Lucy and me. "Will you excuse me, please? I haven't seen my friend in ages."

Before we could answer, Anne was off, and we turned back to the fellows standing behind us. Earl and Harold were lounging against a banister, their long legs casually crossed, and when Earl pulled Lucy over next to him, Frankie and I were left standing by ourselves, unsure of our place in this foreign environment.

Frankie leaned in and whispered in my ear. "You wanna dance, Addie?"

"Sure," I replied, thankful that we could do anything besides stand out like a sore thumb.

He took my hand and we walked out to the large floor, merging with the collection of dancers that swayed to the big band sounds of the Marcus Mendel Orchestra, a local favorite, as Anne had previously informed us. He pulled me in close, closer than I would have expected, but I found it more thrilling than frightening and went along without protest.

Having Frankie's arms wrapped so tightly around me and his face so close to mine offered me the opportunity to show him that I was no longer a young girl, but a young woman who understood the ways of romance. I didn't need any of Scarlett's advice. I knew intuitively what I was doing, and when I breathed softly into his ear that I was having a wonderful time, he gently buried his face in my hair.

He drew me in even closer, and his hands pressing on my back conveyed his desire as they followed my spine, gently pressing on each bone, exploring the contours of a mysterious sanctuary yet unavailable to him. My head on his shoulder, we swayed in time to the music, rehearsing the rituals of suppressed adult love that had yet to be let loose.

After a couple of dances, he guided me off the floor. "I need some fresh air, Addie. That okay with you?"

"Of course," I replied, and followed him out of the auditorium and into the dark of the chilly night. The break was rejuvenating, and as we leaned against the stone rail, I closed my eyes and put my head back, taking pleasure in the cold air that surrounded us.

I felt Frankie's hand gently touch my face, then my throat, following the curve of my neck and sliding down to the top of my dress before he placed his lips on mine and kissed me fervently, his arms wrapped around me. Frankie's presence was vast and flowing—somehow he invaded the empty space around me, moving like languid honey. He found every empty nook and cranny and filled them, taking me over.

Breaking away from him was not easy, but the footsteps and chatter of others out for a breath of fresh air forced us apart. We hurried back inside, our desire postponed by the invading company and the frosty breeze that was no longer invigorating. Earl was hopping mad and gave me the business for disappearing without telling him. He shot Frankie a look of warning, but Frankie seemed miles away, and I don't think it even registered with him that Earl was upset.

After Earl's outburst, I was careful not to let Frankie kiss me, but we danced, bodies pressed together, for the rest of the evening. When the night came to an end and we retired to Anne's dorm, I didn't sleep at all. I couldn't. I relived every moment of our time spent out on that cold balcony, the thrill from his kiss still lingering. I was sure this was the beginning of something wonderful.

We returned to Michigami the next day, Earl driving with Lucy cuddled up next to him and Frankie and I in the back, discreetly holding hands. When we got back to the house, Frankie left abruptly, citing a need to help his daddy with something, and I was somewhat surprised when he didn't make any plans with me.

The knot in my stomach got bigger when I didn't see or hear from him all that week. I worked at the Bijou the following Saturday and held my breath every time I looked up to sell a ticket, hoping that Frankie would show with excuses beyond reproach as to why he hadn't been in touch.

He finally did show, just as I was finishing my shift, but he had a small brunette trailing slightly behind. I was flabbergasted. Why would he torture me like that? Had I just imagined our intense connection the week before? Was he that unfeeling, that he could parade some… *girl* right under my nose and think I wouldn't care?

"Hi, Addie. Two, please," he said softly as he laid his dollar on the counter.

I moved in slow motion, taking the money, giving him his change, and pushing the tickets through the slot in front, my brain fuzzy with trying to make sense of this bizarre situation.

"Enjoy the show," I managed to squeak as my heart took a beating.

He looked over his shoulder apologetically as he and his date entered the theatre. I recoiled as I watched him hold the door open for her.

My shift soon ended, and I wandered in a daze back to the rear of the theatre where I kept my bicycle. I tried to sort through the clutter of thoughts that clouded my head as I began walking the bike down the road home. Nothing made any sense to me and I was forced to come up with various hypotheses as to what had happened. I wouldn't accept the most obvious—that Frankie didn't like me. Every bone in my body knew that he had feelings for me, that he was attracted to me. I knew it by the way he'd held me, the way he'd kissed me. I was convinced that such feelings could not be forged, and I pressed on in my reasoning, sifting through the myriad of possible excuses he might offer for seeming such a cad. Maybe the girl was a friend? Perhaps she was even a relative I had never met? But if this was the case, then why be so secretive? Why not introduce us? Maybe he had already been seeing her and was trying to break it off. But why take her to a picture show to do it? Was he just mean? I had a hard time believing this. I had known his family too long not to have seen that behavior before.

My walk home ended before I had even an inkling of an idea as to why Frankie had shown up at my movie theater with another girl.

The week dragged by, pulling me unwillingly along. My preoccupation with my personal mystery took precedence over everything—school, chores, even my friendship with Lucy. I was too embarrassed to ask her outright if Frankie had another girlfriend, especially after our display at the dance. Now that Earl was home, she was caught up with him anyway. Saturday rolled around, and I couldn't help but anticipate the same scene as the week before. I dreaded going to work, hoping I would get sick or break my arm—anything that would prevent additional heartache.

Frankie showed up again, this time alone and with an explanation.

"Addie, can you have a soda with me after you finish?" he asked. "I can meet you at the five-and-dime."

I wanted so bad to shout out, "Are you crazy?", but I didn't. Setting aside my self-respect, I nodded, and twenty minutes later I found myself facing him, a watered-down Coca-Cola in front of me.

He looked off into the distance uneasily as he cleared his throat. "I know it weren't the best idea to show up at the Bijou last week. I'm sorry, Addie. But I had asked Peggy Louise to the show before me and you... well, before we went to pick up Earl."

"Why didn't you tell me that, Frankie?" I asked, relieved that I had been on the right track with my assumptions.

"Well, it ain't like you and me are going steady. It seemed a funny thing to tell you. I just figured it weren't no big deal." He drummed his fingers on the counter.

Frankie's explanation stung more than I expected. It wasn't really the explanation. It was the crass delivery of the very words that were supposed to make me feel better. Normally I would have let my position be known loud and clear, but I didn't know how far I could push with Frankie before he would fade away. I wasn't willing to take any chances.

"It's not," I said with false nonchalance. "It doesn't matter to me. You're free to do what you want, Frankie, just like I am. I'm not your boss."

"I'm glad you feel that way, Addie. I knew you was different." He smiled at me and took a long swig of his Coke. "Hey, you want to go for a motorbike ride?"

I knew my father would not be happy to see me riding on the back of Frankie's bike, but if I never asked him, he could never say no.

"I would love to," I replied, finishing my drink and standing up.

"Ah… not right now," he frowned. "I meant some other time. Maybe next Friday?"

"Oh, yeah, sure." I mentally kicked myself. Why would I think he meant now? "Um… Frankie? You'd better pick me up at the end of my drive. I'm not sure what my daddy would say."

"No problem, Addie. I'll see you next Friday—around six?" His handsome face beamed. "At the end of your drive."

We both laughed as he said goodbye and left me sitting at the soda counter of the five-and-dime, wondering what in the heck had just happened. There had been no rhythm to our encounter. It had been a staggered exchange punctuated by misunderstandings and confusion, exactly the opposite of our time spent together at the dance.

All week I waited impatiently for Friday, hoping I wouldn't run into Frankie, lest he change his mind. I argued with Maude and Millie over nothing and went out of my way to make sure Jack knew I would be seeing Frankie in a few days.

"I think that's great," he told me.

But it only made me feel worse, not better. I half expected Jack to tell me not to go, that Frankie was not my type.

Friday did come. As I hopped on the back of the motorcycle, my arms wrapped around Frankie's waist, a sense of guilt and wrongdoing passed briefly over me, reminding me of my deceit, but I shrugged it off and forgot all about it as Frankie steered the bike out onto County Road. It was a perfect spring night in Michigan, and even though my traveling career was limited, I was sure there was nowhere as pretty as the mitten-shaped state in May. The summer snow of fragrant apple blossoms drifted down whenever the wind picked up, and we rode under a canopy of oaks, the great trunks lined up along the road like soldiers, their limb-rifles saluting us as we tooled along. Frankie yelled back into the wind every now and then, inquiring as to how I was doing, and his concern bolstered my belief that my previous trepidation was to be ignored.

Frankie drove eight miles out to the public beach at Lake Michigami. The park was deserted. We jumped off the bike and walked down to the water shimmering in the late sun's glow. The ducks were gathering in their young and the grasshoppers had begun their nightly symphony.

I felt a change come over Frankie. He slipped back into the Frankie I'd seen at the dance. We held hands and watched as a deer and her fawn scrutinized us from the edge of the wood, waiting until they deemed us harmless before turning away.

We pulled off our shoes and dug our feet into the sand, the waves calmly traveling back and forth, the sound tranquil and methodical in its simplicity. I glanced at Frankie's profile as he tossed some loose stones into the water, wondering what he was thinking about. I couldn't read him for the life of me, and his paradoxical actions kept me continually guessing as to his plan. This must be love, I thought. Why else would my heart beat so and my stomach work its way into such a knot of apprehension?

Scarlett called out to me from my subconscious, reminding me to use the charms that had previously been so successful in garnering Frankie's attention. Sure enough, when I leaned back on my elbows, shaking out my hair and giving him my most beguiling smile, he noticed and looked over at me.

"Addie, you're so pretty," he said straightforwardly as he leaned over to kiss me.

We found ourselves back in the same situation we had been in at the college dance and the passion returned, stronger than ever. I was comfortable up to a point, but things switched gears a few minutes later and I found myself having to slow the speeding car that I had thought I was driving.

"Frankie," I managed to say as I pushed him gently away. "I can't breathe very well. Can we take a break?" I sat up and brushed the sand from my arms.

Frankie sat back, looking at me a bit like a wolf eyes a lamb, but he acquiesced, sitting up himself and moving over, away from me, just a bit. He reached in his back pocket and pulled out a small flask, opened it, and took a drink.

"Want some?" he asked, holding out the flask.

"Oh... um... no thanks." I wasn't sure what I should do. Did girls drink when they went out on dates? I was pretty confident I knew the right answer—and I knew what my parents would say. But the small voice in my conscience fell on my own deaf ears as I changed my mind and reached for the flask.

"Sure, why not?"

Frankie smiled as I hesitantly took a small sip of the burning whiskey.

"Delicious!" I exclaimed as I wrinkled my nose. Frankie and I giggled as he took back the bottle.

"What do you want to do when you finish high school, Addie?" He pushed his heels through the sand as he spoke.

"I want to go to Hollywood and be a movie star."

"That sounds great." He perked up and turned to me. "How you gonna get there?"

"I don't know, maybe take a train. I haven't told my parents yet so I'm not sure how they're going to take it." I sighed, knowing it would not be an easy undertaking.

"Well, you might just have to go without telling them," he replied.

"Maybe." I couldn't imagine leaving my family without saying where or what I was doing. My parents would be sick with worry, and I had no bone to pick with them.

"Wouldn't that be great, to travel 'cross the country, seein' all the swell stuff on the way, like the Grand Canyon and the Hoover Dam?" Frankie became excited as he spoke. "You could sleep out under the stars, catch your breakfast from the rivers, and make your way to the big city." He turned to look at me. "You could be a movie star, Addie."

He had said all the right things. "Do you think, Frankie?"

"Oh, yeah. You're prettier than any of them movie stars I seen at the Bijou.

And you got a figure like a movie star—you bein' so tall and… curvy-like."

I loved Frankie beyond expression for saying the words I so wanted to hear. Why his approval meant so much to me, I can't say, but I didn't care. I had it, and it gave me the assurance that I could be bold, that I could say anything.

"Do you want to come with me? Do you want to come to California, Frankie?"

"I think I might just do that," he replied as he nodded his head, thinking about the proposed plan.

The thought that Frankie and I could be together was all I needed to start me on a new course. From then on, everything I did centered on being with Frankie and doing what he wanted. We saw the movies he wanted and we listened to the music he picked out. I didn't mind. I enjoyed his command. I had always made my own choices, and it was pleasurable giving that up for the man I loved.

I know my daddy didn't care much for Frankie. I know he thought Frankie was too unreliable and somehow not good enough for me, but he didn't know him like I did. It was a good thing when Frankie started at the filling station his father had purchased, and quit the farm. I didn't want any friction, especially with Jack added to the mix.

I spent my summer taking care of Frankie. He could be moody at times, no doubt from thinking of the pain in his life, and I respected the time he needed alone. The many times he was late or couldn't make our plans, I went looking for him. I knew that he needed me, needed to know that I would always be there, especially during the bleakest of moments.

That September, as Earl and I both began our junior year, he at MSC and I at Midland High School, Maude also started her higher education at Delta College for Women in Midland. She was determined to be a nurse, and with the impending war, it was a suitable as well as a noble profession. Earl, having turned twenty-one, was forced to register for the draft, which did not sit well with my mother and father at all. Having come of age, Earl was legally able to do what he pleased, however, and he explained to them that he felt it was his duty, that he was an American willing to fight if called upon. My parents were despondent. My mother wrote a series of unpopular essays that threatened her position at the paper. In the end, Earl got his way and my parents were forced to accept that their eldest had his own opinions—opinions that differed significantly from theirs.

After having witnessed the drawn-out battle that took place between my brother and my parents, I was less than eager to bring up the idea that I would be moving to California when I graduated. Frankie wanted me to quit school and leave that fall, but I was just seventeen and I knew for a fact that my father would track me down and bring me home, sparing no expense to do so. I urged Frankie to be patient, that winter was coming on anyway and I needed more time to save my money. He insisted that he could support us, that his job as a mechanic could get him work anywhere. I was reluctant to rely on that—on him—just yet.

The winter of 1941 brought news of heavy fighting in England, and the rumor of war threatened to become a reality. Franklin D. Roosevelt began his unprecedented third term as President. His fireside chats drew my aunts and parents together to listen to his forecasts of the United States' impending involvement in the conflict. Times were uncertain for everyone and we all waited anxiously, anticipating bad news every time the phone rang.

Frankie's moods became more obvious that winter. As he drifted, I felt an urgent need to pull him nearer, that if I didn't he might somehow drift away. I had held him off physically for close to a year, but he was growing impatient and I was running out of excuses.

A month or so shy of our one-year anniversary, Frankie and I took the long drive back to his childhood home in Roscommon County. The new owners of the property had yet to demolish the charred remains of the house where his mother had met her death. It stood, an ominous icon, as it had since the day of the fire.

"I ain't been back here since that day," he offered quietly as he got out of the truck and walked towards the pile of rubble that had once housed his family.

The destruction spread out before me was shocking: there was but half a wall standing, the black, jagged edges of the remaining boards standing out against the bright afternoon sunlight. It was a pleasant but cool spring afternoon, and I shivered and pulled my coat closer as I imagined the horror of the scene that must have taken place there.

"When I set out on the errand she wanted, I knew somethin' weren't right." He spoke as if addressing the house, explaining his actions. "Somethin' didn't feel right. Sure enough, when me and the girls come back because I got a bad notion, I seen smoke comin' from the window." He pointed to a window no longer there. "Didn't take but minutes for the whole house to burn to the ground."

I slipped my hand into his and laid my head on his shoulder. "I'm so sorry, Frankie. It must have been horrible."

"Funny thing is," he finally looked at me, "my daddy slept through the whole thing. Passed out in that there barn." He pointed over to the dilapidated but still standing structure. "Never woke until it was all over and she was gone."

I felt the terror that Frankie and his sisters must have felt as they watched their home burn with their mother inside. I knew his mama had had a difficult life with his father. Everyone knew Frank Conklin was as mean as his brother— but to see her life end in such a way must have been horrific.

We walked around the property, inspecting the grounds and what remained of the house. It had all been picked through, but Frankie looked at it like there was some secret he was missing, something that would divulge the reasons for this unfortunate tragedy. We wandered out to the decaying barn and tiptoed inside, peeking around the door as if his daddy were still there, waiting with a switch. A couple barn cats called out their annoyance at being imposed upon, but other than that, the ancient barn was silent, the shadows of the afternoon sun dancing noiselessly through the broken windows.

Frankie put his arm around my waist and drew me in next to him. He looked deeply into my eyes, then kissed me long and hard.

"I wanted you to see to this. I don't know why, I just did," he said, letting me go.

"I'm glad you did, Frankie. You can share anything with me. I'm always here for you." The fact that he had been so willing to disclose this heartbreak and misfortune showed me what I meant to him, and it touched me deeply.

He kissed me again, with an urgency that was disconcerting, and whispered in my ear, "I need you so much. I want you so bad. It's time, Addie. I've waited for you long enough."

I looked into his pleading eyes. Into the eyes of my future husband. Into the eyes of a man imploring me to give my love to him in the most sacred of ways.

And there, amidst the ghosts of the past, surrounded by the truth of the present and the hopes and dreams of the future, I did as he asked of me. I submitted to his request, offering myself as the final bargaining chip in our tumultuous relationship.

I took sick that spring with a bug that sent me to the toilet more than once to throw up my breakfast or lunch. I didn't have a fever, just aches and pains that left me exhausted and lethargic and had my mother warning me that if it didn't clear up soon she would be scheduling a visit with our local doctor. I did shake it off after a couple weeks, perking up immeasurably just as I finished my junior year. I was still working at the Bijou, and Lucy and I were looking forward to seeing the new picture, *Citizen Kane*, that had everyone talking.

I'm not sure when it first occurred to me. It wasn't one single realization, more like small pieces in a big puzzle that finally fell into place. And when it did, I practically laughed aloud at my stupidity. I hadn't come sick in over two months. I'd been so preoccupied with my "bug" that the thought I could be pregnant never entered my mind, but I awoke one morning knowing that I was expecting a child. The clues all added up and I couldn't dismiss any of them.

I was surprised, but not shocked. Jack had told me long ago the facts of life, and though I had never thought it would happen to me, the reality of my situation was blatantly obvious. Frankie and I were going to have a baby.

"You sure, Addie? You positive?" Frankie stood in front of the car he was working on, tool in hand, looking at me distrustfully, like I'd just pulled a fast one on him.

"I'm sure, Frankie," I replied nervously.

I could see his hands shaking as he carefully set the wrench down on a rag and walked over to the sink to wash his hands.

"Well, that's a wrench in our plans," he snickered unpleasantly.

"What are we going to do? My daddy's going to kill me, I just know it." He would probably do more than that. Frankie was not a favorite of his, and I could only imagine what was in store for us.

"What do you want to do?" he asked me.

This was not the assurance I wanted to hear. I wanted him to tell me that he loved me and would take care of me, that this was not what we had planned but we would deal with it together. This pregnancy would be a sacrifice for me as well. My plans to be an actress or to attend college would have to be abandoned, at least for the next couple of years. But I was willing to forfeit my dreams for a life with Frankie. It was an easy decision for me to make.

"What are you saying, Frankie?" His nonchalance was making me tense, and I wasn't sure what he was getting at.

"Nothing," he muttered, turning his back to me as he reached into his icebox for a beer. "I guess we'll just do the right thing," he said as he stood and faced me, a feigned smile on his face. "How about Friday?"

"Friday?"

"Sure. On Friday, we'll drive over to the courthouse and get hitched. How about that? Can you make it?"

His casual manner was irritating to me and I took offense at his words and actions. "You don't have to be a jerk, Frankie."

"I'm not," he said brightly. "I'm serious. Do you have plans?"

"You know I don't."

"Great. Then I'll pick you up. Say around noon, at the end of your drive. That good for you?"

I didn't want this to be the way my marriage started. This was the sort of awkward, jagged conversation that Frankie and I occasionally had, and it made me uncomfortable and downtrodden.

"I'll be ready." I turned to leave. "I'm sorry it has to start like this Frankie, but I'm sure it'll be all right in the end." I walked over close to him and tilted my head, longing for him to hold me and kiss me.

His eyes met mine, and there was no sarcasm in his voice when he said, "I'm sure it will, too, Addie." He pecked me on the cheek and turned back to the job at hand.

I left the shop dejected and miserable, my future scarier and more uncertain than ever before. I thought about Scarlett and realized she was no role model. Her principles and moral code were nonexistent, and I had fallen under her deceptive spell just as Rhett had. "Well, you're in good company," I imagined Rhett saying as I got on my bike and started back to the house. "Don't worry, kid. There's always tomorrow."

Chapter Eight

Jack

I first discovered he was sneaking into my sister's bedroom when she was but six years old. Lucy and baby Cora shared the small room next to the kitchen, and he was so intoxicated one night that when he snuck in, he tripped and fell, hitting his head on the baby's bed and startling Cora so that she had one of her screaming fits right then, in the middle of the night. I was sleeping in the back room, and come busting in to find Lucy holding the baby and my daddy out cold with a deep gash in his forehead that would require six stitches from the Old Doc the next day. Lucy looked at me, her eyes plum full of panic, and from then on I slept on a mat between the crib and Lucy's bed, my eight-year-old self ready to do battle if needed.

When I asked Lucy if this were the first time Daddy ever come to her room, she just kept her eyes down and didn't answer. I took that for a no but was too embarrassed to ask what'd happened, and she didn't offer to say. I just knew that it was no good, whatever it was. For the next year or so, until he married Aunt Bonnie, I became my sister's guardian. He come in a couple times when I was setting guard, but I steered him back to his own bed and he didn't ever bring it up, so it just got forgotten. In all fairness, that's when he was drinking more than not, and he probably don't even remember what he was doing, but I know that don't excuse his behavior for making a claim on his own daughter.

My daddy and my uncle had their share of bad luck—seems their whole lives were full of it. They lost parents, wives, a brother, and even a child, but in the end they found the Lord. That was their salvation, and they begged his forgiveness for all they'd done wrong. Uncle Frank and my daddy even set up shop in the pole barn they built on our back lot—the smell of fresh manure drifted in during the warmest of times. I wasn't one for fire and brimstone preaching, but I appreciated they were trying. Anything was better than the whiskey kind of life familiar to them both.

There ain't too much that ruffles my feathers—it don't even bother me that I took my unfair share of lickings from a drunk, set out to punish his own demons. But the one thing I don't take kindly to is disloyalty. I been let down by many folks, but I can honestly say that the one person that never did me a bad turn was my cousin Frankie. Me and Frankie was born but one day apart, and from the second we come into this world, it's been me and him, together through thick and thin. My earliest memory is of us getting a whack after accidentally throwing a rock through a window in the barn. I remember that we couldn't stop laughing, even after our behinds stung with the wrath of the switch, and we run off to soak our wounds in the cool of the Tittabawassee. We couldn'ta been more than four or five, but even then you had to pry us apart. Once I witnessed my cousin laying down his life for me, and I'm proud to say I'd do the same for him.

For the longest time, till we were almost grown, Frankie and his family lived in the next county over. Until he got his motorcycle, we only seen each other in the summer and on holidays and such. It was the Christmas before Frankie got his finger pulled off, when his family had crowded in with ours to celebrate the holiday. There was seven kids milling about, and the older ones were told to take their play outside. Frankie and me went down to the partially frozen river to throw stones, the girls stayed behind to play dolls in the barn. The freezing point had come early that year, and the river was ice-covered and solid in all but the deepest places. We had to use every ounce of our strength to get our stones to fall in the yet-unfrozen areas about fifty feet offshore.

Looking back, it's easy to see what a reckless decision I made, but I was just an ignorant boy, set out to prove God only knows what. Now normally it would be Frankie showing off, but I remember feeling like it was my turn. Even after

Frankie warned me not to and told me that the ice could be untrustworthy, I danced out farther than common sense would command.

I heard the ice cracking before I actually felt it, but by that time it was too late. I scrambled to try to make it back to safety, but my weight was too much for the thin ice under my feet. I slipped slowly into the freezing water, my arms grabbing at the disappearing edge of the frozen Tittabawassee until I found a solid piece that I clung desperately to. I was mostly in the water—my arms, head, and upper chest were the only parts of my body not beginning to turn into a human ice cube. My hands were frozen flat on the smooth ice, laid out in front of me, and were the only things holding me back from a certain death. My strength began to succumb to the cold. It seemed impossible to find the muscle needed to pull my waterlogged body out of the freezing current that pulled at it.

As I struggled to stay afloat, Frankie grabbed a long dead limb partially buried by the snow and pushed it out toward me, quickly but carefully walking out a few steps onto the unreliably frozen river. I grabbed onto the small branches on the end, and he was able to pull me out, inches at a time, until we both found our footing on solid ground. We lay on the banks of the Tittabawassee, bitterly cold and wet, too shaken to say anything, until Frankie finally looked over and whispered, "It wasn't your time, Jack." He squeezed my arm and continued. "Somehow I knew it."

I wondered how he could have possibly known, and looked at him curiously. We went back to the barn, both of the mind that it would be dangerous to repeat the story to any of the adults. Who knew what the consequences would be? A whipping could be in order, and we weren't taking any chances. I snuck in and went to the barn loft while Frankie secretly told Lucy what had happened and she crept into the house for some dry coveralls. I caught the worst cold I ever had that evening, but I figured it was a small price to pay. For the rest of my life I had a newfound respect for the river. It's strange. I lost my baby brother to the waters that once almost claimed me, and I always wondered how God had decided which of us to take. He musta been needin' some small angels, because for the life of me I can't seem to figure out how the Lord coulda taken him and not me instead.

My mama died before I could even set up my memories, so the responsibility for chores was twofold for us kids, and we were always working. We were farm folk, so our day started at dawn and ended long after the sun had slipped behind the grove of apple trees to the west of the farm. Before Aunt Bonnie come into the picture, Lucy and I also had Cora to take care of. She was a difficult baby and had more problems than we knew what to do with. There were the fits she threw, sometimes daily, that we tried to keep from our daddy. He didn't take kindly to being woke from a whiskey-made sleep by a screaming baby, in addition to the plain fact that she were born without all her faculties. Cora would never age much past three or four and required constant watching, for she could get into just about anything and make a mess of it. When we were younger and had no mama, Miss Pearl sent an old Polish woman out to the farm, Mrs. Gorzynski, who would help Daddy with the baby while me and Lucy went to school. If Mrs. G weren't feeling well or we couldn't pay her that week, we just didn't go to school. Mrs. G. had a way with baby Cora, and until Daddy remarried, she was me and Lucy's saving grace.

It sounds like times were always tough, but when you're in the midst of them, it don't always feel that way. We did what had to be done. We didn't know anything different. When we were eating Mr. Harris's horsemeat because we couldn't afford anything else, we didn't know we were missing out on steak, because we never had it. The horsemeat tasted fine and was tender and juicy, like a combination of venison and beef, and I made a flavorsome stew with some potato and carrot. Some folks turned up their nose at the notion of eating the sweetmeat, but there were plenty who didn't. We kept it under our hat, but it was cheap and it kept our family going during the toughest of times.

We had a pack of farm dogs living out in the barn, and that would be my explanation for buying the large quantities of the ground meat from Mr. Harris. I wondered if he knew that the dogs were just an excuse. He would sometimes look at me in a strange way, like he was trying to see something inside my head, and he often gave me more meat than I had paid for. I looked up so to Mr. Harris, and more times than not I wished he was my daddy. I would pretend that the looks he gave or the words he spoke to Earl were meant for me, or that I was the one he was teaching to drive that fancy car of his. As I got older, I came to appreciate the hardships of my pa's life more. Though I never stopped thinking about being George's son, I knew that one day I could make a family of my own and be the kind of father I never had.

I wasn't the only one thinking about being a part of the Harris family. Lucy woulda been about ten or so when she first told me her plans.

"I'm plannin' on marryin' Earl when I get old enough," she announced one fall day on our way home from school.

"What if he don't want to marry you?" I asked.

"Why would he not want to marry me?" She stopped and looked at me all confused-like.

"Well, I don't know. I was just thinking maybe he had different ideas. Maybe he's thinkin' he's gonna marry Winnie Mae or something." Winnie Mae was always crowdin' around him, saying silly things.

"Earl don't want Winnie Mae, Jack. You'll see. Earl's got his heart set on me. I can just tell." She tossed her blonde curls. "Then I'll go live in their house and have a sink with running water, and a bathroom—no more outhouses." She looked over at me seriously. "And we'll have electricity and a nice car and lots of babies." She thought for a minute. "Jack, why don't you marry Adeline? Then we can all live together. I think that's a swell idea, don't you?" She looked at me hopefully.

"Lucy, you got your head in the clouds," I told her.

Truth be known, I *was* sweet on Addie—always had been. There was something about Adeline that drew me to her. It wasn't her pretty face or her bright green eyes or even her inside plumbing. It was the unexplainable draw that matched green with blue and sand with water. It was a gut feeling, but one I wouldn't act on until I had no other choice but to do so one spring morning when her brother lay on his sickbed. Even though Addie would share her affections at times, she was never committed to me. She couldn't seem to see the invisible connection that brought her back to me time and time again.

Frankie saw this long before I ever said anything. He sensed my feelings, he felt my devotion, and he understood why I could do nothing but wait.

"She's one tough nut to crack," he whispered as we trudged quietly through the back wood early on Easter morning in 1937, our guns poised for shot.

"Who is?" I asked, just as I spied a wild turkey off in the distance. I looked over to my cousin and put my finger to my lips, motioning silence before I pointed off in the distance to what could be our Sunday meal. He nodded his understanding of the situation and we split up, hoping to trap the bird in the thicket past the lowlands the turkey was standing in. Turkeys are fast and have keen eyesight, so our aim was to surprise the bird before he knew what hit him. Snow still sat in large piles, especially in the shade of the evergreens where the late winter sun could not yet reach it, and we calculated every footstep to make as little noise as possible. The sky was clear and the wind cold, but the thought of bringing home that beautiful bird and how to do it took over my every notion.

I could sense Frankie's whereabouts and knew he had made it behind the animal, and I saw from my post it was a male. Turkeys travel in flocks early in the season, but this lone ranger didn't seem concerned that he was a sitting duck, so to speak, and could soon be covered in gravy. His beard of smaller feathers stuck out from his long red neck, and I guessed his weight to be eighteen to twenty pounds. He cocked his head, hearing the smallest of twigs crack under our feet, and I knew we didn't have long before his instincts took over and survival was his only goal. I took aim, but before I could fire I heard a shot ring out, saw the bird drop, and knew Frankie had beat me to the punch.

"He sure is a beaut," Frankie crowed as we carried our prize back to the house. This truly was an Easter blessing, and we were in high spirits as we carried the bird between us.

"Yeah, he is," I replied, thinking about the stuffing Aunt Francine would make. "Hey, Frankie, who were you talking about when you said she was a tough nut to crack?"

"Adeline Harris."

I kept walking like nothing had happened, but my insides jumped when he mentioned Addie's name. "Why do you say that?"

"Jeez, Jack, I can just tell. I know you like I know the backa' my hand. You can't fool me none. I hear the way you talk about her. I can tell." He smiled at me teasingly, but without any meanness.

"I kissed her last year," I suddenly confessed. Until that time I had kept this sacred fact to myself, reliving that morning over and over until it became a movie in my mind, with actors playing the parts so I could appreciate a different view.

Frankie stopped short, and I almost dropped my end of the tom.

"What the heck! Why didn't you ever say nothin'? I tell you everythin'." He looked so disappointed that I felt the need to explain.

"It ain't like I was keepin' it from you for any one reason," I offered. "It just happened, and then I forgot about it. And besides, it weren't no big deal. Yeah, I like her enough, but she"—I struggled for the right words—"she just thinks of me as a friend."

"Well she's crazy if she don't think you're just the cutest thing to come around these days." His voice had turned high, and he mimicked that of a high school girl. "Why, I'd go steady with you in a heartbeat."

I was laughing too hard to even take a swat at him with my free arm. His face was all puckered like he was tryin' to kiss an imaginary girl and I had to stop to take a breath, I was chuckling so.

"All right, you done had your fun on my behalf," I said as I took a deep breath and readjusted the turkey. "I hope you feel better."

Frankie batted his eyes at me and we continued home, our steps light and our banter easy. But as we walked, the turkey between us, I reflected that Frankie wasn't always this carefree. He had his dark side and no one, not even his mama, knew it better than me.

I first seen him have a fit when we were about nine years of age. He was staying with us for a couple weeks in the summer and I awoke to him shaking uncontrollably, his back arched and his eyes rolled back. It lasted but a few seconds, and just when I was getting ready to get Aunt Bonnie, it suddenly stopped. Frankie was dripping with sweat and confused, like he weren't sure what had happened and he weren't sure where he was, and he promptly fell into a deep sleep.

The next morning, when I questioned him about the seizure, he confessed that it weren't the first time, that it usually only happened at night, and that he didn't want anyone to know about it. He said it was his own private demon and weren't no one's business.

A comfortable silence had settled between us as we lugged the turkey homeward. As I hitched up the tom again, a thought occurred to me. "Frankie?"

"Yeah?"

"Did you have a fit that day you put the tractor through the Lewis's hen house?" It had always seemed a bit strange. Frankie was carefree but not careless, especially with a machine.

He avoided my looks, sighing, while he rubbed his forehead. "I don't remember nothin' about that incident, Jack. I guess somethin' like that musta happened. I never woulda lost control like that. Never." He finally made eye contact, and I nodded my head. Frankie was too good with motors and engines. He understood machines better than anyone, and I knew he was telling the truth.

"You can't tell nobody, you hear me, Jack?" he practically threatened. "It don't happen but once every couple years or so, and it ain't no big whoop. I don't want folks thinkin' I ain't right."

I'd never seen Frankie so up in arms over anything before, and I promised him his secret was safe with me. I asked him why he didn't tell his mama and he said he didn't want no extra worries for her; her plate was full. He fell into a mood that lasted for the rest of his visit, and every now and then, after that incident, when I found that same mood invading his otherwise cheerful self, I wondered if he'd had another night fit. He never brought it up again, save once, and I never did neither. I knew his mama had her own demons and I suspected they'd made their way through her bloodline and into Frankie's, inflicting the kind of inner pain that eats slowly away at a person's heart and soul until his inside is but an empty cavern.

I have my share of faults, and one of them is stubbornness. I get something in my craw and it don't easily shake out. When I found out from Rebecca Hughes that Adeline had been talking bad of me, it found its mark on my heart and I took it real hard. I thought she was different from all the other girls and their gossip, but I realized that weren't so and she didn't have the same feelings that I had for her. Even after she apologized and begged my forgiveness, I couldn't seem to shake the chip off my shoulder. I took up with Rebecca, knowing that it was done for spite and Addie would suffer. I weren't trying so hard to hurt her—well, maybe I was, but it was just my way of dealing with the hurt. I ain't saying it was the right way, I'm just saying it was my way.

As bad plans often go, mine backfired, and after a year or so and some distance from Addie, I saw that she and Frankie were falling for each other. He asked me again and again if I still had a soft spot for her, but by then it was too late. I couldn't make any claims on a girl that thought my feelings had died, and I watched in dismay as they took up with each other. I knew as soon as they left that morning to pick up Earl, when Mr. Harris put his back out, that Frankie and Adeline would find each other, and that it would be my punishment to watch.

"Jack, you sure you got no feelin's for Addie?" Frankie asked me for the umpteenth time as he worked on a '26 Buick at the filling station his daddy had recently bought. "Hand me that there belt, Jack."

"That ship done sailed, cousin. She made her feelin's for me known." I tossed him the belt and sat on a pile of old tires.

"Jeez, Jack. That was nearly two years ago. How can you still hold that against her? You known her all your life, she ain't some silly filly. She's got substance. She just made a mistake," he argued with me, pulling out a hose from under the hood. Jack had an instinct for motors, be it a car or a motorbike, and I admired his skill as I watched him work.

"I know," I admitted. "It's just that too much time has gone by. Too much water under the bridge. She's got her sights set on you, not me. And frankly, I don't know if I got the same feelin's for her I once did." I shrugged my shoulders, wanting so badly to believe the story I'd just told my cousin. Sadly, my stubborn nature went along with it.

I wasn't sure if Frankie believed me, but he weren't out to do me harm. He asked me many times about my feelings towards Addie, but I encouraged him to pursue her, told him that I couldn't care less.

Aunt Francine had passed by then, and Uncle Frank had moved the three girls and Frankie to Michigami after the fire that took his house and wife. He took the money from selling Aunt Francine's farmland and bought a Texaco station and auto repair shop. It was a good move and supported my daddy and uncle's preaching, and Frankie took on the position of head mechanic. He was the only one in town, actually. Automobiles were backed up waiting for Frankie to work his magic on them, and Michigami folks no longer had to travel to Midland to have their oil changed or carburetor adjusted. He started staying on the cot in the back room of the station— "too many female folk at the farm," he said—and on my days off I helped pump gas and put air in tires.

Our house cleared out some. I was working and staying at the ranch at the Harris's, and Uncle Frank and my dad slept in the makeshift bedroom out in the pole barn church. Lucy, Cora, and Frankie's three sisters had the run of the house and the five girls settled in nicely, running the house like clockwork and always having a hot meal for any of the hungry menfolk come in from their work.

The Conklins' luck had changed some with the Texaco station and Frankie's automotive knowledge, and the rewards brought electricity, an ice box, and a stove, luxuries that had been out of reach for a long time. Lucy was in her glory, "living like the Queen of England," she said, as she flipped the light switch on and off and watched the pilot light kick the new stove into action.

The year 1940 was not a good one for me. I had managed to graduate from high school that winter, but I was still working at the Harris farm and watching the only girl I'd ever had feelings for fall in love with my best friend and cousin. I had no grudge against either; it wasn't their fault. As much as I thought Frankie knew me, he seemed not to notice the misery that I found difficult to conceal.

Strangely enough, though, Earl did notice. He come home that summer, and with the help of José, me and him took over running the farm and the foxes. Mr. Harris was running for the county board and Mrs. Harris had a position at the paper, and their politics took too much time for their day-to-day involvement in the family business.

"How you doing, Jack?" Earl asked as he tossed me a bale of hay one sunny June morning.

"I'm all right, I expect." I caught the bale and set it down near the stalls. "We still plannin' on fixin' that fence in the southwest corner today?"

"Let's finish up here and then try to head out before lunch. Where's the post hole digger?" He scanned the barn. I had cleaned and reorganized the place while he was away at school, and he was unfamiliar with the new setup.

"I put the tools in the shed behind the ranch," I said. "Hope you don't mind."

"Naw, looks good in here. You're taking real fine care of the place, Jack. I know my dad appreciates it, and I do too." He looked over and nodded his approval. "Looks like Addie and your cousin are spending a lot of time together, huh?"

"I guess." Earl wasn't one for much personal talk, and it took me by surprise that he would find this worth mentioning.

"I always thought you and Addie would make a fine couple. I never really saw Frankie as the type to settle down much." He glanced over at me, and I saw that he wasn't sure how I would take his remark. He stacked the last of the hay bales next to the stall and we headed out to the shed for the tools needed for our fence job.

"I guess you never know," I said, grabbing the shovel. This seemed like a good time to ask him about his intentions with Lucy, but he somehow sensed my notion and quickly changed the subject, putting our discussion to rest, and I didn't bring it up again. He did bring up the draft going into effect in September—the law that would require anyone twenty-one years or older to sign up for military service. Earl would be twenty-one in December.

"My folks are up in arms over it," he told me as we walked out to the fence that we intended on expanding. "They want me to be a conscientious objector."

"A what?" I asked.

"It's someone who doesn't support the war and refuses to fight. They got to go to the local draft board and make their case." He looked at me with a pained expression, and I could only imagine what a difficult position he was in. Earl was no coward, and he wasn't like his parents, who didn't believe in any kind of violence. I knew that if he was able, he would be first in line at the draft board.

"What you gonna do?"

"I don't rightly know," he answered. "I'm all torn up inside. There's no certainty that there's to be a war, so maybe it's all for naught." He didn't sound so convincing, and I wasn't so sure either; Germany had recently invaded France and the ongoing bad news from overseas continually got worse.

"Ain't it funny," he said as he lowered his voice and looked around. "My family, who doesn't believe in violence, makes a living killing animals."

I didn't say nothing, feeling a certain loyalty to George Harris, but I understood his point. Earl musta felt bad too, because that's the last he spoke of it, at least with me. I didn't have any qualms about fighting the Krauts, and I knew my daddy wouldn't have none about me going. I saw it as part of my American duty.

I watched everyone's lives around me moving and growing, changing and expanding, while mine did nothing. Daddy's church doubled in size when the Presbyterian one burned to the ground, and he found his undersized barn overflowing with eager members. We worked diligently to enlarge the small space, pushing out the walls and even adding a small stage for the out-of-work Presbyterian choir members who were impatient to resume their singing duties. I never saw my daddy or uncle so full of honest happiness as when they were at the pulpit, shouting out for the sinners to repent and come forth and let the good Lord Jesus into their lives. My own melancholy heart thumped miserably along as I sat, detached, in the back of the church, observing the congregation full of families and young lovers, hands touching discreetly as they held the hymnbooks and softly murmured the songs set out in front of them.

Lucy and Earl often double-dated with Frankie and Adeline, and Lucy encouraged me to find someone for myself so we could all go together like when we'd gone to the Harvest Moon Dance.

"Come on now, Jack," she urged. "Rebecca Hughes still has a thing for you."

The thought of Rebecca was almost nauseating—I'd had my fill of her. But my excuses were limited. "I'm not feelin' up to any socializin', Lucy. You go on now and have a good time."

She looked at me like she knew my real reasons, but by then it didn't matter. I knew it would be impossible for me to enjoy any evening where Addie wasn't my date. It would be intolerable to watch her and Frankie, laughing and nuzzling up against one another, whispering and, most of all, kissing. Though he was my cousin and best friend, I couldn't believe that she fit with Frankie as well as she did with me, and I was consumed with a silent jealousy that exhausted me and wore down my character, turning me into a bitter man. A man like my father had been. Would it take fire and brimstone preaching to exorcise my demons?

I don't know if time had healed all my wounds, but it certainly allowed for the making of an awful big scab. Over that next while my heartache slowed to a crawl. Though it still pained me to watch Frankie and Addie, I could hear him talk of her and pretend it was someone else.

The dark winter months of 1941 came, and I noticed a change in Frankie. He turned sluggish, and his dark periods, which came and went without warning, seemed to be more frequent and put him in a place that was hard to reach, even for me. When I asked him how he was doing, my code for asking about his fits, he replied that he was fine, never better. I suspected differently and sensed that sooner or later something had to give.

Frankie disappeared on his motorbike more than once, and more than once Addie come out to the ranch looking for him. I knew Mr. Harris didn't have the same fondness for Frankie that most folks did, and that he didn't approve all that much of Addie being Frankie's girl. I knew this because of the way he didn't say anything when Frankie was around, and also because I saw him blow a gasket one day when Addie come home on the back of Frankie's bike, tooling down the road like they was racing the wind. George didn't say nothing to Frankie, but when he'd left, he let loose on Adeline, something I'd never seen him do to anyone.

"What the hell you doin', girl?" he hollered at her as she tried to scoot by him and make her escape into the house.

"What do you mean, Daddy?" Addie asked innocently, but I could tell she was nervous. I was twenty or so paces behind them, raking out a pen, and I kept my head down and my back turned like I couldn't hear.

"I mean you ridin' on the back of that motorbike. That's what I mean." He stood in front of her, blocking her way.

"We were just out for a joyride. Frankie's a careful driver, really." I peeked over my shoulder and caught Addie's eyes, which seemed to beg for help.

"I don't want you anywhere near that bike. You understand?"

"But, Daddy . . ."

"No buts, young lady. No more riding."

Addie didn't reply. As she stomped away she gave me a look like it had all been my fault, like I hadn't done enough to help her out. Well, my days of helping her were long gone. That weren't my responsibility any more. And Frankie... well, I didn't think he saw what was going on much past his own troubles.

It was hard to pin him down. Frankie always went his own way, but now he had responsibilities to his job and his gal that were suffering, and I felt somehow it was up to me to fix it, to fix him. Why this was the case, I can't say—it's just that he was so much a part of me that when he was broke, I felt broke. When he was hurt, I was too. He was all I had. Lucy was my sister, but she wasn't me. Frankie was. I needed Frankie because I needed me. I needed his cockiness, his confidence, his friendship, his acceptance. He filled out the part of me that had been missing or left empty by the dumb luck of fate. But even as I realized my need for him and what he gave me, I had my own suspicions that the monkey on his back was more than I could handle, that it was too big for me to fight.

The first mark of spring 1941 came in the form of a tornado. I happened to be at the station with Frankie, helping him fix a busted brake on a Chevy, when the skies darkened and the wind picked up, tossing loose papers haphazardly about. When a gust knocked over the metal garbage bin by the pumps, we went outside, securing anything not tied down and pulling down the heavy garage door that was the entrance. This was just another spring storm to us, and it was a good excuse to hang about—something we hadn't been able to do for the past few months. Frankie went to his little ice box and brought out a couple of cold suds, and we settled into our wooden chairs to watch the storm blow through.

We sat in silence for a bit, enjoying the chaos swirling around us, until it suddenly became deathly quiet. We walked through the front door of the station and out into the eerily soundless evening. Then, out of nowhere, come the enormous sound of a freight train, growing dangerously close. Now, it ain't no secret what a twister sounds like, and both Frankie and I knew it when we heard it. We looked towards the noise and saw a funnel cloud south of town.

It wasn't heading directly toward us and it didn't look like it was rustling up the ground much, but the sheer thrill of seeing such a storm so close kept us rooted to our spot. We didn't move an inch as we watched the tornado move slowly off into the distance and the rain pick up, coming down in torrents.

"Well, that sure was some show, huh?" Frankie offered as we headed back in, the rain coming at us sideways and forcing us to take cover.

"Never seen nothin' like it before, that's for sure," I added, shaking the water off my jacket.

"You know, I see stuff like that, storms and such, things nature does, and even if it's destructive in ways, it don't scare me none. Like I'm watching some beautiful ballet show that Mother Nature's puttin' on." He picked up an old guitar that a customer had given him in exchange for a new tire and started strumming it.

"I know what you mean," I replied. "Like God is havin' his own talent show."

"Maybe," he said softly as he picked at the strings, absorbed in trying to play a chord.

"What do you mean, 'maybe'?" I pressed. This was the kind of talk that had come over Frankie recently, and for the first time I questioned him about the vague answers he would give.

"Maybe it was God and maybe it weren't." He set the guitar on his lap. "It don't always have to be God doing somethin'. Maybe it's just what nature's doin' at the moment."

"Why are you talkin' like that, Frankie? Here your daddy's a preacher and you're tellin' me that nature ain't God's work?" I felt a panic growing in my gut. He was always one to question authority, but to question God? What could he possibly mean?

"Don't get yourself in a fit, Jack. I'm just sayin' I ain't seen too much from Him in my life, and, I don't know, sometimes I get the feelin' I'm here alone. There ain't no one lookin' out for ole' Frankie Conklin but Frankie Conklin."

"How can you say that? I've always been here for you." I was flabbergasted.

Me and Frankie never had words like that and I couldn't believe he was saying these bothersome things. I got up and paced around the garage.

"Jack, I don't mean that about you." He came over and placed his hand on my shoulder. "You always been there for me. I don't know if I coulda made it, if it weren't for you. You been my brother. You been everythin' to me." He walked off like he had the weight of the world on his shoulders.

"What about Adeline?" I asked abruptly. "What does *she* mean to you?"

He turned around and looked at me. "Why? What does she mean to *you*?"

I wasn't expecting his response, and stuttered as I rushed to explain. "I... I was just wonderin' how she fits into this picture. Does she know how you feel about her?"

"I don't know how I feel about her, cousin." He sat down on the chair and picked the guitar back up. "She scares me sometimes."

"What do you mean, she 'scares' you? She fightin' with you?"

"Naw, nothin' like that. Maybe 'scare' ain't the right word." He picked at the strings and hummed as he tried to play. "She's just... alive, ya know? Full of life." He looked up at me. "I mean, she's got dreams, thoughts, ideas, plans." He picked at the strings again. "Like she knows what she wants. She's got confidence."

I was surprised to hear Frankie saying these things. I'd always thought of him that way. "You got a lot to offer too, Frankie. You got your whole life ahead of you. 'Cept for missin' the top half of your finger, you got a lot of good things goin' on too. Ain't no one a better mechanic." I smiled at him, hoping the joke about his finger would lighten the mood.

"Yeah, maybe. I got confidence about some things, I don't doubt that." He smiled and strummed the guitar hard. "Let's go back to the house and see what the girls got cookin'. I'm starved."

"It's still rainin'," I said, watching the water roll down the windows of the station.

"You scared of a little rain?" he jeered as he continued his invigorated strumming.

"Naw, I ain't scared of that.   Get your cycle goin' and let's go."

I wasn't scared of the rain. I was scared of what lay in the future. What I couldn't see.

Earl came back for the summer from his second year at Michigan State College, and we took up where we left off the previous fall. We worked well together, and seeing as his dad had won a seat on the county board, we were busier than ever. I'd added another bunkhouse to the back of the ranch, and Earl took to sleeping out there and occasionally bringing Lucy over to visit. I didn't mind much having her over, but I began to feel like a fifth wheel and took to taking long walks in the evening, sometimes into town, where I would occasionally find Frankie strumming on his guitar.

I loved walking the banks of the Tittabawassee. Even though I had lost my brother and almost my own life to its grasp, the rushing waters brought a strange comfort to me. I found the beauty and grace of the willows along the edge soothing and reassuring, calming the unrest that stirred in my gut.

It was on one of these walks that I met up with Adeline. I knew she would frequently wait for Frankie, sitting on the post at the end of her drive, but it was a few hundred yards away from that that I seen Frankie drop her off on his forbidden motorcycle. I caught up with her and grabbed her arm.

"What are you doing?" she snarled at me as she shook off my grasp.

"I thought your daddy told you not to ride on that motorbike." I was taken aback that she would so openly disobey her father.

"What's the big whoop?" she answered dismissively, but changed her tone and added, "You aren't going to tell him, are you?"

"I ain't a snitch. I'm just surprised that you would do somethin' he asked you not to." *And that Frankie would, too*, I thought privately, *after all Mr. Harris has done for him.*

"It was just this once," she said, but looked too quickly away, and I knew she weren't telling the truth.

"Addie, I just don't want to see you get into trouble. That's all." I patted her arm where I grabbed her and we walked together back towards the ranch. She wasn't in a talking mood, so it was a silent walk, but not uncomfortable—in fact, it was a pleasant night, and she softened, seeming almost disappointed when we reached her house.

"Thanks, Jack. I'm sorry I was cross with you. I just got a lot on my mind." She touched my hand, and I felt the familiar longing for her that never seemed to waver. *She's Frankie's girl*, I repeated to myself as I watched her walk into the house. *She's Frankie's girl.*

It was a couple weeks later, when I was passing by the Texaco station, that I run into Frankie, his head peeking out from under the hood of a Ford. He called out.

"Hey, cousin. Got a minute?"

"Sure. What's up?"

He wiped his greasy hands on a rag as he spoke. "You think you could come over tonight? I got somethin' I want to talk about with you. You busy?"

"Naw, I'll come over after I close up." I called out as I headed back to the ranch. I was curious about his invitation. What could Frankie want that he couldn't ask me right then?

I spent the rest of the afternoon in thought and hurried to finish up, telling Earl I'd be back later.

"What's goin' on?" I asked Frankie when I returned to the station that evening. He was drinking a beer, and I noticed four empty bottles on the counter next to the ice box.

Our daddies were both drunks. Even so, I got no problem with having a beer every now and then, but seeing all those bottles made me wonder how much Frankie was drinking these days. He paced nervously around the small garage, taking draws on his bottle, and looked at me anxiously.

"Are you all right?" I asked. My first thought was that he'd had another fit.

"I'm in trouble, Jack. Deep trouble." He turned a chair around and sat down facing me. "You want a beer?"

I shook my head as my heart raced. "What kind of trouble?"

He looked off over my shoulder and sighed. "Adeline's set to have a baby," he told me, and met my gaze.

That's one piece of news I never would have guessed. My heart continued its race, but added a thumping so loud I was sure Frankie could hear.

"A baby?" I asked disbelievingly. I must have heard him wrong.

Frankie nodded grimly. "Yeah. A baby."

Still reeling from the left hook this news had nailed me with, I managed, "How could you let that happen? What were you thinking?"

I couldn't imagine what George was going to do. He already seemed to have taken a dislike to Frankie, and though I knew he weren't prone to violence, I worried for my cousin's life.

"You have to marry her, Frankie, you know?" He and Addie would have to get married. My Addie. He was going to marry my Addie. I didn't know who felt worse.

"That's already been taken care of. I'm supposed to pick her up on Friday, and we're headin' to the courthouse over in Midland." He glanced up from his beer. "I'm all set to do the right thing. There's only one problem."

One problem? I thought to myself. *Seems like there's more than one.* But I kept my mouth shut and asked, "What is it?"

"I can't do it." He threw back the last of the beer and got up to get another.

"Whaddaya mean you can't do it, Frankie?" I asked. "How can you not marry Adeline? What's she supposed to do? What are *you* gonna do? You know her daddy and her brother are goin' to come lookin' for you, and her daddy might not believe in violence, but I got a notion that Earl don't feel the same way. And somehow I don't think Mr. Harris is goin' to feel so bad if he leaves it up to Earl to help you change your mind." I changed my mind and helped myself to a beer. "Don't you love her?"

"It ain't that, Jack." Frankie dropped the bottle opener and stumbled a bit picking it up. "I was all set to do the right thing until last night. I had a fit last night, Jack. A big one. I lost all my faculties. I pissed myself, Jack. I pissed all over my bed." His disgust registered on his face, and I found I couldn't meet his eyes.

"Then this mornin', when I'm cleanin' my clothes and bed, I felt this dark cloud movin' over me. I know that feelin' like I know the back of my hand, Jack. It's a bad feelin'. One I can't ever shake. My mama had it, I seen it firsthand, and I know I got it too. I don't know if she ever had fits or not, but I got a black cloud over me. It ain't fair to no one, not Addie or no one, to have to live with a man like me." Frankie sat down hard on his stool and tossed his empty bottle off to the side, the glass shattering against the wall.

"I don't know what to say, Jack." I sat speechless, following his logic on everything. I knew Frankie had demons, I just never knew there were so many.

"She don't know me, Jack." He looked at me with tears in his eyes. "I'm not the man she thinks I am. I would disappoint her. You know that well as I do."

I started to say that it weren't true, but I knew that it was. He was right. Frankie's ways were not ways that were easily followed. I also knew how headstrong Addie was, and I could see nothing but trouble for a marriage between the two.

"What are you gonna do, Frankie? You got a real bad situation. How you gonna make it right?"

He looked at me. "I need your help."

"Me? What can I do?" I asked, confused.

Frankie didn't say anything as he looked around the room, like he wasn't sure what to say. His gaze finally wandered back to mine, and as he looked me straight in the eye, he said, "You can be the one to marry her, Jack."

His words struck me like a Buick hitting a ten-point buck. "You must be drinkin' way too much beer, cousin. That ain't likely to happen."

"You love her, I know you do. You could take her to the courthouse and you can be her husband. No one will know she's pregnant, and by the time the baby comes, no one will remember when you even got hitched."

The thought that he had even spent so much time thinking about this ridiculous plan made my stomach turn. "We ain't gonna fool no one, Frankie.

Everyone knows you been seein' her for almost a year now. She ain't gonna be too happy, either. You told her?"

"No, but the way I see it, she's got no choice."

"That's the way you want to treat the girl—the woman—that's carryin' your baby? She's not some animal that we can trade back and forth. She's real, Frankie. And she ain't gonna be happy about me standin' up to be her husband." I could only imagine what she would say.

"I'm leavin' town, Jack. It's already decided. I have to get outta here. I'm goin' crazy with all this, and it ain't helpin' me none." He wiped his wet eyes and came over to me. "I got the devil whisperin' in one ear, Jack, and there ain't no angel talkin' in the other. It's not in me to do what needs to be done. But I know it's in you. You and Addie can have this baby. You can have my baby, Jack. We got the same blood. It'll still be a Conklin. I just can't be here. I'll wither up, right quick." He walked back over to the window and stared off. "Jack, I need your help. Will you do it? Will you help me? Will you marry Adeline and take on my baby?"

He'd laid it out in front of me, and I knew I would do what he had asked. How could I not? It was in my makeup. It ran through the blood in my veins. It covered every inch of my body. I was capable of doing what Frankie couldn't, and I saw right then that we were not the same. Crystal clear, I saw who Frankie was. He was helpless to do the right thing, and I knew it wasn't because he didn't want to. It was because he couldn't.

"When are you leavin'?" I asked.

"I'm plannin' on headin' out tomorrow. I want to go out to the house and see the girls before I go." He burped softly before he continued. "And I don't want to tell anyone that I'm takin' off," he said.

"Are you gonna tell Addie?" I already knew the answer, but I wanted to hear him say it.

Frankie's face twisted and turned ugly. "What am I supposed to tell her?" he sneered. "She'll figure it out when you show up."

So I would have to do his dirty work with Addie. Maybe I didn't know

Frankie as well I thought I did. I could never wish that darkness on anyone, least of all Addie.

"Where are you goin'?"

"I was thinkin' about Detroit. There's so much work there with the auto industry. Or maybe I'll join the service. Who knows?" He shrugged his shoulders.

I couldn't picture Frankie in the service—he didn't have the discipline, and the fits would get him kicked out for sure, if they were found out—but I could see him in Detroit. He would blend in with the large population and disappear in the chaos of the city.

"You comin' back?"

"I don't know, Jack," he said.

But I did. "Don't come back, Frankie. You can't leave me with this mess and then waltz back in one day, expectin' to pick up where you left off. I won't let it happen."

Frankie looked stunned, like he hadn't thought that far ahead. He shook his head slowly, raking his hands hard through his hair. He closed his eyes, and his lips moved, but I couldn't make out the words. He paced the small room, staring at the oil cans lining the shelf as if they might give him his answer. Then he looked over at me, his eyes empty. "I won't."

He handed me a folded piece of paper. "Can you give this to her? So she believes what you tell her." He certainly knew Addie well enough to know she would require some evidence.

"Sure."

We sat without speaking until I drained the rest of my beer, dragging out my last few minutes with Frankie. I set the bottle on the counter and walked over to him. It was an awkward moment, the circumstances so strange that the years of knowing Frankie seemed to fade to nothing. I wasn't sure if I even recognized the man standing in front of me.

"Well, I guess this is it, Jack." He looked confused, like he wasn't sure whether shaking my hand would be fitting.

I reached out and hugged him close. I was baffled as to how the world could change so quickly, how things could turn so fast. I held him tight as his body shook with sobs, and I couldn't help it as my eyes welled up, too. He patted my back and whispered "Thank you," as I turned to leave.

"You take care of yourself," I said, my voice wobbly and scratched. As I opened the door to leave I turned around one last time, but Frankie's back was to me, his head in his hands. There was nothing left to say. I pulled the door softly shut, leaving my cousin alone with his demons.

I didn't see Adeline the next two days. All I could imagine was that she was getting ready for what she thought would be her wedding to Frankie. The more I thought about it, the more I decided what a bad idea it was. But Frankie had already left. Lucy told me he had dropped by the house, all drunked up, the night before. She had given me a funny look and I had the sense that she figured out what was going on, but she didn't say one way or another.

I borrowed my daddy's old pickup, and on Friday I told George I was taking the afternoon off, had some personal business to attend to. He didn't seem bothered, and I pulled out onto their long road and up next to Addie, who was sitting in a fancy dress on the post at the end of her drive. She waved out to me as if nothing strange were going on, and I sat there, not moving, like I expected her to figure out Frankie wasn't coming. She looked at me, perplexed-like, and for a few moments we just stared at each other as I mentally told her what was happening, practicing for the real thing.

She finally got slowly off the fence and walked towards me, looking around her as if she were anticipating Frankie jumping out to tell her it was all a joke.

She leaned into the car and asked simply, "Where's Frankie?"

"He's not comin', Adeline."

"What do you mean he's not coming, Jack? What did you do?" Her voice was controlled, but I could hear the hysteria pushing out through her words.

I handed her the short note that Frankie had given to me on my way out of the garage those few nights past, and watched her face fall as she read it.

"Why would he do this to me?" she whispered. "How could he leave me like this?"

I wasn't sure whether she wanted me to answer or not, so I didn't say anything. I wondered if she would break down. I never knew her to be a crier, but this was one time it might do her some good.

Still, she didn't start to bawl. She didn't do anything. She stood still as a statue, not moving a muscle, and I could see the wheels in her head turning. She started to speak, then stopped herself, then started and stopped again.

"Get in the car, Adeline," I finally told her. "Let's go for a ride 'fore anyone sees us and gets nosy."

She got in and pulled the door gently shut, and I turned out on the main road that headed towards Midland. We drove in silence for a few miles, Addie turning every now and then to give me a dirty look, until finally I pulled the car off on a dirt road and over to the side, ready to have it out with her.

"Listen, Addie, I don't know what you think, but I got nothin' to do with Frankie's decision.

"I don't believe you."

"What do you mean, you don't believe me?"

"I think you told Frankie something. I think you somehow convinced him he was making a mistake." Her eyes flared and her hands shook when she reached up to pull her hair back.

"What do you think I said?" I retorted, my voice rising. "That he should go off, willy-nilly, to God only knows where, so you could sit back here, with child and without a husband?"

"Why did he go, then? What made him change his mind?"

"Addie. Frankie's got problems, deep problems, and I think when it come down to it, he just couldn't face up to the responsibilities he had."

"What kind of problems? I didn't see any problems, Jack. What do you mean?" She glared at me.

I had promised Frankie I wouldn't tell no one about his demons, and now I was in a tough spot. "I can't say, Addie. But trust me, he had a monkey on his back."

"That's just it, Jack. I can't trust you. I don't know how Frankie could have up and left without saying anything. There has to be a reason."

"What's wrong with your head, Adeline? You think I convinced my cousin to take off and leave you so I could step in and go through this? You're crazy." I couldn't help myself, and hit the steering wheel with the butt of my hand.

She flinched at the noise.

"Why'd he go then, Jack? We had our plans all laid out—then all of a sudden he gets cold feet and you show up to save the day. Once again, I don't buy it."

"Well, good news is, you don't have to. I can let you out here, or hell, I'll even take you back home. I'll scoot right outta the picture and you can figure out this mess all on your own. Frankie's gone, Addie. He ain't comin' back." I stared out the window in disgust.

"I don't want to marry you, Jack. I want Frankie. This is his baby, not yours." Her voice rose as she continued. "You don't have me fooled at all. I know you've been sitting back, just waiting, just waiting until something bad happens, then hey! Here comes Jack to save the day. I know you, Jack. It's what you always do. You're the hero. Ain't that right, Jack? You want to be the hero?" Her face was flushed and her breath came in short gasps as she threw herself back against the seat.

I winced as she hurled her words at me, oblivious to the pain they were causing. But they struck a chord. Did I always come in to save the day? Was I playing the hero again? My mind quickly organized all my insecurities into nice, easy-to-read points, and I began to go down the list. I'd stepped in for Lucy when our daddy was molesting her. I'd stepped in for George when Earl was sick. I'd stepped in for Addie more than once. And now I'd stepped in for Frankie.

Was Adeline right? Had I missed all along that my biggest fault weren't the stubbornness I had previously thought, that it was much worse? That I was a martyr?

I couldn't get my arms around this new idea. It was too much to think about now, here, when I was supposed to be taking care of Addie's problem. I had to set it aside. It was an issue that would take months, maybe years, to really think about. This weren't the place.

"I'm sorry, Addie. You might be right. But I'm just trying to help. Really. You just tell me what you want me to do, and I'll do it. I know you don't want me. I'll take you back home. You can figure this out with your ma and pa." A wave of exhaustion came over me, and all I could think about was finding a nice quiet place and laying my head down.

It took me a minute or two to get my bearings back so I could put the car in gear and start to turn around, but before I could, Addie put her hand on my arm and said, "Stop."

"What?"

"I can't go back."

"What do you want, Adeline?"

"What I want is not possible. My whole life has been flipped upside down, and now I have to figure it out right this minute. I'm thinking, Jack. Please let me think for a minute."

She opened the door and stepped out. The summer breeze had turned sweltering and I got out as well, my fresh shirt wilting in the sizzling heat. I had packed a couple of Coca-Colas for the ride, and I popped the top on one, drinking in the cold liquid. I opened the other and walked over to where Addie stood, her back against a tree. She took it graciously from me and nodded her gratitude, taking a long drink from the frosty bottle. We could feel the humidity rolling in and the heat picking up. Today would be a scorcher for sure.

I took a seat on the other side of the tree, and leaned back and closed my eyes. All I could hear was the sounds of the summer birds, the rustling of the leaves in the wind, and the whoosh of an occasional car back out on the main road. The warm sun beat down on my hat; I removed it, tossing it down on the plush grass surrounding the tree, and let the world around me fade into the background of the perfect spot where I sat.

My thoughts wandered past all that had been laying heavy on my mind, and I went back to a place I remembered as a young boy, where the most important thing I'd had to do that day was my chores, and they was all done. In my youth I could do anything—I could fly, or I could be invisible, or something like—and I imagined all the secret places I could use these fantastic powers... behind enemy lines listening to battle plans or escaping from the clutches of the Germans who had caught me red-handed. I would be rich and travel the world, staying with kings and queens, always enjoying the fanciest of places and eating the finest foods. And when I felt like sailing, I would...

"Jack. Jack, wake up." Addie gently shook my arm. "You fell asleep."

I shook off my dreams and sat up. Addie was standing before me, her face sad and resigned.

"If you're still of the same mind," she stopped and took a big breath, "I'm ready to go to Midland."

She looked lovely standing before me. Her flowered dress blew gently in the wind, still trim at her slender waist. As sad and wilted as she looked, hers was a face from a picture, one that I would forever remember as I watched her push her long auburn hair from her eyes. She was so beautiful to me that I had to close my eyes and wait for the feeling of sheer love to pass through before I could open them and look at her without being undone by the longing I felt.

"If you don't want to... I understand," she offered shakily, mistaking my intentions.

I stood and brushed myself off and picked up my hat, setting it back on my head. "Come on, Addie. Let's go to Midland." I took her hand and we walked back to the car. I opened her door and helped her in. "You sure now, Addie?"

"I'm sure, Jack," she said.

I got in and pulled back onto the road. We drove in silence, both lost in our own thoughts, both wondering how this was ever gonna work. I knew I loved her, and the thought of being with her for the rest of my life was joy beyond any I had ever felt. All I needed was for her to love me back.

Chapter Nine

Adeline - 1941

On a hot, sticky Friday in late June, Jack and I exchanged our wedding vows on the cement steps of the county courthouse in Midland. Two other couples swore their undying love along with us: a farming couple dressed in their Sunday best, and a uniformed officer and his jubilant young fiancée, who was clinging to his arm like a bug on a duck.

Jack and I spoke our vows solemnly but with great trepidation, looking into one another's eyes only once, when we were pronounced man and wife. The awkwardness of the situation was apparent to the other couples and the Justice of the Peace, who all kindly averted their eyes from our unsmiling faces.

Jack pecked my cheek hastily while the other newlyweds shared their wedding kiss enthusiastically, treasuring their first intimate moment as man and wife. After signing the marriage certificate we left promptly, unwilling to bask in the occasion with the other four, who were shaking hands and backslapping with the friendly justice. We hadn't spoken much in the car. Our conversation after the dramatic moments by the roadside had been sporadic and halfhearted, our private thoughts forcibly taking over our attention. I only knew that I had been traded to Jack. For what, I hadn't yet figured out, but I knew that Frankie had given me away like a young boy bartering his favorite marble, and I was completely powerless to do anything.

The day had moved at a snail's pace, my hurt so devastating that it shook me to my soul and coated me with a blanket of apathy heavy enough to squeeze the air from my lungs and the blood from my heart. Why Frankie had left me and why Jack was here in his place were questions I couldn't begin to answer. I was in survival mode, concerned only with getting oxygen to my vital organs and trying to walk without falling.

Jack took my elbow, guiding me gently towards the car and our future together.

"Let's go get somethin' to eat, Addie. I'm starvin'." He helped me into the car. "You hungry?"

"Hungry?" The thought hadn't occurred to me, and I had to think about it. The previous night's dinner had been my last meal. I had been too nervous to eat this morning, and even now the thought of forcing a sandwich down my throat and into the tumultuous pit of my stomach was nauseating.

"Not really," I answered, "but if you are, that's fine."

We headed down Main Street in search of a lunch counter. The heat was sweltering, and my dress clung to the wet skin of my back and arms. I wiped my brow with a handkerchief and felt myself lurch forward as the dashboard of the car rushed up to meet my forehead, knocking me back into the seat.

"Holy Jesus, Addie!" Jack pulled the car over and rushed out to open my door. "Come on. Get out. You need some water and something to eat." He helped me from the car. "Whatcha tryin' to do, kill yourself?"

A diner was located at the end of the block, and we headed for its shelter, moving as fast as the heat would allow. As we pushed open the door, the cool breeze from the fan washed over us, and we gratefully fell into a booth. Within moments, I was sipping on the lemonade that Jack had requested for me. He ordered two pork sandwiches, and when they came I suddenly couldn't eat mine fast enough.

I sat back after finishing and wiped my mouth. "Thanks, Jack. As usual, you saved the day."

He looked over at me, annoyed.

"But this time, I really appreciate it." I forced a smile, the first one I had managed that day.

"You're welcome, Adeline."

"So, Jack… what are we going to do with the rest of our lives?"

Before he could answer, the bell over the door rang out and the farm couple that we had been married with walked in. I saw the girl lean over and whisper into her husband's ear, and he gave me a fleeting look before acknowledging our presence to his spouse. They took a seat on the far side of the diner. I could only imagine what they were saying to each other. They peeked over their menu at us every now and then.

"Sometimes, Adeline, I'm at a loss for words with you." Jack looked away uncomfortably. "I'm tryin' to do the right thing, but you don't make me feel like that's the case. You made your choice and I made mine. I plan to stick by it. We'll do whatever we got to. We'll get by."

"My parents aren't going to be happy."

"No, they probably won't, but what's done is done. We can't change nothin', and we'll just have to make the best of it."

"Make the best of it," I repeated. *I should be sitting here with Frankie*, I was thinking, *not Jack*. "What did we do, Jack? I think we made a mistake."

"Well, it's a mistake you're gonna have to live with." Jack looked crestfallen. As he got up to pay, he leaned over and said, "You're plum crazy, Addie, if you think Frankie woulda made you happy." He walked over to the counter and paid for our wedding banquet as I sat, his harsh words suggesting that I would have misjudged the situation had I listened to my heart.

I followed him out of the restaurant, my chin held high as I passed the other newlywed couple. I sensed their eyes on my back as I walked out the door, and sure enough, when I turned quickly to look at them, I met their surprised faces staring back. I had the most juvenile urge to stick my tongue out at them, but I didn't, and instead opened the car door and got in.

"What's your plan, Addie?" Jack rolled the window down as he started the car.

"What do you mean?"

"Whatcha gonna tell your folks?"

I hadn't gotten that far. My only concern had been not to be unmarried and pregnant. To have Frankie run off and leave me in this condition would have been horrendously embarrassing and disgraceful to my whole family, and it would have shamed them, and me, more than anything. This was not a predicament in which a nice girl found herself.

"I don't know, Jack. What do you think we should say?" I felt relieved that I could share this burdensome task with him, knowing I would have the benefit of his strength and integrity when dealing with my parents.

Jack was silent for a bit, and I didn't want to interrupt his concentration. My thoughts drifted away from the practical and back to Frankie. I wondered where he was and whether he missed me. All that his short note had said was that he wasn't the man I thought he was and Jack was better suited to be my husband and raise our child. He had signed the note "All the best," as though he were a distant relative wishing me well on my birthday. I speculated as to what could have transpired between Thursday, when I had last seen him, and today. Had he really fallen out of love so quickly? I felt my heart clench when the thought hit me that I might never see him again.

When Jack spoke, it startled me, and I realized that even if I did see Frankie, I was now a married woman.

"Are you ready to tell them the truth?"

I stopped myself before I could say "of course." Was telling my father that Frankie had taken advantage of me what I really wanted to do—never mind the fact that he really hadn't? Could I look my mother in the eye and tell her I had betrayed her trust in my judgment? As much as it pained me to lie to my parents, my choices seemed limited.

"I don't think I can. Not right now," I told Jack, embarrassed that he even knew my dilemma.

"Well, they ain't dumb. They're gonna figure it out soon enough." Jack turned onto the road that headed back to Michigami. The air rushing through the car blew my hair around my face and shoulders, wrapping me in a cocoon. I wished I could stay like that forever.

"Addie, I know you ain't in love with me, but maybe in time..." He stared off into the distance, unwilling to utter the words that he hoped would justify his actions.

"Jack, I can't say what will happen." I spoke honestly. "Frankie is gone, and he didn't even say goodbye." My aching heart pushed against my chest and I longed to scream out and cry. As usual, the tears wouldn't come. The agony of unrequited love was crushing me, and I had to suffer in silence. The release that tears might bring was just not to be.

"He didn't even kiss me one last time. My last memory of him is… "

I paused to think. What was it?

"I walked out of the shop, thinking the next time I saw him would be our wedding day. That was it, no sign of anything out of the ordinary, nothing. He left an open door, Jack, and I've got forever to think about why."

"Forever's an awfully long time to be lonely, Addie," he said quietly.

"Maybe it is, Jack. But that's my misfortune. It's my burden to miss him and what we shared."

"You forget, Addie, I known him longer than you. He's my blood and my best friend. We been together since we was born. I know him like no one else, not even you. You think you're gonna miss him? You got nothin' on me." He cuffed the wheel with the back of his hand for the second time that day and sat back, shaking his head. We were still parked in front of the diner.

"As far as I know, Jack, you aren't the one having his baby," I said softly.

We rode back to the farm in silence. When we arrived, I asked him if he would mind waiting until the morrow to tell my parents. The heat was getting to me, and I was dog tired. Suddenly I could barely stand, and longed for the comfort of my own bed in my own room.

"Sure, Addie, no problem," he said, somewhat sarcastically. "Whatever you want to do, you just let me know."

I went upstairs without reply. I was too worn out either to argue or to acquiesce to whatever his plan might be. All I wanted was to lock myself away with my grief. Sharing my anguish with anyone was impossible. No one could possibly know or understand the complete and utter desolation I felt. The thought of my recent marriage only distracted me from my dreams, and I fell asleep wondering how Frankie could fix the situation that Jack was now involved in.

Mother came up early evening, gently shaking me awake, but I told her I was ill and just needed to sleep. She answered that she was worried about me, but I assured her that it was just the heat and I would be down in the morning.

I awoke in the cool predawn and immediately felt the abyss of reality in my gut reminding me that I no longer had the luxury of my dreams to hide behind. My wedding night had been spent alone and miserable, and my future didn't seem likely to be all that much different.

I crept out of the house and walked back to the ranch. I could see that Jack was up, the light glowing from the bunkhouse where he slept. I knocked softly on the door and he opened it. He cradled a coffee cup in his hands. He appeared disheveled and unshaven, wearing the same clothes he had on the previous day. Beckoning me in, he closed the door behind me and offered up some coffee.

"Thanks," I said taking the cup. I sat on the small bed, the same one I had shared with Jack four years ago, and glanced around the room. Not much had changed since I had been there last. His work shirts and pants were neatly folded on the small shelf he had fashioned out of an old crate, and his dishes were stacked in a tidy pile by the rusty sink. It was sparsely furnished with only the necessities, and it suddenly occurred to me that we had nowhere to live.

"Jack . . ." I began. I knew I had been more than a bit ungrateful the day before, and I owed him an apology.

"Don't worry about it, Adeline," he interrupted. "It wasn't such a good day yesterday."

"Yeah, I'm sorry about that. I know this isn't easy for either of us. I really don't want to fight with you." I didn't want to hate him, but I didn't want to love him either.

I surveyed the room again. "Where are we going to live, Jack?"

"I been thinking about that," he said. "Maybe we could stay out here. Me and Earl can fix it up some, put in a bigger kitchen, a bathtub maybe. Get a bigger bed." He looked uncomfortably away.

The thought of living at the ranch made my heart sink. The air felt cold and damp, and the smell of blood was forever ingrained in the paneled wood walls. One door led from the killing floor into the bunkhouse, and it had been left open for so long that it was permanently stuck, the corner digging into the floor. The windowless bathroom was a converted closet with a small toilet and sink, lit by a single bulb hanging precariously from a chain. The kitchen wasn't much better. All I could picture was a filthy baby crawling on the floor crying and me sitting in a chair with a jug of whiskey, drinking and smoking, a hand-rolled cigarette nestled in my toothless mouth. It was the only prospect that seemed likely in this depressing setting.

Jack noticed my gloomy expression and added, "Unless you want to live over at my dad's place with the girls?"

The decision between living in the desolation of the ranch and the desolation of Jack's family home wasn't a difficult one. I would much rather dwell in my family squalor than his. There was no good resolution to our living arrangement. The ranch would have to be where we made our home, assuming that my father was still speaking to me and would give his permission. I told Jack I would come back later when my parents had finished their breakfast, and we could speak to them together then.

Back in my room, my thoughts volleyed from Frankie to the inevitable confrontation with my parents. I knew I had to convince them that Jack and I got married because we wanted to start a life together, so much so that I had dropped Frankie and couldn't wait another day to marry Jack. That I was in such a hurry to get married that I couldn't even stop long enough to inform them of my decision or to get their permission. It was a long shot, but telling them I was pregnant and the father had run off was every parent's nightmare. I knew it would devastate mine.

I rolled over and gazed out my window. My room faced east and overlooked the ranch and even further, past the Tittabawassee River. The heat from yesterday threatened, but had not yet fully returned. As the sun rose, the illumination from the rays tiptoeing across our yard, I thought of Frankie, alone somewhere with no family or friends. If you had asked me then what I missed about him, I probably couldn't have said. He was unreliable, selfish, and emotionally vacant, but I loved him completely. My feelings surpassed his faults, and I knew that given the chance, my strength could have pulled us through.

But I'd never gotten the chance, and there I was, married to Jack. I liked Jack, always had. He was everything Frankie wasn't: reliable, reasonable, and consistent. I knew he would take care of me and my baby. But the exhilaration that Frankie sparked in me was something Jack couldn't match, and I feared my life would be spent comparing the two and waiting for Frankie's return.

The steps creaked as my parents made their way downstairs and into the kitchen to begin their day. I could feel the blood surging through my head, and the pounding in my ears was deafening as I realized that in the next few hours, maybe minutes, my life would change forever. So far, Frankie's departure and the makeshift wedding was Jack's and my secret, but that would soon be common knowledge, and all the world would know my business. I would be forced into the reality of the awful situation in which I had allowed myself to become entrenched, and the music I faced would be akin to Beethoven's "Funeral March."

I dragged myself out of bed, the weariness of yesterday returning as I washed the sleep from my face. I could hear my parents discussing the war as I crept down the stairs, moving so quietly that when I rounded the corner into the kitchen I startled them both.

"Addie," my father sputtered as he set his coffee down, "I didn't even hear you come down the stairs. You're up early."

My mother got up and poured me a cup, uttering a quiet "Good morning." She kissed my head as she sat back down. "Are you feeling better, dear?"

"A little," I offered as I dumped some sugar into my cup.

"It's the heat," my mother said to no one in particular as she walked to the icebox and pulled out some bacon. "It's going to be another scorcher today."

The humidity had suddenly descended with the full rising of the swollen sun, and moisture hung thick in the air even at this early hour of the day. I wiped the perspiration from my brow and imagined that I was still tucked in my bed, this illusory situation an extension of the bizarre dream that would end as soon as I woke up.

But when I heard the quick knock on the door and Jack appeared in the kitchen, the abyss bottomed out in my stomach again. The bile rose in my throat. I could no longer pretend that my life could ever be what it was. My heart beat so wildly I couldn't speak. I knew that no matter what, this was not the time to tell my parents. My whole body was frozen in fear and anxiety.

"Good morning, Jack," my parents said in perfect unison, smiling at each other over the coincidence.

Jack had shaved and cleaned up, and gave no indication that his night had been a turbulent one. He was all business, dressed for work, and his actions seemed deliberate as he walked in and sat down.

"Mornin', folks." Jack glanced over at me and nodded, but looked away before I could signal to him that I couldn't speak, let alone explain the unthinkable to my parents.

"Hot one today, huh?" my father noted as he pushed a plate of biscuits towards him.

"Just coffee, thanks," Jack said, and leaned forward in the chair. I coughed loudly, the action calculated enough to catch his eye, and I shook my head forcefully.

He looked at me curiously, but I saw that he understood my intentions, and the relief I felt was immediate. I watched him sigh and shake his head ever so slightly, but I knew I had been granted a brief reprieve, my world intact once again.

"Still plannin' on extendin' the west fence today, Jack?" my father asked.

"Yep."

"How's that new regulator workin' out?"

"Like a charm." Jack pushed his chair back and stood up. "If you folks'll excuse me, I'm gonna get my day started." No one raised an eyebrow as he headed out the door. "It's only gonna get hotter." He gave me a cheerless nod as he closed the door behind him.

My parents went on with their business, unaware of the drama that was unfolding before them, Mama cooking the bacon and my father consulting his almanac. I needed to talk to Jack and sat there drumming up excuses as to why I had to go to the ranch, when my mother suddenly presented me with an unseen opportunity.

"Honey, I know Jack didn't want anything, but can you run this snack out to him?" She handed me a wrapped bacon-and-tomato sandwich. "He's going to need some energy today."

"Sure," I said as I jumped up.

"Take this jar of lemonade, too." She bundled the food together and I left, anxious to get to Jack and explain my actions.

He was heading out of the ranch when I caught up to him and breathlessly held out my package.

"From my mother. She thought you might want it later."

"Thanks." Jack stood there stiffly.

"Jack. I just... I couldn't say anything in the house. I'm sorry. I just froze up. I just know they're going to be so upset, and I don't know what I'll do." I reached out and touched his arm, which was already clammy from the morning heat. "I'm not trying to make it more complicated. I'm just not doing so well."

"You gotta tell 'em, Addie. Every minute you wait is gonna make it more difficult."

"I know, Jack. I just feel like I've let them down so. I'm finding it so horrible. I'm not yet eighteen and I'm married and expecting a baby." Saying it aloud for the first time was liberating, but I still felt the sting of the shame my actions carried.

"Addie," Jack set the food down and put his hand gently on my shoulder.

"We're in this together now. *You* aren't expecting a baby, *we* are. *You* aren't married, *we* are." He put his other hand on my far shoulder and squeezed softly. "I know this ain't the best of circumstances, but you're my wife and we're starting a family. It's not gonna be easy, but you never have to worry about nothing all by your lonesome. I'm always here. No matter what, you never have to be afraid. Ever."

My gratitude to Jack at that moment was overwhelming, and all I could do was mumble a quiet "thank you." I would be indebted to him for the rest of my life, I knew, but somehow I felt it was all right. He would never call for my marker.

When he took my hand and said softly, "Let's go tell your folks now," I knew it was time and followed him back towards the house.

My parents were just getting up from the table when we walked back in.

"Addie and I have some news," Jack said, taking a deep breath. I detected the smallest tinge of nervousness in his voice, but I had lost mine, so I had nothing but admiration for his courage.

My parents didn't say a word. My father looked hard at Jack and then back at me, like he had been expecting something all along but wasn't sure just what. My mother just looked confused as she sat back down and patiently refolded the dishtowel that she had been holding.

"Addie and me… well, yesterday… me and Addie got married." Jack spoke the words that would forever change all our lives. It was done. There was no turning back.

My mother dropped the towel that she had so nicely folded. "I'm sorry, did you just say that you and Adeline got married yesterday?"

I nodded while Jack said, "Yes, ma'am."

"Now why would you two go and do a thing like that?" My father's voice had an ugliness to it that I recognized but rarely heard.

"Well…" Jack began but my father quickly cut him off.

"I want to hear it from Adeline."

This was the moment that I had been dreading the most. Jack was prohibited from helping. I was on my own. The lies that I would tell would be mine and mine alone.

"I guess," I began, in a voice so small that my father said loudly, "I can't hear you."

"I guess," I began again, "that I realized how much Jack and I meant to each other, that we just wanted to spend the rest of our lives together." I felt my lower lip quiver uncontrollably, and the heat forced beads of sweat to roll down my forehead.

"That so?" My father stroked his chin with his thumb and forefinger. "Just couldn't wait another day, huh? Why, I didn't even know you two was datin'."

"Why, Addie, I thought you were going with Frankie. When did you break up?" My mother was now twisting the dishtowel into knots.

Before I could even begin my second lie, my daddy interrupted.

"Where is that good-for-nothin' cousin of yours, anyway?" He looked at Jack menacingly.

"George!" My mother's voice was harsh.

"Due respect, Mr. Harris," Jack coughed awkwardly, "he ain't good-for-nothin'."

"Okay, son." My father's voice had become eerily calm. "Where's your cousin?"

"I can't say."

"You can't say, or you don't know?"

"I don't know," Jack's voice wavered. He was no match for my father, and his valiant bravado was beginning to crack under the proficiency of my father's drilling.

At that moment, Millie skipped down the steps and into the kitchen, singing out "Good morning," only to be ordered back upstairs by both my parents.

The sun was high in the morning sky, its appearance reminding all that the morning chores were running behind schedule. My mother now used the dishtowel to mop the sweat from her brow. I handed Jack a towel from the pile near the sink and he did the same. My father just stood there, scratching his chin and looking back and forth between me and Jack.

"Addie, what about college?" my mother asked.

"College?" my father practically shouted. "She ain't even finished high school!"

"Oh, Adeline, what have you done?" The tears in my mother's eyes brought a lump to my throat as I whispered, "I'm sorry, Mama."

"It's done and over," Jack spoke up. "We'll just have to make the best of it."

"We'll see about that," my father countered. He got up from the table and started towards the door. "I'm goin' to the courthouse. Maybe we can get it annulled or somethin'."

"No!" someone shouted. I realized it was me, and my face turned red with embarrassment.

"No, Daddy," I said, more softly now but with a newfound authority. "I'm married to Jack. That's the way it is and the way it will stay."

Both my parents looked at me curiously, and I swear I could see the wheels spinning in my mother's head.

"Jack, Addie, please go wait outside while I talk to your father." Mother nodded towards the door.

My father started to protest, but my mother said, "*Now,*" and that ended the conversation. Jack and I went outside, the sweltering heat attacking us like a swarm of mosquitoes, and took a seat on the porch swing. We sat silently and listened to the rise and fall of the discussion taking place on the other side of the wall.

Earl came out the front door, carefully avoiding the early-morning scene that he had just heard unfolding.

"What's going on?" he asked as he headed out to the ranch.

"Jack and I got married," I answered.

He nodded, my reply not seeming to faze him at all.

He looked back towards the kitchen. "They pretty upset?"

"Yeah."

"Yeah, I guess they would be." He walked off, the brief conversation over.

"You doin' okay?" Jack asked.

"I guess so. The worst part is over. I feel relieved that they know." Now I just felt exhausted. Between the heat and the early pregnancy, the coffee and the empty stomach, I couldn't much move. Jack walked out to the hand pump and brought back a large can of ice-cold well water.

"Here, drink this."

I gulped the whole thing down, the cool water spreading relief through my body.

"Thanks," I said, just as the door opened and my mother appeared, dishtowel still in hand. She motioned us in and we filed silently back in the kitchen.

My father was sitting at the table, head in hands, when we came in. He sat up quickly, but didn't meet my gaze. I wondered if they had figured out what was going on. My mother had an uncanny way of knowing everything, and I wouldn't have put it past her to have picked up on the more-than-obvious clues.

No one spoke. We sat there in an uncomfortable silence, my mother folding and refolding the towel, my father staring dazedly out the window, and Jack and I sneaking peeks at each other, wondering what had been discussed. I could hear my sisters moving around upstairs, probably trying to eavesdrop on what was happening below. At least that's what I would have been doing.

The humidity seemed to wilt everything, including us. Condensation was collecting on the inside windows and the still air offered no respite from the extreme heat. Northern Michigan was usually fairly moderate during the summer months, but every now and then Mother Nature's temper flared and she took revenge with a heat so heavy with humidity that you could cut it with a butter knife.

My father finally looked up. He and my mother exchanged weary glances, and when he spoke, it was in a flat, emotionless tone.

"You and Jack can stay out at the ranch for now. We'll do some work on it this summer, so as it's ready for the cold, and with Earl and José . . ." His voice trailed off, and he was silent again.

"We'll try to make it cozy for you, is what Daddy's trying to say," my mother finished for him. "It won't be so bad…we'll put up some pretty curtains, clean the floors, that sort of thing." She smiled a sad smile. The ranch was a dismal home and she knew it.

"Thanks," I meekly offered. I was unsure what to say or do next, and Jack mumbled something under his breath that sounded like an expression of gratitude, but I couldn't be sure.

"Let's get to work." My father spoke suddenly. "We've wasted enough time today. We're behind schedule." He got up and walked out the door. Jack shrugged his shoulders at me and followed him, pulling the screen door closed behind him.

I sat there as my mother ignored me and went on about her business. After a few moments, I got up and left, returning to my bedroom, where I lay back down on my bed. I could hear her talking to my sisters, who had raced down the steps after hearing my door close, and I knew she was explaining what had transpired.

I fell back asleep for a couple hours and was awakened by my mother, who was gently shaking my arm.

"Do you have to work today?" she asked.

I had forgotten that I still had a job at the Bijou. So much had happened in the last week. It seemed like another lifetime ago that I had been sitting in my booth, selling tickets to "Sergeant York" featuring Gary Cooper.

When Jack's daddy found out we had been married by the Justice of the Peace, he insisted that he perform a ceremony in front of God so we wouldn't burn forever in hell. A couple weeks later, close friends and family gathered while Jack and I exchanged our vows a second joyless time, now in front of an audience. We had cake and punch in the small barn-church. The intense heat had passed, but it felt stifling anyway. The congratulations seemed insincere, and there were whispers and glances. My now fuller figure had set tongues a-wagging.

My parents had bought us a full-size bed as a wedding present, and I was now sleeping at the ranch with Jack. Well, not exactly with him—he slept on the small cot that had been moved to the screened-in front porch, our bodies separated by a wall with a small window through which we sometimes communicated. From time to time, the heat or my thoughts of Frankie would keep me awake, and I knew Jack felt the same when I would hear him softly strumming the old guitar his cousin had left him. I wasn't sure whether the melancholy songs he sang were about me or Frankie. Either way, we shared a sadness punctuated by our pathetic situation, and his sorrowful words brought me as close to tears as I've ever been while I wallowed in my misery.

My life drifted back into a routine, a different one than I was accustomed to, but a routine nonetheless. Earl, José, and Jack knocked a wall down and added a larger kitchen and bath to the ranch, and it became a cozy apartment rather than a bunkhouse. Mother and the girls helped me scrub the walls and floors, and a pot of flowers and a fresh coat of paint cheered the room that I had found so dreary. I was trying so hard to remain miserable while everything around me was improving that I often resorted to sarcasm and cynicism, more often than not directed at my new husband.

"Would you like to go for a buggy ride?" he asked one late summer evening. "Might be kinda fun to hitch up the team and go out to the country. Maybe out to the lake?" He had finished for the day and was washing his hands in our new sink, his coveralls undone over one shoulder. "We could even pack a little supper and have us a picnic." He looked at me hopefully as he dried his hands.

"Sounds like a grand time. I hope we can run into some of the gang. Maybe build a fire, throw a ball. Things fat, pregnant, married girls do." I made an ugly face. "If we get real lucky, maybe it'll rain."

He shook his head disgustedly, picked up an apple from the basket, and walked out towards the barn. He had been spending many an evening out there, and it tugged at my heart when I saw that that night it would be the same. I despised myself when I reacted to Jack's kindness that way. I knew how much I owed him, how much he had done for me, how horrible I was. I knew all that, but my anger needed to be directed at someone. No matter how unfair it was, Jack had become my punching bag.

It must have been obvious to those around me, because my father cornered me one day as I walked along the path that led from the ranch back to the house. He stood dead center in my way, making it impossible to pass.

"Excuse me, Dad," I said as I tried to make my way around him.

"Not so fast, sister," he said, holding his ground. "I need to have a few words with you."

"Sure, Daddy." I swallowed hard. My father didn't often confront me like this, and I had a feeling I knew what was on his mind.

"I ain't blind to the way you've been actin' lately, and I have to say I'm just plain embarrassed that you've taken to treatin' the folks who been kind to you with such little regard."

I opened my mouth to argue, but he held up his hand and I stopped.

"This ain't a discussion." He looked squarely at me. "I'm tellin' you, straight forward, that you better knock that chip right off your shoulder or you're gonna find yourself in an even worse predicament." He glanced at my protruding belly. My face went instantly red when I realized that he knew. "You're fallin' from the moon if you think you coulda had it better another way. You're one lucky girl Jack took you on. You understand?"

His face showed frustration but not anger, and I could only nod my head and say quietly, "I'll change, Daddy."

"Addie, you're a smart girl and a good one, and I love you dearly." He choked up as he continued, "But you have to make the best of the road you've chosen. Chin up and move forward." He hugged me briefly and moved out of the path, motioning for me to continue.

My father was a man of few words, but they were weighty ones, and he used them to their fullest. I got his message loud and clear and I knew he meant business. Frankie had been gone almost two months, and the gut-wrenching pain I had endured had been replaced by a dull, constant ache that I would forget about until something or someone brought it to my attention. I vowed to put Frankie out of mind and concentrate on what was right in front of me.

I hadn't thought much about the baby I was carrying except to notice my thicker waist and increased appetite. So far, it had just been the imaginary seed that had blossomed into the root of all my problems. But in late August, as I was lying awake speculating about Frankie's whereabouts and trying to stay cool with a wet cloth on my forehead, I felt the gentlest flutter in my belly, like a butterfly brushing up against my stomach. It caught me by surprise. It was like nothing I'd ever felt before. The tickle came and went again before it occurred to me that I had just felt the first signs of life from my unborn child.

"Jack!" I squealed through the open window, interrupting him mid-song. "I think I just felt the baby move!"

I heard him stop playing, and a moment later he was standing next to my bed.

"Is everythin' okay?" he asked anxiously.

"It's fine," I answered, smiling. "It just took me by surprise, that's all. I didn't mean to alarm you."

"Well, I'll be a monkey's uncle." He shook his head in wonderment. "Ain't that a miracle?" He sat on the end of my bed and for the next few hours we waited for another sign, but nothing happened.

The following weekend we were having Sunday dinner with my parents and siblings. The summer was coming to a close and the heat still hung on, but it was fleeting. Soon enough it would be hibernating for the long winter. Earl and Maude would be returning to college the following week or so, Millie would begin her freshman year at the high school, and I would be doing nothing. It was obvious I was pregnant, and it would be unthinkable for me to start my senior year in my condition.

"I can't believe I actually miss going to classes," Maude was saying. "But I do. I even miss the homework, if you can imagine," she added, giggling. "Do you miss college, Earl?"

"I miss all my friends, stuff like that." He cocked his head. "But I definitely don't miss the homework."

"Do they have a lot of homework in high school, Addie?" Millie asked as she reached for the bread.

"They pile it on. But it's not so bad, you get used to it." I was happy to join in the educational discussion, even though I would not be participating in academic life for the foreseeable future.

"Addie," my mother was grinning like crazy, "I have a surprise for you." She looked around the table to make sure everyone was listening. "I have been speaking with your aunts, and they have agreed to tutor you for a couple of months and then to administer the exams needed for you to graduate. You will be able to get your diploma. "

"Really? I can graduate?" I looked at Jack, and I could see how pleased he was.

Even my father enjoyed my enthusiasm. "You're very fortunate, Addie," he added.

I nodded my head and said quietly, "I know." The fact that my family was so willing to help flooded me with gratitude, and I felt lucky to have them. "Thanks, Mama."

"You're welcome, Addie. I know you'll do your best."

Maude and Earl soon left for college, and the summer leaves began slowly turning to the rich, deep hues of fall. The air turned cooler in the evenings, and the quilt that my Aunt Opal had made for a wedding present was pulled out of storage. Jack was still sleeping on the porch, but I knew soon enough it would be too cold and he would be looking for refuge inside the ranch.

I no longer dreamt of Frankie's returning to collect me and the baby. Fact was, I never wanted to see him again.

"I hate him," I said one night as I pulled the quilt closer around me.

Jack stopped strumming. "Who?" he asked through the window.

"Frankie. I hate him, Jack, for all he's done to us."

"You don't mean that, Addie."

"I do, Jack. I swear I do."

"You're just angry, that's all."

"No. It's more than that." I sat up awkwardly in bed so my voice could be better heard through the window. "What kind of a man leaves like that? What does that tell you about his integrity? His character? He probably would have been a lousy husband anyway," I added.

"Addie, don't speak ill of Frankie like that. You don't know all of the trouble he carries. He's got more crosses to bear than you can imagine." Jack's voice grew distressed.

"I can't believe you would defend him, Jack," I said angrily. " He dumped us on you, and you still stand up for him?"

"I can't say I'm sorry, Addie." Jack's voice now quieted. "He done the best he could. There may be things you just don't know or understand, but he's still my cousin and my kin and I do stand up for him, no matter the sins he's committed." He started to say more, but stopped himself.

"Do you know something I don't, Jack?" I asked.

He was silent for a moment. "Addie, please don't wish ill on him, okay? I ain't never asked you for nothin', but I'm asking now. Don't wish him ill."

I wished I could speak face-to-face with Jack, see his expression, but asking him to come inside would have been heading down a road I wasn't ready to travel. I agreed aloud not to wish Frankie ill, but privately I wasn't so sure I felt that way. My heart still stung from his rejection. Though I thought I could turn my back on him, I couldn't say for sure I would do that if he were standing before me. My feelings were scattered all about—from the highs of the baby's movements and being able to graduate, to the lows of sleeping alone and thinking of Frankie. Every day was different.

September was apple month. Every year we would get bushels of apples from Bach's Orchard up the road and spend days canning sauce and making cider. This year, my mother thought it best that I do my own canning in my own kitchen. I had never done much of the actual work before. I had only watched from the sidelines, picking out the perfect slices to eat and running off when Lucy or something else better came up. But even so, I wondered, how difficult could it possibly be? Even when mother showed up, arms full of jars, lids, and pots, and two bushels of apples sat on my porch, I felt undaunted.

Hours later, I was singing a different story.

Peeling apples is a science. A paring knife needs to just skim the underside of the skin, otherwise the fruit is wasted. If you don't catch enough of the skin, you break the smooth action that should leave perfectly intact ringlets of skin. Done improperly, your thumb ends up cut and your patience tested. This was the lecture I heard more than once from my mother as I edgily waited for her to finish her demonstration and hand the knife over to me. I had peeled many an apple in my life, and I looked forward to one of my first tasks as a new wife and homemaker. Mama relinquished the knife with a shake of her head and a sigh, but I was finally left alone, ready to begin my project.

I set the canning pot on the stove, filled it with water, and picked up my first apple. It looked so perfect and juicy after I peeled it that I ate it. The second apple took a little longer to peel. By the fourth or fifth, my fingers ached and cramps contorted my hands. One of the farm dogs, Sam, kept me company and sat outside the door, nose pressing into the screen, and watched as I stumbled along. The morning moved swiftly, and by noon I hadn't even begun to scratch the surface of the two bushels that sat mockingly before me. The water for the jars was boiling, but the simple syrup that the apples would simmer in hadn't yet been made. I had dropped a cup of sugar water, which had turned the floor into a skating rink, and my thumb was bleeding from two different cuts.

When Jack walked in for lunch, I was knee deep in a mess that only got worse when I took a step and my feet slipped out from under me. I plopped down on my bottom, my bladder bursting from the sudden weight. I was unhurt, except for my ego. Even so, I couldn't help breaking into uncontrolled gales of laughter, especially when Sam started howling away at my predicament and Jack joined in.

"Are you hurt?" he managed to get out between chuckles.

All I could do was shake my head. There was no way I could tell him that I had just wet my pants—that joke was a private one—but I could imagine how silly I looked sprawled out on the floor. I excused myself to change, offering the spilled sugar water as an excuse. When I came back, Jack was wearing an old apron with a pattern of red cherries that set me off again.

"What?" he asked, deadpan. "Can't a fellow help his wife out in the kitchen?"

"You... you look so funny," I practically cried.

"Isn't red my color?" he asked pertly, arms akimbo. We both cracked up again.

My father popped his head in, the loud laughter catching his attention as he walked by.

"Everything all right in here?"

All Jack and I could do was howl with laughter at the whole of the situation. Daddy left, shaking his head, but with a wide grin on his face, leaving us to our own devices.

It took all afternoon and into the evening before we finished the job. But when we were done, jars lined and stacked up like neat little soldiers, we couldn't have been more proud. We both had bandages wrapped around our thumbs and even a few fingers, and our backs ached from picking up the heavy pots. But the kitchen was shining and we were too as we showed off our handiwork to my parents.

"A job well done, Jack and Addie," my father noted. "You two done real good."

"Yes," my mother added. "You should be proud of yourselves."

Jack and I beamed at each other, and when we went to sleep that night we couldn't stop talking about our hijinks in the kitchen.

"Addie, I counted twenty-seven jars of sauce. That'll get us through till the spring, don't you think?" Jack's voice floated in through the window.

"I'm sure," I answered. "We'll be eating sauce till it comes out of our ears."

That set us to quietly giggling again, remembering the fiascos of earlier.

"You warm enough out there, Jack?"

"Yeah, I'm fine, Addie. You better get yourself some shut-eye. You had a busy day."

"Good night, Jack."

"Good night, sweetie."

Jack's use of the endearment had slipped out unbidden and we both lay in silent embarrassment, but it actually felt good to hear the kind word. I hadn't been someone's sweetheart in a while. For the first time in a long time I fell asleep without thinking of Frankie.

The next week, Jack drove me into town and to the library, where Aunt Pearl worked. My father and Earl had built a ramp for her wheelchair so that she could easily get in and out of the building where she held the title of head librarian. I spent most of my fall days studying with her and practicing for the exams that I would take four weeks after my eighteenth birthday. I figured the baby was due the first week of December, so the timing couldn't have been better. Aunt Pearl and I spent six to eight hours a day together, but the whole time wasn't always spent studying. We talked and gossiped and reminisced about days gone by.

"Remember Aunt Opal's apple doughnuts?" I recalled. "Does she ever make them anymore?"

"She hasn't made them in years," Aunt Pearl proclaimed. "They certainly were delicious. If I'm not mistaken, I believe they took first prize in the county fair of '23." She paused for a moment to think. "I'm sorry, it was '24. Did you find Malta?"

I shook my head.

She wheeled her chair expertly around to my side of the large library table. "Here it is," she pointed out, placing a manicured finger on the small European country. "I couldn't see it from the other side," she smiled. "My eyes aren't what they used to be."

Aunt Pearl's blue eyes sparkled with wry amusement. Though forty-three, she still had the smooth porcelain skin of a much younger woman. Of the four sisters, my mother included, she was by far the prettiest. My own mother was not unattractive, but her features were on the sharp side. She lacked the soft, plump skin that always seemed to smell of lilacs and chamomile and the tiny dimples that punctuated my aunt's rosy cheeks. But, as my parents often pointed out, Aunt Pearl was destined to spend her life alone and in a wheelchair and was lucky she had not had polio severely enough to need an iron lung.

She nodded her greeting to a woman who had entered the building. "Mrs. Bedford," she whispered to me, then added, "How are you doing, Adeline?" It was obvious from her tone that the question she had asked was a personal one.

"I'm actually doing well, Aunt Pearl," I said truthfully. "Considering everything has happened so quickly."

"And Jack, how's he doing?"

"He's good." I smiled. "He's busy with Dad since Earl's gone, but they get on well."

"I like Jack. He's smart, but he's also got common sense." She raised her eyebrows at me and grinned. "The two don't always go hand in hand, you know."

We laughed quietly together, not wanting to disturb the two other patrons in the library.

"You're lucky, Addie. He's a good man," she said, suddenly serious. "I know you're young, but trust an old lady, love is a gift to be treasured." She stared off into the distance, elaborating no further.

"Were you ever in love, Aunt Pearl?" I asked softly.

She turned to look at me, a sad smile crossing her face. "I was, Addie, a long time ago."

"What happened?" This was incredible news. My Aunt Pearl had had a great love!

"We were young. He was wonderful." She stared off dreamily. "We read poetry, argued politics, talked of our dreams." Her voice grew animated. "He used to tease me about the silliest things. He called me Madam Blue Eyes. It was his pet name for me."

I was astounded. I had never heard her speak of a past love. I wondered if my parents knew this mysterious man, and I made a mental note to ask them.

"What happened to him?" I asked.

She looked down, the spell broken. "He went off to war. The Great War."

"Did he come back?"

"No Addie, he didn't." She looked at me, eyes full of tears. "He was gone to me forever."

"That's such a sad story, Aunt Pearl. You must have been devastated." My heart ached for my favorite aunt.

"For a while I was." She shook her dark curls as a young girl might. "But then I realized that I had been given the gift of love. And that love never goes away. You can't kill it, you can't bury it. It stays with you for the rest of your life."

She looked at me beseechingly. "It's a treasure, Adeline. One you take out during the difficult times of your life. You hold close the memories and recall the joy and happiness you once felt. It's what makes life worth living and I am blessed that I had it. No, I'm not devastated, I'm grateful." She wiped a tear from her eye. "I consider myself one of the lucky ones."

It was as though I had been hit by lightning. Her revelation shook me from the inside out. I knew something profound had happened. Just recently, I could have sworn that Frankie was my true love, my treasure, who would comfort me in hard times and be with me forever. Somehow now, he was a puzzle piece that didn't seem to fit.

When Jack picked me up that day, I couldn't stop looking at him. Was he my love? Was this the way true love should be? I didn't have the tickle in my tummy or the excitement that I had felt with Frankie, but I also didn't have the anxiety and the reservations that had come with that relationship.

"Did I grow a third ear?" Jack teased as he noticed me gaping.

"Maybe," I giggled.

"What?"

"Maybe."

"What?"

I almost said "maybe" again before I realized he was teasing me.

"You know, a third ear… I can hear better . . ." He looked at me, amused.

"Yeah, I get it." I grinned. "You don't have to tell me three times."

I was getting bigger by the minute, it seemed. My feet were swollen, and putting on my shoes was a gymnastic feat that required Jack's help - never mind lacing them up. I was awkward. I had lost my feminine swagger and found it replaced with an unattractive waddle. Getting comfortable in any position was next to impossible. At night I would pace the small bedroom, occasionally wandering out to the porch to talk with Jack when he was awake. Sitting in the old rocker that had been his mother's, we would chat, sometimes until the wee hours, when exhaustion would take over and my bulky body would give out. I complained to Jack that I was fat and disgusting, but he assured me it was just the opposite.

"You look pretty, Adeline. You have that glow about you. You're pregnant, not fat. Look at your arms. They ain't big at all."

His reassurance consoled me, and I appreciated his kind words. My moods ebbed and flowed. Some days I thought it would never end, that I would be pregnant forever.

On October 11, I turned eighteen. We celebrated with my family in the big house, with a ham dinner and cake afterwards. I received mostly things for the baby. My aunts bought a pram, my sisters some clothes, and Lucy gave me a miniature silver spoon and fork.

It wasn't until after the party, while we were walking back to the ranch, that it occurred to me that Jack hadn't given me anything. I wasn't sure what to say. It was unlike him, but when I glanced over at him he just kept whistling as he ambled along, oblivious to my predicament.

My confusion continued to grow until we walked into the ranch. There, sitting in the middle of the room, was the most beautiful white cradle I had ever seen. I knew as soon as I saw it what Jack had been up to all those late nights in the barn.

My hand flew to my mouth as I caught my breath.

"Oh Jack!" I exclaimed. "It's wonderful."

"Do you like it?"

"I love it," I said, looking over every inch of the baby bed, carefully inspecting his work, as he proudly looked on.

"Your daddy helped me some, 'specially with the spindles." He ran his hand gently over the curve of the back. "But I did it mostly by myself."

"It's a fine cradle, Jack. It really is." I felt the baby wallop me with a swift kick to the ribs. The movement, combined with a peculiar revelation, left me suddenly feeling like the rug had been pulled out from under me.

"What is it, Addie?" Jack asked, his voice full of concern, his face anxious.

"I'm not sure," I answered honestly. I looked into his eyes and felt a connection stronger than I had ever felt together with a longing that had been gone a long time, but not forgotten. My heart cracked opened some, and my long-held resentment started to escape. Suddenly the alchemy that makes love happen was no longer out of my reach. It was real, and it was right there in front of me.

"Addie," Jack began, but before he could finish, there came a quick knock at the door and a sudden rush of noise as Earl and Lucy bounded in. Our moment dissipated as quickly as it had gathered, and the cold air that they brought in was like a slap in the face.

"Addie! Jack!" Lucy's face shone as she closed the door behind her. She stopped and looked over to Earl, who nodded before she continued. She took a deep breath. "Earl and I are engaged! We wanted you two to be the first to know."

She clapped her hands excitedly as Earl beamed and patted her back, his touch newly intimate.

Jack and I were caught off guard, but we quickly found our bearings and offered up our congratulations. Their excitement took center stage, trumping Jack's and my fleeting moment, which slipped quietly away. Maybe for the better, I reckoned, at least for now.

But there was a new and undeniable element to our relationship that kept Jack and me continually dancing about. For the time being, I thought it best to leave well enough alone.

Chapter Ten

Mr. Stacie

To Mr. Jack Conklin,

You don't know of me, but I was friend and employer to a Mr. Frank Conklin. My name is Albert Stacie, and this letter is to tell you the sad news of Frank's passing last month. I would have wrote sooner, but the police just give back all his personal belongings. There weren't much to speak of, no more than the clothes on his back. And Frankie never said much about the whereabouts of his kin, so I didn't know who to tell. But a week ago I found a photo of two young boys by a river, and one of them looked like a young Frank. Your name and address was on the back. I don't know if it's proper to be writing this here letter, but I'm guessing you're his brother, and if I was in your shoes I'd want to know what happened. I weren't privy to everything, but best as anyone can tell, he was in the wrong place at the wrong time.

I own a small auto mechanic shop in Detroit, and Frank come in last July looking for work. The fellow that was working for me had just joined the service, so I give Frank a job and rented him the room above the shop. My business picked up as soon as he started. You probably know he's about as good as them grease monkeys get.

It wasn't soon after that he started running with a rough crowd, and a fellow the police been calling Jimmy P. I met Jimmy a few times, and from the start I wouldn't trust him as far as I could throw him. He was a slick character. It was like he was buying you a soda from the money he stole from your wallet. I didn't think much of him, but Frank, he says that Jimmy's his first friend and he's okay once you get to know him. Jimmy owns a joint over on Eight Mile, one of them speakeasies that stays open to all hours of the night and where they play all that new jazz music. Why a nice boy like Frank would want to get all caught up in that, I don't know, but he takes to hanging out over at Jimmy's place and spending all his money on whores and whiskey. Please pardon my speaking so plain.

I ain't never seen Frank on the marijuana or any other stuff, but when I found him dead in his room, there was a needle nearby. The police figured he got drugs from Jimmy or them Negro musicians, but either way, Frank is the one who paid the price.

Jimmy ain't been around since—he closed his place, then took off. Police can't do nothing until they know his whereabouts and can question him about the night Frank died. I took Frank's last few dollars and last paycheck and laid him to rest at the County Cemetery, off Woodward, in case you ever want to pay your respects. I hope you understand he had to be buried right quick.

I'm sorry for your loss and the way you got to find out about it, but there weren't no other way to tell you. Frank was a good man. He just met with some bad luck.

You two looked awful happy in that picture. It's a shame his young life had to end in such a way. If you're ever down Detroit way, look me up—it's Stacie's Garage in Southfield.

Sincerely,
Albert Stacie

Chapter Eleven

Adeline – 1941

Jack took Frankie's death in a bad way.

It stung me hard and fast, but by then Frankie had lost his hold on me. I regarded his passing with the detached sorrow one might feel at hearing some dreadful news. The initial shock struck a visceral blow, but I recovered more quickly than I would have expected.

The news took a toll on Jack, though, that concerned us all. I had seen him after the death of his mother, his aunt, and his baby brother, and he had held strong and steady, but when I read him the letter from Mr. Stacie, his knees buckled and he dropped to the floor. He crawled into a corner, back against the wall, and stayed there most of the evening. My father had to come out after supper and help me pull him to his feet and into bed, his limbs sagging and weak, his head hanging low.

We slept together that night for the first time as man and wife, but not in the way anyone would have expected. Jack was catatonic and, until the next morning, didn't move—not to eat or drink or use the bathroom. Nothing.

When he finally awoke, he sat at the edge of the bed, holding his head in his hands. I sat down gently next to him and whispered softly that what had happened to Frankie was no one's fault. Frankie had made his own choice to leave. All Jack had done was pick up the pieces.

Jack raised his head, meeting my gaze with a frightening intensity that was out of character for him.

"You don't know shit, Addie," he said in a monotone.

His vicious words cut deep. Apparently I was to blame for both Frankie's departure from Michigami and his subsequent death. I was rattled by the thought that I could somehow have prevented this tragedy—that had I not enticed Frankie so brazenly, he might still be fixing cars at his father's auto shop, and I might be riding the bus to school every day, celebrating my senior year. This whole mess was really my fault. Once again, I had hurt Jack. This time, though, I wasn't sure he could ever forgive me.

I carried my personal cross in my belly, in the form of a baby, and never had it seemed so heavy or burdensome as it did that October of 1941. Jack moved back out to the porch after that night, even though the winds had picked up terribly. When the snow threatened, he covered the windows with old barn wood and brought in extra blankets. It was dark, cold, and damp out there, but he insisted that it was fine and he was comfortable.

The changing weather made it too cold for me to keep the small window open that had been our late-night link, so our nocturnal chats came to a screeching halt. Jack wasn't much interested in talking to me, anyway, whether I was on the other side of the wall or sitting right in front of him. We fell into a routine of politely ignoring each other, but my heart was heavy and I longed for the Jack of old—the Jack who loved me no matter what.

I lumbered through my days, the baby so large that I could feel tiny feet every now and then, pushing out against my ribs. My mother took me to the doctor, who informed me that I still had weeks to go. This news depressed me even more. Some days I stayed in bed until nine o'clock or so, until the rumbling in my stomach forced me to get up in search of a meal.

At night, I thought about Frankie. Not in the way I used to—his death had killed any lingering romantic feelings I had left for him—but as a person, a real person with faults and defects. His imperfections were now glaringly obvious, and I wondered how I could have been so taken with such a troubled man. I had always prided myself on my common sense. With Frankie, I had taken a wrong turn, and boy, what a price I would pay. I thought of my father's old saying about falling from the moon and pictured myself tumbling from the sky, arms flailing, head over heels, until I hit the earth and *splat!* That's where I was now, a puddle of pregnant mess, full of shattered dreams and with a guilty conscience to boot.

Sometimes when I lay alone, the room so dark I couldn't see my hand in front of my face, Frankie seemed an apparition, someone I had only dreamed of, someone who had never been real. I had a hard time remembering what he looked like. The only face I could recall was that of Jack's. No matter how I tried, it was Jack who was burned solidly into my memory.

In early November, I sat for my high school exams. I had always been a good student, and the extra time with Aunt Pearl had been the icing on the cake. I sailed through them, and though I wouldn't get the results for a few weeks, I was confident of my success and the feelings boosted my sagging sense of self-worth. Each day I rallied a bit, my resilient nature buoying me up whether I wanted it to or not. I was resigned to my burdens. There was nothing I could do but move forward, with or without Jack. I was damaged goods, and he had every right to blame me. There was no way out of this situation. Frankie would never come back.

Meanwhile, everyone was busy but me. My siblings were in school, my parents seemed to be running the county. Even my aunts were occupied with a new theatrical production, this time for the church. And Jack—well, he didn't spend much time at the ranch.

Left to my own devices, I made friends with the only one who couldn't avoid me - my unborn baby. I sang the songs I remembered from my childhood and discussed the day's events. He seemed to respond to my voice with small kicks and punches, reminding me that I had a duty to another life. But that in itself was daunting.

Jack eventually came around, but not by much. One night, as the snow drifted gently from the sky, melting as soon as it hit the ground, my father paid an unplanned visit to the ranch. Jack and José had added a wall between the killing floor and the entrance to our apartment, intending to further silence the commotion, but the foxes smelled my dad and began barking when they sensed him, and the noised drifted in through the still of the evening.

"Beg pardon the interruption," he began, "but I was wonderin' if I might have a word with you two."

Jack shrugged his shoulders. I answered, "Sure, Daddy."

He closed the door behind him. "I need to get somethin' off my mind."

I sat in the old rocker while Jack slouched on the edge of the bed. A speech from my father was worthy of attention. I suspected that my mother had something to do with his visit. I looked over at Jack to get his impression, but he was busy cleaning his nails with his pocketknife, apparently less than curious about what my father had to say.

"Jack," he said with enough conviction to make him look up, "you need to hear this, son.

Jack set down the knife and we both sat at attention. The upright position pushed the baby up against my lungs and my breath came in shallow gasps. I wouldn't last too awful long like this, and I hoped for my own comfort that my father would be brief.

"Jack, you're family now, which is why I feel I can take the liberty of talking to you like this." My father rubbed the back of his neck as he surveyed the room. He seemed hesitant to go on, but I imagine that the thought of my mother waiting back at the house for his report urged him forward. He seemed to resign himself to the task, and continued.

"What happened to Frankie was no one's fault. It wasn't your doings and it wasn't Adeline's. You can't possibly take responsibility for another person's choice. That ain't the way life works."

He waited for a response. When none came, he continued.

"Frankie carried his own demons, probably passed down from his mama"—at this Jack looked up—"but that don't have nothin' to do with you. You were his friend, his kin, and I'm sure he loved and appreciated that from you. But the choices he made were his and his alone. You can't say the same thing wouldn'ta happened if he woulda stayed, can you?"

He had Jack's and my full attention now. "He could have just as easily taken off on that bike of his and gone speedin' down some road, only to lose control. Fact is, you don't know what God had planned for that boy. No one does. It ain't your place to be the bearer of his responsibility."

My father stood over Jack. "Let me ask you this, son. Do you think if Frankie were standin' here before you he would place the blame on you for all that done happened?"

Jack didn't say anything.

"I'm askin' you a question, Jack. Do you think he would have found you at fault?"

After a moment, Jack spoke, his voice raspy. "I don't know."

Both my father and I looked at him with curiosity. How could he think that Frankie would have blamed him? This was my fault, not his.

Jack turned to me. "It ain't your fault, Addie." He took a hitching breath. "I told Frankie not to come back."

"What do you mean, Jack?" my father asked.

"The night he asked me to take care of Addie, I told him not to come back. That he couldn't just step back in someday and pick up where he left off." A lone tear rolled down his cheek. "I was afraid he would take away what was mine."

This news stunned me. I could tell from my father's face that he felt the same. Jack didn't blame me, he blamed himself. He felt guilty about his mandate to Frankie. I'd always wondered what had happened the night Frankie left, and to hear that Jack had stood up to his cousin put things in a different light.

Jack wiped his nose with the back of his hand. He looked at my father, and for the first time that night he met his eyes. "He's dead because of me. He knew he couldn't come back, and that killed him."

There was silence. My father cocked his head and held Jack's gaze as he rubbed his chin absently.

"Let me ask you something, Jack. Did Frankie accept your terms?" My father walked over and sat down next to him on the bed.

"Yeah, but…"

"Did he change his mind or express doubt at any point?"

"No, but…"

"Jack?" My father put his arm around Jack's shoulder. "I woulda done the same thing. As hard as it was—is—you made the right decision. Frankie knew what he was doin', and he still did it. He made his choices and now, you gotta make yours. Do you think he would have expected you to grieve for him forever?"

"No."

"Don't you think he would have wanted you to live the rest of your life without the burden of his death? To raise your family? To have a life full of joy, and sorrow? Sorrow that's your own, not his?" My dad stood up. "I'm truly sorry for your loss. As much as I done said about him in the past, I would never wish Frankie ill. I feel the pain of his passin' too, but we got to move ahead. We bury our dead and we move on. You know that, Jack. You've lost more than your share of kin."

My father stopped speaking, and the room fell silent except for an occasional whine from the foxes, who knew he hadn't left. I knew he was a man of few words, but the words he spoke carried their weight in gold.

I closed my eyes, but could barely tell the difference. The room was dark except for the lantern that threw shadows against the ranch walls. The wood that Jack had used to cover the porch windows had almost totally blocked out the light, making our home continually bleak and gloomy.

"Son, you got a lot to be thankful for." My father's voice broke the silence once again. "Me and Mrs. Harris, well, we care for you like you was our own. You got a healthy young family to provide for, and you got your whole life ahead of you. Don't let the bitterness of somethin' you can't control get the best of you. It ain't no way to live your life."

My father spoke with such sincerity it seemed as if he were speaking from experience. Jack lowered his head to his hands, and I could see his shoulders shaking ever so slightly. I instinctively maneuvered my immense self out of the rocker and over to the side of the bed, where I sat and put my arm around his trembling shoulders and hugged him close. He didn't pull away. I whispered into his ear comforting thoughts, just little nothings, but I felt my voice soothing him, calming his nerves. When I looked up, I saw that my father had left and we were alone.

Jack lay down on the bed and I gently rubbed his back. After a time I could sense that he was sleeping and I pulled the blanket up around him. I sat back down in the rocker. The baby had shifted some and I could breathe better, but I wasn't the least bit tired. I turned the lantern down, pulled my shawl close around me, and rocked in the semidarkness as my troubled young husband slept. I wasn't sure how Jack would be in the morning, but my father's words had always made a difference in my thinking, and I hoped they would do the same for him.

With the windows boarded up, it was difficult to tell when the sun rose. The room was still dark when I heard José rustling around in the pens, but I knew it had to be daybreak. I had never fallen into a deep sleep, instead dozing on and off throughout the night, so morning brought stiff limbs and overwhelming fatigue. The lantern still burned, and as my eyes adjusted to the dim light I could see that Jack was awake and looking at me. I had woken once before in the ranch to Jack's watching me sleep. Last time, the moment had ended in a passionate kiss. I smiled wistfully at the memory—we had been so young then.

"Why you smilin' like that?" Jack asked dreamily.

"I was just thinking about the time Earl got sick and I stayed out here with you for the night. Seems so long ago."

"It was," he said, rolling over and putting his hands behind his head. "That was a good night. Except for the fact of Earl bein' sick."

I managed to wiggle my way out of the chair and heaved myself upright, every bone in my body letting me know that a rocker was no place for a pregnant woman to sleep.

"Jack, do you mind if I lie down? I'm so tired I can barely stand." The dizziness of exhaustion settled about me. I felt as though I were speaking in slow motion.

"Heck no, Addie," he said as he jumped out of the bed. "I wasn't thinkin'." He helped me lie down on my side and arranged the blankets around me.

"You get some rest. I gotta get to work."

"Jack?" I asked, as the weariness washed over me.

"Yeah?"

"Do you feel any better?" The words barely made it out of my mouth as I drifted off.

I must have fallen asleep before I heard his answer, because I don't remember his reply, but I could have sworn that he kissed me lightly on the lips before fading away.

That afternoon I woke to a rumbling stomach and a room full of light. While I slept, Jack had removed the barn wood from the windows, and sunshine once again flooded in. I had never been so ravenous. I barely chewed my food as I tried to satisfy my insatiable hunger. Even when I finally felt full, I contemplated when I could eat again and what my next meal would be.

At supper time, Jack showed up and announced that we were going to eat dinner in town. We rarely ate out, but he said he just felt like it and I was already hungry again, so it didn't take much convincing for me to grab my coat and head for the car.

Our conversation during the meal was light and pleasant. Neither of us mentioned my father's visit, nor did we talk about Frankie. When we returned home, full of food and coffee, he asked if I would mind if he pulled the cot back inside the ranch.

"It's gettin' pretty cold out there," he said. "I know it'll make it a bit crowded in here, but I don't want to freeze to death before the baby's even born." He smiled at me.

I longed to tell him to forget the cot and come share the bed with me, but he put that idea to rest before I had a chance to say anything. "I'll stick to the cot for now, if that's okay—I don't want to interrupt your sleep. You need the rest."

Though Jack wasn't lying next to me, he was at least in the same room, and I looked forward to picking up our late-night conversations, especially without a wall between us. Between the coffee and the nap, I was wide awake. I lay on my side, the baby moving about, as I waited for him to get ready for bed.

Jack didn't have the movie star good looks that Frankie had, but his strength of character illuminated his features. When he smiled over at me as he turned down the lantern, he looked positively handsome.

"Addie, you thought of any names for the baby?" he asked as he lay on the cot and propped himself up on his elbow.

"If it's a boy, I thought I'd like to use my father's as a middle name, but I'm still thinking about a first." I considered my next words carefully, but felt I needed to say them. "Jack, I don't want to name the baby Frankie." I glanced over at him, hoping he felt the same. "I just don't want to."

"Nah, I don't think so, either."

"Any ideas?" I asked, relieved that we were in agreement about the Frankie thing.

"What about Earl?"

"Maybe," I said noncommittally.

"David?"

"No."

"Sebastian?"

I raised my eyebrows at him. "Sebastian?"

"What? You don't like it?" I saw him grinning through the dim light.

"How about Ferdinand?" I shot back.

"Too Spanish-sounding. What about Benedict?"

I giggled. "Too… turncoat? I wouldn't be able to trust him."

"Okay, let's just call him Alastair and be done with it." Jack sat up. "Enough discussion. Alastair it is."

"Fine," I agreed with a grin. "Alastair for a boy. But what if it's a girl?"

"It won't be. Girls are too much trouble."

"What?" I said indignantly.

"If it's a girl, we're sending her back."

"Jack Conklin! I can't believe you would say such I thing." I feigned indignation.

"Okay, okay, we'll keep her. She'll come in handy for chores and such."

We both lay back down, the good-natured discussion a pleasure after many days of silence.

"Addie?" The mood changed with the solemnity of his voice.

"Yeah?"

"Someday, I'd like to go down and see Frankie's gravesite."

I wondered where the thought had suddenly come from, and my response was guarded. "Sure, Jack."

"I know what your daddy said is true, and I truly appreciate his words; they meant more to me than you could ever know. But I want to pay my last respects. It's the right thing to do."

"Of course, Jack. I think you should."

"Like your daddy said, it's God's will, but I wish he was still here."

It was funny, but now I couldn't imagine Frankie being here and Jack not. "I like things just the way they are," I said, but added quickly, "I mean, I'm sorry he's passed, but I'm not so sure we would have been... good together."

We lay quietly, each with our thoughts. I regretted the turn the conversation had taken, but Jack seemed to want to talk of Frankie, though I would rather have continued the silly name discussion.

"Your daddy didn't like Frankie much, huh?"

"I guess not," I replied.

"Wonder why."

"Maybe he figured out that he wasn't the one for me," I offered.

"Maybe." Jack rolled over on his back and stared at the ceiling. "I really miss him, Addie."

"I know, Jack. I'm sorry."

"Me, too."

We lay silently for another few minutes before he spoke. "Let's get some shuteye, Addie. You must be plum tuckered out."

I wasn't at all, but I sensed that he wanted to be alone with his thoughts, so I bid him goodnight and rolled over. The big meal and the sleep-filled day had caught up with me, and I could feel my heart racing. I tossed and turned, fighting for a comfortable position, until I finally crept out of bed and went quietly into the kitchen. I didn't want to wake Jack, but the ranch was small and my options were limited. I lit a small candle and tried to read, but soon grew bored. The baby was kicking like a mule and pressing against my diaphragm, making breathing challenging, and I sighed loudly.

"What's wrong, Addie? Are you all right?" Jack rolled off the cot and walked into the kitchen.

"I'm sorry to keep you awake. I'm just not that tired," I sighed. "I'm too big."

"Yeah, but just big with baby." He grinned over at me, drumming his fingers on the table. "Hey, whaddaya say we go for a ride? I'll hitch up the team and we'll head towards the lake. It'll do you good to get some fresh air."

"Now? In the middle of the night?" I asked, surprised.

"Why not?"

I thought of all the times I had turned Jack down. "Sure, why not?"

"Thatta girl. I'll go get the team ready. You get yourself plenty wrapped up and bring some blankets and somethin' hot to drink." He patted my hand briskly and got up to leave.

I nodded and went to change my clothes. *This is crazy*, I thought, but it was exciting as well, and it thrilled me to be doing something so impractical.

The night was clear, but it was cold and crisp, and I bundled myself so that I resembled a large mound. Jack had to get into the buggy to haul me in, the carriage rocking under my weight, but we finally settled ourselves, the blankets tucked around us and the thermos safely between us. Jack slapped the reigns and said "Hee yah!" and we were off.

I couldn't remember the last time I had been in the buggy, and most certainly it hadn't been in the middle of the night. A half moon (was it waxing or waning? I wondered) faded in and out between the wispy clouds, the colors of the night changing from deep purples and blues to grays and blacks. The clippity-clop of the horse's hooves rang clear and clean on the frozen ground, echoing far into the dark. Every now and then an owl called out his warning of our intrusion to the forest. I could see my breath in the chilly air, but I wasn't cold in the least. Still, I snuggled gratefully up to Jack. He circled me with his arm as we sailed through the early winter shadows. For the first time in a long while my mind was peaceful. I was content to enjoy the beauty nature had offered up and the companionship of a man who loved me unreservedly. We rode the countryside until the night's blackness faded and day threatened to break.

I didn't want the ride, or the night, or the peacefulness that had come with them to end. When Jack jumped down, lifted me easily out of the carriage, and kissed me ardently, I knew it wouldn't just yet. I wrapped my arms around his neck, and he carried my bulky frame into the ranch and to bed. When he set me down, kissed me again, and silently returned to the carriage to unhitch the horses, I knew that the morning would see Jack truly become my husband, and I his wife.

My mother had figured the baby was due on Thanksgiving, but when that morning arrived and the baby hadn't, I grew fretful, sure that something was wrong.

"Babies come when they're ready," she told me. "They're on their own schedule, Adeline, even after they're born."

I had hoped to be eating a turkey dinner in the hospital, but instead dragged my overstuffed bulk to the big house to help with the holiday preparations. Mentally, I was as happy as a pig in mud—Jack and I were closer than we'd ever been—but physically, I was miserable. I had been told by more than one person that the baby I carried would be large, and the weight of the unborn infant settled heavily in my loins, a testimony to the likely accuracy of their predictions. I found I couldn't be more than a few steps from the bathroom—any movement could cause undo embarrassment—and things had been happening to my body that I found so mortifying I couldn't even tell my mother. After months of gorging, I had lost my appetite, the sight of food making me sick. My mother told me it was my body's way of getting ready for the birth. I prayed she was right.

Earl was home for the big meal and all the aunts were coming over, so Maude and I set the large dining table for ten people. *Next year*, I thought as I laid the silver down, *there will be a high chair next to my place*.

"Addie, I swear, you haven't learned a thing." Maude sighed as she rearranged the utensils I had mislaid.

"Sorry, Maude, I was just thinking that next year we'll be setting a place for a baby."

She looked over at me goodnaturedly. "I know, Addie. I can't wait to be an aunt. Except for the diaper part." She wrinkled her nose. "I've never been much good with poop."

We giggled. The days of chasing foxes and slipping in dung were long past, but the memory of our old job would stay with us forever.

"Maude," I suddenly remembered, "when I was studying with Aunt Pearl, she mentioned that she had a lover right before the Great War."

Maude looked up, surprised.

"Do you know anything about it?" I asked.

"No, of course not. Are you sure?" Maude had stopped mid-motion, intrigued by the news.

"She told me that they were in love, but he went to war and never returned."

"Really?" Maude was as fascinated as I had been. "I've never heard anything like that. She didn't mention who it was?"

"No, but I thought I'd ask Mother. I'd forgotten about it, with all the hoopla."

"Aunt Pearl had a beau?" Maude thought about it. "Before she took to her wheelchair?"

"I don't know. She was so bothered when she told me, I didn't want to ask her anything that would upset her even more."

"Let's go ask Mother," Maude said as she wiped her hands on her apron. "I'm too curious to do another thing."

Maude skipped and I waddled into the kitchen, both of us singing out, "Mother!"

"What is it, girls?" she asked as she stood over the sink, washing out her delicate crystal gravy boat. Millie sat nearby snapping beans and looked up interestedly at the excitement in our voices.

"Mother," Maude began, beating me to the punch, "Addie just told me that

Aunt Pearl had a lover. Right before the Great War."

"Do you know anything about him?" I added, slightly irritated that Maude had stolen my thunder.

My mother turned slowly, like a ballerina on a music box that was winding down. We all watched in horror as the crystal dish that had been handed down from my Grandmother Suzanne slipped from her hands and crashed to the floor, shards of glass flying everywhere.

"She told you that?" my mother whispered, stunned, seemingly unaware that she had just lost a treasured keepsake.

"Oh, Mother," Maude said, her voice full of concern. "That was Grandmother's."

I didn't know if Maude was more upset about the fact that the gravy boat would never be hers or my mother's agitated state.

Mother stood stock still, dish towel still in hand, poised like a mannequin in a storefront window.

"What's wrong?" we inquired. Why had the question about my aunt's old beau affected her so much? What had happened?

"I'm sorry, girls," she whispered. She looked down, horrified, at the shattered heirloom. "That was my mother's," she murmured, finally aware of the significance of the accident, "from France."

I had never seen my mother cry. Tears at funerals, yes, but for the first time I thought she might break down right then and there. She fought to gather her composure, and we all stood motionless, waiting for her next move, aware of the obvious impact of the question.

A few moments later, she drew a deep breath and spoke. "You caught me off guard. I hadn't thought of *him* in a long time."

"Did you know him?" Maude asked quietly.

"Yes... no. I mean, I knew of him." She bent down and started picking up pieces of glass. Maude and Millie followed, and I grabbed a broom and dustpan.

"Aunt Pearl said he passed in the war," I said, sweeping the glass into a pile.

"Yes, I guess he did. I really don't know much about him." Mother turned her back to us as she continued.

"Did Dad know him?" Millie inquired.

My mother looked up sharply. "No!"

She stood up and rubbed her forehead. "Girls, it was long ago. He's gone, and our lives have gone on. I don't know any details, and if I were you, I'd mind my own business regarding Aunt Pearl. It's obviously painful for her, and I would think you cruel if you brought it up again. Some things are meant to be left alone. Is that understood?"

We all answered, "Yes, ma'am."

"Now I've gone and cut myself." She held up a bloody finger. "Would you girls please finish up for me? I've got to dress my wound." She didn't wait for an answer, but left abruptly, leaving us all standing in the kitchen, mouths agape, wondering what had just happened.

We had told her we wouldn't speak of it again, but that didn't stop us from wondering what had happened so many years ago that could have caused so much pain to my mother and her sister. We exchanged fleeting looks, our curiosity apparent, but no one was willing to disobey Mother's orders, especially so soon after they had been issued. Some secrets were not ours to know, and this would be one of them. At least for now.

Thanksgiving dinner was always a feast at our home, especially when Aunt Opal was in attendance. That year she brought fluffy French popovers, whole-berry cranberry sauce, stuffing with apples and nuts, and an apple crumb cake that seemed to melt in your mouth. Though I wasn't hungry, I had bits and pieces of the feast, afraid that if I didn't, it would be a whole year before I would be able to enjoy the dishes again.

My mother was almost back to normal—she was gracious as usual—but there was a slight sharpness to her that only my sisters and I seemed to notice. When she wasn't looking, we traded furtive glances, and we tried to be extra helpful, clearing dishes and serving dessert since her finger was wrapped in a small bandage.

When Aunt Ruby asked where their mother's crystal gravy boat was, we waited, breath held, wondering how Mama would answer.

"I had an accident. I dropped it this morning when the girls and I were working in the kitchen." She looked at us and nodded, and we understood that we were not to elaborate.

"Oh, Susie!" Aunt Pearl exclaimed. "That was Mother's—from France."

"I'm well aware of where it came from," my mother answered stiffly.

"That's how she hurt herself," Millie chimed in.

"We all saw it happen," Maude added. "It slipped right out of her hands."

"She's lucky she didn't lose a finger," I finished with the defense.

My mother looked at us gratefully.

Aunt Pearl immediately apologized. "I'm so sorry, sister. I know it was an accident. Is your finger all right?"

"I'm fine. I feel terrible about the dish, but what's done is done."

"No use crying over spilled milk," Aunt Opal added.

"It's just a dish," Aunt Ruby put her two cents in. "Now we have an idea for a birthday gift."

My father, Earl, and Jack watched the whole exchange with mild interest. I wondered whether Daddy knew anything of the secret beau. My mother had said not, but somehow I wasn't sure that was the case.

I dropped the thought immediately when I felt a sharp pain, one so severe that it took my breath away.

"What's wrong, Addie?" Jack asked, concerned.

"I think I'm having labor pains," I answered as another one hit.

I became the focus of attention for a while as I was hustled to the couch and made comfortable. The pains came for a few more minutes, then stopped suddenly. My disappointment was obvious. I had so hoped that I would finish the day with a baby, but my body had quit midstream.

The excitement eventually died down. After dessert, we sat around drinking coffee and gossiping.

"So, Earl, tell us about the wedding plans," Aunt Pearl prompted.

"Uh, well, we're getting married in her father's church," he offered, clearly uncomfortable being the wedding spokesman.

"When *is* the wedding?" I asked.

"Sometime after I graduate next year."

"That certainly is a long engagement," Aunt Ruby pointed out.

"Yeah, well, Lucy wanted it that way." He looked over at Jack. "Speaking of which, I'm heading over to your place for a bit. Want to come along?"

Jack looked over at me. "Do you mind, Addie? It'll just be for a couple of hours, but I can stay if you want."

"No, go ahead, I'm fine. Looks like I'm staying put for the night, anyway." I had my feet up and a cup of coffee in my hand, and I was nestled under a blanket. "We can always call if we need you."

He kissed me on the top of the head and left. Over the last few weeks Jack and I had enjoyed an intimacy that was molding a new beginning for us. After years, really, of on and off for our relationship, we had apparently come to solid ground. I knew he loved me, but after Frankie, I wasn't as forthcoming with my feelings—at least not yet. I wanted to be a good wife and mother—I just wasn't as confident as I once might have been. But I knew I was headed in the right direction.

"A penny for your thoughts, Addie." Aunt Pearl leaned forward from her wheelchair just enough to squeeze my big toe slightly.

"I was just thinking about the baby," I replied, only somewhat truthfully.

"Have you thought of any names?"

I watched as my mother whispered into my father's ear and they both quietly removed themselves from the discussion, heading into the kitchen. I would have loved to have been a fly on that wall.

"Jack likes Alastair," I said, grinning.

"Oh, Addie, you can't be serious," Millie jumped in. "How about Orson or Humphrey, or Cary?" She recited the names of the current movie stars.

"What if it's a girl?" Aunt Opal chimed in. "I like Opal, personally."

"I prefer Ruby," Aunt Ruby added, and the small group chuckled.

We all looked to Aunt Pearl, who surprised us by saying, "If it's a girl, I think I would choose a beautiful name. Not that those aren't." She smiled as she looked around the room. "But I would choose one that flows off the tongue. One that's strong and feminine and, well, one that isn't the name of one of us sitting here in this room." She tilted her head and flashed her dimples at us. "Something regal."

We discussed baby names for the next short while, until the aunts decided they wanted to leave before it got too late. I waited anxiously for Jack to get back. I was tired and ready to climb into my own bed. The kitchen had long ago been cleaned, the dishes put away, and the dining room returned to normal. Maude had gone to her room to do some homework and Millie sat at the piano, softly humming as she played. My parents had returned to the sitting room, my mother now wearing her housecoat, and for the first time in my life I felt like an outsider in my childhood home. Not in a bad way, as if I were unwelcome or anything like that, but as if my life were now elsewhere, as if I had my own small family and my own small house.

The evening dragged on. By nine o'clock I began to worry. I asked my mother if she would mind calling Lucy's house to ask when Jack and Earl would be returning.

"I'm sure he's fine, dear. He's probably just spending some extra time with his family, but I'm happy to check."

She got up to use the phone and I heard her asking Dolly, the operator, to connect her with the Conklin's number. The phone was in the kitchen, so all I could hear was a distant "really?" and a "we'll check." I sensed that something wasn't right. My fears were confirmed when she returned, looking concerned.

"I just spoke with Earl. Jack left over twenty minutes ago. Earl was having Lucy bring him back later. He should have been well home by now."

We all looked to my father, who was already out of his chair. "I'll take care of it," he said as he walked out the door.

Maude came back downstairs, and we all sat in the front room and waited. It was unlike Jack to be late. He wouldn't have gone anywhere without phoning, especially on a holiday. We all knew that.

The clock in the hall ticked away. Finally, my mother turned on the radio. The only thing on the air at that point were sermons, and the preacher's voice rose and fell, his words going in one ear and out the other. I tried to read, but after a bit, I put the book down and waited, sure the news could not be good.

Close to midnight, our nerves frazzled, we finally heard a car pull into the drive. We all rushed to the door and watched, relieved, as my father, Earl, and Jack emerged from the car. They walked wearily into the house.

When I could clearly make out Jack's face, I gasped. His right eye was swollen practically shut, a large, deep cut glaring above it. On his cheek was a bruise the size of a handprint, and he walked stiffly, as though his back pained him, his stance giving him the appearance of a wounded prizefighter.

"Oh, my God, what happened?" I cried, hauling myself upright while they peeled off their coats and my mother ran for the first aid supplies.

"Let us get our things off, Adeline," my father admonished me. "He'll tell you everything there is to know in just a moment."

Maude put a pot of coffee on as Jack shook off his wet socks and boots. I watched, my anxiety building, my overdue pregnancy intensifying my already agitated state of mind. I plunked myself in the rocker and rocked back and forth impatiently as Jack settled on the couch, wrapped in a quilt, and began his story. My mother dabbed at the cut above his eye.

"I was set to come home around nine o'clock or so. Earl had decided that Lucy would bring him home later, but I wanted to get back in case Adeline was feelin' poorly." He looked over at me and smiled weakly. "I'm comin' down the road, out behind Eli Peyton's old place," we all knew the area and nodded, "when all of a sudden, an eight-point buck bolts out in front of the car. I had no choice but to hit the dang thing."

We all drew our breath in horror as he stopped for a sip of his coffee. "Well, of course I wasn't expectin' nothin', so it took me by surprise."

I gulped at the image.

"The force from hittin' the deer sent the car off the road and into the ditch next to it, and I think the coffee mug I was carryin' smashed into my head. It musta knocked me plum out, because the next thing I remember is George here shakin' me awake." He looked over at my father gratefully.

My mother leaned back from cleaning the cut. "He may need a couple of stitches here," she announced. "It's started to clot, but I fear it'll leave quite a scar."

"I don't really care about that," Jack replied.

I could only nod my head to agree, the dreadfulness of the whole situation rendering me speechless.

"What happened to the deer?" Millie asked.

"He killed it," Earl answered for him. "We'll get it tomorrow when we go back with the team to pull the car out of the ditch. The meat'll still be good."

"How did you ever find him, dear?" my mother asked my dad.

"His headlights was shinin' straight up from the ditch. I come down the road, headin' out towards the Conklin place, and I see these lights comin' out at a funny angle from the side of the road. Had a feelin' it was Jack." He shook his head. "He was right, he was out cold. He's a lucky young man. He coulda been killed."

The word "killed" sent a jolt of fear through my body, and the commotion of the accident, combined with the misery of my physical state, built up a tidal wave of emotion so great that I couldn't stop it from washing over me. I burst into tears.

My whole family, flabbergasted by my outburst, could only stare as I cried piteously, my body convulsing with sobs that racked my sizable figure. I had been a child the last time I'd had such an outburst, and so young I couldn't even recall when it had been. But the thought of not having Jack plunged me into a morass of emotions over which I had no control. I was powerless to do anything but let my feelings lead the way.

Jack came quickly to my side, helping me to the couch as he comforted me. "It's all done, no use talkin' of it anymore," Jack told the group. "I'm fine, just a little bumped and bruised. Be gone in a day or two."

He helped me get myself under control, my sobs turning into hiccups, my mother still fussing over both of us. After I had stopped sniffling, Maude handed me my wraps and Jack slid his boots on, leaving the laces undone. We bid goodbye to my family, who watched us leave, their expressions slightly glazed with fatigue and concern.

I couldn't seem to shake the jitters that haunted me, and Jack had to help me into my nightdress and into bed, carefully picking up my swollen legs and setting them gently down. He crawled in, pulling me close as he nestled behind me. My tears started once again.

"Boy, when you start, you just don't know when to quit, do you?" he teased.

"Jack," I managed, "I was so scared when you didn't come home. I just knew... I knew in my gut that something had happened."

"Well, I'm here, and everything's fine, so you can relax and get some sleep now. The baby'll probably be here tomorrow."

I sighed, the tears subsiding. "Oh, I hope so."

"You can't get much bigger," he kidded again.

His quip brought a fresh round of tears. Jack apologized profusely and rubbed my aching back. I was not yet twenty, and already I felt like an old woman, aches and pains accompanying every movement I made. The crying added to my misery, bringing with it an insidious despair. I wondered if I would ever be normal again.

We lay quietly for a bit as I calmed down. Jack continued to rub my back as I drifted in and out of consciousness, sleep never quite coming for good. When Jack stopped rubbing, I opened my eyes.

"Is something wrong?" I asked sleepily.

"Addie, how come you never cried for Frankie? Either when he left or passed way?"

I thought about it briefly before I answered.

"I don't know, Jack," I said honestly. "I never felt the urge. I wanted to at times, but the tears never came."

We lay there a while longer before I felt him pull me in tighter and put his lips to my ear. "I love you, Addie."

"I love you too, Jack," I said, smiling to myself as I finally drifted off to sleep, my husband's arms wrapped tightly around my expansive belly.

Jack was wrong. The baby didn't come the next day, or the next, or even the next. I was convinced I would be the only woman in the history of the world who would be pregnant forever. Climbing out of bed was a chore, so most days I didn't. It was cold and blustery outside, the bristling wind sneaking in whenever the front door was open, and the bed was warm and comfortable for my enormous frame. I even took my meals there, the quilts pulled snugly around me.

When I estimated I was almost two weeks overdue, my mother called the doctor. He told her that if I didn't deliver in two days I was to be brought in and labor would be induced. I didn't know what an induction would entail, but it didn't sound good, and I prayed nightly that the baby would come.

Early that Sunday morning, I was awakened by what sounded like a balloon popping under water. I realized with an odd sense of exhilarated relief that what I had heard was my bag of waters breaking in my sleep.

Suddenly, I was galvanized into action. I woke Jack, and we dressed hurriedly and left, stopping at the house to let my parents, who were sitting at the kitchen table drinking their morning coffee, know we were on our way to the hospital in Midland.

We got there in record time, exchanging nervous glances all the way, and checked in at six o'clock a.m. on the dot. Before long, I was in a labor room, surrounded by nurses who shooed Jack out. I wondered why he couldn't be in the room, especially since nothing was happening, and when the doctor came, I asked. After checking me, he said I had a long way to go and that Jack could visit with me for a bit. When the pains got to be too much, Jack would be relegated to the waiting room with all the other expectant fathers.

Jack came in, and we waited anxiously for the pains to begin. We played cards and talked about Earl and Lucy's engagement. I paced the room and he watched. Then he paced and I watched. I held my breath every time I felt a twinge, but there were no real contractions.

Two hours later, nothing had happened yet, and when the doctor returned and found out my status hadn't changed, he sent Jack out and checked me again.

His face betrayed his uncertainty as he listened to my belly with his stethoscope. My heart began to beat wildly. Something was wrong. He rang for the nurses, and after a series of checks with unfamiliar instruments, he called for Jack.

"What's going on?" I begged, my feet still in the stirrups. I looked for Jack, and when he came in I reached for his hand. "Something's wrong!" I cried.

The doctor motioned to Jack. They backed into a corner, their voices too low for me to hear.

"Please tell me what's happening," I said to the nurse who was lowering my legs.

"You'll be fine, Mrs. Conklin," she said, patting my hand reassuringly. "Doctor knows best."

Jack and the doctor returned. Jack looked very upset.

"Someone please tell me what's happening," I pleaded. "What's wrong with the baby?"

"Mrs. Conklin," the doctor began, "two things are wrong. First, for some reason the baby's heart rate is dangerously slow. Second, you should be in active labor, and you're not. We need to put you under and take the baby."

"Take the baby? Where? How? What do you mean, 'take the baby'? Jack?" I grabbed his hand in a panic.

"It's okay, Addie. The doctor knows what he's doin'." But Jack didn't look as sure as his words made him out to be.

I couldn't believe that after all we had been through we might not make it.

"Will we live? Will the baby live?" I looked back and forth from Jack to the doctor.

"You'll be fine, Mrs. Conklin. But we don't have much time. Say goodbye to your husband. We need to get you into surgery." He turned and walked briskly away, shouting out directions to the nurses scurrying about.

"Goodbye?" That sounded like I wasn't coming back.

Jack clearly knew what I was thinking, because he immediately said, "Bad choice of words."

Things got confusing then. People were suddenly running everywhere. Jack left to sign some papers and I was whisked away before he returned. I never had the chance to tell him I loved him—or to tell him any of the things running like a brushfire through my petrified mind.

I was pushed hurriedly down a long hall and quickly moved onto a table in the operating room. Before I knew what had taken place, I had a triangle-shaped mask on my nose.

"Breathe in deeply, Mrs. Conklin, and start counting back from one hundred," said the man who appeared to me upside down.

I was too terrified to do anything but what he'd asked, and the last number I remember was ninety-six before I disappeared into oblivion.

When I awoke, hours later, I was thirsty, my throat dry and scratchy. I learned later that I had already been awake once, in the recovery room, but I had no memory of it.

As my eyes began to focus on my surroundings, Jack came to my side and leaned over.

"How you feelin'?"

"Where's the baby, Jack? Is he all right?" I was groggy, my voice thick.

"The baby's fine." He handed me a glass of water. I tried to sit up, but I was immobile from the waist down.

"What's wrong with my legs?" I asked, alarmed.

"Doctor said the medicine is still keepin' 'em numb. It'll wear off in a few hours."

I sipped the water through a straw as quickly as I could. My stomach started to roil from the sudden presence of fluid.

"The baby, Jack. How is he?"

Jack grinned wildly. "*She*, Addie. It's a girl, a big girl."

"A girl?" I had been sure it would be a boy. "I had a girl?"

"Is everything all right? Where is she? What does she look like?" I couldn't get the questions out fast enough.

"She's absolutely perfect, pretty as a picture, big as can be. She weighs almost ten pounds," Jack said, shaking his head in wonderment. "But she looks just like you—with a little Conklin thrown in. She's in the nursery right now. Maybe a nurse will bring her in."

Jack went to the door and motioned to a nurse, and a few moments later a small pink bundle was carried in the door. "Just for a few minutes," the nurse said. "The missus needs her rest."

We nodded, and I reached gingerly for the package.

Jack was right. She was perfect. Her chubby face was free of wrinkles, so unlike the rumpled faces of most newborns, and there was a fold of baby fat already under her chin. I counted all her toes and fingers, even though Jack said he had already done that, and kissed the top of her fuzzy brown head. Her little mouth opened in a yawn. We both watched raptly, mesmerized by the simple act.

"Jack, I'd like to call her Grace. Grace Marie. Do you like it?" I couldn't take my eyes off her, marveling at every move she made.

"I think it fits her like a glove. 'Grace Marie.' Sounds like a movie star."

"It does, doesn't it?" I said, finally looking up at him. "Maybe she'll be famous."

He laughed. We took turns holding her until the nurse came back in and we were forced to give her up.

"Mrs. Conklin needs her rest," she said as she carried my little girl away.

"But I'm not tired," I complained, yawning.

But of course I was, and within minutes, I had fallen back asleep.

When I awoke again, my parents had joined Jack and were sitting in my room, talking quietly, my father running his eyes over the Sunday paper.

The drugs I had been given were wearing off. Suddenly, I could feel an intense burning near my belly. I tried to cough, and my insides pulled as though I was actually splitting in half. I cried out in pain.

My mother and father looked horrified. Jack called for the nurse, who arrived promptly, shot in hand.

"You'll be very sore, dear," she said, pulling the sheet discreetly back over my bottom, where she had administered the injection. "For a couple of weeks. You need plenty of rest." She looked pointedly to the assembled group, who nodded in assent.

Whatever she gave me worked. Soon I was free of pain, asking for something to eat and inquiring as to whether my parents had seen Grace Marie.

"Oh, Addie," my mother exclaimed, "she's just beautiful. I actually see a little of my own mother in her. Don't you, George?" She glanced over at my father.

"A bit," he said, taking his eyes from the paper. "She's a right fine girl, Addie, and she's plenty healthy, that's for sure."

Just then, Maude and Millie burst in, Millie calling out before she even entered the room, "She's huge, Addie!"

"Millie!" My mother spoke sharply, not only in reference to her volume but to the rudeness of her statement.

"Mother," Maude defended, "she *is* big. She's almost twice the size of any of the other newborns."

"She's just healthy, like your daddy says," Mother admonished.

"Well, I think she's perfect," said Jack, beaming, "and that's all that counts." He squeezed my hand reassuringly. "Matter of fact, I think I'll go see my little girl right now." He leaned over and kissed me. "I'll be right back."

"He's going to make a wonderful father," my mother said softly as he left.

"I know, Mama. It's funny how things work out, isn't it?"

"Always for the best," she answered. "Always for the best."

I had begun to reply when Jack stepped abruptly back into the room, his face pallid, his manner dazed.

"What is it, Jack?" I asked, panicked. "Is the baby all right?" Something was horribly amiss. I struggled to sit up, the stabbing pain returning to my abdomen.

Jack looked at my father, then my mother, and then turned his head slowly to me. "It's all over the radio. The Japanese attacked Hawaii this morning. It looks like we're goin' to war."

I heard my mother gasp and my father sigh. Immediately my thoughts ran to baby Grace. I was thankful that she was a girl. No draft for her ever. But what of Jack? And Earl? What was to happen to my family?

The room was silent. We all felt the sting of the news, our lives forever changed. December 7, 1941, the day my baby was born, was also a day marked by death—the day on which over two thousand men lost their lives at Pearl Harbor, and the day on which the United States would join World War II.

I thought of Grace Marie again. What an extraordinary start to her life. A day stained by tragedy, but also colored by joy. A day when the wonder of birth shared the spotlight with the sadness of death. Would she ever understand the breadth of our emotions that day? How could she? It was our experience... our time. Hers was the future. Hers was tomorrow.

Discussion Questions

1. In the opening chapter, Adeline introduces the reader to the men in her life: George, Earl, Jack, Franklin, and Pops. By quickly categorizing each, she uses her narrative role to influence the reader. What are her perceptions of each of these men? Does her naïveté cause her to think in stereotypes? Who, if any, does she describe objectively?

2. Why does Miss Pearl refuse George's proposal? Does she later regret her decision? Is her stance based on true love or society's expectations? If the novel took place in 2009, how would the outcome differ?

3. Why is Susie a poor match for George?

4. Betrayal and ambition are two themes Shakespeare emphasizes in **_Julius Caesar_**, the play Miss Pearl selects for the children to perform. How do these two themes apply to Adeline, Susie, Frankie, and George?

5. Pops and Susie share an unusually close relationship. What emotional support does each provide for the other? In what way does Pops live vicariously through his son's inability to accept his role as a husband?

6. What does writing provide for Susie? How does the author use Susie as a vehicle to introduce historical/progressive movements?

7. Why does becoming a father alter George's perspective? Why does Susie accept his sudden burst of affection and forgive his neglect?

8. When Adeline confides her misgivings about Lucy and Earl, her mom warns her about making judgments against other people. In fact, Susie provides the same advice as Atticus in **_To Kill a Mockingbird_**: "You have to walk in someone's shoes before you know how they feel." How does this advice apply to the dance and answer questions about Susie's life? More importantly, how does it serve as an introduction to the next chapter, Francine's confession and single narration?

9. Even during the Depression, spousal and sexual abuse is not without any recourse. Why does Francine remain in her loveless marriage? Why doesn't she confide in the Miller sisters? What are her strengths/weaknesses? What does her death inadvertently teach Frankie? How is the adage, "Like mother, like son" or "the apple doesn't fall far from the tree" appropriate?

10. With guns and knives readily available, why does Francine choose to die among the flames and cinders? How is this symbolic? Was it truly her destiny?

11. Throughout the novel, Jack serves as the hero. What are his strengths? What is his one tragic flaw? When does this flaw become apparent to the reader?

12. When/how is Jack's inability to accept Frankie's death foreshadowed?

13. Why is Addie attracted to Frankie? Why does she choose Scarlett as her mentor/confidante? What do the two women have in common?

14. During one of their discussions, Frankie mentions **Of Mice and Men** to Addie. He appears critical of George's decision to take Lenny's life. How does this uncertainty relate to his mother's death and his own suicide?

15. Is Jack a fool to marry Addie? Why is he untroubled by her hesitation? What serves as the impetus of his devotion to Frankie?

16. How does Addie's marriage resemble her parent's union? What advice is unspoken in the final chapter?

17. Why does Aunt Pearl reveal her lost love? What is her underlying message to Addie? What does Susie realize when Addie repeats the story?

18. As part of a marriage ceremony, some cultures deliberately smash a glass. How does knowing this tradition change the reader's perception of the broken family heirloom?

19. What is the significance of Grace's name? How does the child's name reflect the overall theme of the novel?

20. Every main character in the novel faces a major hurdle. While some struggle with physical/emotional disabilities, others strive to overcome sexual/physical abuse. What handicaps does each character face? Why do some succeed and others fail? What challenges await Grace?

Acknowledgments

I do hereby acknowledge the following people
for their influence on my life and work.

Ed and Lois Goulet, who were generous with both their stories and their time.

Lisa (Goulet) Hagenbuch, who (though I don't believe in it—really!)
is an amazing astrologer and friend.

Ed Chupack, author of *Silver: My Own Tale as Written by Me with a Goodly Amount
of Murder*, for his invaluable writing advice and his kindness.

Jeff Comeau, designer extraordinaire, for his patience and his unique vision.

Kelly Russell, lifelong friend and partner in crime for too many years. Love ya, babe.

Stacie Heintze, **Jenny Schmuhl**, **Laurie Rivera**, and **Jaqueline Kurkcu**,
for being the kind of friends and family that read a rough first
draft and tell you it's the best thing they've ever read.

All the girls in the **Esoteric Women's Club**: Bonnie, Connie, Julie, Kristyn, Francesca, Karla,
Laurie, Maria, Peg, Kristin, Lisa, Kelly, Stacie, Jen, Becky, and Jacqueline. You have all
inspired me in countless ways, and I treasure our friendship as much as our debauchery.

My brother-in-law, **Matt Samra**, for his remarkable insight into
story and character development and for all his help way back when.

My sister, **Becky**, for simply being who she is.

My mother and father, **Claudia Lewis** and **Larry Hulce**, two people I never thought
I would turn to for advice or guidance. I take back the words I spoke to you as a teenager—
I really do love you and I'm glad you're alive.

Pete Lewis and **Janet Hulce**, my stepparents, for putting up with the abovementioned.
I know, I know—we owe you.

A big thanks to **Leah Goodwin**, **Leslie Campbell**, **Sally Kim**,
Janet Dooley, and **Brita Higgins** for their third eyes.

A special thanks to **Dawn Wiebe** and **Kristyn Friske**. You complete me.

All of my children, **Marcus**, **Gracie**, **Max**, and **Sam**:
you're everything I'd hoped for and more. I wish only the best for you.

My husband and partner in life, **Craig Arnson**:
I know you always have your hand on the small of my back. Obee.

giving2green

The giving2green symbol indicates that the user has committed to giving monies to the many organizations dedicated to the fight against global warming, decreasing greenhouse gas emissions, saving our rainforests and wetlands, and fighting water and air pollution.

giving2green gives 100 percent of its proceeds to supporting the organizations fighting these battles. Because we feel that saving our planet and the people, plants, and animals inhabiting it is one of the most critical challenges we face today, we request that all our authors commit their support as well.

We feel good about making a difference. Every little bit helps, and today's business should step up to the challenge of not only doing their part, but setting an example—not just because it's good for our environment, but because it's the right thing to do.